ERIS

D. Reneé Bagby

MENAGE AMOUR
Mainstream

Siren Publishing, Inc.
www.SirenPublishing.com

A SIREN PUBLISHING BOOK
IMPRINT: Ménage Amour Mainstream

ERIS
Copyright © 2010 by D. Reneé Bagby

ISBN-10: 1-60601-838-8
ISBN-13: 978-1-60601-838-5

First Printing: August 2010

Cover design by Jinger Heaston
All cover art and logo copyright © 2010 by Siren Publishing, Inc.

PUBLISHER
Siren Publishing, Inc.
www.SirenPublishing.com

DEDICATION

Thanks to my Panya and Jennifer, my beta readers, for helping me get the LARP scene right.

Thanks to Eric D. from the real CGC for answering my many questions about comic grading.

Thanks to Stephanie "Flash" Burke for being a great sounding board and knowledgeable about some of the most random topics—including and not limited to the sound a cat-o-nine tails makes.

ERIS

D. RENEÉ BAGBY
Copyright © 2010

Chapter One

Ranulf stared at the spacious, climate-controlled room in a thoughtful manner. Beside him, Lucien looked through the contents of a nearby box.

"We need to stop putting this off," Ranulf said. "Every year we say we'll get our collection surveyed and every year we find an excuse to avoid it."

"Why do you want strangers tromping through our home? Where does this whim come from?"

"I've forgotten what we own." Ranulf gestured to the boxes. "And can you find anything in this crush? I never get past the first ten boxes before I give up."

Lucien closed the box near him and straightened. He looked around the room then at Ranulf. "Fine."

"Good. I called the company, and they are sending a representative tomorrow morning to give us a time estimate and price."

"Why did you even bother asking me?"

"I like you to feel you have some say in the decision-making." Ranulf threw his arm around Lucien's shoulders. They walked like that back to the main house.

"You'll be meeting with whoever is sent, right?" Lucien asked, shrugging off Ranulf's arm as they entered their shared office.

"You know I will. I know how much you hate meeting new people."

"All we ever do is meet new people. It's annoying."

"The price of eternity. We can't make long-lasting friendships unless we plan to share with them what we are and why we are that way. And then watch them age and die."

Lucien sat at his desk. He searched through a stack of papers, stopped, searched a drawer, stopped and then looked at Ranulf. "Have they found her yet?"

Ranulf retrieved a slim file from his desk and tossed it onto Lucien's. "Nothing. We gave them all the information she gave to us. Nothing, in all this time."

"All the information she gave to us. What information? All we have is her name. She told us nothing."

"She thought we wouldn't believe her."

"It was the thirteenth century. Why would we believe her? Even after..." Lucien trailed off with a soft growl. He shoved the file away and sat back. In a soft voice he said, "Even after she disappeared, part of me still didn't believe we would live to see this age."

"Here we are," Ranulf said in a happy voice with his arms akimbo.

"Your jovial attitude is annoying."

"You have no sense of humor, my friend. Though your sullen nature is more pronounced than usual. Could it be you realize twenty-ten is in a few months? The very year our lovely distraction told us she originated."

Lucien turned away.

"Ah, so that little tidbit hadn't escaped your notice. We've almost reached the fated time. As we are both reclusive types, we have very few venues in which we can meet her, and the private investigators have failed to find her."

"The faire."

"Yes, the ren faire. Ten days when we allow multitudes of unknowns access to our property so they can pretend they know about the era from which we hail."

"How do we find one woman in such a crowd? What if we miss her? Or, she doesn't show?"

"What if she does show? Remember how she was dressed when she arrived, Lucien."

"I remember everything about that time," Lucien snapped. "Even if I wish I could forget."

Ranulf crossed the room and placed a hand on Lucien's shoulder. "I know your pain, but the subject of time remains. As much stock as I place in my own abilities to charm the ladies, I doubt I would have made such a strong impression on her in ten days—if we meet her on the first day."

"You think she arrives before the faire then?"

"It's the only scenario that makes sense. Perhaps at one of the movie premieres or while we're at a business luncheon. Maybe we should make random trips in and about town. We might meet her then."

"And what? Kidnap her and hold her hostage until she falls in love with us...one of us?" Lucien pushed Ranulf's hand away.

"Granted that plan is one way, but I doubt she'd have been so taken with us—this version of us—if that's what we'd done...what we do." He frowned.

"Don't try and figure it out. It's our past tense and her future, but for us it's her past tense and our future. You'll only give yourself a headache if you think about it too long."

"My point is sitting around this mansion will not get her to us sooner. The investigators didn't work, so we must try other tactics."

Lucien unlocked and opened a drawer in his desk. He carefully pulled out a frame. His expression softened as he smoothed his fingers over the glass.

Ranulf moved closer and looked over Lucien's shoulder. The frame held an old piece of parchment with a drawing of a woman whose smiling visage peered out at him. "That was the moment your skills improved the most. Why have you never drawn her again? If you had at least done a quick sketch for the investigators—"

"No." Lucien put the drawing away and locked the drawer. "The next time I draw her, she'll be before me and willingly posing as my model."

"Preferably in the nude." Ranulf laughed when Lucien glared at him.

"That picture is the only way I can remember her face. Any drawing I do now would only be a copy. I..." Lucien paused and passed his hand over his face. "I feel as though I don't remember what she looks like or I won't recognize her when I see her."

"You'll know her. To the depths of your soul, you'll know her. Just as I will. She isn't a woman you would forget."

"Tell me we'll find her."

"We will. We'll find her, we'll make her love us, and then she'll be with us once her journey has ended." Ranulf walked to his own desk, suddenly not as lighthearted as he had been only moments ago.

Knowing they were close to the beginning—or was it the end—made every minute she wasn't with them unbearable.

"Soon," he whispered and met Lucien's gaze across the room.

Both men said in unison, "Eris."

* * * *

"What?" Eris glanced over her shoulder then looked back at her computer screen. She cursed and hit the back button. Her momentary distraction had made her hit the wrong key.

"Are you listening?"

"Yes, Brian, I'm listening. I'm a woman, which means I can multi-task. What do you want?"

"Connie is going on an estimate run tomorrow, and I need you to go with."

Eris shook her head. "Not happening. I'm stuck in the middle of this database."

"It can't be put on hold for an hour or two?"

She stopped typing and looked at him.

He held up his hands in surrender and backed up a step. "Yeah, yeah. You're right. Stupid question."

She nodded and went back to her typing.

"Everyone else is busy, and I like one of the appraisal team members to be with the agent when they do estimations. It makes the clients feel a little more at ease if they meet the people who will be handling their precious babies."

"I agree with you." She stopped typing and thought for a moment. The database was nearly finished. If she stayed late, she might be able to pull it off. "How about this? You authorize some overtime, and I'll get this done tonight. That way Connie won't be solo tomorrow. Deal?"

"You got it. Thanks, Eris, you're a lifesaver."

She smiled at him. "Which flavor?"

"All of them at different times. You're sure you'll be done in time?"

"I'd be done sooner if you would leave me the hell alone."

Brian laughed and walked away.

The man was a great boss but a little clueless sometimes. She smiled over her shoulder at his retreating back. She'd managed to get overtime while making it look like she was doing him a favor.

Accompanying Connie on the appraisal trip to assure a panicky client that their precious possessions were perfectly safe was a small price to pay if Eris could get rid of her current client a day earlier than she'd planned. The man had contacted her at least three times in the last two days. He told her over and over about the importance of the database, hoping it would speed up her pace when all it did was slow her down.

She looked at her watch. "Ten minutes." She could get in a few more entries before lunch.

"Ready for lunch?"

She smiled but didn't look back at Clayton or stop her typing. "No. I've got ten minutes before my lunch starts."

"Fudge it and let's eat. I'm starved."

"Clayton, this is important."

"Are you gonna finish in ten minutes?"

"No way. I've got hours to go, at least."

Clayton grabbed her arm and pulled her. She latched onto the desk with one hand as she continued typing with the other.

"Eris, let go of that keyboard. The work will be here when you get back. Let's eat."

She typed in the last of the data, hit enter and the computer beeped as the information was committed. Letting go of the desk, she swiveled her seat around so she faced Clayton. "Hi."

While dapper and very handsome in his suit, his dyed-black, spiky hair somewhat marred Clayton's corporate appearance. His hair was originally dirty blond, but he liked the darker look so he could appear moody.

Clayton kissed her upturned lips then pulled on her arm. "Me hungry. Want food now."

"Ass." She laughed and followed him.

Half an hour and a filling lunch later, she returned to her desk. "Back to work," she said to get herself psyched up for the coming monotony.

She actually loved her job when she wasn't creating a database for a client who decided a month after the appraisal team finished that he wanted a catalog of his collection—something that was much easier to create during the appraisal process.

Thanks to her overtime though, she only had a few more hours and she could politely—and in a professional manner—tell the client to never call her again. That was something she looked forward to.

She clicked the mouse on the project file. While she waited for it to open, she stowed her purse and got herself situated at her desk.

The computer beeped.

She looked at it then frowned. "What do you mean 'file not found,' you piece of junk?" She clicked the icon again, and the same message appeared. "No, no, no, no! Don't do this to me. That was a day's work you just ate."

No matter how many times she clicked the icon that had worked an hour ago nothing happened. The computer refused to open the file. Normally, she'd have backed it up to her laptop, but Clayton had yanked her away and back-ups were a before-she-left-for-the-day type of thing.

"This can't be happening. All that work."

She called the computer technician and waited frantically for the woman on duty to come to her rescue. It took the technician forty minutes to tell Eris the file never existed in the first place.

"Yes, it does exist. I was working on it all yesterday and most of this morning. I have the beginnings of it backed up on my laptop." Eris snatched up her laptop case and booted the computer to prove her point.

The technician said, "Well, the company desktop just ate what you did today. My only suggestion is to upload the file from your laptop for last night's data and redo today's. I wish I had a better solution for you."

"Here. See?" Eris clicked the icon. Her laptop made that annoying error noise and gave her the same message as the computer.

Without permission, the technician took the laptop from her and repeated her earlier search. "Same thing over here. There's nothing there."

"That can't be!"

"I'm sorry. The file must have gotten corrupted." The technician handed back the laptop with an apologetic expression. "Looks like you're starting completely over."

Eris let her head fall against the back of her chair and resisted the urge to chuck her laptop across the room. It was an expensive laptop with a lot of data on it that she needed. Not to mention, she might hit someone.

"Fine. Thanks for coming out," she mumbled.

"Wish I could have been more helpful. Good luck." The technician walked away.

Eris waited until the sound of the technician's footsteps receded before she looked at the phone. "Ugh."

She dialed Brian's number and then explained the situation to him.

"Tech support couldn't get it back?" Brian asked.

"Nope. She was just here and nada. Even if I stay all night, there's no way I'm getting done in time to go with Connie tomorrow. Sorry, Brian."

"Not your fault. Don't worry about it. Connie's a big girl. She can go on her own. It would have been better with you there, but we'll deal. You do what you can with that file."

"Can you do me a favor?"

"Call the client?"

"Please. I don't want to deal with him again. I already feel crappy enough."

Brian laughed. "You concentrate on that and I'll make sure the client understands and doesn't call you personally."

"Thank you."

"Good luck."

She grumbled under her breath as she hung up the phone.

"This sucks!" She kicked the edge of her desk to add emphasis to that sentiment. That was the extent of her pity party. She retrieved all the hard copies she'd filed and dropped them near her keyboard.

She eyed the computer for a minute. With her fingers crossed, she tried the icon one more time.

The error sound mocked her, and the accompanying gray message box was like the computer sticking its tongue out at her.

"I hate you," she whispered to it before starting her work all over again.

Chapter Two

Lucien looked at his watch and shook his head. "She's late."

The woman Ranulf was supposed to greet had probably gotten lost on her way out to the property. It wasn't easy to find and that's how Lucien liked it. No unknown guests at odd hours—unwanted guests who knew the way were a different matter.

However, Ranulf wasn't there to greet the woman. He'd been called away to an urgent meeting, leaving Lucien to play host—a job he hated.

Lucien had debated calling the company and postponing the meeting until a time Ranulf could do it, but decided against it. Ranulf would never let him hear the end of it. The man's nagging aside, Lucien wanted their collection cataloged as badly as Ranulf.

A quick glance at his watch showed only two minutes had passed. He cursed and glared at the gate. Neither action made a car appear.

Rather than wear a groove into the front porch, he retreated to his office. There was a contract awaiting a final once over that would cede controlling interest to him and Ranulf for a company that had been lucrative in its heyday but had hit a rough patch due to bad management. The current president of the Mizukinawa Entertainment Group didn't want foreigners in her company but needed the collateral Lucien and Ranulf brought to the table.

While Ranulf was supposed to okay the contract before Tokyo opened for business, his meeting couldn't be denied. That left the task to Lucien. Yet another thing Lucien hated. He was better suited to the checking-signing part of the process. He'd been told many times that he didn't have the demeanor for negotiation.

While they both were capable of finalizing contracts, Ranulf's knowledge of business law and his attention to minute details most people overlooked made Lucien feel more confident about signing. Even if Lucien did overlook something that later came back to haunt them, all of their contracts had a loophole buried in legal jargon for a clean, inexpensive escape.

He'd read two lines when his cell phone rang.

"Hello?"

"Sir, a Ms. Connie Depar is here for her meeting."

"Thank you, Grant. Direct her where to park her car. I'll meet her at the door." Lucien snapped the phone shut and stood.

He finished reading the paragraph he had started. He'd rather read the whole thing. The contract was the lesser of the two evils, and the one he'd wanted to do.

With a sigh, he pushed away from his desk, left his office, and went to the front door. The woman topped the stairs just as he opened it. "You must be Connie Depar. I'm Lucien Riordan." He held out his hand.

Connie shook his outstretched hand and smiled at him after looking him up and down. "Nice to meet you, Mr. Riordan. You can call me Connie. I'm sorry to be a tad bit late, but this place isn't easy to find. I thought I got the directions wrong."

"That's normal. You aren't the first. Shall I show you the collection?"

"By all means." She pulled out a clipboard from her bag and followed him. "This is a lovely home you have here, Mr. Riordan."

"Thank you."

She looked at one wall and then another as they walked.

Lucien didn't bother following her gaze. He knew what his weapon collection looked like. He also knew how she would react. The same way everyone reacted when seeing every inch of wall space covered with swords, battleaxes, spears, and various other edged weaponry from around the globe. It was another collection he and Ranulf had amassed over the centuries. And, yet another collection that needed cataloging. He'd have to remember to mention it to Ranulf.

"Does *Mrs.* Riordan mind having all these weapons about?"

"I'm not married," he said.

"Never say so. A handsome man like you isn't married? You must not get out much or else some woman would have run off with you by now."

He stifled a sigh when Connie moved closer to him. It would be rude to push her away, but the temptation was there. He didn't like people invading his personal space, whether it was bodily or his living area. That, at least, was an idiosyncrasy he hadn't grown out of—neither did he want to.

"I don't get out much."

"Now that won't do at all." She dug a business card out of her purse and held it out to him, brushing her breasts against his arm as she did. "Call me. Staying in is boring."

"I prefer it that way."

Connie pouted at him. Then, he remembered Ranulf's words from the day before. They wouldn't find Eris by sitting around the house. He took the card Connie offered him and put it in his breast pocket. "However, a change of scenery may do me good."

"That's the way." She linked her arm with his and smiled up at him.

If the woman knew Lucien only saw her as a means to find another woman, she wouldn't cling to him so much. That information was none of her concern so he kept it to himself.

He led the way down a hallway and opened the door at the end of the walk. "This is only a fraction of the collection."

Connie peered into the room but didn't let him go to get a closer look. "Very nice. Quite a big size." She wet her lips and looked at him, her eyes hooded. "I bet the collection takes after its owner."

He chose to ignore her less-than-blatant sexual innuendo. "This room is where the appraisal team will work. There is a video surveillance system, but it isn't wired for sound. I'm sure your employees are trustworthy, but I take no chances."

"How long have you lived out here?"

He tried to free his arm, but Connie retained her hold. She smiled at him, probably thinking he was playing with her. He swore Ranulf would pay for this. "Years, which is why the collection is so big, and why we wish it appraised and cataloged."

"Yes, the collection." Connie released his arm and entered the room.

Lucien thought the woman's amateur and unwanted seduction was over, but he was mistaken. She bent and placed her bag on the ground, making sure the front of her blouse dipped low. The woman actually had the nerve to check and see if he was looking.

He stared at her because looking away might make her think he was shy. He'd willingly look at any woman who cared to flash him. That didn't mean he was interested, just that he wasn't dead.

She sat on one of the boxes then crossed her legs. Her short skirt rode high and revealed quite a bit of her thighs. She smoothed a hand over her legs as she reached in her bag for a pen.

Lucien opened his mouth to demand she get to the job at hand when she said, "Judging by the amount of boxes, I'd say this is a four month job, no more than six."

"Are you sure four months is an accurate estimate? I don't know how quickly your employees work, but this is a big collection." He waved his hand at the boxes in front of him. "This is only a part of it—a *small* part. There is more in storage, almost five hundred—"

"Not to worry. Not to worry. I assure you this is normal. Not all at once, and from one client, mind you, but still normal." Connie jotted a few notes then chewed the tip of her pen. "I will, of course, assign Erin's team to this job. Hers is the best. She even invented the new cataloging system the company is implementing. Very smart girl."

"I'll take you at your word." He didn't add that he thought the woman wasn't his idea of a trustworthy source since she actually believed her actions intrigued him.

"She was supposed to accompany me on this estimate, but another project had a slight problem, and she couldn't make it. Not to worry though, the problem was nothing she did—computer malfunction." Connie looked around the room again. "It might be a good idea for the team to stay here. You have such a huge house. I'm sure you'd never notice them. I'd make regular visits to ensure they upheld company policy, of course."

"My business is run from this house. My partner and I are busy men. We don't like house guests, especially ones we've never met."

"Partner?"

"He's currently attending a meeting, so I was left to meet you and negotiate the contract for an appraisal on our collection. We have delayed this little project for years. Our collection has only gotten bigger in that time."

"A partner."

Connie's entire demeanor changed. She stood and pulled her skirt to its normal length. Her flirty attitude disappeared, and the businesswoman snapped into place.

Lucien knew the woman had jumped to the wrong conclusion. It was plain on her face. The thought of him and Ranulf in an intimate, sexual relationship with each other made his lunch rise in his throat. He'd allow her the misconception since it made her stop flirting with him.

He didn't even know how he'd managed to live with Ranulf over the centuries. Living on opposite sides of their vast mansion and having wholly separate lives had helped.

It hadn't always been that way. They used to be close friends. Ranulf had saved his life, and Lucien trusted no other with it. But, like all close friendships, the love of a single woman had come between them.

"In any case," Connie said, "if my people will be commuting such a long way every work day then the company requires you to pay mileage. It would be ideal if we could transport the collection to the main office but not practical given its size."

"I don't mean to sound rude, but do you really think I'm worried about the cost of this venture?"

"As well off as you are, I guess not."

"I would like a simple estimate of time and cost and a start date." The woman had run through his patience reserves, which weren't high to begin with. Unlike most long-lived beings, Lucien hadn't gained that particular virtue.

"Sure." She looked at her clipboard and tapped the end of her pen against a miniature calculator. She wrote a few figures on the sheet then held it out for Lucien to see. "That is a rough estimate. It may go up or down once everything is tallied and—"

"Fair enough." He handed back the clipboard. "When will they start?"

"Is the day after tomorrow too soon? I think Erin should be done with her current project by then. I have to check with her once I get back to the office since she's rerouted all her calls to another desk so nothing can bother her. Also, and I'm not certain about this, but I think part of her team is on vacation, or was it assignment? Whichever, they aren't available either." She paused and chewed her pen some more. "Perhaps it would be better to have another team take on this job. I don't know who's free though."

The woman knew nothing for sure. Who had approved her to work as a field agent? That person needed a course in proper placement of personnel.

"Connie, I thank you for your time. When you have all the information finalized, simply fax back the finished contract with the start date." He flipped a business card out of his breast pocket, almost handing back hers. "There are five fax numbers on there, and any of them will do. At this time, I have another meeting to attend."

"I'm sorry this took so long."

So am I, he thought. He walked with her back to the foyer. Leon, the butler, waited near the door. "Have a safe drive back to your office, and I look forward to your company's services. If you would excuse me." He walked away before she could say more and enclosed himself in his office.

Next time, he would leave Ranulf to deal with the annoying, sex-deprived woman while he went to the meeting. Lucien glanced at his watch then at the papers lying on his desk. He had another hour before Tokyo's start of business.

He sat back and stared at the ceiling. Thoughts of his old life crept over him even as he tried to keep his mind in the present. Life had definitely been simpler back in the twelve hundreds, albeit a little more dangerous.

His gaze strayed to the contract. It hadn't reviewed itself while he daydreamed away his time. He straightened with a sigh and got to work.

He flipped to the last page when Ranulf entered the office. Lucien didn't acknowledge him. He had ten more minutes before a very excitable Japanese woman called him to bicker over nothing as had become her custom since the start of the contract negotiations over a month ago.

"When will they be here?" Ranulf asked, leaning his hip against Lucien's desk.

Lucien grunted.

"That isn't an answer."

"If you'd bothered to do as I asked before *leaving the house*, I would have time to talk to you."

Ranulf snorted. "Is that what this is about? You're being pissy because I made you meet someone new? Grow up, Lucien."

"This has nothing to do with my maturity level. Meeting new people means preparing for their eventual demise. I'm getting sick of attending funerals."

"Ha! You were always anti-social, even back when we were mortal. Whereas back then your personality quirk was tolerated because you were a lord, nowadays you're seen as a reclusive asshole."

"Which is why you handle the first meetings."

"And why I leave the tough cases to you." Ranulf smirked as he gestured to the contract.

Lucien picked it up and waved it in Ranulf's face. "This wouldn't be necessary if we had never sold that company back to them three generations ago. Her great-great-great-great grandfather wasn't this much of a pain in the ass."

"You missed a great. Besides, she's like that because she's a woman president in corporate Japan. Their glass ceilings are made out of cement with a large sign that says no girls allowed. She's had to become tough to prove she can do the job she inherited." He chuckled. "Any woman who has nerve enough to yell at you—over the phone or in person—is definitely worthy of heading that company, even if her two predecessors ran it into the ground thus compelling our involvement once more. Or, you could simply let the company flounder and die. Though you did promise her ancestor that you would look out for his family in exchange for having harbored us so many centuries ago."

"You would bring that up."

"Like you had forgotten. You never forget a debt, Lucien."

"Pain in my ass," Lucien grumbled, lowering the contract back to his desk so he could continue reviewing it.

Ranulf crossed his arms. "You know that contract backwards and forwards. Stop fawning over it like it's your baby and answer my question. When will the catalogers be here?"

"The rep wasn't sure." Lucien pushed the contract away and looked at Ranulf. "She sang the praises of a woman named Erin who heads the best team, which she wants to send, but isn't sure when they're available or how much it will cost. The woman was a complete flake."

"Tell me how you really feel about her," Ranulf said with a smirk.

"Her little mind leapt to the conclusion that we're lovers when she misinterpreted a comment I made."

Ranulf shuddered with a look of disgust. "While I know our living situation leaves us open to that assumption, I wish people would stop making it."

"If she has to come back out here, you're dealing with her."

"I would have dealt with her this time if I had been given a choice. You know how this goes, Lucien. We don't choose. Our benefactor does." Ranulf sat across from Lucien and propped his booted feet on the desk. "This time he chose a walk in the park."

"*That* was the pressing business?"

"Genevieve was there."

Lucien frowned. "He can talk to her whenever he chooses. He doesn't need us for that."

"She insisted. According to her, having one of us there humanizes him a little so she can deal with him better."

Ranulf didn't elaborate more than that, and Lucien didn't ask. They went where they were told and then pretended they heard and saw nothing. For that service, they were granted life everlasting.

The fax machine rang, beeped, and then the printer spat out several pages.

Ranulf retrieved the document. He read it over and handed it to Lucien. "Since when is your name Lucianne?"

Lucien looked at the typo on the contract Connie had faxed. The woman had not only emasculated him, she spelled his last name wrong. He'd given her a business card and still she'd made the mistake. "I told you. The woman is a flake."

"Let's hope Erin and her team of appraisers have a better eye for detail—and names."

"We should contact another company."

"No, no, let's give them a chance. They are the number one company for this kind of work, and we've worked with them before, though it was through a third party."

Lucien scraped his pen across the pages, making handwritten corrections so he could fax it back. "I don't know why I still trust you," he grumbled.

"You don't have any choice in the matter."

* * * *

"Erin, I have a job for you."

Eris rolled her eyes and sighed in annoyance. Connie had worked with her for two years and still couldn't remember her name.

"Connie, my name is Eris. Err-ris. Like Iris but with an E. Not Erin."

"I thought that's what I said." Connie shrugged. "I'll get it eventually. Keep reminding me."

Eris bit back the snappy retort about branding her name backwards on the woman's forehead so she would see it whenever she checked her reflection, which seemed to be every minute. Eris said, "You mentioned something about a job."

"Yes. We just picked up a very, very rich client with a nice-sized collection. He wants it appraised and cataloged for insurance purposes. I mentioned your name as one of my best catalogers."

Probably the wrong name, Eris grumbled mentally.

Like every other client Connie had ever referred Eris to, she would have to explain in a professional manner that Erin wasn't her name and Connie was a flake who couldn't seem to remember that fact.

Connie said, "I've already sent over Pete, Chad, and Michael so they can start."

Eris let her head drop against her desk with a loud thud.

"What? What's that for? You don't want the job?"

"Connie, the collection has to be cataloged *first*. The geeks should be the last ones touching them, not the first."

"They said the same thing, but they went anyway."

"They probably wanted to get a feel for the collection."

As if on cue, Eris's desk phone rang. She picked it up. "This is Eris."

"Eris, I have a call from Pete for you. He said you wouldn't mind him interrupting," the secretary said.

"It's okay. Put him through."

"Hold, please."

The phone beeped and music played for a second then Pete's voice came on the line. "Hey, Eris, this is Pete. Has Connie talked to you?"

"She's here now."

"Good, then you know about the new job."

"Yes. She said she sent you and the rest of the geeks out already and you went. Why?"

Pete laughed. "We didn't. We called the client and let him know we couldn't start until tomorrow. Right?"

"I'm almost finished with this last project—thank God—so yeah, tomorrow sounds about right."

"Yeah, we just let Connie think we were going out there. We headed for lunch, and now we're at the shop around the corner for market research."

"Market research, huh? You guys are so bad. So, we're set for tomorrow then. I'll let you guys get back to it, and I'll see you there in the morning."

"See ya."

Eris hung up the phone then said for Connie's benefit, "That was Pete. He let the client know they couldn't start without me, and I'm not available until tomorrow. We'll be there bright and early."

"So long as they informed the client, and he was okay with it. This is a very, very rich man."

"You said that already."

"He has a nice collection and may even invest in the company if we impress him. That's why I'm sending you and the best of the geeks...I mean, of the grading department."

"Connie, just call them geeks like everyone else. You aren't insulting them. It's okay. The geeks of the world have reclaimed the word and made it mean something good. Well, not negative at any rate."

"It's not professional, and I'd hate to slip and call them that in front of a client. Here—" she placed a file folder on Eris's desk, "—is the client info and the directions to his estate."

"Estate?"

"I mentioned he is rich. People with that much money don't live in houses. They live in estates or mansions. It's three miles to his front gate once you leave the highway, and that's all wooded land with call boxes every few hundred feet."

Eris flipped open the file and scanned the contents. "You estimated four months, and he's paying commuting costs."

"Yes, I insisted on that. His collection is much too large to send here, so you're going to it. He suggested the group of you simply board there for the duration, but I talked him out of it. There's too much chance one of you would do or say something unprofessional that might insult him. You know these rich people. They are very sensitive about the oddest things."

"Uh-huh. Well, the geeks and I will endeavor to uphold the company image and finish our job as quickly and accurately as possible."

Connie patted Eris's shoulder. "Good girl. I knew I could count on you. Keep me posted on the progress and have fun."

Something about Connie's tone made Eris think she'd missed some important detail, or Connie hadn't told her something. She'd find out tomorrow morning. Hopefully, the feeling was a false alarm and nothing to worry about. Knowing Connie the way she did, Eris would hope her feeling was wrong but prepare for the worst-case scenario all the same.

Chapter Three

"The appraisal team is here," Leon announced. He stepped out of the doorway and waited.

Lucien looked at Ranulf, but the man didn't move. Lucien cleared his throat.

Ranulf didn't look at him but continued reading over the paperwork before him.

"Ranulf—"

"First you complain when I don't do the final on the contracts, then you complain when I don't greet the guests. Which is it to be, Lucien? You can't have both." Ranulf looked at him.

Lucien left the room. The sound of Ranulf chuckling followed him. He depended on the man entirely too much, and Ranulf knew it.

Leon gestured to the three waiting men. "The Certification Granting Company's appraisers, sir."

Lucien held out his hand to the man nearest him. "I am Lucien Riordan, partial owner of the collection. Call me Lucien. My partner is busy at the moment, but you'll meet him later."

The middle-aged man shaking his hand said, "I'm Pete. Nice to meet you." He gestured to his younger companions. "This is Chad, and this is Michael."

The others shook Lucien's hand. He looked beyond the men for the fabled Erin. "Connie said there was a fourth—your team leader. Where is she?"

"She's not here yet?" Chad looked at the others then back at Lucien. "It's not like her to be late. She hates being late. Let me try her cell phone."

Lucien nodded. "Please. She may be lost."

Michael said, "It's almost guaranteed if she's following Connie's directions."

Lucien didn't have to ask. If Connie had made the same mistakes on the directions as she had on the contract, then there was no telling where Erin was at the moment.

Chad snapped his phone shut. "No answer. I got her voicemail and left a message."

"Call the office?" Michael asked.

Pete said, "There's no way she'd go to the office first then come here. They're in opposite directions." He gave Lucien an apologetic look. "We can't start without her. I'm sorry. I'm sure the company won't charge you for the wait time."

"We're paying by the day, not the hour," Lucien said. Something like this should bother him, but he found he wasn't annoyed. The men before him weren't at fault for their leader's absence. And Erin's tardiness could—and would—be blamed solely on Connie.

He asked, "Have you eaten? The cook has an annoying habit of making king-sized breakfasts, knowing full well Ranulf and I don't eat before lunch."

"Did someone say my name?" Ranulf walked toward the group. "I'm Ranulf Styr, the other owner. Call me Ranulf. Nice to meet you…" He trailed off with a frown as he looked around. "Aren't there supposed to be four?"

"We've theorized she's lost due to Connie's false directions," Lucien said. "They can't start without her, so I've invited them to eat our breakfast."

"Better them than sending it to the main office, I suppose. Enjoy, gentlemen. I only wanted to show my face. I've done that, and now I must get back to work." Ranulf nodded and went back to the office.

Chad, Pete, and Michael looked at each other then Lucien. Michael said, "I never turn down free food. Lead on, Lucien."

* * * *

"I can't believe this. Late on my first damn day." Eris peered out of her windshield, hoping she'd turned off onto the correct tree-lined, deserted road.

Connie said the gate to the client's *estate* was three miles off of the highway exit, but Eris had already gone five. The nagging feeling of being lost wouldn't leave her alone. She was about to turn around and go back for another try when a security guard station and a large wrought iron gate loomed ahead of her.

She pulled to a stop and the guard came to her rolled-down window. "Hi. I'm looking for this address." She held out the paper she'd used for the directions.

"You're here, miss. Your name is?"

"I'm Eris Brue with the Certification Granting Company to catalog the owner's collection. My colleagues should have already arrived." *Two hours ago*, she added to herself.

She only hoped the client—essentially her new boss for the next four months—was the understanding and forgiving sort. Eris prided herself on her punctuality, but today was the exception. One bad thing after another had happened to her that morning, making her late.

The guard said, "I don't see an Eris Brue on the list."

And they kept happening.

Eris held back a sigh and pasted a smile on her face. "Is there an Erica Bree or Erin Burn or some combination thereof on the list?"

"Yes to Erin Burn."

"That's me."

The guard gave her an incredulous look.

"I know how this sounds, but the woman who gave you that name is notorious for getting my name wrong. I'm supposed to be here, and I'm very late."

"Fine, I'll play along."

"Thank you," she said then rolled up her window and waited for the guard to open the gate.

He tapped on her window. She rolled it down again and he said, "Hand your car keys over to my associate, and I'll take you up to the house myself. If you're supposed to be here, we'll park your car in the garage. If not, I'll escort you back."

"Fine, whatever." She rolled the window up, shut off the car and got out with her laptop bag in tow. The car could get stolen and she wouldn't be too upset, but her laptop currently had her life stored on its hard drive.

The guard waited for her in a golf cart. She handed over her keys to the second guard and got on the passenger seat.

She said, "I'm really sorry about this. It's not a scam, I promise you. My co-worker is lousy with names."

"The other three guys checked out fine."

"She's lousy with *my* name."

"Eris—Greek goddess of chaos, right?"

"Yeah. That describes my whole morning from the beginning until now."

During the drive to the front door, Eris learned her driver's name was Grant and he was an avid student of Greek mythology. He insisted on hearing the story of why her parents named her after the goddess of chaos. Eris obliged him, but gave the truncated version to head off more questions since she wasn't in much of a conversation mood.

Grant ushered her to an office to the left of the foyer. He knocked on the door then entered when the man inside said to do so.

Before Grant could present her case, Eris said quickly, "I am so sorry I'm late, sir. I ran into car trouble this morning and then the tow truck guy took forever to get to me and I got a little lost on my way here. I'm not usually late. I prefer getting to appointments early, but—"

"Mr. Styr," Grant said over her, "this woman claims she's with the group from the CGC, but her name's not on the list."

"As I told Grant already," Eris said in a tone she knew was near exasperation, "my co-worker cannot remember my correct name, which is Eris Brue. I'm your cataloger."

But, I'd rather be yours, Eris thought. The man before her was tall, dark and handsome. Well, he looked tall. He was seated behind his desk staring at her and Grant with his tawny eyes wide and unblinking in a state of shock. She guessed they'd overwhelmed him.

His dark brown, almost black, hair was pulled back in, what Eris guessed, a ponytail. She couldn't tell. It could be braided. The length was an unknown in the man's current seated position, as well. She wanted to get up close and personal so she could find out first hand.

"Eris, there you are!"

Eris tore her gaze from the man and looked behind her. "Pete. Thank God. Tell them who I am."

Pete entered the room with Chad, Michael, and another unknown man following behind him. Chad threw his arm around Eris's shoulders and said, "Ranulf, Lucien, this is our fearless leader. Eris Brue. The best cataloger the company's got. When she's done with your collection, you'll be able to find an issue by the colors on the cover."

"I wouldn't go that far," Eris said.

The man with Chad stared at her in the same state of shock as the other. Eris couldn't figure out the problem.

Chad didn't seem to notice anything amiss. He pointed to the man with him and said, "This is Lucien Riordan and that—" he pointed to the man at the desk, "—is Ranulf Styr. They said to use their first names. I've been telling them all about you, well, actually just Lucien. Ranulf has been holed up in here doing busy work."

Eris snapped, "You couldn't have told them my name while you were at it?"

"I didn't know Connie had you listed wrong."

She raised an eyebrow at him.

"Okay, I should have guessed she'd flub your name and made sure the guys at the gate knew, but I thought you'd get here before us."

"I planned to, but my car died on me this morning." She put down her laptop bag, effectively dislodging Chad's arm.

"You should have called. Matter of fact, Chad tried calling you three times," Pete said.

She shook her head. "My cell is lost. I had it last night, and the thing grew legs and disappeared. I noticed it was missing when I decided I should call here and confirm the directions. To add insult to injury, my Internet connection isn't functioning properly either, so I couldn't go to a map site."

"Did Connie's directions get you that lost?"

"Horribly. She had all the exit numbers and names mixed. Thankfully, I figured it out."

"You should have called before you left your house."

"Sorry, *Dad*, but I don't have a landline since I have a cell phone, and I gave up looking for it because I didn't want to be late. I ended up borrowing my neighbor's phone to call the tow truck guy. He was such an ass—uh, excuse me—*jerk* about it I didn't want to ask if I could call here."

"You're here now," Lucien whispered. He cleared his throat and said in a normal tone, "Welcome, Eris. Chad has indeed told me much about you, but he never mentioned your name." He walked around Pete and offered her his hand.

"I'm really sorry I'm late," Eris said, shaking his hand. His grip tightened when she would have let go. She tugged on her hand, and he released her.

"Thank you, Grant. You can go," Ranulf said.

"Sure thing." Grant said to Eris, "Your car will be in the garage when you're ready to leave. Your keys will be on the small table near the front door."

"Thank you. Sorry again for making you come all the way up here," Eris said.

"It's my job." Grant nodded then left the room.

Ranulf came around his desk with his hand out toward Eris.

She shook his hand, and like Lucien, he hesitated before letting her go. Or maybe it was her imagination. Both men wore a weird expression and stared at her as though they couldn't believe she was real.

"Connie said your name was Erin," Lucien said.

"That's Connie for you," Pete said in annoyed tone. "She thought my name was Pat for the first six months I worked with her. Chad was Chris. Michael was the only one to escape."

"She made up for it by butchering my last name," Michael said. "How the hell do you get Kites out of Cates?"

"She—"

"Anyway," Eris said over Chad's reply. She smiled at Lucien and Ranulf. "I know I held everyone up, but I'm here now and anxious to get started."

"This way," Ranulf and Lucien said in unison. They looked at each other.

"Jinx," Eris said. The men looked at her. "Sorry. Silly joke." She gave a nervous laugh and quelled the urge to fidget under the men's scrutiny. "Connie said your collection would take four months. While I'd like to trust her estimate, she has been known to exaggerate."

"If you and your team could finish in four months, I'd be surprised and amazed," Lucien said.

Eris retrieved her laptop bag from the ground, but Ranulf took it from her. "It's not heavy."

"I insist," he said, tightening his grip.

"Thank you."

She walked out of the office with Lucien in front of her, Ranulf beside her and the rest of the guys following. Both Ranulf and Lucien were taller than her—Ranulf by a head while Lucien only had a few inches over her. Lucien's broad back held her mesmerized. She tried imagining what it would feel like to sleep on it. Not against it, *on* it. She didn't know what it was about broad shoulders, but they did it for her.

Both Lucien and Ranulf were blessed with that particular feature. Eris couldn't stare at Ranulf without being obvious so she settled on Lucien.

Sandy peach-fuzz covered his whole head from the top to the outline of his jaw to under his nose—all trimmed to the same length. Eris didn't usually go for guys with facial hair, but she would make an exception for Lucien if he showed an interest in her.

She should feel guilty about imagining a relationship with him while dating Clayton, but it was just imagination. Besides, both Lucien and Ranulf probably had girlfriends who spent all day in spas being pampered so they looked good for the cameras that probably appeared at the functions men like Lucien and Ranulf attended.

Eris wished she were camera-ready. Her head currently sported a colorful scarf that hid her roots. She hadn't seen her hairdresser in over a month. Her dreadlocks needed maintenance badly. Fuzzy described her hair situation best, which meant she'd be wearing scarves until she managed to find a free two to three hours for a hair appointment.

She ran a hand over her head, making sure her scarf was in place. When she lowered her hand, she bumped Ranulf's arm. She apologized quickly, but he only smiled at her.

"Before you got here, Lucien fed us and we were in the middle of a tour. This place is huge," Pete said.

Eris looked at her surroundings. All styles of edged weaponry adorned the walls along with several colorful, medieval banners. "Anyone trying to rob this place is in for one hell of fight. Are the weapons real or decorative?" She looked up at Ranulf for an answer.

"Real," he said. "Lucien and I spend our free time keeping the weapons cleaned and sharpened."

She looked around again. "You must have a lot of free time then."

"We do." Lucien glanced over his shoulder at her but looked away before she could meet his ice blue gaze.

"That's it. I have to ask," Chad said. "Are you two gay?"

Eris reacted. She swung back and smacked Chad's forehead with the back of her hand. "I can't believe you just asked that."

Ranulf chuckled.

"Ignore him. Chad doesn't think before he talks," Eris said, hoping Ranulf and Lucien didn't take offense. She also hoped the answer was no. It would be a shame to waste two such prime specimens of manhood on each other.

Lucien said, "We're not. We are old friends whose joint efforts have made us both rich. Since we work out of our home, it's only natural we live together."

"Besides, we'd only fight over what pieces of our many collections belong to whom if we lived separately," Ranulf said.

The group stopped walking when Lucien did. He opened the door in front of him then stepped back. "This is the room on which Connie based her estimate. I'm not sure she heard me when I told her this was only a small fraction. We have a climate-controlled storage facility separate from the house with the rest of the collection."

Eris walked forward, not believing her eyes. She touched the box closest to the door then looked at the other long, slender white boxes stacked around the room.

"Sweet Mary, mother of God's son," she whispered. "I've died and gone to comic book heaven."

Chapter Four

"Holy shit on burnt toast," Chad yelled. He pushed past Eris and fell into the room. "This is unreal." He removed the lid of one box and then another. They were all full of plastic-wrapped comics.

Pete was rooted to the spot where he stood, looking around in amazement. "Eris? Am I dreaming?"

"I'm right there with you, Pete." She walked farther into the room and turned in a slow circle. "This is only a fraction?"

Lucien said, "Fifty-eight boxes to start. The other five hundred remain in storage."

"Five hundred," Chad squeaked.

"Rough estimate."

Michael wheezed a little then pulled out his inhaler.

Eris whispered, "This is going to take way longer than four months." She sat on a stack of boxes then promptly jumped up with a mumbled apology.

Ranulf said, "You can sit on the boxes if you like. They are sturdy."

She shook her head. "I shouldn't."

Lucien said, "If they can hold my weight without caving then you are fine. Sit before you fall over."

She sat down again only because he insisted but would have rather used a chair. The only ones she saw were across the room. Walking to one of them would have posed a problem since she wasn't that stable at the moment.

Patting the box she sat on, she said, "Five hundred."

Pete said, "On my best day, I can only grade about two hundred comics—two-thirty if I'm in the zone. Each of these boxes holds at least that much—more if you cram them. I'd be here for the next few years."

Chad said, "Even with another team assisting, it would still take two years."

"That is considerably longer than four months," Lucien said.

Eris snapped out of her stupor and looked at him then Ranulf. She had to do something quick before they cancelled the contract. Sure, Connie was an idiot for quoting them such an unrealistic number, but Eris would give her the benefit of the doubt. The woman had probably thought Lucien meant five hundred more *comics* in storage, not comic *boxes*. An easy mistake to make, but that didn't make the situation unsalvageable.

She stood, forcing herself back into business mode. "Gentlemen, I know Connie quoted you four months, but there is no way we could do this job *accurately* in that amount of time with my current team—no company could." Both men watched her attentively. She took that to be a good thing. "While I am sorry about that, I hope you'll give us a chance to make the situation a little more agreeable."

"We're listening," Ranulf said, crossing his arms.

"I'm sure once my boss learns of the size of your collection he'll send more people. That would cost more, but with several teams—possibly two or three on any given day—it wouldn't take more than a year...or, not longer than eighteen months." She hated the pleading quality that entered her voice, but she wanted the job. The collector in her needed to see what the boxes held.

"Unreal," Chad rasped. He lifted a single comic from one of the boxes, holding it like a holy relic and looking at it with the same amount of awe. "This is Investigator Comics number one."

He looked around the room as though seeking confirmation. Pete and Michael gathered around him and stared.

Eris's eyes widened. While she wanted to check for herself, the professional in her kept her rooted to the spot, facing her clients. "Are you sure?" she asked over her shoulder.

"Dead sure. There are only four in existence, and I saw one in a museum. This comic is worth half a million, easy."

"I'm sorry to disappoint you then," Ranulf said.

Everyone looked at him.

He grinned. "Our collection has never been cataloged, and we've never declared any of our assets. That isn't one of the known four, so the value of all of them just went down since we have two copies."

Michael reached in the box and pulled out the second. "Unreal," he said in the same tone Chad had a moment ago.

Chad placed the comic back in the box as gingerly as he could and then walked on his knees over to Eris's side. With his hands clasped, he said, "Please, let us stay. Please, please. I'll work for free. You can't take this away from me. I've waited my whole life to see something this amazing."

So much for being professional, Eris thought. At least Lucien and Ranulf seemed amused at his display.

"I'd say the same thing, but my wife would kill me," Pete said. "I share the sentiment though, Lucien, Ranulf. This—" he swept out his arms, encompassing the room, "—is why I do what I do."

Eris looked at Michael. "You want to add anything?"

He shook his head and took another drag from his inhaler.

"Eighteen months?" Lucien asked.

She couldn't tell if he was annoyed or not at the estimate.

"Make your call then give us an accurate estimate of the cost."

"Thank you," Eris said in a breathy voice. She dug through her purse then patted her pockets.

"You said you lost your phone," Chad said.

"Yeah. That's right. I don't know where my mind went. Give me yours."

Chad unclipped his phone and handed it to her. She dialed the office and asked the secretary to transfer her to Brian as an emergency call.

"Eris, what's up, kiddo?"

"Brian, I so need you to say yes." She shouldered the phone and retrieved her laptop bag from Ranulf, mouthing a thank you.

"To what?"

"Have you spoken to Connie recently?" She sat on the nearest stack of boxes, started the laptop with one hand and dug out her camera with the other. Pete took the camera and snapped a few pictures of the room.

Brian said, "Yes, yes I have. She told me about the big, four-month contract she nabbed the company. Go her. You're there now, right? How's it going?"

"It's not at the moment." She glanced at Lucien and Ranulf then back to her computer.

"What's the problem?"

"Oh, we need about four or five more extended teams and a longer contract." Pete handed her the camera, which she connected to her computer. She knew Brian well. The man wouldn't send more help unless he had tangible proof it was needed. He relied too much on Connie's say-so. It didn't matter if she was the president's goddaughter. Her lackadaisical approach to her job hurt the appraisal teams that had to live up to her underestimations.

There was a long pause. Eris took the phone from her ear and made sure she hadn't gotten disconnected. "Brian?"

"Four or five more *extended* teams *and* a longer contract? What for? This isn't a hard job. You four can handle it."

"Brian, I know you trust Connie's judgment, but this time she is way off."

This time, Pete mouthed.

Eris rolled her eyes in response before she remembered Lucien and Ranulf watched her. She busied herself emailing the pictures Pete had taken to Brian.

"So you need more time? That's something you talk to the client about, not me."

She hit send. "Check your mail."

"Why?"

"Brian—"

"I'm checking. I'm checking. What is this?"

"The room I'm sitting in right now with the clients and my team."

"Merry Christmas, Momma."

Eris smiled. She'd won. "That's just this room. There are another five hundred *boxes*—give or take—in storage."

"I'll send the rest of yours and give you two extra extended teams on a part-time basis."

"But—"

"That's the best I can do, Eris. This project was only supposed to be one team. Rich or not, we still have to consider our other clients."

"True, true." She nodded. "Which teams do I get?"

"You have a choice—Nathan, Gretchen, and Clayton."

"What about Susie?"

"Nothing doing. Her team is second only to yours. I'm not losing her *and* you."

"Fine. Nathan and Clayton then."

"How did I know you would say Clayton?"

"It's not what you think."

"*Sure* it isn't."

"It's not," she snapped.

"Okay, fine. It's not."

"It isn't."

The man laughed at her, and she had to tamp down the urge to set him straight. In front of clients was not the ideal time for her to reiterate her ability to keep work and relationship separate.

She asked, "How soon can I have them?" She gave the men a thumbs up. Chad kissed her calf, and she pushed him away with her foot.

"Nathan's team is free tomorrow. I'll have to talk to Clayton. You can have one team for four days and the other for three. No arguments. Fax or email a schedule for approval so I know when they'll be in the office."

"Will do."

"Good, good. I'll have a new work contract faxed over before lunch. Is that all?"

"That's it. Thanks, Brian."

"Wait, Eris."

"What's up?"

"Do me a tiny favor. Keep an eye out for any of the comics on my want list. It's on my site. I'll pay up to ten percent over graded value."

"I'd say it's a safe bet with a collection this size. I'll keep an eye out and let you know. Anything else?"

"Nothing. Bye."

She pushed the end button.

Lucien asked, "What is the new situation?"

"CGC will provide you three extended teams. We—" she indicated the guys and herself, "—are the basic team. Normally, I would do all the cataloging, while the geeks—that's what we call the graders—evaluate the comics.

"An extended team adds more people so there are fewer things for each person to do. One to scan, one to do data entry, three to grade, and one to seal the comics."

"And there would be three teams?"

"Yes. My team will be here full time while Nathan and Clayton's teams will be here part time." She looked at her laptop where she'd started an email with her schedule proposal for Brian. "The way I figure it, all three teams would be here Wednesday and Thursday. All other days would be two teams." She glanced away from her laptop and met Lucien's gaze. "Unless you care who is here when."

"Not so much."

"Good."

Pete made a thinking noise. "So, Nathan and Clayton, huh?"

Eris froze. He wouldn't dare. Not in front of a client.

"No playing footsie under the table now." He winked at her.

Michael and Chad linked arms and sang together, "Clayton and Eris sitting in a tree—"

"Shut up! Oh my God, you guys are such brats." She said to Lucien and Ranulf, "Ignore them. They didn't mature past elementary school."

Ranulf said, "I take it there is something between you and Clayton?"

"They're dating," Chad said in a little kid voice. He made an exaggerated kissy face, complete with noises.

"If there is a chance of distraction, I'd rather this Clayton person not show," Lucien said.

"No, no." Eris placed her laptop aside and stood so she could face them properly. They needed to know her next words were serious and honest. "Clayton is not a problem. We may be dating, but our relationship has never interfered with our work."

"You're sure?"

"Very."

Lucien and Ranulf exchanged a look Eris couldn't read. It almost looked like worry. That didn't make any sense.

Pete said, "I'm just playing with her, guys. Eris is top notch all the way. She does every job she sets her mind to and is a great team leader. I'm putting that on her evaluation, as a matter of fact."

"Evaluation?" Ranulf asked.

"Pete is the actual team leader," Eris said. "He has stepped aside temporarily so I can assume the role. He's grading whether I'm ready to be a supervisor."

It meant a lot to her that Pete felt she could lead. They'd known each other for years. He was almost like an uncle to her. His approval was something she strove for.

"Between you and me," Pete said, leaning in close to Lucien and Ranulf, "I'm inclined to drag out her evaluation just so I can stay a peon. Not as much responsibility or stress."

Chad got to his feet. "You know, Pete, you could always evaluate me for a supervisor position."

"Good idea. Doing your eval would last until I retire, at least."

Eris laughed behind her hand at Chad's pout. She turned back to Lucien and Ranulf. "Everything meets with your approval then?"

"Oh yes," Ranulf said. "Three teams at eighteen months."

"Rough estimate," she said quickly.

He nodded.

Lucien said, "We will stop in from time to time for observation and reading purposes."

"Of course. That's not a problem. We sometimes have music playing, but you can tell us to simply shut it off."

"That won't be a problem."

Michael cleared his throat in an exaggerated manner. When Eris looked at him, he tugged at his dress shirt and coughed some more.

"I think Michael wants you to mention something about his clothing," Ranulf said.

"Dress code, actually. We're usually a jeans and t-shirt lot," Eris said.

"So long as the clothing is office-appropriate, we don't care what you wear."

Chad put his hands on his hips. "You mean I can't wear hot pants and a wife beater?"

Eris smacked her forehead. Yup, professional had definitely left the building. She grumbled, "Pay no attention to the idiot in the corner."

"Yo, Eris, does this belong to you?" Michael asked as he tossed something her way.

She put her hands out to catch it, but Lucien reached around her and caught it first.

"Nice catch," she said. He handed the object to her, and she stared at it. "My cell phone. Where was it?"

Michael pointed to the laptop case. "Under the laptop. You must have sat the computer on top of it in your rush out the door."

"I wasn't in a hurry when I packed my laptop. I know I left my cell on the kitchen counter next to my keys like I always do." She shook her head. "This day has been doing me wrong since I woke up. First, my alarm didn't go off, but I was already up because I was anxious to get started. My phone grew legs, my car crapped out on me, the tow truck guy got lost on the way to my place then took forever to give me a jump, I got turned around coming out here...argh. I know I'm named after Chaos but enough is enough."

Ranulf smoothed a hand over her head and bent so his face was close to hers. "No worries, Eris. You're here now, and everything is fine. Lucien and I may be a little annoyed at the delay, but it's not anything major."

"I'm so sorry about all of this," she said in a soft voice. He'd caught her gaze and held it with little effort. His hand on her head comforted her as such a motion always did.

"Don't be." He straightened quickly and removed his hand. "You're doing a beautiful job. I'm quite happy with your presence thus far."

"So, now what?" Pete asked.

Eris's stomach chose that moment to growl. She clutched her middle with a look of embarrassment. "I didn't eat breakfast," she whispered.

"That's not healthy," Lucien said.

"You're one to talk. Didn't you say you and Ranulf don't eat breakfast even though your cook makes it?" Pete asked.

Michael snapped his fingers. "That's right. There was still some left over. The bottomless pit over there didn't finish it off." He jerked his thumb toward Chad.

Lucien put his hand at the small of Eris's back and urged her out of the room. "By all means. Come eat while the geeks browse the collection."

"Oh, that's not going to happen." She stopped and looked back into the room. "Guys, you're going to do scanning and data entry for the rest of today so tomorrow you can start grading without having to wait for me to finish each issue, thus slowing you down."

They groaned.

"And I'd love it if one of you could get my scanner and printer out of the car and have it hooked up by the time I get back. Please."

"You got it," Pete said, saluting her.

She smiled at him then looked at Lucien and Ranulf. "So, someone said something about food?"

Chapter Five

Ranulf clasped his hands behind his back as he walked beside Eris to the kitchen. That was the only way he could keep from touching her. His hand on her head earlier had been a mistake. He'd almost kissed her and—God help him—she'd looked receptive to the idea.

He glanced at Lucien, who walked on Eris's other side. Ranulf knew his long time friend was having the same issues of control.

Eris was there. She'd returned, in a manner of speaking.

The Eris he'd known in the past had been quiet and timid, while the woman before him had an air of confidence and a beautiful smile. He never knew she could make such an expression, but she'd never been truly happy when he and Lucien first met her.

She didn't look very different from how he remembered her. A gray pants suit with a rose-colored blouse accented her gentle curves, while her low heels made her hips sway in a manner that would mesmerize if he chanced walking behind her.

Even her flawless sienna-colored skin was the same. And, he noted with happiness, she didn't mar it with makeup. A little glitter dusted her eyelids, and her full lips shined with gloss, but that was the extent of it.

Ranulf had wanted to shout for joy when she'd walked into his office pleading her case, but he could only stare in disbelief. He thought he'd wake any moment and find he'd been dreaming and she'd never been there.

He had to be careful though. They knew her, but she'd only just met them. A too familiar gesture or the wrong words would send her away from them as quickly as she'd arrived.

He asked, "How long have you worked at CGC?"

"Two years. Actually, I worked as a convention representative, peddling our services for a year and then became part of a grading team two years ago. I've always loved comics."

"You have a collection of your own then?"

"No. Absolutely not. I'd be broke, not that I'm not already close."

"Who is Clayton?" Lucien blurted out.

Ranulf snapped, "Lucien! That's none of your business."

Lucien looked at him. Ranulf warned the man with his eyes to watch himself. He then looked down at Eris, who watched them with a small amount of fear. He said in a soothing voice, "Ignore him. He's only being nosy. You've said you and Clayton can do the job. We believe you."

Eris relaxed visibly and nodded.

"Sorry," Lucien whispered. "It's none of my business."

"Clayton and I only recently graduated to couple status. We've been friends and hanging out for months."

"Ah," Ranulf said, feigning interest he didn't have. The last thing he wanted to talk about was Eris's...boyfriend. Even thinking the word made him see red. She was supposed to be single.

Before his thoughts took him in an angry direction, he asked, "What all will your team be doing? I've read about the process but reading and seeing are two different things."

Eris nodded. "Of course. If I had accompanied Connie yesterday, I would have explained the whole process then."

She looked apologetic again. At least that aspect of her character hadn't changed.

Lucien said, "There's no need to worry about that. It was a situation out of your control."

"The process sounds more convoluted than it really is," Eris said. "Saul, who you'll meet tomorrow, will be scanning the front and back cover, as well as the copyright page. For foldout covers, he'll scan the entire image. All those image files will be attached to that particular entry."

Both Ranulf and Lucien made sounds of understanding.

"After Saul, the comics go to Chad, then Michael, then Pete—they are lovingly referred to as the geeks since each is a comic fanatic. Each of them will go through the comic looking for imperfections that may bring down the grade."

Lucien asked, "Imperfections such as what?"

She shrugged. "Dog eared pages, torn pages, missing pages. Sometimes stuff that you as the buyer have no control over, like ink going out of the lines or the staples being off center. All of those things and more can bring the graded value of the comic down."

"I'm sure it's a long list of things to look out for," Ranulf said.

She nodded. "Hence having three sets of eyes going over it to catch what the others miss. All the imperfections are counted and the grade assigned. From there, the graders' notes and the scanned images come to me while the comic itself goes to Megan, the woman who will be sealing your comics."

Lucien asked, "You will not be handling the comics?"

"The less they are handled, the better. I input a long list of things such as the title of the comic, issue number, whether it's part of a series, date of publication, print run, writer, artist, inker, cover artist if the person is different from the interior artist, publisher…" She trailed off with a small smile. "Do you want to hear the whole list?"

"By all means," Ranulf said with a grin.

Lucien said, "No, you don't have to recite the whole list." He shot Ranulf a look and then said to Eris, "Chad mentioned being able to find issues by the colors on the cover. I assume that has something to do with what you input."

Eris said, "He was exaggerating. While I do input characters and words depicted on the cover, I don't input colors."

"Characters should be enough. It sounds like a lot."

"I'm a fast typist. Once the full team is here and my main focus is data entry, I'll move as quickly as the geeks. We should finish a box a day."

"That sounds good." Ranulf pushed open the kitchen door and waved her forward.

Eris sniffed the air. "Smells good."

"Thank you. I try," the woman near the stove said.

Ranulf said, "Eris, this is our cook Liselle. If the food the geeks left isn't enough, feel free to ask her to make more." He grabbed Lucien's arm and kept the man from following Eris when she walked to the table. "Lucien and I have some things to discuss. Will you be able to find your way back?"

"Pretty straight shot. I shouldn't get lost," she said.

"If you're unsure, our butler Leon is usually skulking around. He'll direct you back to the survey room. We'll check on your progress later." He winked at her then walked away with his hand firmly clamped onto Lucien's arm. The man didn't fight him. Ranulf released Lucien before they reached their shared office.

"I don't want him here," Lucien said once Ranulf closed the door. He paced from the door to the desk and back again.

"I assume you mean Clayton. I don't want him here either, but what excuse do we give? Eris said his presence won't be a problem."

"*I* have a problem with him."

"Why? What is the reason you would relate to her boss for his dismissal?" Ranulf held up a hand when Lucien would have answered. "And remember, you and I just met Eris today."

"Damn it!"

Ranulf leaned against his desk. "I have an idea."

Lucien stopped pacing and looked at him.

"We can prepare the rooms on either side of the current one. Each team would have their own room and that means Clayton will be kept separate and away from Eris." Ranulf made an off-hand gesture. "While he's here, at any rate. He won't see Eris during the work-day, and we'll stay away from him. He'll live past his experience on our property, which means we won't have to go into hiding for murder."

"Fine. Good plan. Are we done?"

Ranulf rounded his desk and sat. "No. Go do your work."

"You—"

"We'll scare her away if we crowd her. She's here. We've met. Let the rest play out at her speed."

Lucien threw himself onto his chair. "I had no idea it would be this maddening. She is right here. I touched her. I wanted to do more than touch her." He glared at Ranulf. "You very nearly did."

"I stopped myself."

"See that you keep stopping yourself or Eris will only have one suitor."

Ranulf smirked at Lucien's threat. "You couldn't beat me then. What makes you think you can beat me now?"

"Overstep your bounds again and you'll find out."

* * * *

Eris couldn't help pausing and looking at every eye-level weapon on her way back to the survey room. Each piece was lethally elegant. She reached out to touch one.

"Are you lost, miss?"

She snatched her hand away with a yelp then looked over her shoulder at the man who'd spoken. "You must be Leon, right?"

"That's correct. Have you lost your way?"

"No. Sorry. I'm heading back to start my work now."

"Of course, miss. I would ask that you not touch any of the weapons. They are very sharp. I wouldn't want you to get hurt."

"Sorry." She continued on her way with the butler watching her progress.

Chad, Pete and Michael sat at a table that held a stack of comics. Michael scanned while Pete entered the copyright information into her laptop and Chad did the first round of grading.

"How far are you?" she asked.

"Thirty in. Pete types slow," Michael said.

"You can't type at all," Pete snapped.

"Boys, let's play nice while we're not in the office. I'm sure there's a camera around here somewhere." She looked around the room and spotted a tiny black bubble protruding from the ceiling tiles. There were five others in the room. She pointed at one of the bubbles and said, "Case in point."

Pete vacated the seat before the laptop and sat on the other side of Chad. "I didn't make the name code, since I still don't understand your system for that, but everything else is inputted. Michael's gonna scan the rest of that box, which should see us through the day, and then we're going to grade."

"Sounds like a plan." Eris did a quick check over Pete's work and was satisfied he'd made only a few mistakes.

He may be the actual supervisor, but the database system was her invention. She'd given the company exclusive usage on the basis that she have job security and upward mobility. While the company loved the software, they didn't like the complexities of the naming system she'd concocted to go with it. Even after writing out a detailed handbook explaining how she'd come up with the code, people still didn't get it right.

She entered the name code for Lucien and Ranulf. The computer beeped at her and she stared. "Well, I'll be damned."

"What?" Pete scribbled a note on the paper in front of him then looked at her.

"We've worked with Lucien and Ranulf's collection before."

Michael said, "No way. We'd have heard about a collection this big."

She did a quick search of the company database and found well over two thousand comics listed. The titles were recent.

"It's only their newer titles. They've paid for our platinum service—a rep flies out to the printers and grades and seals the comics as they come off the press." She scrolled down the list. "They get two of every title they collect. One has a sealed grade and the other has an open grade."

"One to keep and one to read," Pete said. "Wish I could do that. My wife promised me pain in a bad way if my collection got any bigger. I've had to limit my collection to the titles I truly love and a few number ones and specials."

"Hmphf. Half my paycheck is going toward a very large, climate-controlled storage unit for my collection," Michael said.

"Lightweights," Chad said. "I talked my friend, who owns a store, into letting me rent space in his warehouse where he keeps the bulk of his inventory and his own collection."

Eris started typing, not bothering to add her comments to the who-has-the-bigger-collection contest since hers didn't even compare. The guys' banter flowed around her. Ignoring them was second nature. Once started, she usually phased out of reality. Her fingers got the job done while her mind wandered.

Its first stop—Ranulf. She'd almost had a close call with him. Maybe it was her imagination again, but she got the feeling he was about to kiss her when he had his hand on her head. Of course, there was no way. Ranulf was probably like Chad, one of those people who liked to touch others while talking to them. With that little idiosyncrasy came a disregard for personal boundaries. That would explain how close he had gotten.

Lucien, on the other hand, didn't seem like the touchy-feely type. Although, he had held her hand for longer than was necessary for a handshake. And, he sounded almost jealous when he asked her about Clayton.

Her imagination had to be working overtime if she thought either man was the least bit interested in her. Lucien wouldn't be jealous over a woman he'd just met. Neither would Ranulf try to kiss her.

Whatever the case may be, she was happy both men seemed laid back and approachable. That would make the coming months much easier.

Chapter Six

"Welcome back, Eris." Lucien looked at his watch. "Early, I might add."

"My phone was where I left it, my car started like usual, I didn't get lost on the way out here, and the gate guard recognized me. So I'm back on track." She held out the revised contract. "This is your copy of the contract. I looked it over for typos. Everything is good."

"Excellent." He took the contract and tucked it under his arm without looking at it.

"The rest of my team, along with Nathan and his extended team, will be here today. The company should have sent along our equipment and the preservation materials for the graded comics."

"Yes, they did. It arrived last night. You're right. Today is going much smoother."

"Good morning, Eris," Ranulf said, joining the conversation. He shook her hand.

"And to you. I meant to tell you both yesterday, but it slipped my mind. I've worked for you two before, in a roundabout way." She smiled when they exchanged confused looks. "Your platinum account with the company to have your newer purchases graded straight off the press. Sometimes I was sent. All the comics I graded have my initials on the information card sent with the comic. I didn't even realize until I gave you a client code and your existing collection appeared in the database."

"Your company has a record of our collection?" Lucien asked.

"The ones you have graded through us, yes. Actually the fine print on your agreement with us states that your collection information—no personal information—will be published on the company website. If an interested party takes notice of a particular comic you own that they want, they can contact you through us to start the negotiation process."

Ranulf said, "Yes, I remember reading that."

"You never told me," Lucien said.

"It didn't seem important."

Eris said, "Once your full collection goes live, I'm sure you'll have offers every minute. Brian has already told me to keep watch for the comics on his want list." She paused and looked at them in turn. "You don't mind, do you? I should have asked that from the beginning. I can't take the collection off the site, but I mean about Brian."

Lucien gave a small shake of his head. "No harm. He's welcome to buy any of our open-graded copies."

"Naturally we want to keep the more valuable of the two," Ranulf said. "Our entire collection is made up of doubles. We always bought two of every issue that interested us."

Eris made a mental note to tell the geeks that later. They had noticed the doubles but thought it was something Ranulf and Lucien had started in recent years. The entire collection being doubles meant the cataloging portion of the project would get ahead of the grading portion.

Ranulf said, "Now that the formalities are out of the way, have you eaten breakfast?"

"I actually had time to grab a bowl of cereal."

"I'll take that as a no."

Eris laughed. "I won't be able to keep my girlish figure if you keep feeding me the way you did yesterday."

At Ranulf's suggestion, he and Lucien had invited the grading team to lunch and dinner. Lucien had also offered to provide all future meals as an excuse to spend more time with Eris. She'd accepted lunch, but had skipped dinner, citing lack of hunger.

Lucien had to remind himself that she would return the next day so he shouldn't try and keep her there. That didn't stop him from thinking of ways to prolong her days.

He said, "You can always use our gym before or after your work day. It has every piece of equipment there is and some prototypes. We also have an Olympic-sized pool, if you like swimming."

"You have a pool?" she asked.

"In a house this big, you have to ask?" Ranulf said with a smirk.

"Actually, in a house this big, I expected you to have your own imitation ocean, but I'll settle for a pool. You'll have to show me where it is later. I'll definitely bring my swimsuit tomorrow."

"We're here!" Chad crowed as he and the others entered the foyer.

Lucien used the distraction and faced the newcomers. Eris's promise to bring a swimsuit had sent his mind into a tailspin, causing his lower body to react. To hide the bulge in his pants, he shrugged out of his jacket and draped it over his arm, which he crossed over his stomach.

A quick glance at Ranulf proved Lucien wasn't the only one affected. Ranulf had positioned himself near one of the many potted plants in the foyer. They would both need to switch to looser pants in the future.

Eris made introductions and handshakes were exchanged.

Lucien was slightly confused at the number of people filing through the front door. Instead of twelve people, there were eighteen. One of the eighteen, a tall man with dyed-black hair, made his way around the others and took Eris in his arms. He laid a kiss on her lips and hugged her close.

The urge to drive his fist through the man's head swept over Lucien.

Eris pulled back and pushed at the man at the same time. He didn't release her. "Clayton, we're at work."

"You're at work. Me and mine are visiting to get a lay of the land before we head back to the office. A company sanctioned field trip." He cupped her bottom and squeezed.

A loud snap drew everyone's attention to Ranulf. He held a severed branch from the potted palm in his hands. "It was loose," he said then walked away.

Lucien had had serious doubts about Ranulf's commitment to Eris when he'd noticed how calmly the man handled the news of her current boyfriend. The snapped branch meant Ranulf wasn't as aloof as he'd pretended.

In truth, Lucien wished Ranulf had snapped Clayton's neck.

Eris pulled out of Clayton's arms completely and walked him over to Lucien. "Lucien, this is Clayton, the head of your third team."

"So I gathered," Lucien said through his teeth.

Clayton held out his hand. Lucien only stared at him. Since he would probably break every one of the boy's fingers if they shook hands, Lucien didn't put his hand forward.

"Okay," Clayton said and dropped his hand.

"I trust you will remember this is a place of business and not a bar," Lucien said.

Eris said quickly, "I'm sorry about that. It won't happen again."

"See that it doesn't." He turned and left the foyer before his temper got the better of him. Something he hadn't let happen in a long time.

She wasn't his, not yet. He didn't have the right to dictate who she touched or *how* she touched them. By God, he should though.

He entered the study and closed the door. Ranulf stood near his desk studying the branch he held.

Ranulf asked in a thoughtful voice, "If I kill him, would Eris cry over his loss?"

Lucien snorted. He didn't get a chance to reply because someone knocked on the door. "Enter."

Eris poked in her head. "Hi."

"Hello, Eris," Lucien said, his dark attitude instantly lifting. "Come in."

She pushed the door open and entered with Clayton at her side.

Lucien's good mood soured once more.

Eris looked around and asked, "Is there any room in this house that doesn't have weapons on the walls, besides the survey rooms? I mean, even the kitchen."

Ranulf said, "The bedrooms."

Lucien asked, "Did you need us for something?"

Clayton said, "We got off on the wrong foot. Sorry about that. I actually didn't come out here to see the comics."

"So we gathered," Ranulf grumbled.

"Uh, yeah." Clayton cleared his throat. "That's not what I meant. I wanted to meet you two. I've attended your ren faire for years. I actually wanted to face off against one or both of you last year, but you didn't make it to the last day like you usually do. That was the only day I could come out. A little disappointing but still a fun day."

"We were busy."

"That was here?" Eris asked.

"You didn't know?" Clayton said then grinned at her. "I guess it makes sense. You slept the whole way here and this house is on the other side of the property, but yeah. Lucien and Ranulf host the ren faire I took you to last year."

"Get out! I didn't even realize. It is a small world after all."

Lucien sat on his desk because standing was beyond him after Eris's words. "You attended the ren faire last March?"

"It was our first real date," Clayton said. "I wanted her to meet you two but, like I said, you weren't there."

"An important meeting called us away. Normally we attend the opening and closing days," Lucien whispered. He looked at Ranulf. The man looked as disbelieving as he felt. That was twice they'd come into close contact with Eris and yet hadn't met her.

Eris said, "It's a shame you weren't there. Clayton spent half the day whining about not being able to duel you."

Ranulf said, "The next faire is almost seven months away, but that's no reason we should wait. As is obvious, we have plenty of weapons around. Simply choose a time." He gestured to the weapon-laden walls.

"You fight with these? I thought they were decoration only." Clayton looked around the room again with an appreciative eye.

"All of our weapons are battle-ready and tested. We would donate them to a museum or sell them if we couldn't use them," Lucien said.

"In that case—"

"No, you don't," Eris said quickly. She turned Clayton and pushed him out of the door. "You said you wanted to meet them. You've met them. Now get out."

"But—"

"No buts. March it, mister."

"Next time, fellas," Clayton called over his shoulder.

"You can bet on it," Ranulf called after them, his lips curving into a menacing smile.

Lucien waited for the door to close and their footsteps to recede before he asked, "How did we come so close to her a second time and not know?"

"We were called away. Both of us, which is rare."

"He knew."

"Of course he did, but why would he delay our meeting?"

"You know he won't answer that question if you ask. He has his reasons. We will find out at a later date or not at all." Lucien looked at the door.

If they had met Eris on that day, would she be dating Clayton now or be with them?

Chapter Seven

Eris coached herself not to fidget. It was hard given the intense way Lucien and Ranulf stared at her while she gave her normal weekly report. She should be used to it after three months, but every Monday she found herself feeling like a bug under glass, being dissected by two sets of eyes.

"All three teams report smooth sailing, as usual. Nathan's team managed to find five comics on Brian's wish list."

"Yes, he contacted us," Lucien said.

Ranulf gestured to his computer screen. "This database is impressive and extensive. The level of detail it offers explains why it takes so long."

Eris ducked her head. "Sorry."

"Not at all," Lucien said. "The time taken is money well spent."

"Agreed. You even managed to find the comics I was looking for." Ranulf typed in something to his computer and then nodded. "Your team just unearthed them this morning, from the looks of it."

Eris raised an eyebrow. "Really?"

"Yes." He stood. "I've been wanting to read this particular storyline again for the last three years."

She laughed and then covered her mouth with a mumbled apology. It wouldn't do to laugh at the boss.

Ranulf nodded. "I know. It is sad, but you must understand, after seeing the disarray of our collection, how hard it is to find anything."

"That's why Megan and her counterparts are here. They are sealing and organizing your collection."

"From what I've seen, she does a great job." He rounded his desk and approached her.

Again, Eris had to tamp down the urge to fidget—fix her hair, make sure her clothes weren't mussed, and all the other little things women did when they thought a man might be paying attention to them. She looked up at Ranulf. "I could bring the series here, if you like. Which is it?"

"I wouldn't want to put you to any trouble. I'll read it there."

"You will?"

Lucien stood and joined them. "Likewise."

Eris looked between them. "Both of you?"

"Is that a problem?"

"No," she said. "I mean, you two have sat in for short intervals and know we aren't exactly quiet. The music might distract you."

"It doesn't distract you?" Ranulf asked.

"I zone out while I'm typing and everything fades away. I don't hear anything." She shrugged. It was a good talent to have when concentration was needed around distracting people. Her team understood her little proclivity and had found a way to get her attention when they needed it.

Lucien smiled at her. "Well, isn't that a coincidence? We're the same when we're reading."

The urge to sigh came over her, but she stopped it. "I warned you. That's all I can do."

Ranulf opened the door and gestured for her to precede them. She walked with them back to the survey room.

"Uh-oh, what did you do?" Pete asked when she walked in the door.

Michael paused the music, and all gazes were on her, Lucien, and Ranulf.

She waved away their concern. "They want to read some comics."

"Does that mean we have to act civilized, like the other times they visit?" Chad asked.

Ranulf said, "Pretend we're not here like usual." He gestured to a pair of desks and chairs across the room.

They were Ranulf and Lucien's workspace when they came and observed. Each survey room had a set. Though, from Eris's understanding, Lucien and Ranulf observed her team more than the others. Her team was the main one, so it only made sense, she guessed.

"Suit yourself," Chad clipped out. He signaled Michael, who hit the play button.

Eris frowned at him. He'd been acting strange all morning. She didn't say anything since Ranulf and Lucien didn't take offense at his tone. They went to their desks after retrieving the comics they wanted to read, and she returned to hers.

As she had told them, she started typing and zoned out. All of the background noise faded away. The computer screen was all she saw, and the click of her keys all she heard.

A loud thump made her jump. She looked around quickly for the source.

Pete had smacked his head against his desk.

"What's wrong, Pete?" she asked.

"Another angst rock. Another one. How many angst rock songs are on that MP3 player? Seriously, can't we listen to something else? I was in a good mood before I came to work today."

Since she hadn't been paying attention, she didn't know how many had played and if Pete's reaction was valid or exaggerated. "It is Chad's day."

"And I'm *not* in a good mood so we're listening to angst rock. Deal with it," Chad snapped. The scratching of the pen as he wrote was almost audible over the music. Eris was surprised he didn't tear through the paper.

Pete shot Eris a look that said he would do Chad serious harm if she didn't do something about the music selection.

She sighed. "Chad, maybe something that isn't so depressing. I'm not saying no angst rock, but could you pick the less suicidal kind?"

"This is what I want to listen to. You don't hear me bitching when Megan wants to listen to that rhythmic nagging known as R&B or Daniel's sickeningly sweet anime crap."

"Chad, I need to talk to you outside." She stood and headed for the door.

Normally, she would play along and let his attitude slide, but not while Lucien and Ranulf were there. She waited for Chad in the hall then closed the survey room door.

"Well?" she asked.

He crossed his arms and looked past her shoulder.

"Say something. You're acting out for a reason. Either tell me what it is or go home."

He sighed, baring his teeth a little. "Joseph broke up with me. I'm sorry for being a dick about it."

"Okay. Do you want to go home?"

"No. I...going home will only piss me off more. That's why I came to work."

"Well, you can't stay here if you're going to act this way, especially with Lucien and Ranulf hanging around."

He nodded. "I just need time to think."

"Will fifteen minutes do it?"

"It would help."

"You've got fifteen minutes then, and you're losing your music day."

He gave her a wry grin. "Tell Pete I'm sorry."

She patted his shoulder and then pointed down the hall. "Get. And you better be civil when you get back or fake it."

"Only women fake it." He saluted her and jogged away.

She entered the survey room and went back to her station. "Free for all day."

"Where's Chad?" Michael asked.

"Collecting himself in his car."

"Problem solved then?"

"Joseph broke up with him."

"Poor guy," Pete said. "I should have guessed the angst rock was because of relationship issues. You did something similar when you and Clayton were having problems a few months back."

"That was back in the beginning of September. Why do you even remember that? I barely remember it."

"You're blocking. I remember because I wanted to go knock his teeth in for whatever he did to make you all upset like that. What did he do?"

She glanced at Ranulf and Lucien and found she had their attention. Why today? Any other day she wouldn't care. But why was all this stuff happening on the day they'd picked to observe?

"It was nothing," she said, turning back to her work.

"Well, if it was nothing then you have no issue telling us about it," Michael said.

Pete nodded.

Eris rolled her eyes but couldn't think of a valid argument. "He was complaining about the scheduling. He wanted his team working the four day shift instead of three. I decided to compromise and do it on an every other month schedule. One month Nathan's team would work four days and one month Clayton's team would. That would keep the confusion to a minimum and people wouldn't be driving out here when they were supposed to be at the office."

"Sounds like a good plan to me. What was Clayton's problem?"

She smiled at Pete, happy that he agreed with her solution. "It was a money thing. There was some huge purchase he wanted to make and working the four day shift here would have helped pay for it."

Ranulf asked, "Does your pay increase on the days you're here?"

Michael said, "Yes, indeed it does. Like a doctor making house calls, us being here means more money. Makes me glad I'm here five days regardless."

"What did he wish to buy?" Lucien asked.

"I don't know," Eris said, shaking her head. She squinted at the computer screen. "I didn't ask. It completely slipped my mind once the whole thing got resolved."

"More like you didn't want to bring it up again and have another fight," Pete said.

"Whichever. The compromise was revamped to the current schedule—they switch off every two weeks and Clayton's team works one Saturday a month."

"So what did he buy?"

"Pete, I just said I don't know. I seriously didn't ask."

"Well, it's late October. I think the problem has resolved itself. It should be fairly safe to bring it up again, right?"

"You're probably right. Whatever. I'll ask him Friday."

"It's Tuesday. You going to remember?"

"Yes, I'll remember. It probably has something to do with our weekly get together."

Pete asked, "Get together?"

Eris clapped her hands. "That's enough chitchat. Chad graciously gave up his music day for an extra fifteen so pick whatever but no more angst rock. Back to work, people." She glanced at Lucien and Ranulf. They were engrossed in their comics once more.

They'd probably only joined the conversation out of idle curiosity. She shrugged and went back to her typing.

Chad came back at the prescribed time. He said a quick apology to everyone and returned to his grading. Eris was glad that crisis had been averted.

She looked back at her computer screen, rubbed her eyes then looked at the issue beside the keyboard. The tiny print of the scanned comic page blurred. She rubbed her eyes again, but her vision didn't get better. With a sound of annoyance, she dug through her purse for her reading glasses. She hated wearing them, but every so often, her eyes refused to see right.

"Eris, you ever consider contact lenses? Those glasses make you look like my third grade teacher. I don't mean that to be a compliment," Michael said.

It was too much to hope no one would notice. She resumed her typing. "Can't wear them."

"Don't like putting your finger in your eye?"

"That's not it." She flipped to a new page and typed some more. "According to my doctor, they aren't a viable option due to the amount and types of surgeries I've had."

* * * *

Lucien looked up from the comic he read. Ranulf did the same. The topic was of immediate interest to him. He never knew Eris had had surgery. Obviously none of the others had known either because everyone gave her their undivided attention.

"What happened?" Michael asked in a concerned voice.

Eris continued typing without answering.

"Eris?" Michael looked at the others.

Chad whistled.

Eris stopped typing with a surprised jerk then looked around. "What?"

"What surgeries?" Ranulf asked. "Were you in an accident?"

"Huh? No...well, yes, but that's not why I had surgery. I wasn't a candidate for Lasik but I was one for permanent contact lenses. It's a new type of lens that is never removed since it fits under the cornea. The doctor even offered me a discounted color upgrade. Sometimes staring at the computer screen for too long makes my vision go blurry so I use reading glasses."

"Your eyes aren't naturally hazel?" Lucien asked.

"Nope. I was born with dark brown eyes." She slid her glasses off and chewed on the earpiece in a thoughtful manner. "That was two years ago."

Ranulf laid aside his comic and stood. There was a look of comprehending horror on his face.

Eris asked, "What's wrong?"

He ignored her question and walked toward the door. Without warning, he put his fist through the wall and yelled, "Son of a bitch."

Before anyone could ask, Ranulf left the room.

"Let me guess. There was a fly on the wall." Chad looked to Lucien for an explanation.

Lucien followed after Ranulf without answering, curious to find out why the man had ruined the wall.

He got to the office and found Ranulf tearing his desk apart searching for something.

"What are you doing?"

Ranulf didn't answer. He opened a file, flipped through the contents then froze. His look of anger turned to rage. He cursed again and hit his desk, cracking the surface.

"No more! You hear me, damn you! No! More!"

Lucien shut the door as soon as Ranulf started yelling. "What? Who are you talking to?"

"You know who." He cursed again before he held out the file that had caused him such ire.

Lucien didn't know what to expect. A photo of Eris wasn't among his guesses. There was no mistaking the woman in the photo was Eris though her hair was in braids and glasses hid most of her face. He stared at the photo a while before he noticed the time stamp.

"What is this?" Lucien whispered. "Why do you have her photo two years before her arrival?"

Ranulf fell onto his seat, shaking his head. "He said he found three girls. Two matched the description but their names were wrong. One had the name and most of the features, but her eyes were the wrong color. She wore glasses then, so he was sure it was her natural eye color.

"I dismissed it without looking at the photos. I knew she would never change her name, and there was no way her eyes could change. She could see clearly then. She could see things farther away than our best scout. I knew...I *knew* she would have no cause to wear glasses." He dropped his head into his hands. "I didn't look at the photos. I buried the folder in my desk without even opening it because I couldn't face more false hope."

Lucien closed the folder and placed it on the desk. He wanted to rage and shout as Ranulf had, but he didn't. It was no coincidence that they had come so close to Eris and yet never met.

"No more. I completely agree," Lucien said. "I want to hear of no more instances where Eris came within our reach, but other circumstances denied our meeting. I've had enough of this game."

"Does he do this to torture us?"

A knock at the office door stopped Lucien's answer. Both men froze.

"Lucien. Ranulf. Is everything okay?"

"Eris," they whispered together.

Ranulf swept the folder off his desk and back into a drawer. He called, "Enter."

As was her usual custom, Eris stuck her head in first and assessed the situation before entering. "What's wrong? Did I do something or did you suddenly feel the need for an indoor window?"

Ranulf chuckled. "No, I...your words jogged a memory which shed light on a deal I let fall through because of my negligence."

"You? Negligent?" She shook her head. "Pull the other one."

Both men laughed, and Eris smiled. She came farther into the room. "Seriously, Ranulf, anger management. First that poor potted palm and now the wall."

"Potted palm? I don't know what you mean."

"Yes you do. The second day we came back here and Clayton introduced himself, you broke off that branch, marring a defenseless tree, and then claimed it was loose. I know for a fact it wasn't because I watched you break it out of the corner of my eye." She shook her head in wonder. "And now you put a hole through a brick wall covered in plaster. I didn't know you were that strong." She moved closer to the desk. "Did you hurt your hand?"

"Not at all." He showed her the back of his hand. "You're right, though. I did let my temper run away with me."

"Yes, you did. I mean, I know Clayton was out of line that one time and I'm sorry about that. But if I did or said something to make you angry this time, I wish you would tell me."

"My anger is not at you, Eris. As I said, your words reminded me of a stupid mistake in my past. That's all."

"Lucien doesn't seem that broke up about it. If it concerns you then it concerns him, right? You should take a page out of his book and learn to control your outbursts before you hurt someone."

Ranulf stared at her with wide eyes. He smiled then threw his head back and laughed. The laughter consumed him until tears ran down his cheeks and he clutched his side.

"Like Lucien," he wheezed and laughed some more.

Eris looked at him with concern. She edged closer to Lucien and asked in a low voice, "Has he snapped?"

"Ranulf has a perverse and inappropriate sense of humor," Lucien grumbled, crossing his arms.

"Sure. So we don't need to phone in a reservation for a padded room?"

"We may, but not because of this." Lucien turned from Ranulf's hysteria and asked Eris, "Why the sudden need to change your eye color two years ago? That seems vain for you. We haven't known each other long, but you don't strike me as the type of woman who would drop good money on something so superficial."

"I wouldn't, but I had one those life-altering things that facilitated, and somewhat necessitated, it." Ranulf's laughter stopped abruptly, and he looked completely serious once more. She frowned at him but continued, "I was in a car accident. It wasn't hugely serious, for me anyway. The car took the majority of the impact and was totaled beyond recognition. Most people were surprised I survived, considering they literally had to cut me out of the car. I just had some bruises and scraps here and there. But, it made me look at my life and its direction.

"My Mommy said that accident helped me grow a backbone and a measure of confidence. She's right. I was the keep-to-yourself-and-don't-make-eye-contact type. I didn't have many friends, and I liked it like that. After the accident, I decided I wanted to know more people and be remembered as being part of the population."

Lucien said, "We're not sorry for your decision. You seem all the better for it."

"I feel better for it. My family physician says my overall health improved when my outlook on life did—less stress headaches and mysterious aches and other stuff like that. And the money from the two insurance companies paid for my new life direction."

"Two?" Ranulf asked.

"I was hit head-on and rear-ended almost simultaneously. The guy who hit me head on had swerved, jumped the median and hit me. While the lady behind me in the tank-on-wheels had been tailgating—like a foot off my bumper—and I couldn't switch lanes to get out of her way. As a result, they were both found at fault for smushing my little compact like a soda can."

"That must have scared you greatly."

"No joke. I didn't leave my apartment for almost a month. I refused to buy a new car for the longest time. I didn't want to drive anymore after that. But, like I said, I looked at my life and realized what I was doing—and not doing—and made a decision not to live in fear. I bought a new car with all the bells and whistles—an upgrade from my last—that will be paid off in four more months, a whole new wardrobe and new eyes." She winked at him.

Lucien said, "Well, I'm glad your experience helped rather than hindered."

"You better be since your collection is benefiting. Until that accident, I was nowhere near a management position. The company hadn't even heard of my database program even though I'd been tweaking it for quite some time. Back then, if my team had been assigned here, I would have faded into the background—or tried my damnedest to. I'm much more of a people person now. I want to know people. I want to leave a mark so somebody somewhere will remember me when I'm gone."

"Time is on your side, Eris. You're not going anywhere for a long while," Lucien said.

"Promise?" Eris smiled up at him.

He almost swore it but didn't. He forced himself to return Eris's smile and retain a joking manner.

She patted his arm. "Well, I ran interference, and there's nothing wrong—with us—so back to work I go. Ranulf, try not to hurt any more inanimate objects."

"I guarantee nothing if they start it." Ranulf winked at her.

Eris laughed as she walked out of the room.

Lucien made sure the door was firmly closed then locked it. Ranulf was on the phone when he turned back. "Who are you calling?"

Ranulf held up a finger. "Yeah, Rachel, this is Ranulf. I need you to issue a ten thousand dollar check to Abram Investigations." He made an affirmative noise. "The address is in our records already. Call and make sure that information is current since it's two years old. Thank you."

He hung up the phone.

Lucien asked, "The reward money?"

"It's rightfully his since he found her."

"True." Lucien thought back over what Eris had said. "I guess he had his reasons for delaying our search for her after all."

"I still don't like it." Ranulf touched the phone then paused. After a moment he snatched it up and stabbed in a number.

"Who are you calling now?"

"Thanus. If her accident was as bad as she says and all she suffered was a few scrapes, then he had a hand in her survival. I know it. He should have told us her location. He knew we were looking."

Lucien walked forward and pushed a button, ending the call. "Even if he did save her, he'll say nothing to you. It doesn't matter if every one of them knew her whereabouts and hid that information from us. That's their prerogative and possibly *his* request."

Ranulf hung up the phone with an annoyed sigh. He nodded. "We can do nothing about the past and yelling at Thanus—no matter how tempting—won't change anything. However, the problem of Clayton still remains."

"He wouldn't be a problem if you'd have let me call his boss when he first arrived. But you're right. He is an obstacle we have to handle with finesse so as not to trouble Eris."

Chapter Eight

A shrill whistle made Eris jump. She looked at Chad who pointed at the doorway. Clayton stood there looking mildly annoyed.

She asked, "What's wrong, Clayton?"

"I called your name five times. Didn't you hear me?"

"No, I was off in my own world. You know how I get when I'm working."

"Yeah, sure. It's time to get gone."

Eris looked at her watch then at the pile of comics next to her.

Before she could even open her mouth, Clayton said, "No, Eris. Let's go."

"We've almost finished this box. It won't take that much longer."

His annoyed look got worse. "We got permission to leave early. Let's go."

"The party starts at seven. It's barely four and Jamie lives around the corner from your place."

"Ten miles isn't around the corner."

"You go ahead, and I'll follow. Besides, it doesn't matter if we don't arrive on time. You're not supposed to arrive on time anyway."

She held her hand out to him. After a moment's hesitation, he crossed the room and took it. She pulled him down for a quick kiss and smiled up at him. "Okay?"

He nodded. "Don't take too much longer. There's a thin line between fashionably late and missed-all-the-fun."

"I'm right behind you."

Clayton gave her hand a squeeze and then left.

Eris was back to her typing before he reached the doorway. She only wanted to finish off the current box and then she would go. There were fifty comics left. Once she got back into her groove, she'd be done in no time.

"That reminds me," Pete said, sitting back and crossing his arms. "Did you remember to ask Clayton about his hissy fit?"

"Huh?" She looked at Pete and then his meaning registered. Turning back to her work, she said, "Oh. No, I forgot."

"I knew it. You're scared to ask."

"I'm not scared to ask. I just forgot. I'll ask him."

"Tonight?"

"If I remember."

"That means no."

"Pete—"

"So are you and Clayton going in matching costumes?" Michael asked.

Eris almost kissed him for changing the subject. She wasn't scared of asking Clayton about the purchase but that night wasn't the time to do it in case it put him in a bad mood. She didn't want to ruin the party.

Chad said, "Couples who do that are doomed to fail. That's what I've heard, anyway."

"That's only couples that dress alike on a regular basis," Eris said. "Having correlating costumes just gives you a chance to win the couples' costume contest. And no, our costumes don't match. Clayton insisted on dressing in his medieval attire."

"Because he's too cheap to go out and buy another costume," Michael said.

She didn't acknowledge his statement, but she agreed. Clayton was being cheap since he already had the costume and wore it to every costumed event they attended. "I didn't want to do the renaissance motif since I'll be doing that for the faire in March. I chose something else." She switched to the next issue and kept typing.

The room lapsed into silence once more. As a side thing, Eris wondered what happened to the music. She didn't ask about it since she had no song suggestions and didn't want to break her stride. Besides, the silence didn't bother her.

"Eris, not to interrupt you when you're on a roll…"

She didn't stop her typing but made a sound to show she was listening.

Pete continued, "…but weren't you supposed to be out of here an hour ago?"

"What?" she yelled. She looked at the wall clock, the clock on her laptop, her watch and finally the new set of scanned comics she'd started without thinking. "Oh crap! I was only going to finish that box and then get going. Why didn't you stop me?"

"Called your name and you didn't answer. Chad refused to whistle."

She shot Chad a look. He stuck his tongue out at her. Getting into an argument wouldn't get back the time she needed. She finished entering the data she'd started and saved quickly. Learning from past mistakes, she uploaded all of the info to the company database before turning off her computer.

"I have to call Clayton." She pulled out her cell phone and hit the speed dial for Clayton's number.

Chad tsked at her. "Standing up a guy for comics. You'd be a woman after my own heart if you were a guy."

"I'm not even going to point out the many things wrong with that sentence." She stuck her finger in her ear when Clayton answered. "I'm so sorry. I'm going to have to meet you there."

"Where are you?"

"I'm still at work."

Pete mouthed, *ask him.*

She waved him away and turned her back to the room. She could almost hear Clayton grinding his teeth about her answer.

"Still at...Eris, you said you wouldn't stay much longer."

"I know. I know. I didn't mean to. Look, I have my stuff with me. I can change here and meet you at the party. It's no big deal."

Clayton sighed. "Fine. I'll see you there then."

He hung up before she could thank him for being so understanding about her absent-mindedness. She snapped the phone shut then stowed it in her pocket. Once Clayton saw her costume, all would be forgiven and everything would be right with the world.

First things first, she had to get changed and get to the party. She headed for Lucien and Ranulf's office. The door was cracked so she poked her head around the edge.

"Lucien? Ranulf?"

There was no answer. She walked into the office. Neither man was there.

"If you are looking for the masters, they are out back," Leon said, coming up behind her.

"Out back? Doing what?" she asked, facing him. "In the past three months, I've never seen them leave this office during business hours. Well, they split their time between this office and peeking in on the survey rooms, but you know what I mean."

"Yes, miss. Be that as it may, they are currently out back."

"Cool. I need to talk to one of them. So, where's out back?"

"This way, miss."

She smiled at his resigned tone. The man had warmed up to her. In the past, she would ask him the location of something in the mansion and he'd simply walk away, expecting her to follow.

On a few occasions, he'd had to rescue her since she'd gotten turned around and then lost. The fourth time she had gotten lost, he'd finally spoken to her and it was to tell her that he planned to buy her a homing beacon and a bell. She'd laughed but had gotten the feeling he hadn't been joking.

Leon opened a sliding glass door for her at the end of winding path she knew she wouldn't be able to backtrack. He stepped back so she could pass him. "Do me a favor and call for me if one of the masters doesn't see fit to escort you back. It would save time."

"Oh, come off it. You'd be bored to tears if I wasn't here to entertain you."

He walked away without answering, but Eris thought she saw him hiding a smile. The man was all talk—when he bothered to talk.

The clang of metal against metal drew her attention to the middle of the well-manicured lawn.

Lucien and Ranulf fought sword to battle-axe. Both men were topless and sweating. The lethal dance distracted Eris from why she had sought them out. She watched them in silence.

Some part of her felt they looked more natural holding weapons. They definitely looked more relaxed. She couldn't hear what they said to one another because of the distance between them and the noise of the weapons clashing, but their laughter carried, and she could see them smiling.

No wonder Clayton wanted to face them. Eris might not know much about fighting with edged weapons, but Lucien and Ranulf looked like they would be hard men to beat.

Ranulf knocked the sword from Lucien's hands then swung the battle-axe towards Lucien's stomach. Eris gasped. She didn't know how Ranulf heard her, but he stopped his swing short and looked her way. Lucien followed his gaze.

"Eris," they said in unison.

"Hi." She walked forward when they beckoned her closer. "I didn't mean to interrupt."

"Not at all. We need a break," Lucien said.

"*You* need a break. I was winning," Ranulf said.

"I'm sorry," Eris said.

"Don't worry, Eris. You are a welcome distraction always. Did you need something?" Ranulf shouldered the battle-axe and signaled her to walk beside him back toward the house.

Lucien retrieved his sword and joined them.

"I was hoping I could borrow a shower."

"Finally remembered your swimsuit?" Lucien asked.

"It's too cold to think about swimming."

"The pool is indoors and heated."

"It is? You didn't tell me that."

"Then I was remiss, but yes, it is."

"Huh. I might have to actually find my swimsuit now."

Ranulf said, "I thought your excuse was forgetfulness."

"Out of sight, out of mind. I kept forgetting it because I never bothered to find it. I'll change my mind about that and find it later, but not today." She glanced at her watch. "I really need to get changed and get going. I would love it if I could borrow one of the five million showers in this place. Please?"

"What's the occasion?"

"Halloween party. I was supposed to change at Clayton's and then we would go together, but I stuck around here to finish up a few more issues, got distracted, and lost track of time. It would save time if I went straight to the party from here." She stopped her little explanation and smiled. "Which works out since I'll have my own car. I already told Clayton I would meet him at the party at seven, so I can make a slight detour and take the munchkins trick-or-treating. It shouldn't take long to run them around a few blocks." She nodded since the idea sounded even better aloud.

"Munchkins?" Lucien asked.

"My nieces and nephews. They wanted me to take them, but there was no way if I had gone to Clayton's first. I guess my absent-mindedness works in my favor this time."

"It sounds more like prudent planning to me," Ranulf said.

"I didn't plan anything."

"Consciously," Lucien said. "By all means, use the room at the top of the stairs."

"Great." She took one step then stopped. "How do I get back to the stairs?"

Both men chuckled. Lucien handed his sword to Ranulf and then slung a towel over his shoulders. "I'll lead you back. I need to check on something in the office."

Ranulf bent and whispered in her ear, "He means he needs to get his energy back before facing me again."

Eris hid a smile behind her hand.

"Come," Lucien said in a gruff voice.

She knew Lucien must have heard Ranulf, but he didn't rise to the baiting. He entered the house. She jogged to catch up with him, waving goodbye to Ranulf over her shoulder.

"Do you two fight often?" she asked once at his side.

"On the odd occasion. When we aren't busy."

"It looked dangerous."

"We never hurt each other."

"Then these scars aren't from your matches?" Eris touched a scar on Lucien's arm near his shoulder. He stopped abruptly. She jerked her hand away. "Sorry."

"No, it's all right. You only surprised me." He brushed his fingers over the scar she'd touched. "Ranulf didn't cause this."

"So he's the cause of one of your other scars then?"

Lucien's chest, back and shoulders were covered in scars of differing lengths. She'd never seen them before, but she'd never seen Lucien without his shirt before.

The scars were all old and long healed. Looking at them made Eris imagine the pain Lucien must have been in when they were caused. She shuddered.

"He's only responsible for this one," Lucien said, pointing at the seven-inch long puckered scar over the left side of his rib cage. "That was an accident. The others are mementos of my rambunctious and hardheaded youth."

To lighten the mood, she knocked lightly on the side of his head. "Doesn't seem that hard now. Guess you learned your lesson."

"I learned it the hard way, but I did learn."

"So what did Ranulf do to cause this one?" She pointed at the scar on his side. Though she didn't touch him, Lucien sucked in a breath.

"Don't you have a party to get ready for? I thought you were in a hurry."

"I am, but I'm also curious."

"Your curiosity will have to wait for another time then. I wouldn't want you blaming your tardiness on me." He resumed walking.

Eris caught up with him and asked, "Are you and Ranulf doing anything for Halloween?"

"I'm sure we are."

"You don't know?"

"Ranulf likes springing things on me. He says it keeps me from becoming complacent."

"That would drive me nuts. I hate surprises."

"We have that in common then." He stopped at the foot of the stairs. "And here we are."

"Oh, good. Thank you, Lucien, for leading me back and letting me borrow the bathroom. You're a prince." She braced a hand on his chest and laid a quick kiss on his cheek. "I have to get my bag out of my car." She patted his chest then walked away.

She wasn't sure why exactly she'd kissed him. He didn't say anything. It had been spur of the moment and completely stupid on her part. If he didn't bring it up, she'd be happy to forget about it.

* * * *

Eris's actions so surprised Lucien that he could only stare as she walked away. Slowly he touched his chest where her hand had been then his cheek.

She'd kissed him.

A mere peck but still a kiss.

She'd touched him earlier, and the surprise had made his brain stop along with his feet. Such a simple thing and every memory of her in his arms, moaning with pleasure, came back to him with crystal clarity.

Most of the last few centuries were a blur, but his time with her had never faded. He growled and walked to the office.

Sweet though some of those memories may be, he knew the true reason why his recollections hadn't grown fuzzy with time. His guilty conscience wouldn't allow him to forget or taint the memory with rationalizations and pleas of ignorance.

He touched the wound at his side, the one he'd told Eris was an accident. It was a half-truth and one of the few times Ranulf had ever truly wanted him dead. Ranulf had meant to impale him, but Lucien had dodged.

Their entire existence had changed that day. For the better or for the worse, Lucien still wasn't sure. He looked at his desk, half tempted to pull out the drawing he'd done of Eris so long ago. It made no sense to stare at it when the real woman was only a few feet away.

He moved to his desk but the door opening stopped him before he would have opened the drawer containing the picture.

Ranulf entered. "Have you been staring off into space this entire time? You took so long I thought you had decided to forfeit the day to me and be done."

Lucien looked away from Ranulf to the desk drawer.

"Lucien? Did Mizukinawa call again? Was that the delay?"

"She kissed me," Lucien whispered. He touched his cheek again. "Eris kissed me. It was a gesture of gratitude."

Ranulf shook his head with an amused sound. "Poor girl doesn't know what she's doing to us. The other day she hugged me."

Lucien looked up quickly, annoyance with an edge of anger mingled inside him. He kept himself from acting on either emotion, barely. He bit out, "You didn't tell me that."

Ranulf made a dismissive motion. "It was a fluke. Like yours, a gesture of gratitude. I found her car keys." He chuckled. "Somehow they ended up in the refrigerator. I don't remember her being this absent-minded."

"Being carefree and having few worries does that to people," Lucien grumbled. He moved away from his desk and the temptation of Eris's portrait. Doing so didn't help him escape the memories.

The weight of them forced him onto the couch near the door. He dropped his head. "We should stop," he whispered. "This isn't her choice. It's our whim and what will it get us? What will it get *me*? She hates me."

"You don't know that," Ranulf said in equally quiet tones.

"Don't I?"

"If she hates you then she does me as well. We are equal in this, Lucien."

Lucien rose from the couch, his anger rising with him. "She never hated you. Stop acting as though she did so you can pretend you sympathize."

"Lucien—"

"Enough!" He touched his side and the wound there. So much anger had caused that wound. Ranulf hadn't apologized in all the centuries since he'd inflicted it. He'd wanted Lucien dead so he could have Eris all to himself. Perhaps that was best. There was never a need for both of them—only one.

Lucien said, "I'm changing the rules. It's her choice. She did what she did in the past for self-preservation. There's no need for that now. Whomever she chooses, we'll abide by that."

"She accepted us both. There's no reason to think—"

"We forced her hand. I won't do that again."

Silence fell between them. The staring match had started. After so many centuries, heated words didn't solve their problems. Only two things settled things between Lucien and Ranulf—armed combat with the weapons that lined the walls or determination of will.

They hadn't raised a weapon in anger against one another since the first few decades of their immortality. Even if Ranulf had wanted to settle things in that manner, Lucien refused. He needed Ranulf to see how serious he truly was.

Even if it meant losing Eris forever, Lucien would do it. He would do that and more simply to see her happy.

Ranulf looked away with a sigh. He nodded. "If that's the way you want it, so be it. We'll let it be her choice." He raised his eyes to meet Lucien's gaze once more. "I won't let you give up, though. We've come too far and been through too much. I refuse to be declared the victor because you forfeited."

"It's my choice."

"No, it's your guilt. You—"

"Whoa, Momma!"

Chad's exclamation made Ranulf and Lucien look toward the cracked door of the office. A faint jingling tickled Lucien's ears.

"Foxy lady." Chad made wolf noises. Pete and Michael added their sounds of appreciation to Chad's.

Ranulf and Lucien exchanged a look then exited the room. Lucien followed the men's gazes and forgot how to breathe.

Eris descended the stairs, jingling all the way. Each step revealed her bare legs before the curtain of her floor-length, purple tasseled-skirt hid them again. The jingling came from the belt of coins riding low on her hips and the coins decorating the bra that matched the skirt.

She stopped three steps above the men and held out her arms. "Ta-da!"

Michael sidled up to her and asked, "So, if Clayton comes up missing in the next hour, can I take his place?"

"Ha ha, Michael." She descended the last few steps and set her bag on the floor. "Does it really look okay?"

"Hell yeah."

"I agree," Chad said. "I didn't know you looked so good. Where have you been hiding that body this whole time?"

"Under my clothes." She twirled. "Think I'll win the costume contest?"

"Sexiest for damn sure," Pete said.

"Dude, aren't you married?" Chad asked.

"Married, not dead."

"Same thing according to my dad."

Lucien said, "You're beautiful."

Out of the corner of his eye, he saw Ranulf jerk. It was a small movement. Lucien would have missed it if he didn't know Ranulf as well as he did. The man had probably been in a stupor until Lucien had spoken.

Ranulf said in a breathy voice, "Ah, but my question is whether or not the costume is for show, or can you truly dance?"

"Show. I want to take lessons though." She swayed her hips a little, which made the coins jingle.

"You are gonna freeze your ass off," Michael said.

"I'm borrowing my sister's trench coat when I take the kids out. So, I should be okay." She looked Lucien's way. "But, if I get sick—which I seriously doubt—I'll have Brian send a replacement for me."

Lucien said, "Keep warm. I'm sure a replacement wouldn't do as good a job."

Chad said, "No joke. Her archiving system is a work of art, but it almost takes a Ph.D. to work the damn thing. And let's not forget that finicky-ass laptop. I tried to get on the Internet the other day, and the screen went black."

Eris put her hands on her hips and gave him a stern look. "So you're the one who did that. Remind me to kick your ass later. I had to hard boot the system and re-enter seventeen comics' worth of data." Eris flipped open her phone then closed it. "I have to put that on my to-do list as I am going to be late. Everyone enjoy your Halloween. I plan to."

She waved as she jogged away, jingling all the way.

Pete called, "Don't forget to ask Clayton about that purchase."

She didn't acknowledge him.

"Eris."

She walked out of the front door.

Pete crossed his arms with a harrumph. "That little chicken shit isn't going to ask."

Chad nodded.

Michael said in a wistful voice, "I wish I'd had the nerve to ask her out before Clayton. Lucky bastard."

Lucien knew Clayton would be a dead bastard soon if he and Ranulf couldn't figure out a way to end Eris's relationship. It may be October but March was fast approaching. Lucien felt the hurried feeling of three months ago overwhelming him again. Nothing he thought of would alleviate it. He only had a short time to win Eris's love, or else he would lose her forever.

Chapter Nine

Eris huddled into her cape, thinking warm thoughts to ward off the December chill. Halloween night had been cold and she'd worn less and had been fine, even when she'd gone trick-or-treating with the kids. Ever since Halloween, it had been unseasonably warm. She thought the trend would continue. Except Mother Nature had dumped rain all through Thanksgiving weekend and then the freezing weather started.

She wanted to turn up the heat in the car, but it was as high as it would go.

"It'll be warm at Jamie's place." Clayton glanced at her. He rubbed her arm for a bit before returning his hand to the steering wheel.

"I know but I still wish I'd brought my coat." She glanced over her shoulder at Clayton's cloak. It was part of his gaming costume. As such, she didn't even bother asking. Clayton was nutty about his costume and the props that went with it.

The light of a street lamp glinted off the hilt of a sword buried under the cloak. Suddenly, Pete's nagging voice entered her thoughts. He'd spent all of November bugging her daily about the mysterious purchase Clayton had made. Every evening she found some reason not to ask, which only made Pete nag her more the next day.

No time like the present, she thought. She still didn't want to ask but Pete's insistence had finally peaked her own curiosity. Her hope was that the topic wouldn't lead to an argument.

"Clayton, I almost forgot to ask. You remember back in September you said you were making some huge purchase?"

"Yeah, what about it?" Clayton pulled into the driveway of Jamie's house, put the car in park, and then looked at her.

"What was it?"

"I thought I showed you the Damascus." He reached behind her seat and hefted a long, cloth-wrapped parcel with the hilt poking out. He brought it forward and unwrapped it, revealing the rest of the sword. "I've been bringing it to our sessions all this time. I know I showed it to you. You never noticed?"

"You know I can't tell one sword from another. I just thought it was one I hadn't seen before. You're very secretive about your collection."

"Yeah, well, not all of us can be like Lucien and Ranulf and have it on display for the world to see."

"You're just jealous."

He snorted but didn't reply.

Eris knew he was jealous. He always studied the various weapons lining the walls when he went to and from the survey rooms. Once he even tried talking Ranulf, or was it Lucien, into giving him a full tour of the collection. Both men had had prior business engagements and couldn't do it. Of course, Clayton complained about that for a few days.

Eris had to talk him out of bugging the men about a tour. She didn't want him bothering them. They always seemed annoyed with Clayton anyway. Her only guess was that Clayton's first impression had been a lasting one they didn't want to forgive.

"You ready?" Clayton asked.

She took a bracing breath and jumped out of the car. The cold December air hit her, and she yelped. "I should have brought a coat."

"We'll be inside in a minute." Clayton rushed around the car and threw his arm around her shoulders. He pulled her in close, ushering her to the door.

It opened before they had a chance to knock. Eris rushed in and did the get-warm dance for a few seconds. "It is *freezing* outside."

"You're not exactly dressed for the weather. Nice outfit though," Spencer said, looking her up and down.

Patty whistled as Eris opened her arms, lifting her cape out of the way, and turned in a circle.

"Very nice," Jamie said.

"Glad you like. I patterned it off of an elf I saw in an anime," Eris said. "I think I did a good job."

"Damn straight you did." Clayton grabbed her close and kissed her.

She returned his kiss then pushed him away when his hands started wandering. He always did that. She didn't mind a little petting but not when they had an audience—an avid audience at that.

The others watched them without shame. She smiled at them all, and they smiled back.

She disengaged herself from Clayton and straightened her clothes. In doing so, her hands bumped against the fold of her belt where she'd stashed her keys and clipped her cell phone. The keys slipped loose and hit the floor.

Jamie asked, "You got enough keys on there?"

Eris laughed a little. "Believe it or not, I don't even know what half these keys go to. This is the only way I can make sure I don't lose them."

Patty held out her hand. "You can leave them on the kitchen counter if you want. That way you don't have to worry about dropping them. The cell too."

"My cell is on a clip, so it's not going anywhere. Just don't let me forget my keys." Eris handed her keys to Patty, who walked over and laid them in plain sight on the kitchen counter.

Clayton asked, "Are we picking up where we left off last time or are we doing a different quest?"

"Left off." Patty showed everyone to the living room. "Jamie is hunting some mystical root in the forest and has gotten lost because the trees keep moving around. I'm waiting in a tavern and about to leave 'cause Jamie is late and he's my contact."

"My dwarf is waiting for an antidote made out of Jamie's lost root and Gabe couldn't make it so I'm playing his bridge troll for the night," Spencer said.

Clayton said to Eris, "He's guarding the bridge we stopped at last time."

She nodded.

"Let's get started then," Patty said.

Spencer jumped out from behind the couch with a bat in his hands. It was supposed to represent a club. He bared his teeth at them. "Hold there, sirrah. What right have you crossing my bridge without payment?" Spencer said in a heavily accented, rough voice.

"What did he say?" Eris asked, pretending not to understand. She was a dark elf mage who didn't speak troll and Clayton's character's traveling companion, though not by choice. He had her magically bound to his side, and she was actively trying to find a way to break the spell.

Clayton held up his hand for her silence. He faced Spencer with his other hand on the hilt of his sword. "These are free lands. You have no claim to them. Give way."

"Hah! You humans always think to set boundaries without thought to others. I built this bridge and lived in this land far longer than you existed. That makes them mine. Pay my toll or go another way."

"What is your fee then?"

Spencer looked Clayton over. His gaze settled on Clayton's sword. "'Tis a nice bit of metal you've got. Dwarf made, I'd wager."

"It is, and you won't have it."

"What is he saying?" Eris asked in annoyance.

Clayton leaned over and repeated the conversation for her.

"I could put him in a trance if that would speed things along?" Eris crossed her arms with an impatient look.

"Have you even learned the song for trance magic? Your English is horrible. You could end up killing him."

"Would that be considered bad?"

"Let me handle this. No singing."

Spencer looked at Eris. He smiled wide. "Or perhaps a time or two with your elf. Yes. I like that better. It's been quite a time since I tasted flesh of the fairer sex."

Clayton translated that as well.

She huffed with a look of disgust. "It'll be a whole lot longer too."

Clayton said, "Silence, woman."

"I will not be silent. I'm not—"

Clayton grabbed her arm and pulled her to the side.

Spencer called after them, "Don't go too far with my elf."

Clayton whispered to Eris, "Don't worry. I have a plan. Just play along. We'll get across the bridge without giving up my sword or sullying your virtue."

"Whatever you have planned better work." She jerked away from him and faced Spencer.

"I have a proposition—a wager," Clayton said, returning to Spencer.

"I'm listening," Spencer said.

"You duel me sword to sword. If I win, we pass without having to make payment."

"When I win, I get three times with the elf."

Clayton relayed the terms of the deal.

Eris yelled, "What?"

"You took too long talking amongst yourselves. If this talk goes much longer, I change my mind to four." He leered at her. "Yes, four be a better number."

"Like you could really go four times," Jamie said with an amused snort.

Patty laughed then covered her mouth with an apologetic look.

Clayton glared at them. "Jamie, shut up. And call O.O.C. when you do that shit."

"Jamie, stop going out of character, and let's hurry this along. Clayton is going to accept the duel. Just do it," Patty said.

Spencer cleared his throat and got back into character. "I want her word. You lose and she's with me four times."

"Three," Clayton said.

"I know haggling when I hear it, even if I cannot understand the words. How about not at all?" Eris snapped. She opened her mouth to start singing.

Clayton slapped his palm over her lips. "Just stand there. I can handle this."

Spencer said, "If she won't do it, then your sword be mine."

"Fine, because I know I won't lose. Let's do this."

Patty pointed at the sliding glass door. Eris didn't want to go out into the cold but couldn't argue the matter. The last time the guys had dueled in the house a three hundred dollar statue had been broken. Everyone chipped in to replace it, but things had gotten a little heated and the rest of the night had been strained.

Everyone filed into the backyard for the battle. Jamie handed both Clayton and Spencer kendo practice swords surrounded with foam. Clayton never dueled with the sword strapped to his side for fear of bruising the blade. And, the foam caused less damage if someone miscalculated and hit their opponent.

The fight started. Both men went all out. Dueling was the one thing they didn't fake or leave to a roll of the die. Even magical duels needed the actual incantations spoken in the appropriate language, after which a die roll would determine the damage done.

Eris had had to memorize all of her spells in elven language—a fun but somewhat annoying venture. A few times she tried to flub her way through, but her companions ruled she botched the spell and the damage she'd rolled had fallen on her character instead of her opponent. She later discovered song magic, which could be done in either elvish or English. No one complained about the spell-casting change, or her lack of elvish, since they loved hearing her sing.

She debated a song to speed along the duel but decided against it. Clayton, in or out of character, wouldn't appreciate her interrupting his chance to show off his sword-fighting skills. It was his biggest conceit, and Eris had learned to handle it with care lest they have a pointless argument.

Clayton swung wide at Spencer's chest, leaving himself open. Spencer lunged and stopped with the point of the sword against Clayton's neck.

"You lose, knight."

Eris couldn't believe it. Clayton never lost. Not in all the time she'd known him had he ever lost. He took his swordplay seriously and hated losing. She stared in shock. She wasn't the only one.

Clayton didn't get angry. He let the point of his sword fall to the ground and bowed his head. "You are a better swordsman than I, it seems."

"I knew that already," Spencer said with a bark of laughter. He dropped the sword and headed for Eris.

She pointed at him as she backed away. "Stay away from me."

"I hate speaking elvish," Spencer grumbled. He grabbed for Eris and said, "He lost."

"I didn't say I'd copulate with you. Take the stupid sword. And stop butchering my language while you're at it."

"I speak well enough. Don't want the sword. I'd rather have you."

Clayton said over Eris's reply, "I'll go on ahead. Catch up when you're finished." He trotted back into the house with the others following.

Spencer pulled her into the house and up the stairs. She followed him to the guest bedroom then flopped on the bed.

"O.O.C. I know this is a game but why would he throw that fight? Clayton hates to lose," she said.

"How do you know he threw the fight?"

She looked at Spencer like she thought that was the stupidest question in the world and it was. Spencer knew Clayton longer than her. In fact, Spencer had warned *her* to never play games with Clayton as the man was a sore loser.

She'd taken the advice to heart and had avoided anything that pitted her against Clayton. When she witnessed his temper tantrum at a lost poker game, she'd been thankful for Spencer's advice.

"How long do we stay up here? Or can we go back down now?" she asked.

"We don't leave until we finish. Don't worry about the others, they'll play around us," Spencer said, removing his shirt.

Eris jumped off the bed in alarm. She pointed at him when he reached for his belt. "What are you doing?"

"Easier to have sex when your clothes aren't in the way. Or so I've heard."

"We're not having sex. Not for real."

"Clayton lost the bet."

"A *fake* bet. I knew you guys took this game too seriously." She dodged around him to get to the bedroom door, but he blocked it with his foot. "Move."

"I knew this would happen. I told Clayton to be up front with you. He said you'd be more open to it if you could use the excuse of this being part of game play."

"What are you talking about? Forget it. Just move before I scream."

He moved his foot and stepped back. She jerked the door open and took one step when Spencer said, "The bet was real."

She stopped and looked back at him. "Excuse me?"

"The bet. It's real."

She faced him but said nothing.

Spencer said, "You're right. Clayton threw the fight but only because he'd already lost."

"You two fought a real duel over me?"

"Nah, I'm not that callous, and we didn't fight. It was a bet on whether or not I could raise enough of a stink to get a TV network to reconsider canceling a show. I made a site and hit the chat loops and forums. I won.

The execs announced another season and filming has already started. They even mentioned my site as one of the main reasons for bringing it back."

"What were the stakes?"

"I win and I get his nine hundred dollar Damascus steel sword. He wins and he gets my second gaming laptop. They're about equal in price since that laptop is old but it's souped up enough to run rings around most of the newer models."

"So you get a sword. What's that got to do with me?"

"He didn't want to give it up when the bet came due. *He* actually suggested you instead."

Eris shook her head and tried very hard to keep herself calm. This was all a misunderstanding. "Clayton wouldn't do that."

"He would, and he did. I didn't think you'd go for it and told him to fork over the sword. I'm glad he thinks you're worth nine hundred. Frankly, I think you're worth more than that, but he hatched this scheme of making the whole scenario part of our gaming night." Spencer shrugged. "It's up to you now that you know what the real deal is. I'm all for it. I'd rather you were dating me instead of him, but I kept my mouth shut because he's my friend. Since he's offering you around, I figured I should step up."

"Clayton wouldn't do that," she whispered again.

"Eris—"

"Don't touch me!" She smacked his hand away when he would have touched her shoulder.

Spencer backed away with his hands raised.

"Clayton!" She had to yell again before Clayton's heavy footfalls could be heard.

He appeared in the doorway with a curious look on his face. "Finished already? That was quick, Spence. Also kind of scary. You're like a machine gun."

That was all the proof Eris needed. She reacted and slapped Clayton as hard as she could. "You asshole! You wagered me in a bet!"

She tried to hit him again but he blocked her and moved out of reach. "It's a game. Just play along. You'll probably enjoy it."

"I told her," Spencer said in a calm voice. He pulled his shirt on but didn't refasten his pants.

Clayton glared at Spencer. "What the hell did you do that for?"

"She wasn't buying your performance. Maybe if you had acted pissed and thrown a tantrum like you normally do after losing *anything*, she might have believed it." Spencer gathered the rest of his gear and walked out of the room. He turned back to Eris and said, "Sorry about this." With a small nod, he walked down the hall toward the stairs.

"Spence-man, come back. It's just a small misunderstanding," Clayton called after him.

"I'll pick up my sword in the morning." Spencer waved over his shoulder.

Clayton's face flushed red as he faced Eris. She didn't care if he was mad. His anger didn't compare to hers.

"Why are you such a fucking prude?" he yelled.

"You traded me to keep some stupid sword. Why are you such an insensitive, self-absorbed piece of pond shit?"

"I see the way you and Spence are together. I figured you'd jump at the chance to be with him since you're always cock-blocking me."

"I'm being nice to your friends."

"Then drop the other shoe so I can keep my sword. It was hard to find and cost a mint. I'm still paying it off."

Eris couldn't believe her ears. The more she thought about it, the less sense it made. Clayton thought more of a sword than he did of her simply because she wouldn't have sex with him.

She whispered, "I want to go home. Now."

"Have fun getting there then. I'm not driving you."

"What?"

"You heard me. Thanks to you, I have to give Spencer my sword."

"I didn't make the bet!"

She left the room before Clayton could reply. Whatever he said would probably be something he thought would sway the whole course of the argument but it would only make her madder.

She got down the stairs and saw Spencer had already related the story to Jamie and Patty. They watched her with pitying eyes. She knew they probably heard her argument with Clayton too.

She ran out of the front door and down the driveway. Someone grabbed her arm and pulled her to a stop. She lashed out without looking to see who it was.

"Whoa. Stop, Eris. It's me," Spencer said, ducking her hand. He let her go and held up his hands.

"Leave me alone." She could hear the tears in her voice. They threatened to spill over any second. She couldn't cry in front of Spencer no matter what. To make sure, she presented him with her back.

"I wanted to offer you a ride home," he said.

"I've got one."

"You sure?"

"Bye, Spencer."

He sighed and walked away. "Sorry about all this, Eris."

She didn't reply, only waited for him to go back to the house and leave her alone. A breeze made her shiver and pull her flimsy cape around her more securely. She took out her cell phone and looked at the time. None of her friends would be awake at that hour, weekend or not. Those that were awake—the club-goers—would be in no condition to drive.

Ranulf's number caught her eye. She remembered him saying he and Lucien were usually up late doing business with the other side of the world. He might be awake. Hopefully, he wouldn't be busy.

His number rang and rang and then switched to voice mail. Her throat constricted, leaving her unable to speak. What should she say?

She snapped the phone shut.

Even if she had left a message, there was no telling when Ranulf would get it. She didn't want to stand out in the cold for too long. And, going back to the house to beg for a ride was out of the question.

She opened the phone and tried Lucien's number. Luckily, he answered.

"Eris? What's wrong?"

Hearing the instant concern in his voice made the tears start falling. She sucked in a shaky breath.

"Eris? Say something. Are you all right?"

"Lucien…" Her voice broke.

"I'm right here. Are you crying? Eris, what happened? Where are you?"

"I couldn't think of anyone else to call."

"That's fine."

She tried to stop it, but a sob escaped her lips and carried over the phone. Lucien cursed.

Of course he'd be angry. He didn't want to have to put up with a weepy employee.

She whispered, "I shouldn't have called."

"Eris! Eris, don't hang up!"

She waited.

"Eris?"

"I...I need a ride home. I didn't know who else to call and Ranulf didn't answer his phone and I didn't mean to bother you and—"

"I wasn't doing anything. It's okay. Tell me where you are. I'll come get you right now."

"You're sure?"

"Yes, very sure. Where are you?"

She gave him the directions, having to repeat half of it because her voice kept breaking.

"Okay, I've got it and I'll be there soon. Are you safe at the moment? Will you be okay to wait? Should I stay on the phone?"

"I'm okay."

"You don't sound like it."

"I'm okay."

There was a long pause. She wiped her eyes on her cape and sniffed loudly.

"Eris—"

"I'm sorry."

He sighed. "Don't apologize. Just stay safe until I get there."

"I will."

"I'm hanging up and I'll be there soon."

"Okay." She closed her phone and wrapped her arms around her waist, hoping Lucien would get there before the cold weather made her sick.

Chapter Ten

"Dan, Lucien and I are staring at the contract, and we don't see the problem. It's more than generous to you and your company." Ranulf rolled his eyes at Lucien.

"I had a few questions," Dan said through the speakerphone.

"Of course, of course. Fire away. We're here to make everything clearer."

Lucien wrote a note and held it up for Ranulf to read. *I'd rather be anywhere but here.*

Ranulf nodded, pointed to himself, and mouthed, *Me too.*

These contract meetings were all the same. The client thought he and Lucien were out to take their company away when all they wanted to do was help.

Dan had a good glove manufacturing and distribution company, but he didn't have the contacts or know how to get the company recognized. It wasn't getting the business it should, so it was floundering even though the product was one of the best.

Ranulf and Lucien were ready to step in and give a financial and technical helping hand. All they asked for in return was controlling votes on the board, which meant a large share of the stocks.

Dan asked question after question. Ranulf answered them all diligently. Truthfully, Lucien didn't need to be there. He only attended to keep abreast of the happenings in the company and give his input from time to time.

Ranulf's cell phone rang, but he pushed the end button without looking at it, sending the call to voice mail. "Sorry about that, Dan. Keep going."

"Like I was saying, this merger would be a great help to my company but—"

Lucien's cell phone rang. He glanced at the caller ID then snatched the phone off of his hip. "I need to take this." He gave Ranulf a look then rushed out of the room.

"Is something wrong, Ranulf?" Dan asked.

"No, don't worry about it." Ranulf frowned at the open door, trying to figure out what Lucien's look had meant. Ranulf brushed it off as something Lucien would have to explain later. "Dan, I appreciate your misgivings about this. Lucien and I are willing to give you as much time as you need to think it over. However, your creditors aren't so generous. Our contract clearly states none of your current employees would be sacrificed and business operations would proceed as normal. That is more than the other companies are willing to offer you."

"That is true."

"I know it's a little scary handing over majority vote and controlling stock to an unknown party, but you are still the owner. We would consult with you before making any drastic changes. The contract states that as well."

"Yes it does."

"If you know all that, then I don't see the problem, Dan." He laughed to take the annoyance out of his voice. "Or did you just want to talk to me? People have told me I have a sexy phone voice."

Dan laughed while Ranulf pantomimed hitting his head against a wall. The whole ordeal wouldn't be so annoying if it didn't play out the same every time he and Lucien went through it.

If they could announce to the world how many companies they really had control over, people like Dan would be falling over themselves to sign with them. But, Ranulf and Lucien had to keep a low profile. Immortality was tricky like that.

"I guess you're right, Ranulf. I just wanted to make sure I'm making the right decision."

"You know you are. Just sign and let's get your business in the limelight where it belongs. I have a webmaster all lined up who is itching to make your site look better. She sees it as a challenge."

Dan laughed.

Ranulf looked up when Lucien returned.

"We need to go. Now," Lucien whispered so Dan wouldn't hear him over the phone.

"We need to finish this conference call," Ranulf replied in like manner.

"Fine. You finish the call. I'll go get Eris."

"What!"

Ranulf didn't get an answer because Lucien had left the room.

"Is something wrong, Ranulf?" Dan asked.

"Dan, we'll have to pick this up tomorrow. I'm sorry for cutting you off but I have an emergency."

"I hope everything is okay."

"As do I. Thank you, Dan. Bye." Ranulf ended the call then ran out of the office. Lucien was already out the front door but he'd left it open so Ranulf could follow him.

Ranulf ran out of the door, slamming it in his wake, and jumped in the passenger seat of the car Lucien had backed out of the garage. "What's wrong with Eris?"

"She called in tears and asked for me to go get her. I thought you'd want to come."

"Damn straight." Ranulf opened his phone. "She called me first. Damn! I should have answered."

"I did, and we're on our way. That's what matters."

"Where is she? Why does she need a ride? Why would she call us?"

"She's someplace without a car of her own, and we were the first ones she thought of. I'm not questioning it."

Ranulf nodded and sat back. He wouldn't question it either.

Eris couldn't think of anyone else to call. That made him ecstatic. Up until that moment, he hadn't been sure where they stood with her. Calling them for help had to mean she felt they were friends, at least.

That was a start.

It took Lucien forty minutes to get to Eris's location. She stood near a lamp post at the end of a nice-looking row of houses. Ranulf was glad the neighborhood seemed safe enough. He didn't want to think about Eris in danger while she'd waited for them.

She huddled more into her cape and stepped closer to the lamp post when Lucien pulled the car closer. A defensive gesture that annoyed Ranulf, but he was glad Eris was smart enough to be wary of an unknown car approaching her.

"What is she wearing?" Lucien asked as he pulled the car up to the curb.

Ranulf ignored the question and got out. Eris looked instantly relieved when she saw him. He smiled at her and gestured to his vacated seat. "Your chariot, my lady."

Eris slid onto the seat. He closed the door for her and then got in the backseat.

"Thank you so much. I couldn't think of anyone else to call. I'm so sorry about this," Eris said between sniffs.

"What happened, Eris? I barely understood you on the phone," Lucien said. He pulled a u-turn and got back on the highway.

She shook her head and sniffed again.

Ranulf placed a hand on her shoulder. "It's all right. You don't have to tell us. We'll take you home."

"Home." She looked down at herself. "Oh no!"

"What?" Lucien and Ranulf said in unison.

"I left my keys."

"We can go back," Lucien said, slowing the car.

"No! Please, don't. I don't want—"

"He won't," Ranulf said quickly, wishing he could hold her and ease some of her agitation. "You can come back to our place. We have plenty of guest rooms."

"Thank you," she whispered. "I'm sorry."

Lucien said, "Stop apologizing. We were awake, and we weren't doing anything important."

On that point, Ranulf agreed. Nothing was more important than Eris to them. Not even a multi-million dollar business deal. What was a few more million? They had plenty of money. They only bought and revamped companies to keep from being bored.

Eris sneezed.

Ranulf reached across the divide and turned on the heat full blast. "You're not dressed for the weather."

"No."

"Were you at a costume party?"

"No."

He wanted to ask more, but Eris started crying again. Lucien gripped the steering wheel. Ranulf knew his friend was as frustrated about the confines of the car as he.

They reached the house, and Ranulf had to resist the urge to sweep Eris into his arms and carry her into the house as they walked to the door. Lucien had no such qualms. She had taken two steps before Lucien swept her up high on his chest.

Eris didn't protest being carried.

Instead of taking her to a guest room, Lucien carried her to the office and placed her on the couch. She sat up and would have stood, but Lucien placed a hand on her shoulder, holding her in place.

"What's happened? Why are you crying?" Lucien asked in a low voice. He crouched in front of her and waited.

She didn't answer, just looked uncertain.

Ranulf sat beside her. "What is this flimsy thing supposed to be?" He fingered the thin material of her cape.

Better to talk about a neutral topic until Eris felt she could tell them what had happened. He was dying to know, and he knew Lucien was too, but Eris seemed very shook up. Ranulf didn't want to push her.

"A cape," she whispered then laughed. The sound broke on a sob she held back when she bit her lip. "I...I always wanted a cloak—a real one complete with lining and hidden pockets and a hood. But, this costume cape is all I can afford at the moment." She took a shaky a breath. "I didn't bring my coat because we wouldn't be outside that long, and it would have been a pain to deal with it."

"We?"

"Clayton and me."

Lucien looked ready to kill. Thankfully, Eris didn't notice his expression since she stared at her lap.

Ranulf asked in a low voice, "Where is Clayton, Eris? Why didn't he drive you home?" She looked at him with an apologetic expression. He patted her hand. "We don't mind. Truly. But, it makes no sense for you to call us when he was there."

It pained Ranulf to say the words, but truth and reason had to override desire in that instance.

Eris didn't look like she would answer. Ranulf resigned himself to not knowing. He knew Eris wouldn't talk if she didn't want to. He didn't want to force her and ruin his chances with her. A stern look at Lucien ended the conversation.

Or would have…

"You know what live action role-playing is?" Eris asked.

"LARP. Yes," Lucien said.

Eris looked at Lucien then Ranulf. She opened her mouth, but no sound came out. Seeing her like that pained Ranulf.

"If you don't want to tell us, then don't, Eris. It's none of our business," Ranulf said, knowing full well he meant the opposite.

She shook her head and collapsed against him. The joy of feeling her in his arms once again couldn't even be marred by her crying, though it did make him angry. He held her tight as her tears soaked his shirt.

Eris related the entire incident between sniffling sobs. At the end, she said, "I can't…why would he think…*we* haven't even…" She pulled away from Ranulf and looked up at him. "Why would he do that?"

"I have no answer for you. I'm sorry he did that to you, but I'm happy the situation didn't get out of hand. That Lucien and I were able to get to you in time."

She sat back, pulling out of his arms. He wanted to continue holding her but settled on keeping his arm around her shoulders.

"God, I'm a mess." She rubbed her eyes on the edge of her cape. "I must be near my period for me to be crying this much. I always get so weepy around that time. It's annoying." She glanced at Lucien and then Ranulf. "Sorry. That was TMI."

"So, this situation isn't as traumatic as we think it is?" Ranulf asked.

"Probably not. I'm in mood swing hell—laughing to tears in five seconds or less and with no discernible cause."

"You had plenty of cause tonight," Lucien said. "Forgive me if this sounds insensitive but what type of sword was it? You said it cost nine hundred."

"Damascus steel."

"Ah. Strong blades made of quality metal. Nine hundred is pretty cheap for a true Damascus. *If* it was a true Damascus."

Eris opened her mouth then shook her head with a laugh. "God, I was about to ask a stupid question."

"What?"

"I was going to ask 'how do you know about Damascus steel?' But, duh…" She gestured to the swords gracing the walls of the study.

"Your momentary mental lapses are excused. You've had a rough night." Ranulf gave her a squeeze.

"Well, since you know about it, does that mean you have one?" she asked.

"Quite a few, as a matter of fact. Why?"

"I want to get a closer look at my competition." She stood.

Lucien straightened and looked at her with a worried expression. "You can't be thinking of staying with Clayton after what he did?"

"Somehow *hell no* just doesn't adequately convey my feelings on the matter, but it's the only thing I can think of to say. As far as I'm concerned, he ended it when he decided to *sell* me to his friend. I just want to see the weapon that means more to him than me."

"The man is an idiot. No weapon could mean more than you," Ranulf said, standing.

"That's sweet."

"It's true," Lucien said.

"Thanks for saying so. My self-esteem needs a boost after tonight."

"Glad to be of service." Ranulf put his hand on the small of her back and guided her out of the study and up the stairs. He entered the third door on the left and flipped the switch. "The far wall holds a small portion of our Damascus steel collection."

"You two are fond of small portions of the whole, aren't you?"

"Though this house is big, it is nowhere near big enough for us to display all that we have collected over the years." Lucien took charge of her and ushered her closer to the blades.

Eris reached out then jerked back with a mumbled apology.

"Why do you apologize? You can touch them. It won't hurt the blades."

"When I almost touched one the first day I came here, Leon got all huffy with me."

"Ah, well that is a different matter. One of my ex-girlfriends purposefully injured herself on one of the blades downstairs so she could sue us for injury while on our property."

"That's such a crap thing to do. Had you just dumped her or something? She didn't win, did she?"

"Yes, I had broken off our relationship, and no, she didn't win. Our security system caught the whole episode on tape, and we showed it to the judge, who then dismissed the case." Lucien gestured to the swords. "Touch them if you like. Actually..." He took one off of the wall and held it out to her, hilt first.

She gripped it, and he let go.

"Good Lord," she cried when she almost dropped it. Her first instinct was to let go, but she didn't want to bruise the sword since it was worth a lot. Instead, the tip of the blade imbedded in the flooring and she supported the hilt. She'd just barely missed hitting Lucien's foot. "I'm sorry. I'm so sorry. I thought it was lighter. You held it so easily. How the hell did people fight with these things way back when?"

"You grow accustomed to the weight when you practice with them day after day."

She tried to lift the blade but couldn't and shook her head as she passed the hilt back to Lucien. "No way. Too heavy. Holding it for that little bit made my wrists hurt, and I was only propping it." She looked at the hole in the wood flooring. "Sorry about the floor."

"It's an easy fix. Don't worry about it," Ranulf said. "And you can't expect me to believe that blade was too heavy for you. A woman who lifts comic book boxes all day should at least be able to hold that sword."

"That's what you think. I don't lift a damn thing. I bat my eyelashes at the nearest guy and ask him to do it in a cute little voice." She cocked her head to the side and blinked her eyes in a cutesy manner. "Times like those, it pays to be female."

"Yes, yes. Feminine wiles are the undoing of all men everywhere." Ranulf let a woeful expression cross his face. It didn't last long since he grinned at her when she laughed at his antics.

Lucien placed the sword on the table behind him and faced Eris in time to see her hide a yawn behind her hand. "I think you should get some sleep."

"I'm really sorry about this."

"We've already told you we have plenty of room. It's not a problem. The guest rooms are kept ready because we never know when we'll have visitors."

"You're just saying that."

Ranulf said, "No, he's not. It doesn't seem like it since it's been quiet for the months you've worked here, but we do have many guests. They often times stay for extended periods of time."

"Oh, okay. So long as it's not a bother," Eris said.

"It's not."

She followed them to the guest room directly before the stairs. It was the one she'd used at Halloween.

Before she retreated inside, Lucien asked, "Do you need anything?"

"A spare shirt to sleep in, if you have it."

"Be right back." Ranulf ran down the hallway. He disappeared into a room and then returned with a shirt in his hand. "Here you go. Direct from my closet to you."

She looked down the hall and then back at him. "That's your room?"

"Yes. Why?" He wiggled his eyebrows at her. "Going to sneak in while I'm sleeping?"

"Um, no. For some stupid reason I thought you guys stayed on a different floor, which makes no sense when I already know this place only has two floors."

"As well as the attic, basement, and dungeon."

"Dungeon?"

Lucien said in a dry tone, "He means wine cellar."

"Yes, but dungeon sounds more ominous." Ranulf gestured over his shoulder. "That's my room." Then he gestured past her shoulder at the opposite end of the hall. "That's Lucien's."

"Good to know. I guess." She took the shirt from him. "Thank you for this. I'll make sure to give it back."

"Or you can keep it if you like."

She looked down at it then back at him. "Are you sure?"

"I never wear it."

* * * *

Lucien wanted to shake his head at Ranulf's blatant lie. The man had given Eris one of his favorite soccer team shirts. Ranulf had collected them since the team was created and had started handing out merchandise. But, it was Ranulf's prerogative.

Besides, the man was probably counting on Eris being with him soon, so the shirt would come back into his possession.

Eris said, "I would ask if you could wake me up before everyone gets here tomorrow so you could take me home without being seen, but I don't have my keys. I'll just hide out in here until I can get Clayton alone and can ask for my keys back." She stepped into the room and inched the door closed.

Lucien had almost forgotten it was a work-Saturday for Clayton's team. It only occurred once a month, and yet Fate had conspired to have Eris stay on that very Saturday. He would have liked for her to spend the day with them. Her co-workers' presence would make that impossible.

He smiled when Eris glanced at him. "Call us if you need anything."

"Okay. Thanks again. Good night."

"Good night," both men said in unison.

She closed the door, and they stood staring at it.

Ranulf whispered, "Why don't we have a camera in there?"

"Because what you're thinking of is illegal in this state." Lucien turned away against his will and went back to the previous room. The Damascus remained where he'd left it.

He went to the desk and flipped through some of the papers there.

"What are you looking for?" Ranulf asked.

He didn't answer. Several certificates caught his eye. He picked up one and then another. They all looked alike. He shook his head. It didn't matter so long as it named the Damascus. He put it in a folder then picked up the sword.

Ranulf asked, "What are you doing with that sword?"

"Not what I truly want, unfortunately." Lucien slid the Damascus blade into a nearby matching scabbard. "I'm retrieving Eris's keys."

Ranulf crossed his arms with a smirk. "With a blade in tow? I think I'll go with you."

"I don't need a chaperone."

"I'm not—"

"Or an accomplice. I have no intention of hurting him."

"No intention but you don't know what your temper will make you do."

"As angry as I am, I'm also happy. Clayton's idiocy has given us Eris."

"She's not ours, but I agree with your sentiment." Ranulf let his arms fall back to his sides. He waved Lucien forward. "Fine. I'll see you in the morning."

Lucien nodded and left the office.

He made it back to the place where he'd retrieved Eris and paused. She'd stood at the curb. He wasn't sure which house was the one he wanted.

Again, Clayton helped him without knowing. The boy stalked out of a house three down from the corner where Lucien had stopped. Clayton snatched open his car door, threw his belongings inside then himself. After starting his car, he rolled down the window and tossed out something before driving away in a hurry.

Two men and a woman stood in the doorway watching Clayton leave. The woman walked to the item Clayton had discarded. She said something to her companions before taking the item back to the house. The others followed after her. Lucien waited another few minutes before he pulled his car into the driveway and made his way to the front door and knocked.

"Clayton, I already told you—" The woman who answered the door stopped with a surprised look. "I'm sorry. I thought you were somebody else. May I help you?"

"Yes, you can. Is this the place Eris Brue attended a LARP session?"

"Yes."

"Good. She left her keys. I've come to retrieve them."

"Oh. Okay. Come in."

The woman stepped back, allowing Lucien entrance. He looked at the costume-clad men sitting on the couch.

"I'm Patty. That's my husband, Jamie. This is our house." She walked past Lucien into the living room. "She left her cell charger too."

Jamie said, "No, she didn't. Clayton chucked it out the car on his way out, which was a shit thing to do."

Lucien agreed silently. Patty handed him the keys and charger, which he pocketed.

Patty asked, "Is Eris okay? We...I didn't know what to do for her when she stormed out. I thought I would give her a chance to cool off and then bring her back in the house once we got Clayton to leave."

"Took his damn time about it, arguing the whole way," Jamie grumbled.

Lucien said, "Yes, Eris is well. My friend and I took her home." He didn't specify which home because Patty and the others didn't need that information.

Patty looked at the others then back at him. "Did Eris tell you about what happened?"

"Yes."

"Well, Spencer told us, and I got pissed. I never really liked Clayton, but Jamie knows him from online and they've met at several conventions. I tried to be nice, but what Clayton did to her was the last straw. I kicked him out of the house."

Jamie added, "I kicked him out of the group, which he felt the need to bitch about for over an hour. He's not welcome any longer. However, if you could tell Eris, we would love to have her over again. She plays a great dark elf mage, and everyone enjoys her company."

"I'll be sure to tell her." He turned his gaze to the one person who hadn't spoken. The boy seemed to jump. "Spencer," he said with a nod.

Spencer sighed. "That's me. I'm sorry if she's angry with me. I would have never gone along with Clayton's plan, but he said she'd be into it. When she freaked out, I backed off."

"Yes, I know. She told me that." Lucien crossed the room and held the sword out to Spencer. "This is for you. She said you won it."

Spencer took the blade, straining under the weight as he gripped it with both hands, and pulled it out of the scabbard. He looked at it then Lucien with wide eyes. "How did you get Clayton's sword?"

"That isn't Clayton's sword. That is a *true* Damascus blade made in the seventeenth century. It is worth far more than nine hundred dollars." He held out the folder he'd carried with the sword. "This is the provenance. I put your first name on it..." He trailed off with a raised eyebrow.

"Oryel. Spencer Oryel. O-R-Y-E-L."

Lucien took out his collapsible pen from his back pocket and scrawled out the name. He then handed Spencer the paper.

Spencer took it and stared at it. "Why would you sign this over to me?"

"I doubt you will see Clayton again or the sword he owes you. Since you did not take advantage of his wrongfully proposed offer, I feel as though I owe you. This is my debt repaid."

"Who are you? How the hell do you own a sword made back in the sixteen hundreds?"

"Sorry, I didn't introduce myself." Lucien held out a card from his breast pocket. "I'm Lucien Riordan."

"*The* Lucien Riordan who puts on the biggest ren faire in the country every March?" Jamie yelled.

"The same," Lucien said with a smile. "I take it you all attend."

Everyone nodded dumbly.

"Well, Eris's company is in the process of cataloging my comic collection, and we've become friends. I do not like seeing her hurt." He returned his attention to Spencer. "So I thank you for not making a bad situation worse."

"You sure this is okay?" Spencer asked, glancing down at the sword.

Lucien said, "I own several. I'll hardly notice the loss of one."

"Your collection must be amazing if you can go around giving away pieces of it."

"Feel free to stop by and you can take a tour. Call first and I'll make sure the gate guard has your name."

Spencer gaped at him, opening and closing his mouth several times but not making any sounds or talking.

Jamie asked, "Are you for real? We can go to your place? Your actual house?"

Patty smacked Jamie's shoulder. "He was talking to Spencer, not us."

"My invitation extends to all of you. I'm happy to entertain friends of Eris." He flashed his best statesman smile and made a mental note of foisting his volunteer work onto Ranulf when the group arrived, as he knew they would. His charity ended with the errand and the invitation. He didn't entertain, not even for Eris.

He handed Patty one of his cards. She took it with a look of awe on her face. Lucien would have rolled his eyes but he didn't want to be rude. "I have to leave now. Thank you for Eris's belongings. Enjoy your new sword, Spencer. And, I will see you all when you arrive for your tour."

Patty walked him to the door. He bid her goodbye one more time then went to his car. Before he closed the car door, the sound of the trio shouting happily reached his ears. He shook his head.

"Simple joys," he whispered.

Chapter Eleven

Eris opened the bedroom door at six and peered out. No one had arrived yet. She still had another hour and a half, but she was hungry. It was best to get food while no one was there to see her. Once everyone was situated and doing their jobs, she would figure out a way to get Clayton alone so she could get her keys back, assuming he'd bothered to get them from the kitchen counter. Eris hadn't even thought of the possibility that Clayton had forgotten the keys too.

That changed matters completely. She would have to catch a ride to Patty and Jamie's house before she could go home. That would mean imposing on Lucien or Ranulf further. She didn't want to do that since they had already done so much.

"Good morning, Eris," Lucien said.

She looked down the long hallway. Lucien exited his room carrying a bundle. Suddenly feeling shy, she whispered her greeting to his neck.

Worry over the location of her keys waned as the realization that last night actually happened settled around her. She'd stayed overnight, wearing one of Ranulf's shirts. Said shirt barely reached her knees. She inched behind the door so Lucien wouldn't notice her state of undress.

Lucien said, once he neared her, "The bathroom has toiletries you can use. They are generic. I'm sorry for that."

"It's okay, and thank you." She'd noticed, her first time using the bathroom, the pre-packaged toothbrush and toothpaste, as well as the other bath items. They were there again, or still there, but she hadn't disturbed them since she didn't want to use anything without asking. Lucien and Ranulf had already gone above and beyond by letting her stay the night.

"I also brought you something a little more comfortable to wear and your keys." He held out the bundle to her.

"My keys?" She took the clothes—a pair of jeans and a large shirt. Her keys and cell charger rested atop the clothes. "My charger? How? I left that in Clayton's car."

"Clayton felt the need to throw the charger away when he left. Patty rescued it and handed it and your keys over to me when I went back."

"Went back." The more he said the more confused she felt. "You went back? You didn't have to do that."

"There's no need for you to deal with Clayton if you don't have to." Lucien smiled. "Retrieving your keys gave me a feeling of usefulness."

"You've already done so much. Now I feel like I owe you."

"Good morning, you two," Ranulf called.

Eris looked down the other end of the hall. Ranulf grinned at her as he neared them.

"What are you doing awake?" Lucien asked. "And coherent? That's unlike you."

"I've been up for the last three hours. I wanted to make sure I woke in time to take Eris home." Ranulf grinned at her. "Did you sleep well?"

Eris said, "Yes. That bed is heavenly. I wouldn't have woken up if I hadn't set my phone alarm."

"We would have roused you. We know you're anxious to get home."

"Lucien went and got my keys for me."

"Yes, I know. When you're ready, I'll drive you home."

Lucien said, "I'd come with, but I have a meeting to attend this morning, which I would have let Ranulf do if I'd known he be awake."

"Don't pout, Lucien. It's infantile," Ranulf said.

Eris looked between both men. "I'm really sorry about all this. I will find some way to repay you. To start, I'll be out of your hair in no time." She looked down at the clothes. "I'll put these through the wash and bring them back on Monday."

"There's no need to rush off," Ranulf said.

Lucien said, "Agreed. And, you owe us nothing. We're happy to help."

"Since you're here, you might as well eat."

"No, I should get going." Her stomach chose that moment to growl.

"Your stomach disagrees," Lucien said. "Stay and eat. I'm sure you'll be out of here long before any of your co-workers see you."

Eris nodded. "It's probably no big deal, but I don't want to give them something to gossip about. I really shouldn't have called you. You're clients of CGC."

Ranulf stepped closer to her and placed his hand on her arm. "We'd also like to think we're your friends, Eris. We don't mind that you called. Besides, there's nothing for you to feel guilty about."

That was true, but it didn't change the fact that she did feel guilty. Lucien and Ranulf had gone out of their way and still were. Even though they said not to, she planned to find some way to make it up to them.

She took a deep breath then smiled. Ranulf and Lucien smiled with her. She said, "I'll get changed and head for the kitchen then."

"Good," Ranulf said. "It'll be a quick meal and then you're on your way home."

Lucien glanced at his watch. "You two have fun. I have to go. I'll see you Monday, Eris."

"Have a good day."

"Oh, I already am."

She didn't know what that meant, but smiled and waved as Lucien walked down the stairs. Her attention went back to Ranulf, who didn't look like he would leave. She inched back as hint of her intention to go back to her room.

"I'm going to change," she said.

"I'll meet you in the kitchen then."

Those were his words, but he didn't move. She inched the door closed and finally shut it. A few seconds later, Ranulf walked away.

There was something different about both men that morning. Up until the night before, they seemed reserved around her. One emotional incident later and they were grinning as though all was right with the world.

Maybe something had happened—like a major deal going through—after she had gone to bed. That could be the reason for their change in attitude. She was just happy she'd gotten them on a good day.

A violent sneeze caught her off guard. She barely had time to turn her face away from her clothes.

"Oh, please don't get sick. I really don't want to be sick," she pleaded with herself. Hopefully her body would listen.

She'd managed to avoid getting sick Halloween night, and she'd been wearing next to nothing compared to her elven outfit. Then again, she had been moodier than usual lately as evident by her crying fit the night before. It would be just her luck that she was starting her cycle. And, around her time of month she was more susceptible to germs and the like. She'd stood out in the cold waiting for Lucien and Ranulf for almost an hour.

"Stupid period," she grumbled.

It was probably nothing, and she was worried for no reason. She'd go home and down some vitamin C before soaking in a chamomile and eucalyptus bath. That should stave off anything. A glass of lemon and honey tea wouldn't hurt either.

She laid the clothes on her bed and looked at her cell phone. Even though she had her keys, she still needed to talk to Clayton. As far as she was concerned, their relationship had ended. But, did Clayton see it that way or had he interpreted last night's blow up as just a lovers' quarrel?

Her cell phone rang, and she jumped.

"Speak of the devil," she whispered as she looked at the caller ID. She flipped open her phone. "What do you want?"

"Why aren't you at home?" Clayton snapped.

"Why the hell is that any of your business?"

"I'm at your house to get my stuff."

"What stuff?"

"My sword and the chainmail I left there the last time I changed at your place."

She was about to deny the existence of the items when she remembered. They were occupying floor space in her hall closet. He'd left them over a month ago. They'd managed to keep forgetting about them—out of sight, out of mind.

Clayton asked, "Well? You coming back so I can get my stuff? I have to get to work."

"After what you did, you're calling me this early in the morning about some stupid gaming gear?"

"I want it back before I head in to work. Get home."

"Go to hell. I'll go home when I damn well feel like it, and it won't be any time soon." She huffed a little bit to calm herself down. "I can't believe you called me about this."

"Why else would I call you?"

She almost snapped her phone closed, ending the call, but that wouldn't solve anything. "I should…you…" She stopped and shook her head. "You know what? I'm not even going to be trifling like that. You can get your stuff at the front gate of the mansion."

"When?"

"When it gets there and you better be damn happy I don't throw that shit in the garbage. Lose my damn number." She snapped the phone shut. As much as she wanted to toss it across the room, she didn't. Her phone had cost too much to abuse it.

She set it down and worked at bringing down her heart rate.

Well, at least there was no confusion about the end of their relationship. Now she only had to worry about how the break-up would affect their work life. Everyone was bound to notice.

Would Clayton tell all or be too embarrassed—as he should be—to relate the real reasons?

She didn't care if he took the credit for ending the relationship. If that assuaged his ego and kept him out of her hair, then she'd let him have the last word.

Pushing all thoughts of the future out of her mind, she focused on the present. She got dressed, gathered her stuff, and then exited the room headed for the kitchen.

Ranulf was already there, grinning at Liselle, who was serving breakfast.

"There she is," Liselle said in greeting. "When Ranulf said you were here, I dished up your favs."

Eris's face grew hot. What had Ranulf told Liselle?

The woman said, "It's a shame about your car breaking down on the way here. Why you wouldn't wait until Monday to fix that glitch—or whatever it was—is beyond me. Dedication to your job, I guess. But, it's a good thing you had your cell phone and could call the house."

"Yeah, it was a good thing." She looked at Ranulf who winked at her. She gave him a thankful smile.

Liselle placed a plate of food on the kitchen island and then held out some napkin-wrapped flatware. "Eat up so you two can get away before the crowds arrive. Nosy people are known to make stuff up if the truth isn't as interesting as they'd hoped."

"You're a jewel, Liselle," Eris said, taking the utensils. She sat on the barstool and inhaled the aroma of the food.

Ranulf said, "That's why we pay her so much."

"Funny, I thought it was because I could cook around the world," Liselle said.

"That too."

Eris ate her food with flourish. Her secret was safe. All she had to do was get home and the day would be saved. Except, she still had to come back out and drop off Clayton's gear.

She sighed.

"Something wrong?" Ranulf asked.

"No. Nothing." She smiled at him and then turned that smile to Liselle. "Thanks so much for breakfast. It was great."

"You're welcome. Now hurry up and get out of here." Liselle gathered the plates with one hand while shooing them out of the kitchen with the other.

Ranulf escorted Eris to his car and they left the property. He glanced at her several times. Finally he said, "There's something wrong. What is it?"

"I'm just annoyed that I have to come back out here."

"I'm sorry. I didn't realize we bothered you that much."

Eris jerked and looked at him. "Oh no, that's not what I meant. I meant today. I…Clayton left some of his stuff at my house and he wants it back. Rather than have him at my place, I told him I'd drop it off at the gate."

"I see."

"I love this project. It's a lot of fun."

Ranulf nodded. He glanced at her then back at the road. "Why not throw it away?"

She laughed. "As much as I'd like to play the vindictive ex, we work together. I'd be borrowing trouble with loads of interest if I decided to be petty. I'm just going to give it back and that'll be the end." She thought about it a little bit and then added, "Besides, I'm not the vindictive type. Getting even never solves anything, and I'd regret it later. Avoidance is more my way of dealing with a bad situation."

"Ah."

"What about you? How do you deal?"

"I like to get everything out in the open so there are no questions or misunderstandings."

That made her nod. "You seem like the type."

"Don't I? I wasn't always like that, but I've found it makes things easier." He grinned at her. "What type do you think Lucien is?"

"He's hard to read." She rested her chin on her hand and her elbow on her arm, which she crossed over her stomach. "I think Lucien is the type to leave it up to you."

"Go on."

"Well, I mean, he always seems to step back from every situation and let you handle everything. Maybe it's because he knows you can handle it and he trusts you like that. You two complement each other very well."

"We're not gay."

She gaped at him. "I didn't say that. I didn't mean to imply it either."

"It's true we've lived together for a while, but we've never once considered intimacy with each other." He shuddered. "The very thought makes my breakfast beg for freedom. Let's talk about something else."

"Sorry."

He patted her knee. "I'm just teasing you, Eris. I'm not mad. I know how our living situation may seem like more than just friends and associates to outsiders."

"You do complement each other though. *If*—that's a very big if and I'm not implying or suggesting anything by it—you two were a couple, you'd be amazing."

Ranulf threw back his head and laughed.

Eris was scared he would swerve off the road. She clutched the passenger handle and braced her other hand against the dash. Despite her precautions, the car remained steady.

Ranulf continued laughing.

At least her words had amused rather than insulted. She smiled with him but didn't see why he found it so funny.

He said, once he sobered, "I'm sorry. I don't mean to laugh at you. It's simply many of our past girlfriends have said something similar. They felt they couldn't compete with our friendship."

"Yeah, I can imagine. I feel sorry for any woman trying to get between you two."

"Oh, I don't know. Having a woman between us might be fun."

Eris's face turned into one giant flame. She only hoped Ranulf couldn't tell.

He said, "But, we should talk about something a little more appropriate. Like the directions to your house. I've seen your address before, but I'm not sure how to get there once we leave the highway."

"You have?"

"What?"

"Seen my address."

"Yes. Yours and your co-workers. It was needed to calculate the mileage using the most direct route. Not that we don't trust you all, but we're not paying you to drive the scenic route to work."

"Makes sense." She pointed at the sign ahead. "You need to exit here and turn right."

She guided him through the maze of roads that lead to her apartment complex and was thankful for the distraction. Why had her mind immediately put her in the middle of Ranulf and Lucien when Ranulf had said that? More to the point, why did that image feel so right and perfect? She didn't want a relationship like that and had always vowed to avoid it.

But…

She glanced at Ranulf.

"Eris?"

She blinked at him. "Huh?"

He grinned at her. "I asked how it is you get lost at the mansion but can navigate this mess and get home?"

"Oh. That's because I know these streets. I've been living here for a long time. I've explored every road so I know the best ways to get in and out. Your mansion is huge and unknown. I'm scared to go exploring since I might get lost and never find my way out."

"Lucien or I would search for you."

"Yeah, right. Probably to find the source of the rotting corpse smell."

Ranulf didn't say anything. Eris got the distinct impression her words had upset him. She pointed ahead of them to a row of townhouses. "That one on the end."

He pulled into the carport and put the car in park.

"Thanks so much for the ride." She gathered her bundle. "I'll get everything washed and back to you on Monday." She braced for the cold air and then opened the door.

"I'll take it back for you," Ranulf said in a low voice.

"Excuse me?" She looked back at him.

"Clayton's things. This is your day off. You shouldn't have to drive all the way back to the mansion, and over something so trivial. I'm headed back that way. I'll take it."

"You're sure? I don't…you and Lucien have already done way too much."

"I insist."

There was something cold in his voice. It made her shiver, or was that the cold air?

She nodded. "I'll be right back. Or, did you want to come in?"

"No, I'll wait here."

"Okay. I'll only be a second." She closed the door and rushed to her house. Once inside, she dumped her bundle and went to the hall closet where Clayton's belongings were stashed.

Thankfully everything was in a small gym bag. A small, *heavy* gym bag as she discovered when she tried lifting it. She really needed to think about working out. The sword from last night was one thing, but she should at least be able to carry a chainmail shirt and whatever else was stashed in the bag with it.

She lugged the bag out to the car. Ranulf took charge of it and tossed it in the back seat like it weighed nothing.

"I told him I'd drop it at the gate," she said.

"Then that's where he'll get it. Don't worry. He won't know that you didn't drop it off." Ranulf got back in the driver's seat and closed the door. "I'll see you Monday."

"Yes, you will, and thank you."

He waved as he backed out of the carport and she watched him drive away.

Ranulf really was a nice guy. Ranulf and Lucien both. She only hoped she could pay back all their kindness one day.

A sneeze made her rush back in the house for hot tea and a chamomile soak. She wouldn't be able to repay Ranulf and Lucien at all if she had to call in sick.

Chapter Twelve

Ranulf closed his eyes and let the darkness surround him. When he opened his eyes again, he'd be back in the office ready to start his Monday routine.

"Ranulf," Lucien said in a soft voice.

"Back."

"Likewise."

Ranulf looked at Lucien who looked just as weary as he felt. "Double duty, I see."

Lucien nodded. "A rarity and always taxing."

"Where did he take you?"

"Gezane."

"That far? I thought Genevieve wanted to stick to Earths similar to this one. I went to Conclave."

"It's a waste of time is what it is. Stupid Genevieve and her stupid quest."

Ranulf laughed. "She'll get you back for that. You know it."

"Whatever." Lucien leaned back in his seat.

Neither of them was in much of a hurry to turn on the lights and resume their normal work lives now that their errands had ended.

The door to the office opened and Eris entered. Ranulf frowned a little that she didn't knock as she usually did. But then, it made him happy that she felt comfortable enough to simply enter.

She took two steps then stopped, noticing him and Lucien. "Oh crap. You two are here."

Ranulf smirked. "That's not your usual greeting."

"The lights were off. I thought you were at a meeting and I could crash on your couch for an hour."

"Feel free." He gestured to the couch.

"I don't want to bother you."

"You're not," Lucien said.

She looked at the couch then back at them. "You're sure?"

"Please," he and Lucien said in unison.

She sat on the couch and let her head fall against the back.

Ranulf and Lucien watched her but said nothing. Ranulf was curious about her behavior but would rather let her tell them the problem if she felt like it.

In a slow, tired voice, she said, "We finished the room so we're taking a short break while the comic boxes get switched out. The team said it should take no more than an hour." She sighed. "I thought of lying down in the den, but the guys discovered your game system and some medieval fighting game."

"One of Lucien's better ideas," Ranulf said.

Eris lifted her head and looked at Lucien. "You came up with that game?"

Lucien nodded.

"Nice job. It looks lifelike. That spiked ball hanging off a chain causes a lot of damage."

"Flail," Lucien said.

"Is that what it's called? Well, Pete got a character using that and Chad got some huge guy with a giant hammer."

"Warhammer," Ranulf said.

She rubbed her temple. "Anyway, the guys are into it and yelling and carrying on, so there was no way I could sleep in there. I was going to ask to borrow a room—"

"You can if you like," Lucien said.

"—but if I lie down on a bed, I might not get up until after sunset. I thought I would crash here since you guys weren't here, but you are here. Why is the light off?"

"We are hiding from work," Ranulf said.

"Ah. Sorry to interrupt."

"No bother. What's wrong?"

She sighed again. "This headache has been kicking my ass since the weekend. I thought I'd headed off the problem at the pass, but this cold won't be denied." She sneezed into the crook of her elbow, proving her point. "I didn't feel that bad this morning when I came to work, but it's just been getting worse. Hopefully a good night's sleep will knock it out, and I'll be okay."

Ranulf approached the couch. He pulled the wrap off the back and gestured for her to lie down. "Go to sleep. We'll wake you when it's time to go back."

"Thank you." She complied and cocooned herself once he covered her with the blanket.

"Comfortable?"

She made an affirmative noise.

Lucien smiled.

Ranulf asked, "Do you need anything? An aspirin maybe?"

A negative noise.

"Sleep well then."

She mumbled something that sounded like a thank you. Ranulf resisted the urge to touch her. He stood by her side a little longer then returned to his seat.

Both men watched her. They gave their best impression of statues, barely breathing, so as not to disturb her.

A little over an hour later, Chad's voice filtered through the door. "I don't know where she went. Should we check upstairs?"

Lucien exchanged a look with Ranulf and then walked to the door. He exited the office, closing the door softly behind him, and faced Chad and Pete. "Eris tells me you all availed yourselves of our games. Did you enjoy them?"

"And how. You do good work," Chad said with his thumb up.

"Thank you."

"Have you seen Eris? The room is ready to go. It's time to get back to work," Pete said.

"She's not feeling well and is sleeping at the moment."

"Huh. She has been looking kind of strained today. She said she caught a bug over the weekend and was over it. I guess not."

"So it would seem."

"Guess we can work without her then."

"Or, you and your team can take the rest of the day off."

Chad perked up. "You're not joking? We can have the rest of the day with pay?"

Lucien nodded. "It's only two hours, but yes."

"Thanks!" Chad ran off toward the survey room, probably to inform the others.

Ranulf exited the office and pulled the door softly shut behind him.

Pete said, "That was generous."

Lucien said, "She'll feel bad if you work while she sleeps, and I have no intention of waking her. This heads off the problem before it starts."

"Good thinking. Or would this be planning for the future?" Pete gave them both an assessing look.

"I don't know what you mean."

"Don't you?"

Lucien was about to answer when he noticed Clayton approaching them. Pete followed Lucien's gaze then faced the newcomer.

"I hear tell we get the rest of the day off," Clayton said.

Ranulf asked, "Your team finished your room as well?"

"No."

"Then why would you have the rest of the day off? Eris's team is being rewarded. When your team finishes your room, you will be treated in like manner, not before."

"Just thought I'd ask to be sure," Clayton said before walking back the way he'd come.

Lucien sneered at the boy's back.

Pete said under his breath, "Lazy ass." He looked at Ranulf and Lucien. "You didn't hear that. However, you will hear me when I say if you two are playing with Eris, I'll burn this place to the ground, starting with the survey rooms."

Lucien didn't bother looking at Ranulf since he knew the man probably wore the same intrigued expression he did.

"I'm not blind, and neither are the other people on our team. Eris may not have noticed the way you two look at her, but we have. It's one thing if you two are being serious..." Pete trailed off with a hard look.

Ranulf said, "Whether or not Lucien or I or both of us begin a relationship with Eris now that her relationship with Clayton is over is entirely up to her. While I do admit we've done everything in our power to steer Eris in the direction of seeing us as possible romantic options, none of it was done with the intention of hurting her."

"Why do you care?" Lucien asked.

"I'm her friend and mentor. I've known that girl a long time. I recruited her into CGC. It set my teeth on edge when she started dating that waste of space Clayton."

"I take it you don't like him."

"And make no excuses about it. He's a slacker and an opportunist. I still don't know how he managed to become head of his team. But he's not a problem anymore, from what I hear. You two are."

"We aren't a problem, not to you or Eris," Ranulf said.

"I'd like to believe you, but guys like you see girls like Eris as a form of entertainment until the novelty wears off."

"We'll put it in writing. Will that ease your mind? If we do end up hurting Eris then you can sue us."

Pete looked to be considering the offer. He nodded. "In writing then. However much I sue you for would probably be a drop in the bucket to you two though."

"Have faith. You may not have to sue us at all." Ranulf ducked back into the study. When he returned, he had a handwritten contract stating he and Lucien had no plans to harm Eris and would do nothing in the future to bring her harm.

All three men signed it. Ranulf handed it to Pete. "I hope this settles matters."

"For now," Pete said, folding the paper and putting it in his back pocket. "She's in there, isn't she?" He nodded to the office.

"Sleeping. She is sick. We'd like her to rest."

"I'll come back later and drive her home. No arguments, either. She's not staying here."

Lucien said, "Yet."

Pete looked at them both in turn then walked away.

"I like him," Ranulf said.

Lucien snorted. "Like him or not, he better not interfere. Our moment has come. Anyone who gets in our way will be dealt with."

* * * *

Eris startled awake when someone shook her shoulder. She looked at Pete, who grinned at her.

"You awake?" he whispered.

She sat up and regretted it as her head started pounding. "Unfortunately," she mumbled.

"Well, it's time to go home."

"What!" She looked around the room for a clock. It was almost five. She'd slept the last three hours. "Oh no. Oh crap. I didn't mean to sleep so long."

"You needed it," Lucien said.

She looked at him and then Ranulf. "You said you'd wake me."

"We lied," Ranulf said with a shrug.

Pete said, "Don't worry. We didn't work without you. They gave us the rest of the day off with pay. Chad and the others have been playing video games all this time. I've been reading comics." He patted her shoulder. "But, it's time to get you home and to bed."

"Oh. Okay." She stood, and the room swam.

Pete grabbed her arm to keep her on her feet. She was happy for the support. "I'm driving you home, and I don't want to hear any of your crappy little excuses or denials."

"Yes, sir."

"Good girl. Say thank you to the nice men for letting you use their couch and then goodbye."

Eris couldn't help grinning at the way he was treating her. She nodded to Ranulf and Lucien. "Thanks for letting me rest. I feel a lot better."

"You don't look it." Lucien's voice was gruff with annoyance. "If you come in here looking like that tomorrow, I'll be very angry with you. Take care of your health. Our comic collection isn't going anywhere."

She nodded. "Good night."

Ranulf and Lucien said in unison, "Good night."

Pete helped her to his car. She hated leaving her car at the mansion. That meant she'd need to catch a ride in the morning. But she'd hate getting into an accident even more.

"You need to be careful around those two, Eris." Pete glanced at her and then back at the road.

"What do you mean?"

"You really do go off into your own world when you start typing, don't you?"

"You knew that already."

Pete sighed and shook his head. "I'm saying the wolves are at the door, and you're inviting them in for tea and cakes."

"Ranulf and Lucien? Wolves? After me?" She laughed. "You're nuts. Men like them don't want someone like me. They're just being friendly to an employee."

"And gullible is in the dictionary twice."

"I'm not being gullible."

"You're sure as hell acting like it." Pete pulled off on the side of the road and looked at her. "Listen to the voice of wisdom and experience. Those men are after you. I don't know what they have planned. I don't care. I just don't want to see you hurt."

"You're reading too much into the situation."

"Humor me and be careful around those two."

"Pete, I'm happy you care, but you really are seeing things. Ranulf and Lucien aren't after me. I'd be flattered if even one of them was, but the possibility of both is not even registering on the radar."

Pete harrumphed and pulled into traffic once more. "Maybe not for you, but it is for them."

"I'm not like that."

"You don't *want* to be like that. I'm betting those two could change your mind."

She crossed her arms and forgot all about her aching body and her struggle with the cold virus. "Pete, it won't happen. They aren't interested, and even if they were, I wouldn't do it."

"You know what they say about apples and trees, right?" He glanced at her.

She didn't answer him. He was wrong. She wasn't like that. Even if she thought for a second that Ranulf *and* Lucien did want to be with her, she'd set them straight. She wanted a committed, *monogamous* relationship.

That wouldn't happen with them. She'd already said as much to Ranulf, in a roundabout way. Ranulf and Lucien were a package deal. Anyone who spent more than five minutes with them would realize that.

Package deals weren't for her.

Chapter Thirteen

"That's strange," Ranulf said.

"What's strange?" Lucien closed the file cabinet drawer and opened the one below it.

"I'm looking through the database and there are about twenty issues without full information."

"The team must still be working on them." Lucien left his search, came around Ranulf's desk, and looked at the screen. He shrugged at what he saw and went back to his task. "Don't worry about it. I'm sure they'll fix it."

"This is marked as finished a month ago." Ranulf looked over the file closely. "I wonder if Eris knows about this."

"Stop trying to find excuses to go to the survey room."

"That's not what this is."

"Fine, I'll go tell her then."

Ranulf stood and met Lucien at the door. He pulled the other man back and said with a knowing look, "Now who's trying to find excuses?"

They stood staring at each for a long a while until they both grinned. Ranulf crossed his arms, and Lucien chuckled.

"Fine. Fine. You tell her." Lucien returned to the filing cabinet and his earlier search. "It might be an oversight and they meant to go back to them."

Ranulf nodded and left the office. He made his way to Eris's survey room. Everyone worked diligently. Only Pete bothered glancing Ranulf's way when he entered.

Learning from the past mistakes of others, Ranulf made his way to Eris's side and bent close to her ear. "Eris," he whispered.

She jumped and looked up at him. "Geez, you scared me. Something wrong?"

"I need to steal some time and show you something. If you could come with me."

"Sure. Let me type in this one last thing."

Ranulf stepped back. He smiled at the others who looked his way but decided not to volunteer his reasons for taking Eris away from her work. If she felt the need to share the situation with them later that was her choice.

She followed him back to the study and he showed her the computer screen. Before he could explain his worry, Eris said, "This isn't right. Half the information is missing."

Without asking, she sat in his seat and started scrolling through the page. He placed one hand on the desk and the other on the back of the chair and leaned over her shoulder. She said nothing. As much as he should be concerned with the matter before him, he couldn't help inhaling the scent of her hair.

Apricots and shea butter. He liked her better wearing roses. Just thinking of the day when she would wear roses again for him had him wanting to lay kisses over her bare neck. He lifted his hand from the back of the chair and moved slowly to touch her neck. She wouldn't feel the barest of caresses. If she did, he could excuse it as a slip of his hand.

"What in the world?" Eris whispered.

Ranulf pulled back, startled and a bit guilty. He replaced his hand on the chair and looked at the screen. "What?"

"This is very wrong. I mean, not wrong. The information present is correct, but it's not complete. I don't know how this could have…" She trailed off.

Ranulf looked at the top of her head. "What's wrong?"

"Excuse me. I'll go check on this right now. Thank you for bringing it to my attention," she said before rushing out of the door.

"You're welcome," he said to the space she once occupied as she'd fled too quickly to hear him.

Lucien asked, "Did you enjoy that?"

"What can I say? I'm a dirty old man." He stroked the chair, enjoying the lingering heat, then bent low and inhaled Eris's scent. He definitely liked the roses better.

* * * *

Eris couldn't believe her eyes. Clayton's team had surveyed all of the comics with incomplete information. It was lucky Ranulf hadn't known the team codes or he would have seen that for himself.

She only hoped it was just those few and not more. A small nagging feeling told her the situation was bigger than she realized. She returned to her computer to give the problem a thorough check before confronting Clayton with it.

They hadn't had a conversation in two weeks. He avoided her, and she was happy he did. No one mentioned their break-up. It looked like Clayton hadn't told anyone the particulars.

"What did Ranulf want?" Pete asked when she entered the room.

"There's a glitch in the database. I have to check it out and then let him know I fixed it. He didn't want to mention it in front of everyone and embarrass me."

She hoped Pete forgave her that little white lie if he ever found out the truth. The whole situation wasn't clear yet. She wanted to know the extent of the damage before she accused anyone of anything.

Two hours and one sore scrolling finger later, Eris came to the realization that the error wasn't a glitch and it wasn't an accident. A few comics with incomplete information were an oversight. Seventy boxes of comics—months of work—with the same errors was deliberate laziness.

Clayton's team—either with or without his knowledge—was cutting corners so they could get finished sooner. And what was worse, Ranulf had noticed.

Even though she didn't want to, she had to talk to Clayton about the situation since he was the team leader. She only hoped he was ignorant of it.

She went next door and, like Ranulf had done with her, she went to his desk. "I need to talk to you," she said in a low voice. She nodded when he looked up at her.

He made an annoyed sound, stood and followed her out to the hall. Once the door was closed, he said, "This isn't the time to talk about apologies."

"Yes, you do need to apologize to me, but that's not why I called you out."

"Me? Apologize to you? You've got that backwards, lady. You're the one that screwed up."

"I…" She stopped and took a breath. This was not the time. She started over and tried to remember to keep things professional. "Ranulf pointed out several comics with incomplete information. I checked the database and found well over seventy boxes worth of comics with a similar problem."

"And?"

"They are issues your team graded, Clayton. Thankfully Ranulf doesn't know the team codes."

"And you're going to tell him, right?"

"No. I'm coming to you first. I thought maybe you didn't know. Just talk to your data entry person, okay?"

"Tony is doing the best he can with this stupid new system you had the company implement. No one needs to know who inked the issue. All they need is the title, issue number, date, print run, artist and writer. Who cares who edited or translated or who the president of the company was at the time of comic release? That information is superfluous."

"It's part of the copyright and therefore part of the database, Clayton. Ranulf and Lucien expect that information to be present on all the issues. If they didn't care, Ranulf wouldn't have brought it to my attention."

"That makes it your problem, doesn't it?"

She narrowed her eyes. "You knew about this already."

He crossed his arms.

"I thought you wanted more money. Why are you cutting corners?"

"The bonus."

"The what? What bonus?"

He smirked at her. "Brian didn't tell you about the bonus?"

"What bonus? Just spit it out already."

"Three teams, each does one-third. The first team to finish their third gets LA."

She barely kept her mouth from falling open. "No. Brian wouldn't do that. He promised Pete and me LA."

"He changed his mind then. Too bad, huh? At the pace we're going, we should be out of here in no time."

At the pace they were going, seventy boxes worth of comics translated roughly into a little over two months. The company had been working Lucien and Ranulf's project for four months.

"You son of a bitch," she said in a low voice. "You sold me out. We only broke up two weeks ago but you've been stabbing me in the back this entire time."

He shrugged. "What do you need LA for?" He waved around him. "This is your dream job. You can flirt with Lucien and Ranulf all you want."

"I do not flirt with them."

"That's not what I heard."

She snapped her mouth shut before she said anymore. They weren't in high school, and she had bigger problems to solve.

"You aren't going to LA. Your third isn't anywhere near finished since you need to go back and augment the comics you already entered."

"No one cares about that missing information but you. The work is done. Leave it alone or fix it yourself." He returned to the survey room and left Eris staring.

"I don't believe this," she whispered.

She returned to her own desk but not her work. The shock of the situation had her confused on how to proceed.

She'd spoken to Brian on several occasions. He never mentioned LA or the fact that she might not go. It was the biggest comic convention in the whole of the United States—she wanted to say the whole world, but she didn't know for sure. The event was invitation only, and only people in the industry were invited. As a comic grading company, CGC was automatically invited. The cataloguing teams vied all year to be the representatives of the company. Brian had promised that spot to her team thanks to her software.

She stared at her screen but it didn't offer a solution.

A whistle made her look up at Chad. He pointed at Pete. She blinked at him. "Did you say something?"

"What's the prob? You okay?" Pete asked.

"Fine. It's complicated."

"Anything we can help with?"

She shook her head and went back to staring at her screen. The list of incomplete issues sat staring back at her. The only solution she could think of was to do it herself. The task was too much for one person, though. Then there was the problem of the movers having to bring back all of the boxes—something Lucien and Ranulf wouldn't overlook and would want explained.

"Eris, it's time for lunch," Michael said as he passed her.

She nodded but didn't move. Hunger had fled in the face of this dilemma. She watched the others file out of the room and turned back to the mess of Clayton's creation.

She had one more option—if he wouldn't listen to her, then he would listen to Brian. She hated to be a tattletale, but there was no help for it. Besides, she wanted to know if Brian had really given away her trip to LA.

She dialed Brian, who was still in his office.

"Hi, Eris. What can I do for you?"

"Brian, I hate to call you like this, but there's a problem."

"Uh-huh, what's that?"

She took a steadying breath and looked around to make sure no one would hear her. "There are sixty to seventy boxes worth of issues with incomplete information. I brought the problem to Clayton's attention, but he doesn't seem concerned about it."

"Why Clayton's attention?"

"The boxes were ones his team graded."

"You know for a fact all the issues were done by Clayton's team?"

She nodded. "The code said it was Clayton's team."

"And none of them were Nathan's team?"

"Nathan? No, all the ones I saw had Clayton's team code."

"So you accessed nearly seventy boxes worth of data—over twelve thousand comics—to see which teams did them or if the comics were truly missing the information?"

"Not every box. But, Brian—"

"Look, Eris, Clayton already called a little while ago and told me that you two broke up on bad terms."

"What?" she yelled. She immediately looked around to see if anyone had heard her outburst. No one came forward to inquire about her tone. She lowered her voice and asked, "What does that have to do with anything, Brian? I'm telling you, something is wrong with—"

"I never thought you would do something so petty just to get Clayton off that project. You're in two different rooms from what I understand. If you don't want to see him, then just avoid him. It shouldn't be that hard. There's no reason to sabotage him."

"I'm not sabotaging anyone," she ground out through clenched teeth. Some part of her knew Brian didn't believe her. She didn't know if it was because Clayton was a guy and Brian felt the need to side with his gender or because Clayton had called Brian first.

"Eris, I'm going to trust that this call was bad judgment on your part and ignore it. Okay?"

She clutched the phone but said nothing.

"Eris?"

"Fine. You do that." She snapped the phone shut before she said something she would regret.

The nerve! How dare he accuse of her of being vindictive?

Here she was trying to save the company from being embarrassed and he accused her of being a jilted lover. She had half a mind to let the mistake slide and let what happens happen. But, her conscience wouldn't let her do it. Such negligence wasn't fair to Ranulf and Lucien, and she owed them. It would be one thing if she didn't know about it, but she did and that made it her responsibility.

She sighed. Then she remembered she hadn't asked Brian about LA. Well, she wasn't going to call him back. Not yet, anyway. First she would prove Clayton wasn't doing his job and then she would deal with LA.

Now the question became how she would fix the entries without tipping off Ranulf and Lucien to the real problem or sending Clayton crying to Brian about harassment.

While she should be surprised at Clayton's immaturity, it was a part of his character she'd known about and ignored. No longer.

She walked to the office and knocked.

"Come in," Ranulf said.

She poked her head through the doorway before committing the rest of her body. Ranulf and Lucien looked at her expectantly. She smiled, and they smiled with her. "I had a favor, or actually, a request."

"Yes?" both men asked in unison.

It was funny how they did that sometimes. That only reinforced her opinion that they made a good pair.

She chewed her bottom lip as she tried to think of a way to phrase her request so neither man would be suspicious as to the real problem. Finally, she decided to blame the one thing that had screwed up once before.

"It seems there's something off with my database. That's why the information is missing. Rather than take up time during the work day to fix it, I was hoping I could stay late?"

"If you like," Lucien said.

His ready agreement made her instantly relieved. "You're sure?"

"As we've said before, Eris, the services of CGC are by the day, not the hour. Even if it was hourly, a little overtime wouldn't bankrupt us."

"Well, there's that, but I thought you both appreciated getting your house back at the end of our work day."

"You are only one, Eris, and hardly an intrusion. Past events should have proven that already."

"Thank you for that. Picking me up, I mean."

Ranulf said, "We could do nothing else."

She nodded, getting back a small measure of her confidence about the situation. Ranulf and Lucien weren't bad guys, which made it hard for her to deceive them about the real situation.

Though, the task might end up being more than her now that she thought about it. If the data was screwed up, what else was wrong? She hated to think the grading might be wrong as well. While she was perfectly capable of grading, she'd be forever and a day trying to do data entry and grading on seventy boxes worth of comics.

"I might need one of the graders to stay too. Not tonight, but if I find the database is screwier than I think, I will need some help."

"We leave that up to your discretion."

She shook her head as she smiled. "You guys are too nice."

"Only to you," Lucien said in a very honest voice.

As much as she wanted to think he was joking, he looked too serious. She glanced at Ranulf, but he didn't correct or deny Lucien's words.

Instead, Ranulf said, "No one else is worth the effort."

"Effort?" she asked with a raised eyebrow. Suddenly Pete's words from the other day surfaced.

Could he have been right? Were Ranulf and Lucien interested in her? Surely not *both* of them. Nah, she was reading too much into an innocent statement.

Lucien looked pointedly at Ranulf, who seemed to ignore the look and said, "There is a movie premiere in three weeks. We wish you to accompany us."

Eris asked, "Movie premiere?"

"You like movies, right? I've yet to meet a comic fanatic who wasn't enamored of the movies as well."

"Oh, I love them."

"Good. One of the projects Lucien and I financed is having a premiere. It's a period piece of the Middle Ages."

"You don't mean that new Crusades movie, do you?"

"The same," Lucien said. "It struck a chord with me when I read the script. I had to see it made and wasn't happy until the perfect actors and director were chosen. It was one of the few projects where my tyrannical side surfaced."

"You have a tyrannical side?"

A shadow flitted across Lucien's face and his mood turned somber. Eris didn't know what it meant, but there was a marked difference in his attitude. She scrambled to think of a way to fix it.

"You said the movie premiere is in three weeks? In January?"

Lucien said, "That's right."

"This is a red carpet affair, right? One of those things with tons of nasty reporters who trash the people who show up looking less than perfectly amazing?"

"So it would seem," Ranulf said.

"Why invite me?"

Both men smiled the same knowing smile. Eris suddenly gave every word Pete had said more credence. It made no sense though.

Why her?

Lucien said, "Beautiful women should always accompany men to events such as this."

"Both of you?"

"Yes," they answered in unison.

"Umm, wouldn't it make more sense for you each to have a date...uh...escort...I mean...person who will accompany you?"

Good. That sounded nice and innocent. There was no way they were inviting her on a double date minus the second woman.

"We want you to accompany us both." Ranulf sat back in his seat with a sly look.

Eris said, "As repayment for helping me the other day."

"As an enjoyable evening spent together with charming company. Otherwise known as a date."

"With you both."

"Is that a problem?" Lucien asked.

She met his gaze, not sure how to answer the question.

"This isn't an ultimatum, Eris. You don't have to look so scared."

Ranulf said, "You have to have noticed our interest in you after all this time."

She shook her head.

"You didn't?"

"No, and I'm not exactly all gung-ho to jump into another office relationship, especially not with *two* men."

Lucien nodded. "Understandably, but that's not what Ranulf and I are proposing."

"Proposing?"

"Suggesting," he said with a grin. He stood and walked to her side.

She could only stand there, unsure whether she should leave or let them continue.

Lucien cupped one of her hands between his. "Ranulf and I wish it to be your choice."

"Between the two of you?"

"Yes," they said in unison.

"Isn't this sudden and kind of from left field?"

"It's only sudden because you never noticed our interest before this moment," Ranulf said. "And, we wouldn't have presumed to tempt a woman already taken."

"So, you both want to take me to this premiere as a way for me to choose which one I want to date?"

They nodded.

"What if I don't want to date either of you?"

Lucien said, "We would accept that and remain friends."

Eris snorted and gave Lucien a skeptical look. "Uh-huh. Are there unicorns in your land of make-believe?"

"Yes, dragons too."

That made her laugh. She couldn't help it. He'd answered with such a straight face.

Ranulf said, "The friendship would probably be strained, but it would remain."

She stopped laughing and looked at them both. "You're serious?"

They nodded.

"What *type* of date is this supposed to be?"

Both of them started to talk at the same time again, but Lucien waved Ranulf forward. "The movie, the premiere party, and then we'll see you home."

"That's it?"

"We expect nothing from you except your fully-clothed-company for the premiere."

Well, that answered that question. She looked at Lucien's hands surrounding her own. Was he shaking or was she? It had to be her. There was no reason for him to be nervous.

A red carpet movie premiere.

With her free hand, she touched her hair. She'd have to make sure it looked perfect, not one single strand out of place. That was easily managed so long as she made an appointment with her hairdresser. The real problem was her lack of appropriate attire. She didn't have anything red carpet worthy.

"I'm a mess," she whispered. "I can't go to a red carpet anything looking like this."

Lucien smoothed his hand over her hair, bumping her hand. "You look fine."

"I don't have a dress that is even remotely worthy of such an occasion."

"Don't worry about that. We'll pay for the dress."

She stared at them both in shock. "No. No. That's too much for a first date." She paused and let that word float around her skull a little while.

A first date. It truly was a date with both Ranulf *and* Lucien.

She pushed that thought to the back of her mind and focused on the matter at hand. "I can't let you both pay for a dress as well as take me to the premiere."

Lucien released her and returned to his desk. He scribbled something on the back of a business card and then held it out to her. "Take this. When you find the dress you like, call the number on the back. The payment will be transferred to the establishment."

Eris said, "Okay, did what I said register at all?"

"It registered, but the argument holds no substance. We have invited you to an event you have professed you aren't ready for. This is our way of making sure you are comfortable." Lucien walked the card to her. "Call it an early Christmas present."

"I hadn't planned on getting you both anything."

"You've made it so we finally know what's in our collection. That's gift enough."

"That's my job."

Lucien smiled at her. "Then it is a gift you do it so well."

She reached for the business card with a shaking hand. "Is this even allowed? I'm pretty sure there's an EEOC violation in all this somewhere."

Ranulf said, "Your job is not contingent on this arrangement. We have given no ultimatum and never will."

"We're mature enough that we can separate our business and personal lives," Lucien said.

That was a relief, because she knew someone who wasn't. She kept that thought to herself though.

Thinking of Clayton and his immaturity reminded her of the real reason she'd come to Lucien and Ranulf's office in the first place. She put her hand to her head and almost scratched herself with the edge of the card Lucien had given her.

She looked at the numbers scrawled on the back.

"Do you need a list of dress makers?" Ranulf asked.

"No. I know exactly where to go." She pocketed the card and gave herself a mental shake. "Okay, that totally threw me off why I came here in the first place."

"You wish to stay late to fix the archiving system," Ranulf said.

Lucien said, "And you think you may need one or two members of your team to stay with you."

She nodded. "Yes."

"It's fine. Do whatever you feel is necessary to ensure a job well done. We trust you."

There was a wealth of meaning in his words. She felt it as though it had been tangible.

She said, "Thank you for that then. And, thank you for letting me figure this mess out after hours. I'll try not to stay too late."

"If you find you are too tired to drive home, I would prefer you utilize the room you used on your last visit rather than driving home fatigued," Ranulf said. "I insist on that."

"I don't think I'll stay that late, but you can be sure I'll stay over if it looks like I'm too sleepy to drive. But only because I'm too sleepy to drive, nothing else." She gave them both a pointed look.

"Do you find us so untrustworthy?" Lucien asked in an amused voice.

"You're men. So, yes."

They laughed at that. After a moment, she joined them. She only hoped they would keep laughing together after the movie premiere.

Chapter Fourteen

Eris rushed out of her survey room ten minutes before lunch officially started, headed for Clayton's. After a week of overtime, Eris had definitive proof that Clayton's team was being negligent. She'd checked every single comic book entry and found not only missing information, but incorrect information. That meant having to do all of the boxes over again rather than augmenting what was already there.

One of the key things missing was some of the grader notes, specifically Mr. Sebastion's grader notes. Mr. Sebastion was the company hard ass. The man never gave any comic mint status, not even the ones fresh off the press. He'd trained Eris and Pete and several others in the company, so it was very suspicious when mint status comics showed up in the boxes Clayton's team had graded and Mr. Sebastion's notes were missing.

Old age had only made Mr. Sebastion ornerier. What's more, the man had eyesight better than a hawk. Eris knew his grades had probably been left off on purpose. She planned to add them to the database, thus changing the grades on most of the comics. But first, she had to get Mr. Sebastion's notes.

Her only obstacle was Clayton. If he figured out what she was up to, he would be on the phone to Brian in a New York second. She mentally shook her head in disgust because she'd put up with his childishness for so long.

She got a reprieve that day. When she peeked into Clayton's team's room, she saw that Clayton was gone as well as most of his team, except Mr. Sebastion.

Perfect, Eris thought.

She entered the room. "Hello, Mr. Sebastion."

Mr. Sebastion looked up at her, harrumphed, and then turned his gaze back to the comic he was grading.

So far as greetings went, that was Mr. Sebastion's version of a fond hug.

Eris took that as a good sign. "I was hoping to borrow your grading notes. I'll give them right back when I'm finished."

"What for?"

She knew he would ask that and had her lie all prepared. "I'm doing a random check of all the comics. I'm using the grader notes from the strictest grader on each team and matching them against the database. I've already gotten Pete and Angie's notes. I just need yours."

Well, it wasn't a total lie. She did have Pete's notes since she'd typed them herself, and she had gone to Angie for her notes the day before just in case Mr. Sebastion went to verify her story.

Mr. Sebastion finished scrawling a few words on the paper before him. He closed the comic he'd been grading and then looked at her. "Which notes?"

"All of them, if you please."

He stared at her with narrowed eyes.

Eris kept herself looking calm.

"All of them, huh?"

"Yes, sir."

Mr. Sebastion smiled. "Very thorough. That's what I like about you, Eris."

Internally she sighed with relief.

He reached for the briefcase beside his chair, opened it, and then pulled out five spiral bound notebooks. "Here you go." He put them on the desk. "You still read shorthand?"

"I learned it just for you and haven't forgotten, sir." Eris approached the desk. She picked up the notebooks and held them to her chest like the treasure they were.

"I want those back in the same condition they left, missy."

"Yes, sir."

Mr. Sebastion opened another comic and turned to a clean sheet of paper.

Eris asked, "Aren't you going to eat lunch?"

"My wife is buried and I left my nagging daughter at home. I don't need another busybody female in my life. Shoo." He flicked his hand at her a few times.

She grinned but left the room like he wanted. She would have Liselle fix him something after she dropped off the notebooks in the fourth survey room.

Away from the others, on the other side of the house, the fourth survey room held every single comic box Clayton's team had touched. Eris had requested a room away from the others so no one would know she was pulling overtime. Lucien and Ranulf had agreed without question.

Once the normal work day was over, she took an hour break and then jumped into Clayton's mess. She normally worked another four hours before Lucien or Ranulf stopped her for dinner. After eating, she would head home to get a little bit of rest before coming back the next day.

She hadn't told Lucien and Ranulf yet, but she had every intention of coming on the weekends until the problem was fixed. Hopefully they would be as giving about that as they had been about everything else.

"What the hell is this?"

Eris gasped and spun around, confronting Pete. He'd followed her to the fourth room. She had been so caught up in her own triumph at getting the notes from Mr. Sebastion without too much fuss that she hadn't even noticed him.

Pete walked passed her into the survey room. He looked around then back at her. "Answer me, Eris. What's going on?"

"It's another survey room."

"Oh yeah? For who?" He gestured behind him. "There's only one desk and one chair and, unless I'm mistaken, that's your laptop case. What are you doing?"

She stared at him with wide eyes.

"I came back last night because I forgot my MP3 player. When I saw your car, I got pissed since I thought you might be doing something with Ranulf or Lucien after I warned you not to."

"Pete—"

"After seeing this, I only wish you were. Tell me you aren't pulling overtime just so we finish this project by the eighteen month mark."

"No. This…" She looked around at the room.

No matter what she said, Pete would be angry. She sighed.

A sense of inevitability closed around her. She walked the notebooks to her workstation and set them down before she faced Pete.

"Well?" He crossed his arms and gave her his best disapproving father look.

"These are all the comics Clayton's team graded. They're all wrong."

Pete dropped his arms and looked around again. "What do you mean they're all wrong?"

She put her hand on the stack of notebooks. "For one thing they are missing Mr. Sebastion's grade notes."

"Mr. Sebastion? What the hell is he doing here? He's on Clayton's team now?"

"He and Susie had a falling out a few weeks before this project started. Brian swapped him for one of Clayton's graders to keep the peace."

"More like to keep Mr. Sebastion from shoving his cane up Brian's ass."

Eris agreed silently.

"Okay, that doesn't explain why you're the only one in this room."

As quickly and precisely as she could, Eris explained the situation from the moment Ranulf brought her attention to it until the point Pete followed her.

Pete clenched his hands at his side. "I don't know who I want to kill first—Brian or Clayton." He faced the doorway.

Eris grabbed his arm and pulled. "No, Pete. Don't. It's not worth it."

"The hell it isn't!" He yanked his arm away from her and then faced her, his eyes blazing with his anger. "Why they hell did you lie to them, Eris? This is bullshit. You don't fix other people's problems. You make them do it. What the hell type of team leader are you?"

Eris stared at him in shock. He hadn't yelled at her like that since she was in high school.

"I can't believe you didn't open up your mouth and tell someone. Anyone. Me! Why the hell didn't you at least tell *me*?"

"Pete, stop," Lucien said in a cold voice.

Eris almost hit the floor.

Lucien and Ranulf stood in the survey room doorway. Neither man looked very pleased.

How many people had followed her? Was anyone else waiting to yell at her?

It didn't matter. All of her precautions had met with ruin. She sank back against the desk with her head in her hands.

Pete put himself before Eris, guarding her. "This isn't her fault."

Ranulf said, "So we heard."

Eris wanted to cry at the disappointment she heard in his voice. She'd betrayed a trust. And, after she had promised herself that she would repay them for all the kindness Ranulf and Lucien had shown her.

Ranulf stepped out of the doorway. "Pete, walk with me."

Pete didn't budge.

Lucien walked forward, stopping one stride before Pete. "Leave."

There was a wealth of danger in that one word. It made Eris's skin crawl. She'd never heard Lucien sound so angry before. She actually witnessed Pete slinking out of Lucien's way. Pete never backed down from a fight.

He walked passed Ranulf, who gave her a long look before closing the survey room door.

Eris looked at Lucien. "I'm sorry," she said in a small voice. She wanted to sound more forceful but she couldn't.

"Don't apologize." Lucien's tone was just as soft. He reached out and took her hands in his. "Why were you hiding it?"

His gentleness confused her. "Aren't you angry?"

"Of course I'm angry, Eris. I want to put one of my swords through Clayton's gut and then run him over with my car. I'm also angry about Pete yelling at you like that. More than that, I'm angry that you felt you couldn't tell Ranulf and me the truth."

"That's not..." She gripped his hands. "I wanted to fix it. I didn't want you two to find out and think the company was bad. It's not. Clayton's team is one of our best."

"Why are you defending him?"

She shook her head. "I'm not. It's just that the new system I had the company implement is radically different from the old system and it's taking some people longer to adapt than others."

Lucien freed one of his hands and cupped her cheek. "Why are you blaming yourself?"

She looked at him, helpless to figure out what he wanted her to say or what would make the situation better. "I can fix it."

Lucien gave her a sad smile. "I know you can."

"You shouldn't have to though," Ranulf said as he entered the room. He closed the door behind him.

Eris pulled her other hand away from Lucien and stepped back. She looked behind Ranulf and then at Ranulf. "Where's Pete?"

"I locked him in the entertainment room and told him not to come out until he worked off some of his aggression. I don't want fighting on the premises." Ranulf clasped his hands behind his back as he approached. "Now then. We have a problem."

"I can fix it," Eris said in a more forceful manner.

"It's not your problem to fix."

"Please, let me fix this."

Ranulf looked at Lucien. There seemed to be a silent communication between the two of them.

Lucien looked back at her first. "I would rather call Brian."

"No!"

"But, I doubt it would do any good."

Eris sagged in relief. The last thing she needed was Ranulf or Lucien calling Brian. The man would probably find some way to spin the situation so it sounded like Eris put them up to it. That would only get Clayton more sympathy.

Ranulf said, "The problem is that trip to LA, so far as I can tell."

Eris nodded. "Like I told Lucien a minute ago, Clayton's team is one of the best. The only one better is Susie's team."

Lucien grumbled, "Why couldn't we get her team then?"

She didn't answer since she figured it was a rhetorical question. Besides, he wouldn't like the answer.

Ranulf said, "If LA is the problem, then let's take it out of the equation. I'll call Brian and tell him to award the trip to Clayton's team."

"What?" Eris and Lucien yelled at the same time.

Ranulf held up his hands. "Hold on. Let me explain."

Lucien crossed his arms with a grunt.

"Once Clayton's team is assured they have the trip with no strings attached, they'll perform better, right?" Ranulf looked at Eris.

She nodded. "More than likely. But—"

"That means this mess will end here." He gestured to the room.

"Yes," Eris said in a dejected voice.

His solution was sound. Pete was right. Her actions proved she wasn't a team leader. As such, she shouldn't be allowed to go to LA.

Ranulf put one finger under her chin and tilted her head up so she met his gaze. "That means I can invite you and your team to LA as our guests."

She blinked at him. "Huh?"

Ranulf straightened away from her with a grin. "Lucien and I get invites to LA every year. We have controlling stock in Black Horse Comics as well as KyotoPop. We're allowed to bring anyone we please."

Eris stared at him. "You own Black Horse Comics and KyotoPop?"

Ranulf and Lucien nodded.

"And you're inviting me and my team—my *whole* team—to LA as your guests?"

Ranulf said, "Which means you can enjoy the convention rather than having to work. How's that sound?"

"It's too much," she whispered, shaking her head. "I lied to you. Why are you rewarding me?"

Lucien said, "We lied to you when we said we would wake you the other day and didn't."

"That's not the same," Eris snapped.

Ranulf lifted her hand to his lips. "Give in and go with it. If you haven't noticed, we like spoiling you."

"What happened to keeping work and personal separate?"

"It's just the three of us—" Ranulf made a big production of looking around the room before lowering his voice to a seductive rumble, "—and that makes this personal."

Eris couldn't help laughing.

He wiggled his eyebrows at her.

Lucien rolled his eyes. "That is one problem solved. The only one left is this mess." He looked at the stack of boxes. "You aren't doing this, Eris. I don't care what you say."

"I'm the only one who can read shorthand." She pulled away from Ranulf, picked up Mr. Sebastion's notes, and flipped to a random page so Lucien and Ranulf could see what she was talking about.

Lucien opened his mouth but Ranulf cut him off. "We lose."

"I'm sorry," she whispered.

"Fine," Lucien ground out. "I'm still calling Brian. It is wholly unacceptable for you to handle this mess alone. Since Susie's team is so great, they should have no issues helping you fix whatever mess Clayton's team made."

She wanted to argue but Lucien shot her look that made her snap her mouth shut. She nodded instead.

"Good." He pointed to the door. "Lunch. Now."

"You don't have to talk to me like I'm a child."

"Obviously, we do," Ranulf said. "If I find out you're hiding anything else from us, I'll turn you over my knee."

Eris said, "That doesn't sound like a punishment coming from you."

"Who said anything about punishing you?" He winked at her as he offered her his arm. "Let's get you fed while Lucien deals with Brian."

She linked arms with Ranulf but looked back at Lucien. He already had his cell phone to his ear. She only hoped everything worked out.

That was the second time Lucien and Ranulf rescued her from Clayton. Both men were entrenching themselves in her life so solidly that she wasn't sure she would be able to choose between them after the premiere. But, she couldn't have both.

That was something she refused to do.

Chapter Fifteen

Eris stopped typing and covered a yawn. Her overtime was catching up with her. Even with Susie and Caroline coming out to the mansion three days a week, Eris still stayed late so she could type in Mr. Sebastion's grader notes. The comics were already scanned, so they only needed two other graders to go over them before resealing them.

Brian had been happy to provide Susie and Caroline free of charge. Eris was happy about that. He even apologized to her and offered the LA trip. She turned him down since Ranulf had already invited her. She would much rather go to play than to work.

She yawned again.

"Stop it. You'll get the rest of us doing it," Pete said without looking up from the comic he was grading.

True to his prediction, Michael yawned.

Chad said, "Must be all of those late nights." He grinned at her.

She looked at Pete and then back at Chad. "What do you mean?"

"I heard you've been staying late. And, rumor has it you're going to a movie premiere this coming Tuesday."

Eris didn't bother looking at Pete again. He obviously hadn't told Chad the truth behind her late nights since it sounded like Chad thought she was having personal time with Lucien and Ranulf. How many others thought the same?

Megan said, "Dish."

Eris gave a resigned sigh and sat back. "Yes. I'm going to a movie premiere."

"I knew it." Chad held his hand out to Pete, who pushed his hand away with a grumble of annoyance.

"Who told you?" She turned her gaze to Ranulf.

He was busy talking on his cell, negotiating a contract. With the earpiece in place he probably hadn't heard the question. Even if he had, she didn't need him to tell her what she already knew.

Ranulf and Lucien both prized their privacy above all else. They wouldn't have said anything. Besides, they knew she wanted her co-workers kept in the dark—for privacy but also because the higher-ups wouldn't look too kindly on her dating a client. *If* she decided to date one of them.

The possibility was tempting, but the implementation was irresponsible, and she should know better.

Chad said, "I overheard Frank, the guy driving you all to the premiere, telling Liselle about it."

Before she could say anything, Ranulf slammed his hands on the desk and stood. He ended the call he was on and then used the walkie feature on his phone and barked, "Grant, I want Frank in my office now!" He ripped his earpiece off and left the room.

Chad whistled. "That man is gorgeous when he's angry." He winked at her. "You're a lucky woman."

"I think you just got Frank in trouble," Eris said.

"I didn't mean to, but enough about him. Which one are you going with?"

She chewed the end of her pen and tried to think of a way to get out of the conversation. Though, she doubted her companions would let her. "As *friends*, we're all going together."

"Friends, huh?" Chad nudged Michael, and both men laughed.

Pete gave her a disapproving look that she ignored. She'd heard his warning and had taken it to heart, but she wouldn't miss the premiere of a movie she'd been anticipating for the last year. It would be easy enough to keep the entire evening platonic and then let the guys know she had no intentions of dating either one of them.

They might try to persuade her otherwise. She actually anticipated it. Her counterargument was simple—she wasn't ready to be in another relationship.

End of story.

Clayton and his antics had put her off dating for a while.

"A little birdie told me something interesting."

Speak of the devil…

Eris didn't bother looking at the doorway where Clayton stood.

"Looks like someone is bucking for a new job." He cackled to himself. "Or maybe she's just bucking."

In that moment, Eris regretted letting Clayton have the LA trip. She should have told Brian to give it to Nathan's team, except she knew Nathan wouldn't appreciate the gesture. He would want to have earned it, not win due to a technicality.

She decided to ignore Clayton in the hopes he would go away.

Clayton entered the room fully and walked to her work station. "I'm betting that little birdie hasn't reached Brian yet. Maybe someone should let him know what his head cataloger is doing while his back is turned. News like that might make that someone the new head of this project."

She said without looking up, "I suppose that someone would be you?"

"One good snitch deserves another."

She faced him then to tell him just what she thought of him. The sight of Ranulf standing directly behind Clayton, looking as angry as when he'd left moments ago, stopped her.

Ranulf said in a low, cold voice, "Perhaps you should also tell Brian about your tendency of stealing time."

Clayton swung around and confronted Ranulf. "What?"

"Each of these survey rooms, in fact most of the house, is under surveillance. We have well documented accounts of you arriving late, taking long lunches and unscheduled breaks, and leaving early."

"You're supposed to tell people when you're recording them."

Pete said, "They did. It was in the contract Brian signed. Eris told us about it. Didn't he tell you so you could tell your team?"

Clayton looked at them all in turn. He huffed a few times and then left the room.

Eris waited a bit before facing Pete. "Brian didn't tell me about the cameras. I just noticed the bubbles."

"He didn't? Gee, I could have sworn you mentioned Brian's name at the time." He shrugged. "My mistake."

"The contract states the survey rooms have cameras," Ranulf said.

It was Eris's turn to shrug. "I just assumed. Rich people don't get rich by being stupid."

Chad asked, "Where are these cameras exactly?"

Ranulf grinned at him. "If you're wondering if I saw your little excursion to the den to play a round rather than the bathroom like you told Eris..." He trailed off and grinned wider when Chad cursed.

Eris pinned Chad with a look. "You and I are going to talk after lunch."

"Yes'um."

She looked at her watch. "And lunch is now. See you all in an hour." She kept her gaze on Chad as he passed her. "Especially you, Chad."

He hung his head in an exaggerated manner and stuck out his bottom lip.

Michael said in a sing-song, "You're gonna get it."

Eris hung back. She noticed Ranulf did too. He gave her a questioning look once everyone had gone. "Not hungry?" he asked.

"I'm curious to know where those cameras are located."

"Every room on the first floor is monitored and only the hallways of the second floor."

"That's it?"

He moved closer to her with a sly smile. "If you'd be willing to sign an agreement, I could *put* one in the bedroom at the top of the stairs for the sake of future visits."

"That would be a no."

She knew he was joking. That's why she didn't take offense at the question. The insinuation that she'd use the room at the top of the stairs again—and possibly for an extended period—needed to be addressed, however.

After putting a little distance between them, she said, "Ranulf, I don't think it's a good idea for us to continue thinking of this movie premiere as a date."

"Then don't."

"Huh? I thought you and Lucien wanted me to choose between you."

"We do." He held up a hand to stop what she would have said next. "Tuesday's invitation was for entertainment purposes only. I think we confused you when we presented the evening out and the idea of choosing one of us at the same time. I apologize for that. We have no intention of rushing you. We've barely spent any time with each other that wasn't work related."

"I agree."

"I'm a patient man and perfectly capable of waiting a few days before you decide to pick me."

She let her mouth drop open.

Ranulf chuckled. "I'm kidding. Take all the time you need…to pick me."

She laughed. "I'm telling Lucien on you."

"Tell him. See if I care."

"Tell me what? You're talking about me, right?" Lucien entered the room and looked between her and Ranulf. "What's the joke?"

Eris was about to tell him when Ranulf covered her mouth and said, "Nothing."

She called him a chicken shit, but his hand muffled her words.

Lucien asked, "What's going on?"

Ranulf shook his head at Lucien. "Nothing." He nodded at Eris. "Right, Eris?"

She nodded with him. He removed his hand slowly but she kept her mouth shut. Once he stepped back, she jumped behind Lucien and said, "Ranulf said I should choose him."

"I was kidding. A little joke to lighten the mood." He faced Lucien. "I didn't mean anything by it."

"Yes, you did. You said it twice." Her voice was high like a child's, and she pointed at Ranulf.

Lucien said, "He's not wrong. You should choose him."

His deadpan statement brought an end to the joking atmosphere. Eris felt he meant every word in all seriousness.

Ranulf put his hand on Lucien's arm. "I was only joking, Lucien."

"Were you?" He pushed Ranulf's hand away. "You really think you were joking?" Lucien didn't wait for an answer. He pulled out from between Ranulf and Eris and left the way he'd come.

Eris looked at the doorway then looked at Ranulf. "What was that?"

He didn't answer, only stared at the doorway.

"Ranulf, what's going on? Why was Lucien so upset?"

"It's nothing."

"The hell you say. You two said nothing would change, no matter what my choice—*if* I choose."

Ranulf looked at her then. "If?"

"I will not be the reason your friendship is ruined. I refuse." She backed away when he would have touched her. "No. As a matter of fact, I'm putting a stop to this right now. Thank you for the invite, and I would have dearly loved to go, but—"

"Eris, you're jumping to conclusions."

"—it seems I must decline. I'll repay the money for the dress. And I hope this whole situation won't hurt our *working* relationship."

"Eris—"

She left the room before he could finish. He didn't chase her.

It surprised her how much it hurt to say what she had, to put them back into the roles of employee and employers. She didn't even know Ranulf and Lucien that well and yet ending their not-even-started relationship hurt more than she thought it would.

In her current mood, the kitchen was out of the question. Everyone would know something was wrong the moment they saw her. The only safe place was her car.

The path was blessedly free of nosy people. She got in the driver's seat and let her head rest against the steering wheel.

"Pete's going to have an hour's worth of I-told-you-so's when he hears about this," she muttered.

That thought only depressed her more.

* * * *

Lucien looked up when Ranulf slammed the office door.

"I hope you're happy," Ranulf snapped.

Lucien stood and confronted Ranulf's anger with his own. "You stab me in the back and then have the gall to be angry? I'm the one who should be angry. What happened to all that talk about not winning by default?"

Ranulf sliced his hand across the air. "I was joking around with her. But you—" he jabbed his finger in Lucien's direction, "—had to ruin the mood with your pity party. Now, she doesn't want either of us."

"What does that mean?"

"She cancelled the premiere. She refuses to go. She said she'll pay back the money for the dress."

Lucien dropped back to his chair. "Why?"

"Besides not wanting to date clients of her company, she won't be responsible for ruining our friendship. That was her excuse. That's *always* her excuse."

"Too late."

Ranulf grunted his agreement.

Eris had ruined their friendship a few hundred years ago. They couldn't tell her that though. She wouldn't believe them. Rightfully so. Theirs was a story that they barely believed, and they were the ones living it.

Lucien watched Ranulf stalk over to his desk and throw himself onto his chair.

"We need to fix this," Ranulf grumbled.

"Granted. How?"

"If I knew that, I would have done it already." He pulled his hand down his face with an irritated noise. "When she walked into this office and told me who she was, it was the happiest I'd been in decades. I couldn't believe our luck. Now, I think having her working for us is more hindrance than help."

On that opinion, Lucien agreed. Convincing Eris that his and Ranulf's friendship wouldn't suffer—even though he knew it would—once she chose between them was an obstacle easily overcome. Her constant worry about workplace propriety was another matter entirely.

The whole situation almost made him wish for the days when he first met her.

Almost.

Chapter Sixteen

Eris let Pete pull her to the side. She didn't want to hear what he had to say, but knew he wouldn't leave her alone until he'd said it.

"I don't know what happened between you and Ranulf after we left for lunch, and I don't care. I do know you shouldn't do another late night."

"I'm in the middle of a project, Pete."

"You have Mr. Sebastion's notes and remote access to the database. Do it at home. With Susie's team coming on the weekends to clean up after Clayton's team, *you* don't need to stay here."

"It's not just about augmenting the comics. I've decided to work up a second version of my software."

"You made the first version at home. You can make the second one there too."

There were so many ways she could answer his statement, but she wasn't in the mood to argue. She gave him a sad smile. "I know you're worried about me."

"Then go home."

"Pete, I'm a grown woman—"

"You don't act like it."

"—and I'm capable of taking care of myself. I set things straight with Ranulf and Lucien. It was a fun delusion while it lasted, but it's over now. Okay?"

"You think so, but do they?"

"I'm still here, aren't I? They said whatever this was wouldn't interfere with my job, and it hasn't. Leave it at that and let me work."

"That's my point. Your work is over. The day is done. It's time to go home."

She nodded. "I will, just like I do every night. After—"

"After you finish whatever it is that's so damned important you have to stay here."

"Yes."

"Why are you so stubborn?"

"I blame Mother."

"Oh yeah? Which one?"

She laughed. Pete gave her an annoyed look before he joined her.

He patted her shoulder. "Fine. I'll stop mother-hen'ing you and take my own advice and get the hell out of here. You're okay, right?"

"I'm fine."

"I'll see you Monday then."

"You too." She waved at his back as he walked away.

Pete was a really good friend. Not only because he looked out for her, but because he knew about her wacky family. He took her bouts of what he deemed odd behavior in stride and attributed much of it to her upbringing and left it at that.

Odd behavior.

Was it really odd for her to stay on the project knowing how Ranulf and Lucien felt? Maybe she shouldn't have taken them at their word.

But how would it look if she gave up the project?

She sighed and went to the fourth survey room. It was too much to think about. She needed to save her brain cells for the night ahead.

"I didn't think you would be staying tonight." Lucien leaned against the doorjamb of the survey room. He must have been waiting for her.

"Do you want me to leave?"

"That's entirely up to you."

She nodded. "Pete thinks I'm crazy. But, I'm taking you at your word. You said nothing would change."

"It won't."

"With that in mind, I have work to do." She waited for him to say something more.

He remained silent, so she figured the conversation was over. She walked past him into the survey room.

"Eris, you misunderstood my earlier response to Ranulf's teasing."

"I don't think I did."

"There is more going on than you know."

"All the more reason for me not to get involved and complicate the situation further." She glanced at him to see how he took her statement. He looked annoyed.

Despite his appearance, his voice sounded normal when he said, "We still wish you to accompany us to the movie premiere."

"I don't think that would be wise." Not to mention, Pete would chew her a new one. She left the last part unsaid.

"The one has nothing to do with the other."

That made her laugh. "You're deluded if you really believe that." She set out Mr. Sebastion's notebooks in preparation of her coming task.

"No, I don't, but I thought you might."

"I'd like to think I'm not that gullible." She looked at him. "Lucien, I really appreciate the invite, I really do. But, like I told Ranulf, I don't want to be the reason you two stop being friends." She waved her hand at the room around them. "You two have done way too much together to let me, or any other woman, break that apart."

"You make us sound like a married couple," he grumbled.

"I know you two aren't together sexually, but you are together emotionally."

His face screwed up into a look of distaste.

"Deny it all you like, but it's the truth."

"That's an argument for another time. My immediate concern is convincing you to accompany us to the premiere."

"I already said—"

"And I refuse to acknowledge that reason. My friendship with Ranulf will not suffer because of this."

"It's against company policy—"

"Brian strikes me as the type who would sell out his mother if it meant getting him what he wants. I'm sure he wouldn't notice your involvement with one of us if I simply *give* him one of the more expensive comics on his want list."

That caused her to raise an eyebrow. Lucien wasn't wrong. Brian was a mercenary to the umpteenth degree. How Lucien figured that out after so little contact with the man was the surprising part.

She said, "You wouldn't give away something you could sell."

"Don't be so sure of that. I've already given away one of my swords for your sake. A comic isn't a big loss."

She startled and blinked at him a few times. Sure she had misheard him, she asked, "You did what?"

"I gave your friend Spencer the Damascus you nearly dropped."

She gaped at him.

He nodded. "I'm surprised he didn't tell you."

"I haven't been back in a while. With all the overtime I've been pulling, I haven't had time." She tried to ask five questions at once but could only get out one. "Why?"

"A debt repaid. I always repay my debts no matter the cost."

"Spencer didn't do anything for you."

"He remained chivalrous. For that, I am deeply grateful."

"That makes no sense. You don't give someone a piece of expensive antiquity because of something like that."

Lucien smiled in a sad manner. "If he had acted in any other manner, something like that could have changed your entire outlook on life, again. He deserved the sword." He straightened and took one step toward her. "Come to the premiere, Eris."

She wanted to say no but found herself hesitating. "Give me one good reason."

"To go to the premiere or to date one of us?"

"Both."

Lucien approached her. "One good reason. That's all?"

She nodded.

He snaked his arm around her waist and hauled her against his chest as his lips descended to hers.

She only had enough cognitive thought to brace her hands against his chest before everything turned hot and liquid. He pressed her lips apart, rather than wait for her to open for him, and slipped his tongue past her lips.

No one had ever kissed her so deeply or thoroughly before. He tasted her, drew from her and dared her to do anything other than respond to his passion.

He tightened his hold when she leaned into him. She breathed in his scent and felt her inner muscles clench.

Her body's reaction was a surprise. She'd never had such an instant reaction to anyone. When Lucien's free hand caressed high on the back of her thigh, all she wanted was for him to move his hand a little more forward.

She shifted against him, pressing herself closer.

Lucien made a sound of satisfaction two seconds before he pulled back. He held her away from him when she leaned into him once more. "You said one." His voice was breathy and rough with need.

"One." She repeated the only word that made sense but didn't comprehend what he meant.

"One reason." He traced his thumb over her lips and followed the path of his finger with his eyes. "Was that reason enough to reconsider?"

His question brought the real world back.

She'd just kissed Lucien!

She pulled away from him and stared at him with wide eyes. "You kissed me."

"You wanted a reason."

"I thought you would use words."

"Why? That was faster." He gave her a soft smile. "And you enjoyed it."

Yes, she had, but that wasn't the point. "Do you normally kiss women to convince them to give in to you?"

"Only the stubborn ones who aren't impressed with my wealth. So, just you."

"Sorry I'm not like the gold diggers you're used to."

"I'm not." He held his hand out to her.

Her hand placed itself in his before she realized what was happening. He pulled her close enough that she thought he would kiss her again. Instead, he grinned down at her.

He said in a low voice, "Don't make me beg. I might not be able to stop at just kissing."

She swallowed at his unspoken promise of more pleasure. Her body begged her to tempt fate and see how far Lucien would really go.

In the end, thoughts of Ranulf checked her libido and brought back rational thought. Until that moment, if she'd had to make her choice right then, she'd been prepared to choose Ranulf.

He was easier to approach and talk to. She had no issues relating to him. He didn't have the air of tension around him that Lucien normally did.

One kiss later and she was ready to brave the tension for physical pleasure.

She released Lucien's hand.

"Eris?"

"I'll go to the movie with you."

Lucien sagged with a thankful smile.

"As for the other, I still think it's a bad idea."

"My friendship with Ranulf will endure."

She snorted as her response. Of course, she didn't believe him. She didn't know anyone who would.

"We'll change your mind." Lucien cupped her cheek.

She found herself leaning into him without thinking. He moved his fingers so they brushed her lips. "I'll let you get back to your work. Don't stay too late. I don't want you driving tired."

"Okay."

He lowered his hand and left the room.

Eris blinked a few times and straightened.

Lucien had officially become dangerous. With only one kiss, he'd completely hijacked her higher brain functions. One touch and she was ready to agree with anything.

Something told her she wouldn't fare much better with Ranulf.

"Those two are dangerous. I better keep my guard up at the premiere or else…" She shook her head violently. "Don't think it! Get your butt to work so you can finish and go home."

She faced her work station and the waiting notebooks.

No matter how much she urged them, her feet wouldn't move. She was rooted to the spot while her mind and body relived Lucien's kiss.

With mechanical movements, she packed her laptop, gathered up her purse and headed out of the survey room toward the office.

The door was open. Ranulf looked up at her as she approached. He smiled and beckoned to her.

"Coming to work in here?" he asked.

"No, I'm going home."

Lucien asked, "Why?"

She didn't look at him. That didn't stop her body from reacting. "I'm more tired than I thought. I can't concentrate."

Lucien made a smug noise that almost made her look at him. She kept her gaze firmly on Ranulf.

He smiled at her. "Have a good night then. Drive safely and we'll see you on Monday."

She nodded. "Bye."

"See you on Monday, Eris," Lucien said in a low voice.

The man was fighting dirty, and it wasn't fair. She nodded again and left the house as fast as she could. So long as Lucien was in the other room, her body would insist on a repeat of his earlier performance with extras.

Putting an hour's worth of distance between them would solve all problems, for now. Tuesday night was another matter altogether.

Chapter Seventeen

"Come on, Eris. Let me go."

Eris continued ignoring Chad's whining in favor of finishing her work. She'd have to stop soon and get ready for the premiere, so she had been pushing herself at her top speed almost all day to make up for the two hours of work she would miss.

"Please."

Pete said, "Chad, give it up. There's no way she's giving up her ticket for you. She's been looking forward to this movie since summer."

Eris made an affirmative noise.

"And the cute men escorting her aren't a bad bonus either," Megan said with laughter coloring her voice.

The topic of conversation had been the same since lunch. Eris held off telling her team she'd be leaving early as long as she could to avoid the ribbing and teasing.

Chad whined, "Can't Ranulf or Lucien get another ticket? They fronted the money for the movie, didn't they?"

"Enough already, Chad," Michael snapped. "The movie comes out this Friday. Just suck it up."

"I would if that would get me a premiere ticket."

Eris said, "I doubt Lucien or Ranulf would appreciate that sentiment."

"You're right." Ranulf's words came from her right shoulder.

The heat of his chest radiated through the chair and warmed her back. She was happy he was there and not Lucien. That wasn't to say she didn't react to Ranulf, because she did. Her mind went to naughty thoughts, and it was hard to sit without fidgeting. But, with Lucien, her imagination had past experience to work with and thus her visualizations were more intense, as were her reactions to him.

Ranulf's breath tickled her ear as he whispered, "You said to stop you at three. It's two after."

She gave in to a tiny shiver. Oh, tonight was going to be hard. Ranulf and Lucien would see to that. Any sane person would bail, sensing the trouble on the horizon. But, she wasn't any sane person.

She looked at her watch then confirmed the time with her laptop. "She's late."

Ranulf straightened. "Who?"

"Hold on." She pulled out her cell phone and punched in the third speed dial option. The phone rang three times before someone answered.

"Brue speaking."

"Hi, Daddy."

"Hello, my lovely daughter. How do you like the dress?"

"I will probably like it just fine when I see it. Who did you send?"

"Stephanie. What do you mean *when* you see it? She's not there yet?"

"No."

"She left almost two hours ago. She should be there."

"Well, she—"

Ranulf's cell phone rang.

"Hold on a second, Daddy." Eris watched Ranulf answer his cell.

He nodded and said to the person on the other end, "Yes, Grant. She's sitting beside me." He asked her, "Are you expecting a woman named Stephanie?"

"That I am."

Ranulf said to Grant, "Let her through."

Eris said to her dad, "Never mind, Daddy. She's here. Sorry to worry you."

"Don't forget to mention me."

"I won't forget."

"Have fun."

"I plan on it."

"Don't do anything stupid."

"Bye, Daddy." She snapped the phone shut and stood.

"Stephanie?" Ranulf asked.

"Yup. She's my dress's courier, and she's helping me get ready."

"Why would you call your father to find out about your dress?"

She smiled. "He made it."

"He did?"

"Yup. My father is a designer of couture formalwear. When I told him what I wanted the dress for, he gave me half off the price."

"I saw how much was charged to the expense account. That is still fairly steep for half off. Besides, you're his daughter. Shouldn't you have gotten it for free?"

She snorted. "You don't know my father. I don't even think free is a word in his vocabulary. But, he said he'd refund the money if the shop is mentioned on TV or in a magazine."

"How mercenary of him."

"My father dreams of celebrity clientele. If my showing up on the red carpet in one of his creations gets him that, then I'm more than happy to oblige him with a plug."

Ranulf opened his mouth to say more when a loud, feminine voice cut him off. "Eris! Where are you, hon? We've got work to do."

Eris's smile turned into a grin. She called back, "I'm coming, Stephanie."

"Hurry the hell up. Have you taken your shower yet? Did you do the upkeep on your locs yesterday? Where are you?"

Eris didn't get a chance to answer as the woman walked into the survey room. Stephanie's tall, lithe form commanded the attention of everyone present. She looked over the people in the room before her gaze settled on Ranulf.

She held out her keys to him. "You can unload my car. Take him—" she pointed at Chad, "—with you. And be careful with the equipment. It's fragile."

Eris said, "Stephanie, you can't—"

"Why are you still standing there? Get your ass up those stairs and take a shower."

"But he—"

"—is perfectly capable of carrying my stuff."

Ranulf said, "Eris, go and get ready. Chad and I can handle the unloading."

"You're sure?" Eris asked.

Stephanie said before Ranulf could answer, "That's what he just said. Your shower is calling. Get." She held out the bag she carried. "Here's your underwear and shoes."

"I have underwear."

"Your dad sent these. He made them specifically for that dress."

Eris took the bag with no further argument. If her dad had made the underwear, a rarity in and of itself, then she chanced the wrath of hell by not wearing it.

"The room at the top of the stairs," she said.

Stephanie nodded.

Eris turned and almost ran into Lucien.

His mischievous grin let her know he'd snuck up on her purposefully. He reached past her, brushing her arm with his chest, with his hand out to Stephanie. "Lucien Riordan."

Stephanie took his hand and shook it. "Available."

Lucien laughed. He stepped closer to Eris as he released Stephanie's hand. "I'm not."

Eris dodged around him. "I have to get ready."

She ran all the way to her room and shut the door.

How was she supposed to get through the night if just being near Lucien had her all hot and bothered? It was just a simple kiss.

She sighed.

It may have been a simple kiss, but it had held the promise of much more.

At least Ranulf's presence meant Lucien couldn't do so much. What he still could do had her worried. Not about what Lucien would do but how she would react to it.

"Here's to a memorable evening." She toasted with a fake glass then pushed away from the wall and headed for her shower.

* * * *

Ranulf looked at his watch and then the stairs.

Chad asked, "What the heck is taking so long? She's been up there for three hours. Don't you all have to be there in two?"

Lucien said, "Fashionably late is all the rage now, but you are correct."

"Did I mention you two look damn hot?"

Ranulf chuckled and shook his head. "I'll take the compliment. Thank you."

"We're still not gay," Lucien said.

Chad shrugged. "Just because I'm not buying doesn't mean I can't check out the real estate."

Ranulf would have shot off a snappy comeback, but Eris's bedroom door opened. Everyone quieted and looked up in expectation.

Stephanie stepped out with a huge grin on her face. She cleared her throat in an exaggerated manner then spread her arms wide. In a typical announcer-style voice, she said, "Ladies and gentlemen, I give you, straight from the creative genius of Gordon Brue, a vision of loveliness all men will want to bow down and worship and a masterpiece of—"

"Stephanie!" Eris snapped.

The woman stepped out of the doorway. "Eris Brue."

Eris stepped out of the room. Ranulf's heart stopped. He was sure it had because time froze in that moment.

The vision before him smiled shyly at them all as she waited for a reaction. Eris wore a shoulder-less blue medieval-style chemise that conformed to her waistline with the help of a black and gold, Celtic knot design waist cincher corset.

The chemise dragged on the ground around her but had a slit up one side that left her entire right leg bare and showed off another Celtic knot pattern drawn on her upper thigh. The pattern followed the outside of her thigh, twisting and curving down her leg until it met her blue slipper heels where it continued around the curve of the shoes.

"Turn so they see the full effect," Stephanie said.

Eris complied. When she glanced over her shoulder once her back was to everyone, Stephanie pushed her head to face forward again.

"I want them to see your hair." Stephanie waved at Eris's head. "This is what took so long. And, it is a masterpiece of epic proportions if I do say so myself."

"Lovely," Lucien whispered.

Ranulf agreed. He was used to seeing Eris's locs in a ponytail. Stephanie had somehow French-braided the locs. The braid snaked down the back of Eris's head and curved in on itself at the end. A blue brooch with matching ribbons that brushed Eris's shoulders finished the braid and tiny blue gems decorated her entire head, completing the look.

Eris faced them once more and started down the stairs.

Ranulf propped his foot up on the third to last step and held his hand out to her. She smiled at him, placed her hand in his, and let him guide her the rest of the way down. He bowed over her hand and kissed her knuckles. "You are breathtaking, Eris."

"Thank you."

"Truly a work of art that was worth waiting for," Lucien said, joining them. He kissed Eris's other hand.

Ranulf could only smile when she ducked her head, completely embarrassed by their attention.

Chad stepped forward. "I'd just like to say—" he dropped to his knees and bowed so his nose touched the floor, "—I'm not worthy." He repeated his sentiment over and over.

Michael and Megan joined him. Soon the others of the survey teams joined in on the gag.

Pete said over the commotion, "If those magazine people dare say anything mean about your outfit, I'll personally hunt them down and beat them."

Eris said in a shaky voice, "You guys are too much."

Pete said, "You look beautiful."

"Yes, she does." Stephanie descended the stairs with camera in hand. "Okay, you three stand together. Time to get some camera practice in."

Eris said, "Stephanie—"

"Don't Stephanie me. Your father wants pictures." She waved them together.

Ranulf tucked Eris's hand into the crook of his arm while Lucien brought her other hand to his lips.

Stephanie clicked a few pictures. "Good. Thanks. You three have fun. I have to get out of here." She pointed at Pete and Chad. "Help me get my stuff to my car."

Before Eris could say anything, Ranulf said, "We have to go."

Eris looked uncertain but nodded.

Lucien released her. "Won't you be cold?"

"Oh! I almost forgot." Eris broke away from Ranulf and turned back to the stairs. Stephanie stopped Eris with a long, blue piece of material held out toward her. "Thanks."

"Don't do anything I wouldn't do," Stephanie said with a wink.

Eris wrapped the cloth around her shoulders. Ranulf was saddened to see her cover up since he enjoyed admiring the swell of her breasts. One good tug and the twin globes would be free for the world to see. But, he didn't want the world to see them. Just him, and maybe Lucien.

Once situated in the waiting limo and on their way, Eris asked, "How long will it take to get there?"

"An hour and thirty," Lucien said.

"I should have rushed a little more."

"Nonsense. Beauty should never be rushed." Ranulf kissed her hand again. "And you are beautiful."

"Well worth the cost." Lucien brushed his finger over her exposed thigh and the knot design there. "I especially love this."

Eris breathed in quickly and wet her lips. A reaction not lost on Ranulf who was all but convinced Lucien had done something to her and had not mentioned it. Whatever it was, it had gotten Eris to accompany them to the premiere, but it had also made Eris very skittish around Lucien. Not scared-skittish, but cautious.

"I'm surprised Stephanie had the time to be so intricate," Ranulf said.

"Oh, she didn't." Eris touched the design, brushing her fingers against Lucien's. "This is the design on my stockings."

She yelped when Lucien caressed her thigh from knee to hip.

He said, "Ah, they are all but invisible, but they are there. The designer is genius."

"Yes, my father does good work."

Lucien nodded. "I think I shall hire him to make more things for us."

"He'd appreciate it, I'm sure."

Ranulf asked, "Is there a reason you aren't in the same field?"

"Couture work?"

"Yes."

"Oh, I would love to if it weren't for the customers. I've designed a few things and even used to help out at my father's shop over the summers. He loved that because of the wedding rush. But, it's too stressful. Some customers are never satisfied. At those times, my father becomes unbearable to be around." She shrugged. "It's a nice talent to have but not a career I would have enjoyed."

"I'm sure that disappointed your father."

"Not at all. He taught all of us, my sibs and me, the basics of hand sewing and machine sewing. If we wanted to learn more, he taught us. But it was never with the expectation that we follow him."

Ranulf nodded. "Well, I'm glad you didn't. Who knows what the catalog of our collection would look like without your program. I hear you're doing a second version. How is that going?"

Lucien said over Eris's reply, "No business-talk this evening. You are off the clock and so are we." He looked pointedly at Ranulf.

Eris nodded.

The limo lapsed into silence.

Ranulf realized they didn't have much to talk about outside of business. He tried to think of something to engage Eris in conversation. Talking would keep his mind from imagining the many ways of getting her out of her dress.

Actually, getting her out of it was no hard task. Getting her back into it so no one could guess what they'd been up to was another matter entirely.

His hand twitched at his side, eager to take up the challenge.

"You mentioned siblings," he blurted out.

Eris nodded. "Yes. I have one older and one younger brother and one younger sister."

He waited for her to continue, but she didn't. Usually people jumped at the chance to speak about their families. If anything, Eris seemed more nervous than when Lucien had touched her thigh.

That reaction to such an innocuous topic intrigued Ranulf, but he wouldn't pursue it. Not at the moment. He didn't want to add any stress to a tentative situation.

Lucien had convinced her to join them. That was only one step toward their goal. The next step was having her choose one of them. While she said she wouldn't, Ranulf knew otherwise.

He glanced at Lucien over Eris's head. The man shared his knowing look.

Their time had come.

Chapter Eighteen

Eris tried hard to stay relaxed and breathe evenly. There was something about a man in a tuxedo that made her mind go to naughty places quickly. It must be a weird fetish she picked up while working with her dad during the summers. Whatever it was, she was having a hard time thinking non-sexual thoughts.

Even though she currently stared at the seat before her, she had gotten a good look at both men before getting in the limo. Both wore all black tuxedos, including their shirts.

Ranulf's was a traditional, non-vented single button tuxedo with a silver tie and matching vest. Lucien wore a mandarin-style tuxedo with matching shirt. The collar of the shirt and the jacket sported silver buttons.

Eris wished they had told her they would be wearing silver and black so she could have had some silver in her outfit and matched them just a little. That small gesture would have made her feel less out of place.

She touched her hair to make sure everything was still in place and bumped Lucien's arm. When she shifted away that brought her against Ranulf. She didn't understand why both men had crammed themselves and her onto one seat when there was a whole other seat across from them. The limo had enough room so they could all be comfortable.

Then again, she doubted rearranging them would make her feel any less uneasy.

The more she thought about it, the more she felt she shouldn't have agreed to go. Lucien had already taken several opportunities to touch her thigh and arm, possibly because he liked seeing her react.

If Ranulf hadn't been there, she might have invited Lucien to do more. Though, it wasn't like Ranulf was much of a deterrent. She felt the same vibes coming from him that radiated off of Lucien.

What had she been thinking?

Simple—she'd thought they'd be at a movie premiere surrounded by throngs of people and press. She'd forgotten to account for travel time.

Small talk was out of the question. The less they talked about her family, the better she felt. Thankfully, Ranulf hadn't pressed the issue. Since she hadn't been forthcoming about her family, she didn't feel right asking either man about theirs.

Bringing up the weather felt trite, and Lucien had already outlawed business talk. Did that include asking them about other movie ventures?

She looked at Ranulf and then Lucien, who raised an eyebrow at her. "I didn't mention how good you two look. No magazine would dare say anything bad about you."

"Thank you." Ranulf raised her hand to his lips. "I do fill out a tux quite well, don't I? Maybe I should model."

Lucien grumbled, "You're already an airhead. You might as well drop the other shoe."

"I'm the airhead you trust to finalize all of our contracts. What does that make you?"

"If you finalized all of the contracts then I wouldn't still be arguing with Mizukinawa almost every morning over the placement of a comma."

Ranulf tutted and wagged his finger at Lucien. "Ah, ah. No shop talk."

Lucien looked like he wanted to reach around Eris and hit Ranulf. He leaned forward slightly, probably preparing to do it. Eris wasn't sure if she should dodge or try to stop him.

She said quickly, "Uh, I've never been to one of these functions before, obviously. Is there more to it besides the chaos when we enter?"

Lucien looked at her and then settled back. "The chaos aside, this is like any other trip to the movies."

Ranulf added, "Except this is a black-tie affair, the actors and director are sitting nearby, and there is an after-party."

"No pressure, huh?"

Both men chuckled.

"Will I be allowed to ask for an autograph without being considered tacky?"

"Let me guess, you want Van Petrol's autograph?" Lucien asked.

Eris smiled at the huffy quality in his voice. "Of course. This is a once in a lifetime situation, and the man is gorgeous. I love his movies. I've seen all of them at least fifty times." She sighed and made a dreamy face.

Lucien's annoyed look only grew.

"I hope someone gets a picture of me standing beside him." She bounced a little and said in an excited fan-girl voice, "Oh my God, I will be standing close enough to hug Van Petrol. Life is perfect."

Ranulf put a finger under her chin and turned her head so she faced him. "I think I'll become jealous if you keep speaking about him that way."

"Why ever for?" She let her lips curve into a coy smile.

"Don't start games you aren't prepared to play, little Eris." He trailed his finger down her neck.

Her heartbeat sped up. He leaned into her, and she knew he was going to kiss her. Would his kiss be as devastating to her senses as Lucien's?

Someone's cell phone rang. She jumped, bumping against Lucien.

Ranulf made a knowing noise as he released her and sat back.

Lucien answered his phone. The person on the other end couldn't have said much before he yelled, "No!"

Eris pulled away from him in surprise.

"Not tonight, damn it. Why does it have to be tonight?" He gripped the phone. Eris was sure he'd crush it.

Lucien said, "You are so fucking petty. Fine. When?"

She looked up at Ranulf, but he only stared at Lucien with a look of curiosity.

"After the premiere then." Lucien snapped his phone shut.

Ranulf asked, "Well?"

Lucien looked at Eris and then Ranulf. "Last minute meeting. I've stalled until after the showing."

"Give them hell when you get there."

"Without question or fail." Lucien crossed his arms and looked out of the window.

Eris wanted to say something, but what? She looked at Ranulf.

He smiled at her and patted her knee. "I hope you won't be disappointed with just me at the after-party."

"We don't have to go. I only want to see the movie, really."

"Go." Lucien bit out the command in a gruff voice. He faced her. "You need to attend the party if you want the full effect. And..." He trailed off as his gaze moved to Ranulf. He faced the window once more.

From fun to fuming in under six seconds.

The meeting had to be something truly important if Lucien couldn't put it off. At least he'd be able to see the movie.

Eris wanted to say that much, but she got the feeling Lucien wouldn't appreciate the sentiment.

The limo slowed.

"We're here," Lucien said.

Eris looked over his shoulder out of the window.

She'd always seen the red carpet premieres on television, but the actual event was much more daunting. Screaming fans were everywhere. The small locales the fans didn't fill were occupied with cameramen and reporters carrying microphones.

"Oh God, I was out of my mind to want to do this," she whispered. "Is it too late to go back? These windows are tinted, right? They can't see us. We can sneak out and pretend we were never here."

Lucien's answer was to open the door once the limo stopped moving. He exited to the excited screams of the spectators and then held out his hand to her.

She looked into his eyes.

His annoyed look of earlier was replaced with a soft look of understanding. In a low voice, he said, "Pretend you know something they don't."

"Like?"

Behind her, Ranulf whispered against her neck, "Lucien is wearing boxer briefs that feature an elephant motif."

She jerked back and looked at him. "How do you—"

He cut off her question with a quick kiss. "The crowd is waiting." He gave her a little push to get her moving.

Eris took Lucien's hand. He provided a steady support so she could rise from the limo with a grace she didn't feel.

"Don't look at the cameras," he whispered seconds before hundreds of flashes nearly blinded her.

"Mr. Riordan! Mr. Riordan! Over here!"

Eris didn't know who was calling.

Lucien slipped his hand around her waist and moved her two steps to the right just as another flash went off.

Ranulf joined them. He kissed her hand for the cameras.

"Well, well, well. Lucien Riordan and Ranulf Styr, the financiers of one of the most anticipated movies this year." A woman in a long red evening gown walked forward and held out a microphone.

"Nonsense," Ranulf said, flashing the reporter a winning smile. "The year has barely started. I'm sure there's some highly anticipated summer blockbuster that has eclipsed our little production."

"Everyone is dying to know why you planned the release of this movie now and not this summer. Care to comment?"

"The movie takes place in winter," Lucien said. "I don't know about you, but I abhor watching winter movies in the summer and vice versa."

"And your lovely companion. What does she think of the release date?"

The microphone was shoved in Eris's face, and she said the first thing that came to mind. "I think if Lucien had delayed the movie until summer I might have hurt him. I would have also accused him of trying to keep me away from Van Petrol out of jealousy."

"Lucien does strike me as the jealous type. And where is your date for this affair?" The woman turned her attention to Ranulf. The hungry look in her eyes said she'd probably jump at the chance to fill the role.

Ranulf laid a kiss on Eris's shoulder. "Right here."

The woman stared at all three of them in mild surprise.

Eris found it easier to smile after seeing the woman's reaction.

That's right. She was there with two of the hottest men at the premiere, except Van Petrol. And she happened to know what type of underwear one of them was wearing, something the reporter would never find out.

The reporter recovered quickly. "And she is dressed for the theme, isn't she? Who are you wearing?"

"Gordon Brue," Lucien said.

He slipped Eris's shawl from her shoulders while Ranulf gave her a slow twirl. The crowd cheered while the cameras flashed.

Ranulf kissed her hand again, and the men escorted her farther up the red carpet and away from the reporter.

"Was she finished?" Eris asked.

Lucien shrugged. "Do we care?"

They were only stopped a few more times. Each time Ranulf or Lucien dropped her father's name while showing her off for the cameras. She wasn't sure if they were doing it because they were proud to be with her or because they wanted their money back for the dress.

Once inside the theater, it was much quieter. Eris couldn't believe the difference. People still talked, and it was loud, but not at the deafening volume of the outside.

"Ranulf, Lucien, nice to see you made it in alive." A man walked over to them. He looked Eris up and down several times. "And with such a lovely guest."

"Matthew," Ranulf said in a cool voice.

The man took Eris's hand from Lucien's arm and bowed over it, laying a kiss on her knuckles. "Matthew Danger, the villain of this masterpiece."

Eris rescued her hand and returned it to Lucien's arm. "I'm sure you do the part justice."

"You'll have to tell me what you think after the showing."

Ranulf cut between her and Matthew so the man wouldn't get any closer. "I'm sure she'll be too busy fawning over Van."

"From the sound of the screaming outside, I'd say he just arrived." Lucien looked over his shoulder at the doorway.

Sure enough, Van Petrol entered the theater with his wife beside him. He was all smiles.

Eris frowned.

"What's that look for?" Ranulf tapped the back of his finger against her forehead.

"I'm not used to seeing him smiling. At least not happy-smiling. Even as the good guy, he always has that I'm-going-to-kill-everyone-in-the-most-painful-manner-possible smile. It is the sexiest thing about him." She looked at Lucien. "Do I meet Van now or wait until afterwards?"

"After. Let's go to our seats."

They left Matthew behind without so much as a farewell or a see-you-later.

"And here I thought Matthew would be your type," Ranulf said.

Eris said with an edge of disgust, "Men who constantly stare at my breasts annoy me."

"Ah, then I must be annoying you quite a bit."

"That's not the same. I know you won't do anything."

He bent close to her and whispered, "I make no promises once the lights go out."

"Try it and I'll sic Lucien on you."

"A task I'd do with pleasure," Lucien said.

"Any time." Ranulf made a beckoning motion with both hands. "I'm sure there's a pair of swords around here somewhere. We could tell everyone it's a mock battle for the premiere."

Eris looped arms with Ranulf and then Lucien. "Now, now, boys, let's play nice."

Lucien said, "With you between us—"

"—we can play very nice," Ranulf finished.

She looked at one and then the other. They watched her, probably to gauge her reaction. In a cautious voice, she reminded them, "You agreed we were doing this as friends. *Nothing* else."

"We're only teasing," Lucien said.

She nodded.

"But that doesn't mean we can't try and convince you to change your mind." Ranulf's statement gave her a sense of foreboding for the evening to come.

Just to be on the safe side, she said, "I want to *watch* the movie. That's why I'm here." She looked at Ranulf. "Not to fend you off when the lights go out." She switched her gaze to Lucien.

"We have no intention of molesting you during the movie."

Ranulf nodded and made an affirmative noise. "Too risky with all these people around waiting for one or both of us to slip up so they can blast it all over the news and internet."

"Thank God for small favors then," she said with a sigh.

"The after-party is a different matter altogether though." Ranulf winked at her. "And Lucien won't be there to stop me."

That's what worried her. She already knew the effect Lucien had. She was two types of anxious—worried and anticipating—about what Ranulf would do to her.

Chapter Nineteen

"See? I was a perfect gentleman throughout the entire movie *and* the after-party," Ranulf said.

"Yes. You were." She took in his wolfish grin and knew she was about to fall into a trap. "It would be a shame to spoil it now."

"Would it?"

He held his hand out to her.

When they'd entered the limo headed home, she'd parked herself on the opposite side near the driver. She thought Ranulf would join her, but he hadn't. If he thought she'd move, he was sadly mistaken. Nothing good would come of switching seats.

"Not going to happen," she said, shaking her head.

"It seems I didn't give you nearly enough alcohol," he said, lowering his hand. "My devastating good looks swathed in black tie chic aren't working either."

"The movie was amazing."

"And she even switched topics." Ranulf hung his head. "I must be losing my touch."

Eris said in a firm voice, "We've already been through this, Ranulf. I refuse to jeopardize your friendship with Lucien, and nothing either of you says will convince me a relationship with one of you wouldn't do just that."

"Why does it have to be with *one* of us?"

"What does that mean?"

"You could be with both of us."

She had no doubt he meant his words in all seriousness. His joking tone had disappeared, and his gaze held hers. Not even the width of the limo and the darkness of the interior could diminish that look or its intensity.

Even still, she tried to play it off as a joke. She smiled and forced laughter into her voice when she said, "Like Lucien would ever go for that."

"He would."

"You don't know that."

"Yes, I do."

The heat of his gaze made her pulse increase. The limo turned hot. She had to stop from fanning herself lest Ranulf realize what his words had done to her.

"You're not serious," she whispered.

Ranulf leaned out of his seat, headed to her side.

She held out her hand. "Don't!"

He went to one knee in the middle of the expanse, watching her.

His gaze was predatory as though he was waiting for her to show even the slightest bit of weakness.

Anger came to her aid. "You really think I'm dumb enough to fall for this? First it's my choice, and then it's why-choose-when-I-can-have-both. Pete was right. You two are playing with me."

Ranulf didn't answer. That only proved it.

"I should have known it was way too damn convenient that Lucien was called away. He had his alone time with me, and now it's your turn."

He remained silent, and his expression didn't change. He continued *hunting* her.

"Let me guess. You two were both going to take turns seducing me to see if I wouldn't mind going back and forth and then you'd casually suggest a threesome. After which, you'd both treat me like yesterday's news."

She thought he wouldn't answer again. He said in a low voice, "You're right about the first part. However, Lucien's meeting was not planned. If he could have stayed and kept you from being alone with me, he would have."

"I'm not playing. Just stop it."

"This isn't a game, a train or a joke." He bridged the distance and knelt at her feet. "Give me the chance to prove it."

"Fine. Get back on your side of the limo."

He grinned at her. "That's not what I meant."

"You're not movie-burger-backseat'ing me. I don't care how fancy the movie was or how expensive the burger, or that we're in a limo."

"Ah, that's not what I meant, either."

She eyed him. "What then?"

"A kiss."

"What will that prove?"

"My restraint."

"Until Lucien shows up so you can two can take turns."

Ranulf laughed. "Do you expect him to drop through the sunroof while we're driving down the highway?"

"I wouldn't put it past him."

He cupped her cheek. "That's what I love about you, Eris. You embrace the improbable so easily."

"Yeah. Like I'm embracing the fact that a kiss isn't all you want."

"No, it's not all I want. Not by a long shot. But, it's all I ask...for now."

He rubbed his thumb over her lips, but she turned away, from him and the way his touch made her feel.

"You said as friends," she pleaded. If he kept pushing, he'd break through her resolve.

She got the distinct impression he was aware of that fact.

He said, "We attended the premiere as friends and the after-party as friends. You said nothing about the trip home."

"That should be implied."

She knocked his hand away and dodged around him to go to the other side of the limo. Just as she took one step, the limo jerked and threw her off balance.

Ranulf caught her. He cradled her in his arms, and she stared up at him.

Gathering her close, he leaned into her. Just as his lips were about to touch hers, he said, "Give in. Fate is conspiring against you."

She didn't get a chance to answer.

His lips contacted hers. She wanted to push him away but ended up bunching her hands in his jacket.

He traced her lips with his tongue before moving deeper.

Try as she might not to, her first instinct was to compare his kiss to Lucien's. Ranulf coaxed whereas Lucien had demanded. Despite that difference, both men had her reacting the same.

She opened fully for Ranulf and tugged on his coat so he would deepen the kiss.

Instead, he pulled back. "Only a kiss," he whispered.

She watched him, prepared for more.

Ranulf hugged her tight. He bowed his head over her and said in a gruff voice, "Don't look at me like that. You'll make me go back on my word."

"It's your fault."

He nodded.

After a moment, he loosened his hold. He moved her so she was upright once more and then released her altogether.

"Ranulf?"

He looked at her.

"What is this? What do you want from me?"

"Just you."

"Until what?"

"Until forever."

That gave her pause. His tone was as serious as before.

He urged her back onto the seat and then took up the position next to her.

She wanted to ask what he meant. He couldn't possibly mean what she thought. There was no way.

"I was serious about what I said earlier, Eris." He glanced at her. "If you won't choose one of us then choose both of us."

"That's not going to happen." She searched his gaze. "Why are you two rushing this? We barely know one another. Why can't we just be friends?"

He touched her cheek. She drew in a sharp breath that left her lips parted and waiting for his assault. He leaned into her. She felt herself moving to meet him despite not having been conscious of the action.

"Yes, why can't we just be friends?" he whispered. His lips brushed hers as he spoke.

She moved the last little bit to complete the contact, but Ranulf moved to keep the distance between them. She pulled back and snapped, "Now you're teasing me."

"It's only fair. You've been teasing us since you entered our home." He traced a finger over the swell of one breast. "Little touches here and there."

She gasped when his finger dipped below the fabric of the chemise.

"Standing too close so we can't help but be tormented with your scent." He pushed the fabric away, baring her breast. "Flirting in the way only women can when they want to tease without seeming to do so." He swirled his finger around and around her nipple.

"I wasn't flirting," she said in a breathy voice.

"Not consciously." He leaned into her. "Always playing oblivious every time I moved close to you when we both know you were fully aware." His breath tickled the skin of her breast. "And waiting for my touch."

A surprised squeak left her lips when he kissed her nipple.

"No more teasing. No more games." He raised his head so their gazes met. "You know I want you. You know Lucien wants you as well. Stop torturing us and say we can be together."

Her heartbeat thundered in her ears.

Ranulf would continue his sweet ministrations if she simply said yes. She could feel his mouth again with the utterance of one word.

"Friends," she rasped.

That wasn't the word she meant to say but hearing it jarred her back into reality.

Obviously, it wasn't the word Ranulf expected either. He straightened. "What?"

"Friends." Saying it again firmed her resolve and brought her errant hormones under control. "I want us to be friends. Or else..." She looked down.

Ranulf reached for her but she knocked his hand away. "Or else?"

"Or...or else nothing at all."

He jerked.

She met his gaze once more. He looked spooked. Why? What was so horrifying about being friends instead of lovers?

"You mean that," he whispered.

She nodded unable to say the words.

"Eris, I...we..." He stopped with a frustrated noise. "Friends," he gritted out.

"Thank you."

Ranulf said nothing as he moved to the other side of the limo. He looked out of the window, ignoring her.

She wanted to be mad at him, but his actions were for the best. Any more said could lead them back to dangerous ground while in such a confined space.

She resituated her dress so she was covered once more. That didn't feel like enough, so she wrapped her shawl around herself and hugged her arms.

Though Ranulf agreed to it, she doubted friendship would result. In fact, she didn't think anything would be the same again.

* * * *

Lucien could barely stop himself from running out to meet the limo once it pulled up to the house.

As he'd predicted, the meeting had lasted the entirety of the after-party. He'd only arrived home moments ago. When he'd called to say he was on his way, Ranulf told him not to bother since he and Eris were headed home as they spoke.

Lucien had heaped all of his annoyance at missing the after-party on one woman and told her about it in great detail once he saw her. She'd brushed off his ire like so much lint on her dress suit then proceeded to pretend he hadn't just spent ten minutes yelling at her as she rattled on about the reason for summoning him in the first place.

It was in the past though, and his obligation was at an end.

He walked to the limo and opened the door. Instead of Eris's smiling face greeting him, Ranulf exited the limo and pushed past him. The man took the stairs three at a time and disappeared into the house.

The anger Ranulf left behind made Lucien turn back to the limo with a sense of foreboding.

"Eris?"

She put her legs out of the limo first.

He held his hand out to her. She took it but only long enough to get out of the limo and then she pulled away.

Lucien was immediately angry. "What did he do?"

"Nothing," she whispered.

"The hell he didn't. You're shaking." He reached out to her, but she pulled back quickly, almost falling back into the limo. "Eris?"

"I have to get home and get some sleep. I'll see you tomorrow, Lucien. Thank you for allowing me to see the movie." She met his gaze for only a moment and looked as though she would say more. She turned away and trotted to her car.

Lucien watched until her taillights were two red pinpricks in the night. Only then did he face the house.

Anger the likes of which he hadn't felt in centuries rushed over him.

"Ranulf!" he roared at the top of his lungs.

The man didn't answer his challenge.

Lucien charged into the house. "Where are you?"

His answer was a sword tossed in his direction. He caught it just as Ranulf charged him with a battle cry.

Lucien didn't ask. Mostly because he didn't care.

Sparks rained around them as their blades clashed. This wasn't an exercise match. If one of them landed a blow, the other man would be grievously injured.

Knowing that didn't give Lucien pause. He attacked and defended and fought as though his life depended upon it. He fought the way he had when he and Ranulf had first put on immortality. They had been trying to kill each other back then. They hadn't. They couldn't. Their benefactor wouldn't let them. Knowing that had never deterred them though.

The battle was decided when Lucien's sword broke in half. Ranulf tossed his sword away with a disgusted sound.

Before the man could leave to fume, Lucien grabbed his arm. "What did you do?"

"She wants to be friends."

"What?"

Ranulf yanked out of Lucien's grasp. "You heard me. She wants us to remain friends."

"The hell she does! I know how she reacted to me. It was the same as then."

"For me as well."

"For you as..." Lucien's eyes narrowed. "You bastard."

Ranulf waved him off. "Save your righteous indignation. You have no argument. I did little more than you probably did."

"When I was done with her, she was ready to be ours."

"No, she was ready to be friends. She merely reiterated that sentiment with me. I had always thought she'd exaggerated about us being friends, but perhaps she'd spoken the truth."

"Bullshit. You know that cannot possibly be true. It wasn't then, and it isn't now. We'll convince her of that."

"We'll lose her completely if we try."

Lucien froze and stared at Ranulf. "What does that mean?"

"She gave us an ultimatum. Either we're friends or we're nothing."

"You two or all three of us?"

The look Ranulf gave him answered the question better than any words could. Lucien cursed long and loud. "This is maddening. How can it be true that we were only friends? We've had her already, and she acted at the time as though it were only natural. Why is it so hard to be with her now?"

"That was a different time. We've already seen that she's a different person from the woman we met so long ago. The rules have changed."

"Yes. This time she's making them." He cursed again. "Fine. Friends we shall be." He eyed Ranulf. "I mean that the way it sounds, Ranulf. You will not pressure her. I won't lose her now. Not after everything we've gone through to get her back."

"I agree and was about to say the same to you."

They nodded at each other.

Ranulf sighed. His anger seemed to sink away. "What was the meeting about?"

"The same as the last few."

"Again?"

"She is persistent. Why *he* doesn't curtail this lunacy is beyond me."

Ranulf clapped his hand onto Lucien's shoulder. "You mean to say why he didn't stop her from interrupting your time with Eris is beyond you."

"That as well."

"Not that having us both there would have made the situation better. You saw how spooked she was before the movie."

Lucien nodded.

"We need to give her more time."

"We don't have that much more left," Lucien bit out. "It's January already. The faire is in March."

"I know that."

Yes, they were both very aware of the days and how quickly they passed all of a sudden. This latest blockade didn't help their cause.

But, it was one they could only surmount if Eris allowed it.

"Friends." Lucien spat the word like it was a curse. To him, it might as well be.

Chapter Twenty

"Eris, lunch is this way," Pete said, pointing in the direction he was facing.

"I'm going for a quick swim." She walked away from him before he could answer.

"Trying to clear your head?"

Her steps faltered, but she didn't turn back. "I don't want to talk about it."

"Just tell me one thing."

When Pete didn't continue, she looked back at him.

"Is it their fault or yours?"

She gave him a sad smile. "Mine," she whispered and then continued on her way.

The present situation was completely her fault. No one else could be blamed. Ranulf and Lucien continued their normal routine the very next day following the premiere. Except, they didn't touch her or stand over her any longer.

Cool was the word she'd use. They said no more than they had to and found every excuse not to be alone with her. Everyone had noticed the difference immediately.

She sighed as she changed into her swimsuit and went out to the pool. A few quick laps would work off some of her excess energy and probably help her think. Swimming to clear her mind was a habit she'd picked up in college. It hadn't steered her wrong yet.

After taking her mark at the pool's edge, an imaginary whistle blew. She sliced into the water and pretended there was a gold medal waiting for her at the end of three laps.

She broke the surface after her last lap and then yelped.

"Sorry," Lucien said. "I didn't mean to frighten you." He stooped with his arms resting on his legs. "Not hungry?"

"It's easier to swim before lunch rather than after."

"You could compete."

"I did in high school. I stopped in college because my grades started to suffer. Priorities." She shrugged and moved away from Lucien to the ladder and climbed out.

"Don't stop on my account." There was an edge of annoyance to Lucien's voice.

"I just finished, actually. Plus I need to get lunch."

"Such a shame. Watching you swim has become one of my favorite pastimes."

She wrapped her towel around herself then hugged her arms. "I didn't know you'd been watching me."

He pointed at the ceiling over his shoulder.

One of the black camera bubbles was situated near the entrance of the pool. The bubble made it impossible to see in which direction the camera pointed. She had no doubt Lucien had had the camera trained on her whenever she'd gone swimming.

Any other woman would have freaked out. Knowing Lucien watched her while she swam, even after what had happened the week before boded well.

Her swim had had the desired effect, also. She decided that a relationship with Lucien *and* Ranulf wasn't the end of the world. More like par for the course. While she had tried very hard to be different, giving in to normal hurt less.

No, that wasn't right. Giving in to normal felt right.

She met Lucien's gaze. His look wasn't cold. He looked the same as any other time. That gave her hope. Maybe regaining the ground she'd lost wouldn't be so hard after all. But then, they were only following her lead.

For once, the unbeaten path wasn't the smartest way to go.

She couldn't just do an about-face though. Lucien and Ranulf deserved better than that. And, she didn't want to waste too much time trying to find the right way to approach the situation.

Just thinking about returning to the closeness of before and then going further warmed her body and soul. She felt the heat rising to her cheeks.

"I, uh, I need to take a shower and get changed so I can go eat." She turned away quickly and tried to look like she wasn't rushing when she was.

"Is this what you wanted?"

Her hand froze on the knob of the bathroom door. She stopped herself from blurting out the first thing to come to mind.

Tell him! Just say it and everything will go back to normal, she yelled at herself.

She opened her mouth.

Say it!

"Eris, we—"

"I'm sorry." She rushed into the bathroom and slammed the door behind her.

God, she was such an idiot. Lucien had handed her the perfect out to the mess of her own creation. She could have told him she had been an idiot for giving him and Ranulf the "just friends" speech.

Except, she couldn't say the words.

Why?

Rather than berate herself over the lost chance, she went to the shower.

The time hadn't been right. She wouldn't have felt right if she'd told Lucien she wanted to be with him and Ranulf after denying them so adamantly.

They deserved to know why she had been so against the idea of a threesome. Once they understood, she would apologize and ask for a do-over.

But first she needed to call her father and apologize to him.

* * * *

"Hello, lovely daughter o'mine," Gordon said when he answered his phone.

Eris couldn't help smiling. "Hi, Daddy."

"To what do I owe the pleasure this time?"

She waved at Pete as he left the room. Everyone else had left already, happy to be getting out of work early since they'd finished the room three hours before the end of the work day.

Pete was the last one to leave. He made the call-me sign. She gave him a thumbs-up then turned her attention back to her phone conversation. "Did you see the dress? On TV, I mean?"

"You know it. I even taped it. I've already gotten five phone calls from different celebrities requesting I design something for them. As soon as I got the first call, I refunded the payment on your dress."

"It was gorgeous. Everyone at the after-party couldn't say that enough."

"Let me know the next time you do another red carpet. I'll do the dress for free."

"Wow. Those must have been the best five phone calls ever for you to say something like that."

"Not only that. I'll make sure those men of yours match. That was the only thing that had me gnashing my teeth. Their tuxes didn't match your ensemble. Mandarin-style to a medieval movie. Really? If I had known they were going to do that, I would have insisted on fitting them as well."

"You're just saying that because you want to meet them."

"Damn straight. They are dating my daughter."

"No, actually, they aren't."

There was a long pause.

Eris pulled the phone away from her ear and checked to make sure the call hadn't dropped. Gordon said something she didn't catch and she replaced the phone. "What? I didn't hear you."

"What do you mean they aren't? They aren't what?"

"Dating me."

"Then what was all that touching and kissing I saw on screen. So help me, Eris, if you bring another baby in this house without a man to go with it—"

"Dad! I am not my sister. You know me better than that. And that's not what I meant." She took a deep breath and sighed into the phone. "We went to the premiere as friends."

"It didn't look that way to me or your mother."

"I know. I...Daddy, I wanted to say I'm sorry."

"About what?"

"For being a bitch about your relationship with My Mommy all these years."

Gordon made an understanding noise. "I see."

"I'm sorry, Daddy. I really am."

He chuckled. "Eris-baby, don't beat yourself up. You're not the only one who thought to break the mold, shouted it from the rooftops and then had to take it all back. In that respect, you take after your dad."

Eris blinked a few times. "Excuse me?"

"I told Big Daddy a thing or two myself when I was young. Then I had to go back and eat crow once I met your mother. Just like you're doing. I'm sure all this madness will repeat with one of your kids as well, or Kaylie's."

There was silence on both ends and then they said in unison, "Kaylie's."

They both laughed.

Gordon asked, "You see now though, right?"

"Yes."

"So this just-friends thing is going to become more?"

She nodded. "That's my hope. I kind of said some things, and I need to set the record straight with them."

"So, they are straight, then?"

"Dad!"

"Well, are they? You said they live together."

"Yes, Dad. They are straight."

"You're sure?"

She huffed into the phone as her answer.

Gordon laughed. "When am I meeting your new additions?"

"I don't know."

"How about Sunday dinner?"

"No!"

"Why not? It's the perfect time. You know how your mother likes to do it up on Sundays."

"No. That's final."

"Then when am I going to meet them?"

"Any day but Sunday."

"Fine. Saturday."

"Daddy, how about I actually get into a relationship with them before you try to scare them away?"

"If they were real men, they wouldn't be intimidated meeting your parents."

Her father hadn't even met Lucien and Ranulf and already he'd started insulting them. To her, that meant the conversation was over.

"I have to go, Daddy."

"When are you bringing them over?"

"I'll let you know."

"You better. Don't make me sic Mariko on you. I will."

"Bye, Daddy." She snapped the phone shut before he could say more.

Lord have mercy. The thought of Sunday dinner with Lucien and Ranulf in attendance was enough to make her start drinking. There was no way she would last more than five minutes.

But, that wasn't something she had to worry about. Even if...*when* her relationship with Lucien and Ranulf started, she would *never* take them over to her parents' house for Sunday dinner. Not ever.

She wondered if Kaylie had ever taken her family to Sunday dinner. Since her younger sister was one of the two people she'd wanted to apologize to, Eris planned to ask her.

A quick glance at the wall clock confirmed Kaylie should be home. The phone rang three times before someone answered.

"Mommy!"

Eris pulled the phone from her ear, looked at the caller ID to confirm she'd called Kaylie's house, placed the phone against her ear once more and then said, "Minnie, what the hell are you doing at home, young lady?"

"It's not my fault."

"What's not your fault?"

Minnie didn't answer as the voice of an older woman in the background yelled, "What are you doing on the phone? Hang up and get back to your room."

"It's Mommy," the little girl whined.

"Give me that."

There was rustling as the phone passed from one to the other.

"Get!" Kaylie yelled.

Minnie mumbled something Eris didn't catch. It sounded as though Kaylie had muffled the phone. Eris asked, "Kaylie, what's going on? Why is Minnie home from school?"

"Oh, let me tell you about *your* daughter. She punched some boy in the eye. Normally, that would be a talking-to and some sort of in-school punishment. But no, not *your* Minnie. She KO'ed him. The boy was rushed to the hospital with cranial bleeding and a detached retina."

Eris would have fallen over if she'd been standing. "Is Minnie taking martial arts lessons you didn't tell me about?"

"No. The school accused her of the same. I have to find some way to prove Minnie has never had any sort of training or this could be so much worse." Kaylie sighed.

"Did Minnie say why she punched him?"

"He touched her butt and made lewd comments to the other students. Serves the little punk right for putting his hands where they don't belong—" she sighed, "—is what I'd like to say. But no, I have to suck it up and volunteer to pay the hospital bills."

"Have you called Alphie?"

"Oh yes, let me just rush out in front of *that* bus."

"She can help."

"I know that. Lord knows I'll need a lawyer after all is said and done. I'll call her later once I've calmed down. But I know you didn't call about Minnie since I haven't had time to tell anyone yet. Why are you calling?"

Eris's throat closed.

"I saw you on TV with your *two* gentlemen friends. Daddy made sure everyone and their mother was watching."

"I'm a hypocrite," Eris whispered. "I'm sorry."

Kaylie was silent.

"I'm sorry I was a bitch to you and to Daddy and Mother all these years about your relationships. I didn't understand."

"You do now?"

"Yes. God, I wish I didn't."

"Why? You should be happy. Those two are hot. I'm totally jealous."

"Agreed, but I think I may have ruined it."

A smacking noise carried over the phone, and Eris knew Kaylie had hit her forehead with her hand.

"What did you do?" Kaylie asked.

"It's not my fault."

"Okay, now you sound like your daughter."

Eris made a face at the phone. "I just...I don't want to be like...that."

"Why not? What's wrong with it so long as all parts of the relationship are happy? Do they not want to share?"

"They suggested it."

"Then it's all good. I could see the problem if they were pitching a bitch about the whole threesome thing, but they aren't. It's just you. As usual."

"Sorry to be a pain."

"If sorry solved the problems of the world, we wouldn't need prisons."

"You're no help." Eris looked at her watch and then confirmed the time with her laptop. "Look, I'm still at work, but I wanted to call and apologize for all the grief I gave you over the years."

"Apology accepted. You didn't have to, but I'm glad you did."

"Tell Minnie I'll call her later."

"She'd like that."

"Tell the other munchkins I miss them."

"Will do."

"Call Alphie."

Kaylie grumbled under her breath before the phone beeped, signaling the end of the call.

Eris snapped her phone shut. Everything was still. She could hear the blood rushing through her veins as the weight of her decision settled around her.

Lucien and Ranulf were a package deal. As it turned out, she wanted the package. The only downside was the fact that she had already stamped it "return to sender."

"Now what do I do?" she asked the air.

"About?"

Eris gasped and whipped around in her seat.

Ranulf stood in the doorway grinning at her. "Do you normally talk to yourself?"

"Yes. Intelligent conversation is so hard to come by in this day and age."

"Ouch. And here I thought I was fairly intelligent." He entered the room and walked to her work station. "What's the conundrum?"

She opened her mouth and then closed it.

How was she supposed to take back all that she'd said?

"Oops, my bad" didn't seem very appropriate to the situation. The timing still felt off. It took her a moment to realize why.

Lucien wasn't there.

Earlier, Ranulf hadn't been present. Both men needed to be there before she could explain herself.

She looked beyond Ranulf, but he'd come to the room alone. Asking him to call Lucien or go with her back to the office felt awkward.

She sighed and turned back to her computer. "Nothing. I'll figure it out."

Ranulf placed a hand on the back of her chair. If she leaned back, she could feel his warmth. She stayed sitting upright.

"I didn't think you'd be staying late any longer," he said in a soft voice.

"I finished inputting Mr. Sebastion's notes, but I'm still doing the revamp of my database program."

"I see." He stepped back, removing his hand. "Well, our offer to stay still stands. We don't want you driving if you're tired."

She nodded.

"Good night."

"Good night," she whispered back.

Ranulf left the room. Only when she was sure he was gone did she chance looking at the doorway.

Just a little bit longer. Once everyone had left for the day, she'd go talk to them.

Chapter Twenty-one

"She's not playing fair."

Lucien agreed with Ranulf's words.

They both stood in the doorway watching Eris. She'd fallen asleep at her work station.

Lucien hadn't even realized she was still there until he left the office to get a snack and noticed a light from the direction of the survey rooms. When he arrived, Ranulf was already there, staring at her.

It would be so easy to wake her with his mouth roaming over her body. Her silly notion about remaining friends would completely disappear. A dirty tactic, to be sure, but one Lucien would enjoy. He knew she'd thoroughly enjoy it as well.

Ranulf asked, "Now what? Do we wake her?"

Lucien shook his head. "No." He entered the room and went to Eris. Careful not to jar her, he lifted her against his chest.

Ranulf nodded at him and stepped out of the way.

Despite what Ranulf's grin implied, Lucien had every intention of putting Eris to bed—alone. He would have said as much but didn't want to wake Eris. Ranulf would see what he was doing soon enough.

Ranulf kept pace with him up the stairs. They reached the room Eris normally used, and Ranulf opened the door. Lucien walked in, and the door closed behind him.

He looked back, but Ranulf wasn't there. He'd closed Lucien in with Eris.

What did that mean?

Lucien wouldn't dwell on it. He lowered Eris to the bed. She shivered a little and murmured something he couldn't make out but otherwise didn't wake.

Bent over her as he was, he couldn't help touching her. He trailed his fingers over her cheek.

Eris jerked, and her eyes snapped open. "Lucien?"

He straightened. "I didn't mean to wake you."

"Wake me?" She sat up and looked around. Her confusion turned to surprise. "Oh no! Oh crap! I must have fallen asleep."

"Feel free to continue. You've looked tired these last few days. Good night." He turned to leave. There needed to be distance between them before he did something he regretted.

"Wait, Lucien. I…"

He faced her. "What's wrong?"

"Nothing." She shook her head. "Nothing. I need to get home."

"No, you need to go back to sleep."

"Yes, as soon as I get home." She got off of the bed and walked to the doorway. That was where she stopped because Lucien refused to move so she could pass.

"Excuse me."

"Eris, Ranulf and I have said many times already, we don't like you driving when you're fatigued. Stay here tonight."

"I can't. Besides, I'm fine."

"Why can't you?"

She pursed her lips, and her uncertain look of that afternoon at the swimming pool returned.

"Do you distrust us so much that you don't think you can stay here without it meaning something else?"

"No, that's not—"

"You said for us to be friends, and we have abided, yet you are keeping your distance."

She frowned at him. "Me? I'm not the one who's been avoiding you. You both have been avoiding me. Is that what you call friendship?"

"We're only doing what we must to…" He trailed off with an angered sound. He faced away from her and yanked open the door. "You're staying here."

He tried to close the door behind him, but Eris got in the way and held it open.

"No, I'm not. I have to go home."

"Why?"

"I just do. Please move." She pushed at him.

That was his breaking point. He lifted her once more, which made her yelp in surprise, and carried her back to the bed. Unlike last time, he dumped her and then pinned her down when she would have risen.

He said, "I don't care if I have to lock the damn door. You are not driving home at three in the morning while you're tired. That's final."

"I'm not tired," she whispered.

Her wide-eyed look of shock was his undoing. Before he could contemplate the consequences or stop himself, he lowered his lips to hers.

He expected Eris to push him away or hit him. Instead, she sighed against his mouth and opened for him.

Feeling her respond to him was a surprise, a welcome one at that. He slipped his free hand beneath her shirt as he deepened the kiss.

Still she didn't object. She even pressed herself against him.

"My, my, don't you two look cozy?"

Lucien pulled away from Eris and looked at Ranulf.

Eris mumbled something incoherent before she bolted from the bed and out of the room.

"Damn it," Lucien bit out.

He made to chase after Eris, but Ranulf beat him to it. He caught up with them at the front door. Ranulf had Eris pinned bodily with his front pressed to her back and her front pressed to the door.

"Calm down," Ranulf whispered. He made soothing noises as he backed away a little.

Eris stayed huddled around the doorknob.

Lucien touched her shoulder, but she jerked away from him. "Eris, I didn't mean for that to happen."

"I'm sorry. I'm sorry. I'm so sorry," she said quickly.

That confused him. Why was she sorry?

She faced them, looking at him and then Ranulf and then back again. Her whole body sagged, and she leaned heavily against the door.

"Eris?" Ranulf asked.

"We need to talk," she whispered.

Lucien took in her resigned look. Whatever she had to say, he didn't think he wanted to hear it. Despite that, he still stepped back and gestured to the office. "We should sit then."

Eris nodded and led the way. She went to the couch, sat down and then stood again. Her gaze flitted around the room.

"Eris, calm down," Ranulf said. He sat on the couch and patted the cushion next to him. "What has you so agitated?"

She shook her head. "Lucien."

"Yes?" Lucien looked at the couch when she gestured to it. He sat one cushion away from Ranulf, leaving room for Eris.

She remained standing, looking between the two of them. "I'm sorry."

"You said that already. I'm confused why you feel you need to apologize," Lucien said.

"I've been apologizing all day—yesterday. I…" She trailed off and shook her head. "I don't want you to think I'm indecisive or scatterbrained."

"The thought never crossed my mind," Ranulf said with a small amount of laughter in his voice.

Lucien shot him a look to keep his humor to himself. Eris seemed to be having enough issues. He didn't want to add to them by making her think they were teasing her.

He turned his attention back to Eris and asked the most pertinent question of the night, "You've changed your mind and decided to be with us?"

"Yes. I'm sorry."

"All this apologizing has me worried. Why are you sorry? We asked you to be with us. I know being in a relationship with two men isn't exactly normal but—"

She laughed. "You have no clue what my definition of normal is." All at once, the nervous energy she exuded disappeared. She stood straighter. "Along with my father, I was raised by three mothers."

Lucien let his jaw drop. Of all the things she could have told them, the possibility that she was the product of a multi-partnered relationship had never crossed his mind.

He was jerked out of his stupor by Ranulf's laughter. The man threw his head back and a single tear rolled down the side of his face. His amusement was short-lived. He wiped his face and shook his head. "Now it's my turn to apologize. I just got the punch line of a very old joke." He waved Eris to continue.

She frowned at him but said, "Multi-partner relationships are what I consider to be normal. My whole family—extended family too—is comprised of multi-partnered relationships. It's the way I grew up. For a long time, before I started school, I thought everyone had multiple mothers or multiple fathers."

"If you consider that to be normal, why reject us?" Ranulf asked.

Eris lowered her gaze to the floor. "I hated it. When I learned that it wasn't normal to have more than one of either parent, I resented my parents for teaching me otherwise." She paced a little. "I got picked on in school. It's the reason I was the keep-to-myself type for so long. I wouldn't have to explain about my parents if I wasn't close to anyone."

That made sense, and Lucien would have said so, but he got the feeling Eris needed to say her piece without interruption. Besides, he was still digesting the news that she had three mothers.

"My older brother got into fights at school almost constantly. My sister Kaylie and I were harassed whenever the boys found out what type of background we came from, which got my brother into more fights. And poor Declan." She made an angry noise. "Dad and the moms went on a romantic get-away to Thailand when I was six. They convinced some local woman to have fun with them, and she got pregnant. Nine months later, she tracked Dad and sent him Declan with a note that said she didn't want him. And then Minnie..." She trailed off and rolled her eyes.

"Who?" Ranulf asked.

Lucien elbowed him to be quiet.

Eris waved that away. "Never mind. That's a whole other conversation I don't even want to start. Suffice to say, life outside of home wasn't the greatest for us. We had to hide the truth about our family and that caused us all a lot of stress. I didn't even date until after college because that kept guys from finding out about my family and making assumptions."

Lucien didn't need her to explain what type of assumptions. He had a pretty good idea. He also didn't hear anything that was convincing him Eris would go forward with their relationship once she was done talking.

"Benkei, my older brother, and I both declared we wouldn't be like our parents. We planned to be in monogamous relationships."

Again Ranulf laughed. It wasn't as loud as the first time, but he was still very amused about something.

Lucien asked, "Same joke?"

Ranulf laughed more but waved Eris on again.

"If you think I'm joking—"

"I do not." Ranulf shook his head. He cleared his throat and pasted a serious look on his face. "Believe it or not, I'm laughing with you."

"Huh?"

"Never mind. Continue your story."

Though she seemed annoyed, she continued. "Like I said, Benkei and I didn't want to suffer upholding the family tradition, and we didn't want our kids to have to go through what we did. We very adamantly told our parents the same. He followed through and has been with his wife in a monogamous relationship for five years. Mary has already told him she is not the type of woman to share. Benkei is the same, so it looks like they will remain that way."

Ranulf got off of the couch and went to Eris. He lifted her chin so she looked at him. There was no trace of his earlier humor. "What about you?" he asked in a soft voice.

She cupped his hand and gave him a sad smile. "I called my dad and apologized for turning out to be a hypocrite."

Lucien joined them. When she looked at him, he cupped her other cheek. "I don't mind that you're a hypocrite."

His gaze lowered to Eris's lips. They were begging to be kissed. Now that he knew she wouldn't turn away from him or hide under the excuse of remaining friends, he planned to indulge.

Just as he moved closer to her, Eris dodged back.

"Eris?"

"Well, that's solved. I need to go home." She turned toward the door.

Ranulf and Lucien moved in perfect synchronization. They each grabbed one of her hands and pulled her back.

Lucien said, "Say that again."

Eris looked back at them, and they released her. "I told you. I need to go home." She wagged her finger at him. "And you can't say I'm too tired to drive since I'm wide awake now."

"Why won't you stay here?"

"Isn't that a bit fast?" She edged back as she asked that question.

Lucien followed her. "Should I take offense that you are assuming Ranulf and I have morals on par with Clayton?"

She didn't deny his accusation. He didn't like that one bit.

Ranulf said, "Eris we have no intention of pouncing on you once you let your guard down."

"Even still, I don't think I should be staying here." She looked between them with hope. "Why tempt fate and all that, right?"

"Are you scared we'll find out you're a virgin?"

Eris gasped.

Lucien said, "You are, right? You said you didn't date until college. Given your reticent attitude toward Clayton's advances, and your skittishness now, it's a perfectly reasonable conclusion."

Her gaze locked with his. "If I am?"

"If you are," Ranulf said, drawing her attention, "we congratulate you on accomplishing what amounts to the impossible in this day and age."

"This isn't a joke," she snapped.

Lucien said, "I agree."

Ranulf made an offhand gesture. "I'm not joking. She's twenty-eight and still a virgin. I'm impressed. Actually, shocked awe is a more apt description."

"Good night." Eris turned away again.

Lucien went after Eris while Ranulf laughed. He stopped her at the door. "Eris, ignore Ranulf. He's an ass."

"Just call me pathetic and be done."

He urged her to look at him. When she did, he said, "You aren't pathetic. You also don't have to worry about Ranulf or me. We'll wait until you're ready."

"Uh-huh. Is this going to turn out like the friends-thing did?"

He chuckled. "While I admit we weren't trying very hard, this is different. Very different." He wanted to stress how much he and Ranulf would respect her wish to remain a virgin. And, it had nothing to do with being chivalrous.

Not only did he not say any of his thoughts, he couldn't. She wouldn't understand and trying to explain it would only scare her away. She had agreed to be with them, even if the relationship was platonic for the time being. Lucien wouldn't ruin that.

"Are we okay?" Lucien asked.

Eris met his gaze. "This isn't lip service? You'll really wait for me to be ready?"

"You can stay here with no fear of being compromised." Ranulf grinned. "Though we will steal the occasional kiss."

"Lucien was doing more than kissing earlier."

"With a body like yours, can you blame him?"

Her wary look returned.

Ranulf said, "You can be sure neither of us will touch you, Eris. We'll be too busy fighting over who will be your first. If I catch Lucien trying, I'll kick his ass."

"Likewise," Lucien said.

Eris looked amused. Lucien only wished their words had been said in jest.

Chapter Twenty-two

Eris looked at herself one last time in the full-length mirror. Nothing was amiss. No one would ever be able to tell she'd spent the night. Not that she'd done anything to feel guilty over.

She simply stayed late working on her program. When it came time to leave, Ranulf had barred her way and refused to let her out of the door. She had no choice but to stay.

That was the story she planned to tell everyone.

She left the room and headed for the stairs.

"What the hell?" Pete asked.

His voice so startled her she almost fell. She looked at her watch and then him. "What are you doing here so early?"

"Catching you in the act, obviously."

"You're exaggerating, Pete."

"Am I?"

"Yes. I stayed late. Rather than drive home, I stayed here."

Pete raised an eyebrow. "You accidentally stayed late with a change of clothes. Sure." He pointed a finger at her. "I'm telling your father."

"Go ahead. He already knows about Lucien and Ranulf."

Ranulf joined her at the top of the stairs. He asked in a sleepy voice, "Is there a reason you're being so loud this early in the morning?"

"Did I wake you? I'm sorry."

He tilted her chin up and pressed his lips to hers. "Forgiven." He gave her another kiss and then turned back to his room. "Keep it down. Good morning, Pete. I'm going back to bed."

Eris looked down at Pete.

He didn't seem pleased.

She couldn't think of anything to say that would make him feel better so she didn't try. He had to trust she could handle herself.

He waited for her to get to the bottom of the stairs and then said, "I'm really dubious about this. They've already put you through the wringer, and you weren't even dating them then."

"At least I'll never be bored." She grinned at him.

He didn't echo her amusement. "Be careful. Promise me that."

"Everything will be fine." She linked arms with him. "Since you're here so early, let's go eat. Why did you say you're here so early again?"

Pete balked at first as she tried to lead him away. He sighed and followed her. "I thought I'd take a page out of your book, but decided my wife would be less pissed if I left for work early as opposed to staying late."

They entered the kitchen and found Lucien eating.

"Ah ha!" she and Pete said at the same time.

Lucien looked at them with a piece of bacon hanging from his lips like a cigarette. "What?"

"I thought you didn't eat breakfast," Eris said in an accusatory tone.

"I don't. This is an anomaly."

Liselle said, "It is. He would have caught me off guard if I didn't normally have breakfast ready regardless." She set two more plates of food on the island and gestured to the seats. "Eat up. There's plenty."

Eris said a quick thanks and started eating her food.

"Should I be telling everyone your car broke down again?" Liselle winked at her.

Pete swallowed his bite of food then yelled, "What?"

"It's not what you think," Eris said, shooting Liselle a look to say she didn't appreciate the woman's idea of a joke.

"This isn't the first time you've stayed over. How can it be anything else?"

Eris tried to think of how to explain.

Lucien said in a calm tone, "Ranulf and I rescued her from Clayton. She left her house keys and didn't want to deal with him to get them back, so we invited her to stay here." He looked over at Pete. "Or would you rather we had left her there?"

Pete held Lucien's gaze for several breaths. He nodded and said, "Thank you."

"You're welcome." Lucien wiped his mouth and stood. "I have work to..." He trailed off as a shocked look crossed his face.

Eris turned in the direction of his gaze. Ranulf shambled into the kitchen, pushed Lucien out of the way, and dropped onto the seat Lucien vacated.

"Ranulf, I thought you were going back to sleep," she said.

"Already awake. Might as well stay that way," he mumbled. His head drooped forward, and he blinked several times.

"You don't look it."

He didn't say anything. In fact, she was sure he'd fallen asleep again. She touched his arm, and he jerked upright. "Huh?"

Lucien smacked him on the back of the head. "Go back to bed if you aren't awake."

"Can't sleep." Ranulf turned and hugged Eris tight. "I want an Eris-pillow."

Pete grumbled, "I'm going to be sick."

"Not in my kitchen you aren't," Liselle snapped. "And don't waste my cooking like that either."

Eris disengaged herself from Ranulf even though he tried to retain his hold. "Maybe you should drink some coffee."

"Never touch the stuff. It's poison." He let her go. "Liselle, espresso, please."

"Usual cup?"

"Yes."

Liselle nodded. She pulled a cup out of the cupboard that was usually reserved for cappuccino.

"Li...Liselle, he said espresso," Eris said.

"I know. This is how much he usually drinks when he wants to wake up."

Eris's gaze snapped to Ranulf, who again was sleeping while sitting up. She whispered, "He's going to kill himself."

Lucien said, "I should only be so lucky. Don't worry, Eris. A cup that size will hardly even faze him."

"He should just take the caffeine intravenously and be done."

"He tried. No doctor, in good conscience, would do it." Lucien checked his watch. "I have to get to work. I'll see you later." He kissed the top of Eris's head and then left.

Liselle placed the cup before Ranulf who drank it with a sleepy sound of satisfaction.

"That stuff is going to kill you," Pete said. He finished the last of his food, thanked Liselle and jogged out of the room.

Eris watched him go. She hoped he was going to the survey room. She didn't want Pete grilling Lucien about what happened the first time she'd stayed the night. It was none of his business, and it was in the past.

* * * *

"Hold up, Lucien."

Lucien stopped and looked back at Pete. "Yes?"

"Just what did you save her from?"

Lucien knew that was coming. He signaled for Pete to walk with him and continued to the office. As they walked he related the incident.

"That son of a…I should sucker punch him the second he walks through the door." Pete hit his open palm with his fist.

"Tempting, but don't. Having to put up with the fallout from workplace violence will only upset Eris." Lucien held the office door so Pete could precede him, entered and then closed it.

"Why is he still here?" Pete sat across from Lucien's desk.

"No valid excuse to get rid of him, until recently. Brian can't deny the proof any longer, not with a fourth team coming out to clean up the mess."

Lucien's cell rang. He looked at the caller ID and then hit the call button. "Yes, Grant?"

"There is some eight—"

"Ten!" a little girl yelled.

"*Ten*-year-old at the gate demanding to see Eris. She arrived by cab without enough money to pay the fare."

"I only had a fifty," the little girl yelled again.

Lucien was about to talk but something that sounded like a scuffle ensued on the other end.

"Hey! Give that back!" Grant yelled.

The little girl came on the line. "Eris Brue is in there, right?"

"She is," Lucien said with amusement. "And to whom, may I ask, am I speaking?"

"I'm Minuet Angelique Grey."

"Well, Miss Grey, if you would be so kind as to return the phone to the angry gentleman beside you, I will have him bring you to the house. Is that agreeable?"

"Yes, thank you. Hold on."

Grant snapped once he got the phone back, "I don't get paid enough for this."

Lucien said, "We'll discuss a raise at your review next month. Pay the cab, get a receipt, and bring Eris's guest to the house. Thank you, Grant."

He replaced his phone in its holder then met Pete's questioning gaze. "It seems Eris has a visitor."

"Visitor?"

"A Miss Minuet Grey."

Pete jumped out of his seat. "Minnie? She should be in school. What the hell is she doing here? How did she get here for that matter?"

"You sound like you know her," Lucien said, standing as well.

Suddenly Eris's guest was of immediate interest to him. She had mentioned a Minnie last night. If it was the same little girl on the way to the house, Lucien would be meeting a member of Eris's family.

Pete signaled Lucien to follow him as he left the office. "Of course I know her. I know most of Eris's family. I went to high school with a few of her uncles."

"You did? I didn't realize you and Eris went that far back."

"It's not that far considering Eris has uncles that are still in middle school. Obviously I didn't go to school with one of them, but I wanted to make that point."

"Middle school?"

Pete made a thinking noise. "She might even have some uncles in elementary school."

"Excuse me?"

"Ah. She didn't tell you about Big Daddy yet."

"Who?" Lucien was lost.

"Guess that means you don't know about Minnie either."

Lucien shook his head. His curiosity took on a sense of urgency. He wanted to urge Pete to talk faster but kept himself looking and acting mildly interested.

"Minuet is Eris's—"

"Mommy!"

Lucien froze. He stared at the little girl who had just screamed at the top of her lungs as she ran into the house.

There had to be some mistake. It was impossible for Eris to have any children. She was a virgin. He knew that for a certainty.

Grant tried to hush the girl with a hand over her mouth, but she yelled again.

Eris ran from the direction of the kitchen. "Minnie?"

The little girl broke from Grant and ran to Eris. "Mommy." She latched onto Eris's waist and hugged her tight.

Lucien could only stare. Behind Eris, Ranulf stood in slack-jawed surprise. He looked from Eris to Lucien and then back again. He also looked wide awake. The shock seemed to have done the job the espresso couldn't.

"Minnie, what are you doing here? Where's Kaylie?" Eris asked.

The little girl tightened her hold. "You said you'd call, and you didn't."

"I'm sorry, but I've been busy. It's only been one day."

"You hate me."

Eris gathered Minnie close. "I don't hate you. Why would you say that?"

"Because of what I did to that boy at school. Kaylie hates me. Father does too. They want to get rid of me."

"No, they don't."

Minnie pulled away from Eris. "Yes, they do. Papa said so."

Eris blanched. "You must of have misunderstood. Paul would never say something like that." She looked around, and her gaze settled on Lucien.

She looked a little surprised, as though she hadn't realized he was standing there. She glanced over her shoulder at Ranulf and finally looked at Pete.

"I'm sorry." She tried to turn Minnie, but the little girl wouldn't cooperate. "This is Minuet, Minnie for short. She's my niece, my younger sister's daughter."

"Niece? She called you mommy." Lucien tried to keep the accusation from his voice.

"Yes, she does that because I raised her. Kaylie was still a sophomore in high school when she had Minnie. I graduated a year early and decided to

take a few night courses rather than go away to college right away." She
shrugged. "I became the designated babysitter."

Minnie buried her face below Eris's breasts. Eris patted her back. "For a
long time, Minnie thought I was her mother. It wasn't until she was four that
we could make her understand that I'm her aunt. By that time though, she
simply refused to call me anything else, which drives Kaylie insane."

"Don't care," Minnie grumbled.

Eris sighed and turned her attention back to Minnie. "What happened?"

The little girl spoke, but Lucien couldn't make it out.

Ranulf skirted around the pair and went to Lucien's side. He lifted his
cup to his lips, pretending to take a drink, and whispered, "Do you feel
that?"

"Yes," Lucien answered in a whisper of his own. "I thought it was my
imagination."

"That little girl is host to a lot of power."

"Indeed."

Lucien looked Minnie over. The little girl leaked power from every
pore. It wasn't magical, not yet. If she had the proper training, it could be.
Whatever vocation she chose in the future, she'd be a force to be reckoned
with.

"No, they don't," Eris said.

"They do! Papa said get rid of me, Daddy acts like I'm a nuisance, and
Old Man is always glaring at me."

"Minnie, to be fair, Old Man glares at everyone. I don't even think he
likes Kaylie."

"Good, I don't like her either."

"Stop saying that. Right now," Eris snapped. She lifted Minnie's chin so
the little girl looked at her. "I mean it. Don't say that again."

"Sorry, Mommy," Minnie whispered. "I want to stay with you. Can I?"

"Minnie—"

"Please. I'll be good."

Eris sighed.

Ranulf said, "If she needs to stay—"

She made a negative motion with her hand behind Minnie's back but
mouthed a thank you. Turning her attention back to Minnie, she said, "Tell
me what Paul said and why he said it and why you were eavesdropping."

"I wasn't. Kaylie and Papa were yelling. Everyone could hear them."

Grant interrupted what Eris would have said next, "Sirs, Angel is escorting a woman and her children to the house. She says she's the mother."

"No, I don't wanna!" Minnie broke away from Eris and ran.

Ranulf shoved his cup at Lucien and caught Minnie with one arm. He hoisted her onto his shoulder, took back his cup, and took a sip of his espresso. The little girl flailed and screamed but he held her with little effort. He even managed to drink without spilling.

"This is a mess. I'm sorry, Lucien, Ranulf," Eris said in a dejected tone.

"It's all right. You had no control over it," Lucien said.

A woman in a business skirt and blazer, carrying a baby in the crook of one arm and a diaper bag on the other, with two little boys trailing after her, entered the front door. Her gaze snapped to Ranulf and his burden. "Minuet Angelique Grey, I should beat the black off of you. Don't you *ever* run off like that again."

Eris gestured to the woman. "My sister Kaylie."

"Nice to meet you," Kaylie bit out. She walked over to Eris, dumped the baby in her arms and dropped the diaper bag on the floor. "I was out of my mind until My Mommy called and said Minnie was probably headed for you."

"Now how did she know?" Eris shifted the baby to her shoulder and rocked her.

"My Mommy told her where you work."

"That woman…" Eris trailed off with a shake of her head. "I'll deal with her later. What is going on? Why is Minnie here? Why does she think you want to get rid of her? And why did you bring the kids with you?"

"I have a house to show in less than an hour. It was luck that it's out this way so I won't be late. Father isn't home, and I can't leave the kids by themselves."

"What happened to school?"

"Oh, don't even get me started." Kaylie glared at Minnie. "Miss *Thang* got a bug up her ass when she found out Allen wants to see her."

"I don't blame her. Allen hasn't wanted to see her in all this time. Why now?"

"Who knows? The courts say he can though, and I have to produce her for weekend visits or else. Paul opened his yap and told me to just give her to him for good."

Eris jerked back. Lucien was sure she'd drop the baby, she looked so shocked. She held the little girl, but her expression turned dark. He'd only seen anger like that grace her face once before.

"I hope," Eris said in a cold voice, "you put your foot up his ass for that."

Kaylie waved that away. "Oh, you know I did. I almost took a page out of Minnie's book and decked him. That's my firstborn he's talking about. Just because she isn't his isn't a reason to get rid of her." She looked at her watch and made a frustrated noise. "I don't have time for this. Watch the kids. I should be back in no more than four hours."

"Four hours! Kaylie—"

"Thanks. Love ya. Bye." Kaylie breezed out of the room without a backward glance.

Eris stood staring after her.

One of the little boys pulled on her pant leg. She looked down at him. "What's wrong, Emil?"

The little boy pointed around her to the far wall.

Lucien, and everyone else, followed that little finger and saw the other little boy reaching for one of the swords at his level.

Before Lucien could think of what to do to stop him, Eris barked, "David Anthony Grey, touch that sword and I'll beat you into next week."

The little boy gasped loudly and jumped a good three feet away from the wall. He turned back and looked at Eris with wide, scared eyes. Lucien didn't blame the boy for being frightened. Eris's threat and the tone with which she'd delivered it had him a little scared.

Eris pointed at the spot in front of her with a grunt.

David inched his way closer to her as slowly as he could.

"Now!"

The little boy yelped and ran to her. He cringed back when she reached for him.

She put her hand on the top of his head and made him look up at her. "This is not your house. You do *not* touch anything without permission. And you will behave or I'm calling Alphie."

Who is Alphie? Why is he such a threat? Lucien thought. Looking at Ranulf showed the man was as ignorant of the answers as he.

Emil took a deep breath and let loose a long, loud wail.

Eris looked back at him, her expression softening. "What's wrong, sweets? Why are you crying?"

"Don't wanna see Alphie. Don't wanna."

Eris stooped to his level. After rummaging through the diaper bag, she pulled out a tissue and wiped his face. With a little coaxing, she got him to blow his nose. "If you promise to behave, I won't have to call her, will I?"

Emil shook his head.

She looked at David.

"I'll be good," he said quickly.

"Good." Eris straightened, heaved a sigh then looked at Lucien. "This is Emil, David, and Olivia." She bounced the baby, who cooed and made burbling noises. "Kaylie's offspring, who I seem to be stuck with. I'm sorry."

Pete stepped forward. "Let's get you all situated in the den." He took Olivia and jerked his head toward Minnie and Ranulf. "Deal with her. I've got them."

"You're sure?"

"Please. These monsters are tame compared to mine." He grinned at her. "You think you could whip mine into shape."

"It's the fear of Alphie that does it."

"I think it's the fear of you." Pete chuckled as he led the boys away.

Lucien looked at the children. Like Minnie, they each had untapped potential. The little boys didn't boast the type of power Minnie had, while Olivia seemed like she would surpass her sister when she was older.

He'd even felt a small fraction of Minnie's power coming from Kaylie. In contrast, nothing like that existed in Eris. But, there were multiple mothers in Eris's family. Perhaps the two were half sisters. That would mean the power came from Kaylie's mother.

Eris walked over to them, staring at Minnie's rump the whole while. "Let's take this to the office. Everyone will get here soon."

Ranulf did an about face and walked away. Lucien stayed put, waiting for Eris to move.

"I'm sorry about this," she said.

"Not the way I would have liked to meet your family, but it isn't much of an issue."

She met his gaze with a questioning one. "You're sure? If you're mad, just say so. I'll completely understand."

He kissed her lips. "I'm not mad or even upset. A little surprised, maybe, but not mad." Slipping his arm around her waist, he ushered her to the office.

Ranulf had Minnie situated on a seat. Eris walked over to the little girl while Lucien closed the office door.

"First and foremost, young lady, you will apologize to Mr. Lucien and Mr. Ranulf for barging into their house unannounced and uninvited," Eris said, her reprimanding parental tone returning.

Minnie mumbled something Lucien didn't catch.

"Speak up!"

The little girl flinched. "I'm sorry."

Eris sighed. "Now. Paul is an idiot. We won't contest that. Kaylie will deal with him, so that's not something *you* need to be worrying about. She won't get rid of you. Understand?"

Minnie nodded.

"Words."

"I understand."

"Thank you." Eris placed her hands on her hips. "The thing with Allen is non-negotiable. You have to—"

"But I—"

"Don't talk over me!"

Minnie pulled back and mumbled another apology.

Lucien exchanged a look with Ranulf. He found the entire conversation amusing. He didn't know Eris could be so forceful.

"Allen is your biological father, and he has a right to see you," Eris said. "Be happy it's only the weekends. If you refuse to see him, he could sue to take full custody, and you'll never see any of us again."

Minnie jumped out of her seat and looked like she would say something. She snapped her mouth shut and sat down again.

Eris stooped so she sat on her haunches and rested her hands on Minnie's knees. She said in a gentler voice, "I know you're scared, little bit, but you have to know we aren't going to get rid of you. Kaylie loves you. I love you, and there's no way Pop-pop is going to let one of his children out of this family without one hell of a fight. You've got well over sixty great-uncles who will see to that."

Sixty uncles?

Lucien barely kept himself from blurting that question out loud. How big was Eris's family?

Beside him, Ranulf choked on his sip of espresso.

Eris glanced back at them with an amused look. "I told you, multiples is normal in my family. Big Daddy, my father's father, has over one hundred kids by fifty-some-odd women. Ten of those are his wives, another fifteen are his girlfriends, and the rest are flings and one night stands."

Ranulf sat his cup aside. "I'm awake."

Minnie said, "Big Daddy had twins last month with a twenty-year-old. Kaylie said so. She said that was sick."

"The man is in his late seventies. It is sick." Eris shook her head. "It doesn't help that he looks like he's in his fifties."

"Mommy?"

"Yes, Minnie?"

"What if Allen wants to take me away, and Pop-pop can't stop him?"

Eris ruffled the little girl's hair. "If Pop-pop and the uncles can't stop him, then I'll sic Alphie on him."

The little girl's eyes got wide. "Really?"

"Yes, really. You belong to us and that's forever. Okay?"

"Okay." Minnie sat forward and hugged Eris. "I still want to stay with you."

"Kaylie would miss you if you did." Eris straightened and pulled Minnie to her feet. "You are going to join your brothers and sister in the den. I'll get you all situated with some food and then you'll behave until your mother comes for you or else Allen won't be the only one I sic Alphie on."

Minnie nodded quickly.

"Good girl."

Ranulf held out his hand. "I'll take her."

Minnie ran to him before Eris could say anything.

Once the door closed after them, Lucien asked, "Seventies and he's still having babies?"

"Yup. Big Daddy always said he wanted a dynasty."

"The man has a civilization. How can he afford all those children?"

"All of his wives work, some of the kids moved near home and they help out, and he comes from old money. He's put all his children through college. Those he didn't put through college went to a trade school. Big Daddy can't stand lazy people." Eris grinned up at him. "Scared yet?"

"I'm in awe and a little disbelieving."

"If you want to beat a hasty retreat, now would be the time."

He hugged her to him. "What did you say to Minnie? You belong to us and that's forever."

"Just remember you said that." She turned her face up so she could get a kiss.

Lucien obliged her. He wouldn't forget his words. He only hoped Eris wouldn't either.

Chapter Twenty-three

Eris flopped onto the couch in the den and let loose a sigh to beat all sighs.

Ranulf chuckled at her. "Tired?"

"Between doing my normal work and checking in on the kids, I'm exhausted."

He lifted her feet, sat down, and then placed them on his lap. "We told you we could watch them. Pete and Megan even volunteered." He started massaging her calf.

She snorted. "They just wanted to get out of work and you two as well, for that matter."

Lucien sat on her other side and coaxed her into lying down so his thigh cushioned her head. He reached for her hand and proceeded to massage her arm. "You handled them admirably."

"I already told you, I raised Minnie. Mother and Daddy decided to give me one of those real-world experiences parents always harp about so they didn't help me in the least. I totally didn't think that was fair since I wasn't the one who got knocked up." She shrugged. "I don't regret it though. Minnie is my heart."

"She seems to love you quite a bit as well." Lucien kissed her fingers. "The sight of you with them made me wish for children of my own."

"Lucien!" Ranulf snapped.

His tone made Eris jerk. She glanced back at him and then looked at Lucien. "What's wrong?"

Lucien shook his head.

She thought his words were a bit premature, but Ranulf's reaction made it out like Lucien had said something wrong. Even Lucien acted like he'd committed a faux pas.

She touched his cheek. When he looked down at her, she said, "Let's see how the dating thing works out first. Besides, you all haven't met Alphie yet. That could be a deal breaker for you."

"Who is Alphie? I kept hearing the name but no explanation."

"One of my mothers. When speaking to or around people who don't know about our family dynamic we refer to all three as Mother. Each of them has a title that distinguishes them since we can't call them by name without getting into serious trouble. Kaylie's mom is Last Mommy, so named by me because I didn't want my father bringing home any more women."

"How jealous of you," Ranulf said with a chuckle.

"I was three at the time. What do you expect? My Mommy is my mother."

Lucien chuckled. "I assumed."

"Well, that's her title as well. It was a thing between me and Benkei. I'd call her My Mommy and he'd mimic me, which made me mad. After a while, it just became her title."

"Which leads us to Alphie, Gordon's first wife, I take it?"

Eris nodded. "Alphie is short for Alpha Bitch. I was big into wolves as a little kid. After watching a nature program, I learned some of the titles."

Ranulf laughed out loud. "How old were you?"

"Three. All this took place while I was three. I went up to my parents and declared for one and all that Mariko was the alpha bitch of the family. She was pissed and thought my father had put me up to it since they'd had a fight earlier that day."

"Mariko?" Lucien asked.

"Alphie is Japanese. Daddy met her while doing a bridal expo in Japan." She giggled. "Alpha Bitch wasn't something the parents wanted us kids saying, so it got shortened to Alphie. And even then, no one says it to Mariko's face. Not without a death wish."

"She's that scary?"

"Alphie is a deputy district attorney. She wanted to concentrate on marriage law, but her teachers said she was too cutthroat. They suggested criminal or corporate law."

"Sounds like an interesting woman."

Eris nodded. "Kaylie's kids do the same thing with their three fathers. Papa is Paul, Daddy is Stephen, and Old Man is Marcos. Collectively known as Father."

Lucien said, "A good system."

"You two are learning an awful lot about my family, and I've yet to hear anything about yours."

Ranulf shrugged. "I was a foundling. The man who raised me taught me a lot about life and women. I've learned much more since then."

"I'll bet. When do I get to meet him?"

"You don't. He's dead."

"Oh. Oh, I'm sorry."

Ranulf kissed her calf. "Don't be. It was a long time ago."

"My parents and sister are also dead," Lucien said. He smoothed his hand over her forehead. "While my parents lived a long life, my sister died when she was two of influenza. I miss them, but don't be sad for their loss. I don't like it when you're sad."

She nodded but couldn't help feeling sorry. Here she was with family coming out of the woodwork. All Lucien and Ranulf really had were each other.

Now more than ever, she was happy she hadn't chosen one or the other and broken up their friendship. She still felt like she was coming between them though.

She couldn't brood over it for long because of Lucien and Ranulf's ministrations. She made a sound of appreciation and wiggled a little. "That feels wonderful."

In a normal situation, one or both men would have taken advantage of her position. It didn't seem like Lucien or Ranulf were going to try anything. They both kept their hands firmly situated on the lower part of her extremities.

That annoyed her a little. She wouldn't mind if they did try something. She liked when they touched her.

"I think we're spoiling you," Ranulf said.

Lucien said, "There is no think about it. We are spoiling her."

"Call it what you want. Just don't stop."

She shifted again and pulled Lucien down for a kiss. He obliged her and even traced the outline of her jaw with his finger, but that was it.

Thinking he just needed a little coaxing, she smoothed her fingers up the inside of his thigh. He sucked in a breath and grabbed her hand. She smiled against his lips and tried to free her hand.

"Stop, Eris," Lucien whispered, tightening his grip.

"Why?"

Ranulf said, "I might get jealous."

She smiled at him over her shoulder as she slipped her foot between his legs. "That better?"

Like Lucien, Ranulf caught her foot and held it so she couldn't move.

"You're not making it easy to keep this relationship a celibate one," Lucien said.

"I'm not trying to make it easy." She freed her hand from him then trailed her fingers over the very noticeable bulge in his pants. It jumped beneath her fingers. "I'm trying to make it hard. Very hard."

She was about to undo his zipper when Lucien unseated her and jumped off the couch. He paced to the far end of the room, breathing hard and shoving his hand over and over his head.

"Lucien?" She watched him with concern.

Ranulf stood as well.

Her gaze switched to him. "Ranulf?"

Lucien rasped, "You could tempt a saint, woman."

"You're not a saint." She got off the couch and went to him.

He kept her at arm's length when she would have hugged him. "You said you wanted to wait."

"There are a lot of things we can do while we're waiting. Those things might even convince me to change my mind."

"You can't take us both," Ranulf said. "We still haven't decided who will be your first."

"Shouldn't that be my decision?" she asked.

"Choose then."

"Right now?"

Both men nodded.

She wanted their relationship to progress, but she hadn't thought they'd put her on the spot. All things told, she pretty much put herself there.

Lucien asked, "Well?"

"I…" She looked at Lucien and then at Ranulf.

"You can't, can you?" Ranulf said, crossing his arms.

She rolled her eyes with an annoyed sound. "Fine. Then you two decide."

"We can't," they said in unison.

"This is stupid." She dug through her pockets. "I'll just flip a coin."

"How romantic of you." Ranulf winked at her when she glared at him.

Lucien touched her shoulder, and she faced him. "Why the sudden urge to do this now when you denied us so adamantly last night? And even denied yourself for so long before us?"

"I never said I denied myself. I may be a virgin, but that's only a technicality since masturbation doesn't count."

She thought her words would shock them, but they showed no reaction. Lucien watched her with an expectant look.

"It's different with you." She looked back at Ranulf. "Both of you. I always said I would never be part of a polyamorous relationship and here I am." She faced Lucien. "Everything is different now. All my other relationships always felt awkward and forced. This feels right, and I want more."

Her words should have made them happy. Or at least gotten a response with similar sentiments.

She waited three more breaths for one of them to say something. When they remained silent, she asked, "Why does it feel like you're pushing me away?"

"We're not," Lucien said.

"Then what is this?"

Ranulf asked, "Is it so strange that we want to wait?"

She laughed. "A willing woman and men who want to wait. That has to be one of the signs of the coming apocalypse." She searched Lucien's eyes for some sign of what he was thinking. "You don't want to, do you?"

"Want?" Lucien grabbed her to him.

Ranulf said his name in that tone of warning again, but Lucien ignored him. He shoved his mouth against Eris's.

The force of the kiss and the urgency behind it scared her just a little. She tried to pull away for a little breather, but Lucien's hold only tightened.

He pushed his hand under her shirt and cupped her breast. His other hand went to the front of her jeans.

"Lucien!" Ranulf yanked Eris back and warded Lucien off with an outstretched hand.

Eris couldn't help moving closer to Ranulf. She hugged his arm, and he shifted so his body shielded her more.

Lucien had a wild look in his eyes, but he made no move to get to her. With a growl, he turned his back to her. He rasped, "Want has nothing to do with it. You aren't ready."

"Lucien, I—"

"Please don't." He glanced at her. With a shake of his head, he switched his gaze to Ranulf. "Thank you for stopping me."

Ranulf nodded.

Eris felt like there was more going on than just her close call. She wanted to ask, but there was a thread of tension running between all of them.

Lucien straightened. "I have something I must do," he said in a voice that was a little deeper than his usual. He walked away without another word.

Eris attributed that to the emotional scene. She looked up at Ranulf. He didn't return her gaze until Lucien had left the room.

Ranulf said, "You're playing with fire when you tempt us."

"Whose fault is that?"

He laughed, but it was strained. "Granted, but seriously, Eris, it's best if we wait. I know it seems like we're putting you off, but we aren't. We only want to make sure you're ready."

"Avoiding the issue and holding back won't make me ready."

"Rushing into it won't either."

"Is this a catch twenty-two or a Charybdis and Scylla situation?"

He looked at her. Real amusement returned to his eyes. "With us it's both." He pressed a chaste kiss to her lips. "Just let us stall for the time being."

"You know, there are a lot of things you two can do that don't involve full intercourse."

He hugged her. "You just don't know when to quit."

"Or I could do some things to you two." She trailed her fingers between their bodies.

Ranulf grunted and squeezed her. "Lucien isn't here to stop me."

"And?" She smiled up at him, still caressing her fingers over the zipper of his jeans.

"And unless you want to be walking funny tomorrow or at all, I'd stop if I were you."

There was a genuine threat in his words. She kept her smile in place even as she stopped teasing him and stepped back. "I'm not going to let you two keep dodging this issue. We're in a relationship, right?"

"We are." He drew her near, took her hand, and shoved it into his pants.

She looked up at him with wide eyes as he curled her fingers around his length. "Ranulf?"

"This quite eager and hungry fellow wants very badly to be buried in that cute, round ass of yours." His free hand squeezed her behind.

"I...I don't think it'll fit." She wet her lips at the thought of him trying.

He pulled her hand free with a shuddering breath. "When you think it will, let me know, and we'll move forward." He kissed her pouting lips. "Do you think that's fair?"

She grinned at him. "Not in the least. That's all mine, and the women of the world are weeping and gnashing their teeth in envy."

Ranulf laughed. He kissed her fingers and then pulled her to him for a deep kiss. Only when she was panting did he pull back. "You are a little imp who doesn't know her place."

"Oh, I know my place. It's between you and Lucien." She glanced down. "But, I think I need some preparation."

"Just say the word. I have a wide and varied assortment of toys that could help you. It would give me a perverse sense of joy to think of you wearing one while working. I have a vibrating one with a remote that works over one hundred yards away." He wiggled his eyebrows at her. "That could be fun."

She pulled out of his arms. "Oh no you don't. You aren't making me into your own personal toy."

"I'm not? I thought that's what you wanted."

She backed away, and he followed her. "I think I'll be going to bed now."

"No. I think we need to talk about this."

"I've decided you two were right. We should totally wait." She walked away quickly, grinning the whole way.

Ranulf chased her. "And I've decided you were right. We should prepare you for the coming intimacy."

It wasn't long before they were running through the house. Eris sprinted up the stairs, laughing the whole way. She entered her bedroom, slammed the door shut, and then waited.

"Eris," Ranulf said in a sing-song. He tapped at the door.

"Nobody here by that name. Would you like to leave a message?"

"Ah, well if you see her, tell her Ranulf has two or three toys he thinks she might make use of."

"Good night."

"Spoilsport."

She listened to his retreating steps and his laughter. After a moment, she opened the door and peered down the hall toward Ranulf's room. He stood in the doorway waving a rope of beads at her.

"Oh my God, you pervert. Put that away," she said, pointing at him.

He ducked back into his room and came back with a black something-or-other that looked like a giant rubber stopper. "Would you prefer this one?"

"Where are you...why do you have that stuff?"

"Prototypes from my adult toy company." He waved the stopper at her. "You know you want to."

"You own an adult toy company?"

"One of my most lucrative and innovative companies. I have several samples if you want to try them out. I would, of course, have to watch so I could take notes for the development department." He wiggled his eyebrows. "Camera's all ready. Just say when."

She slammed her door.

"Another time then," Ranulf yelled.

She opened her door long enough to yell, "Go to bed, you sexual deviant."

"*Your* sexual deviant. Just remember that." He laughed again. "Next time then."

His door clicked closed. Eris shook her head. She didn't know how the situation had dissolved into an adult toy showcase, but the whole thing was incredibly funny.

Funny, but still pertinent. Somehow it had slipped her mind how the act of being with both men would actually play out. There needed to be preparation and lots of lube.

She looked down at her hand.

Lots and lots of lube.

"That should be a crime," she whispered.

Chapter Twenty-four

"The grapevine is curious," Clayton said, hanging over Eris's desk.

She staunchly ignored him. If Ranulf or Lucien were there, he wouldn't even think of coming near her. They had retreated to their office to work after lunch with the excuse that she distracted them. Like that was her fault.

"Don't you want to know what they are curious about?"

"Couldn't care less," she bit out as she switched to a new comic.

"They are wondering who that hottie from yesterday was? Friend of yours?"

Eris stopped typing and looked at him. "You aren't serious."

"Hell yeah I am."

She returned to her work. "That was my younger sister, and she's married and those kids were hers."

"Oh." Clayton straightened from her desk. "I thought she was someone Lucien and Ranulf knew."

"Obviously thinking isn't something you're good at. You should stop while you're ahead."

Her cell ringing cut off whatever Clayton would have said next. She flipped it open, ignoring him, and said, "This is Eris."

"Ah, sweetie, I need you to come over."

"Huh? Mother? Why? What's wrong?"

Her phone beeped. She looked at the caller ID and nearly dropped the phone.

"Hold on a sec, Mother." She clicked through the other call. "This is Eris."

Mariko fired off in rapid Japanese that Eris could barely follow. Eris tried to get a word in but the woman didn't slow down.

"Wait…I…slow…"

"You better fix it before I get home," Mariko snapped in English and then hung up.

Eris clicked back to her original call. "Mother, what did you do?"

"What makes you think I did anything?"

"Alphie just called my cell and yelled at me in Japanese. She was talking so fast I couldn't get a word in. What did you do?"

"Oh, I knew I shouldn't have called her first."

"What. Did. You. Do?"

The woman sighed. "The computer—"

"Oh God."

"What? I was checking my email just like your father showed me and then poof."

"Poof? What poof? Computers don't poof. What did you do?" As she spoke, Eris started gathering her belongings and shutting down her computer. It didn't matter what her mother had done, Eris would need to get home before Mariko or all hell would break loose.

"It's probably nothing," her mother said.

"I doubt that."

"What do I do to fix it before Mariko gets home?"

"Nothing. *You* don't touch it. I will be there as fast as I can. You hear me? Don't touch it!"

"Fine. Fine. I won't touch it. But you could probably just tell me—"

"No touch!" Eris snapped her phone shut and ran toward the door. "Family emergency. I'll be back in a few hours."

No one said anything because she didn't give them time. She checked her phone.

Mariko had called from the office. If Eris hurried, she could probably beat Mariko to the house by twenty minutes. Maybe thirty. That should be enough time to fix whatever her mother had done and avert disaster.

She just had to let Lucien and Ranulf know she was leaving and would be back as soon as she could.

The office door was cracked.

"We can't keep doing this. You saw what almost happened yesterday. Every day we're with Eris it gets harder. And what about when she returns?" Lucien asked in a rough voice.

Eris stopped with her hand on the knob. She? What she? They weren't talking about her. She hadn't gone anywhere.

Ranulf said in hushed tones Eris strained to hear, "Stop thinking about it. Eris is here now. That's all that matters."

"No, it isn't. You're a fool to think otherwise. Everything will change when she comes back. You know that as well as I do."

"What do you want to do? Do you want to tell her?"

"We can't. She wouldn't understand."

"Well?"

Lucien heaved a long, annoyed sigh. "Fine. You're right, as usual. We'll worry about it when it happens."

Every part of her wanted to burst in the room and demand to know what they were talking about. Every part except the scared part. She backed away quietly.

Whatever it was, she didn't want to know. Not right that moment. It was cowardly, but she didn't want to find out what they were keeping from her and then end up losing them.

She walked quickly to the front door. First, she had to save the family computer from her mother, and then she'd worry about Ranulf and Lucien and their secret.

"Eris? Where are you headed?" Ranulf called.

She didn't stop walking or even look at him when he caught up with her. "I have to leave for a little bit. My Mommy called with an emergency."

"Nothing serious, I hope."

"No. She's just trying to kill the computer and I have to stop her. I'll be back in a few hours." She wanted to get away from him and think about what she'd heard.

"I'll come with you then."

She stopped and looked up at him. "Excuse me?"

"I want to meet her. This is as good a time as any."

Lucien joined them. "Good time for what?" He looked between them.

Eris couldn't believe how they were acting like nothing was wrong. They both smiled and joked. She wanted to scream at them. Instead, she said, "Nothing. I'll be back."

Ranulf caught her arm before she could walk away. "Eris, is something wrong? You seem angry."

What are you hiding from me?

Who is this other woman you were talking about a moment ago?

When is she coming back?

They were all questions she wanted to yell. Looking into Ranulf's eyes, she couldn't utter one of them. She took a breath and shook her head. "It's nothing. I'm just distracted."

He cupped her cheek, and she stopped herself from pulling away. "If you don't want me—"

"Us," Lucien corrected.

"—to go, then we won't."

She shook her head. "No, it's not that. You can come. I'm sure she'd love to meet you."

What was she thinking? She didn't want them meeting her family if they would be dumping her soon. And what about last night and all that talk about being prepared?

"Eris?" Ranulf leaned into her.

She turned away quickly and headed out the door. "If you're coming then you need to move it. I have to beat Alphie home and fix whatever My Mommy broke."

Lucien said, "I think I'm looking forward to meeting Alphie the most."

They piled into Eris's car. She left black skid marks in her wake.

"In a hurry?" Ranulf laughed as he grabbed the door handle.

"You don't understand. My Mommy has already nuked five computers—the fifth one was literally. We're still not sure what she did, but the stupid thing caught fire. Mariko swore to open the gates of hell if My Mommy destroyed another computer."

Eris checked her watch and wove around the cars that were going too slow. She kept watch in her mirror for cops. Hopefully, they were all taking a break or elsewhere.

Lucien said, "It's hard to believe your mother is so bad with computers when you're practically a programmer."

"It was a trade off. I got computers. She got cooking."

"You can't cook?"

"Not if you want to live to see tomorrow."

Both men laughed.

"I'm not joking. I'm to cooking what My Mommy is to computers. Daddy and My Mommy actually banned me from all things cooking for the betterment of all mankind."

"That doesn't sound like you," Ranulf said.

"I'm usually pretty good at everything I put my mind to. But, in matters dealing with the kitchen, I tend to live up to my name."

"I've always wondered why your parents named you chaos," Lucien said.

She glanced back at him in the rearview mirror. He grinned at her.

His words of earlier filtered through her brain. Why was he acting like this would last? For that matter, why was she too chicken to actually ask that question aloud?

She said, "Alphie did it. According to the parents and Benkei, My Mommy was a walking disaster before she became pregnant with me. That's how she and Daddy met. She was in his shop for a bridesmaid dress fitting, tripped over a fixture, and nearly pulled down the entire window display on her head. Daddy saved her."

Ranulf said, "Kismet."

"The beginning of the end, you mean. My Mommy is extremely accident-prone unless she's in the kitchen or around me. No one understands it. In the kitchen, she is poetry in motion and everything she makes is fantastic. And from her pregnancy until the moment I left for college, she never had another accident. One hour—literally one hour—after I was out the door, she fell down a ditch and broke her arm."

That memory made her laugh despite the apprehension she felt. She shook her head. "According to Daddy, the second I was born the hospital had a black out. The backup generators took a little bit to start. In that time, the doctor managed to knock himself out, the attending nurse tripped over something and broke her nose, and several of the machines burned out all at once."

"Quite a welcome you got there," Lucien said.

"No joke. Alphie thought it was prophetic. She had the baby registry people put Chaos on my birth certificate since she figured I would be a clone of my mother. Daddy wanted to change it, but My Mommy decided she liked it and just changed it to something more feminine sounding, hence Eris."

Ranulf said, "I know I haven't been bored since you came into our lives."

"Likewise," Lucien said.

Eris stared straight ahead. They were almost at her parents' house. She'd rush in, fix the computer, and then get them all back to the mansion where they could go their separate ways.

Why had she let them come with her? It was stupid. Every thought led her back to the earlier conversation and what it meant for them.

She sighed.

* * * *

If Ranulf heard Eris sigh one more time, he was going to make her pull the car over and talk to them.

He said, "Eris, you are completely distracted, and I think it's more than just the problem with the family computer. What's bothering you?"

"Nothing."

Lucien said, "It's not nothing. What—"

Lucien's words were cut off when Eris slammed on the brakes. The car fish-tailed a little, but she didn't seem to notice. She stared out of the windshield with wide eyes. She even blinked a few times like that would change what she was seeing.

"Eris?" Lucien and Ranulf asked in unison.

"It can't be," she whispered.

Ranulf followed her gaze. A man, who couldn't be more than a few years older than Eris, stood in the open doorway of a nearby house talking to an older woman. The man looked over his shoulder when the woman gestured at the car. He waved in a grand manner with his arm over his head.

Eris threw open her car door, jumped out, and ran toward the pair. "Benkei!"

She jumped on the man, hugging him with her arms and legs. Ranulf instantly wanted to break every bone in the man's body. It took a moment for the man's name to filter through the haze of his blind jealous rage.

Benkei.

Eris's brother.

"Shit!" Lucien grabbed the steering wheel as the car started rolling forward without a driver to control it.

Ranulf jumped out of the backseat, got in the driver's seat and aimed the car for the driveway. All the while, he listened to the conversation between brother and sister.

Benkei said, "Hey, brat. Long time no see."

"Long time? Long time! It's been five years," Eris yelled. She half strangled him as she hugged him tight.

He made choking noises and laughed at the same time. "I missed you too."

The woman beside them asked, "Eris-sweets, who is that parking your car, which you left in the middle of the road?"

Eris looked at the woman and then looked at her car. Ranulf pulled it into the driveway and shut off the engine. She disengaged herself from Benkei and walked over to the car.

"Sorry. Sorry. That was rude."

Ranulf exited the car and said with a pout, "You never jump on me like that."

"Disappear for five years then." Benkei leaned on Eris as he held out his hand to Ranulf. "Nice to meet you. I'm Benkei, Eris's older brother."

"Ranulf, her boyfriend." He clasped Benkei's hand then almost dropped it. Ranulf knew the man felt the same thing he did and at the same time because Benkei looked as shocked as he felt. They stared at each other. "Nice to meet you," Ranulf whispered.

Benkei nodded in a mechanical fashion.

Lucien took Benkei's hand before Ranulf could figure out a way to warn him. He had a similar reaction but managed to keep his cool. "Lucien, the other boyfriend."

Ranulf met Lucien's gaze when the man looked at him. That was one hell of a surprise. First Kaylie and her children and then Eris's brother.

Benkei ruffled Eris's hair. She made an annoyed sound and pushed him away. He said, "Glad she finally found someone to put up with her." He thumped her on the head. "Though it was supposed to be *one* someone, not *two*."

"Oh, leave her alone. Love is love no matter what the number of participants." The woman who'd been speaking with Benkei joined the group.

Eris got away from Benkei and held out a hand to the woman. "Lucien, Ranulf, this is Cherish Brue. My Mommy."

Ranulf held his hand out to her, prepared for another surprise.

Cherish walked around the car and grabbed him in a big hug. "Don't be rude, young man. Hugs are a requisite in this family."

"Only for you, My Mommy," Benkei said.

"Hush," she snapped over her shoulder.

Ranulf returned her hug. Nothing weird came off the woman. He was thankful for that.

She squeezed him one last time and then went and hugged Lucien. "It's so good to finally meet you two. Gordon has bitched nonstop about nothing else since the movie premiere. Always whining about Eris not wanting to bring you two over."

"I would have gladly come if I had known," Lucien said, looking at Eris.

She rolled her eyes. "Daddy was insisting on Sunday dinner. No way in hell."

"What's wrong with Sunday dinner?" Ranulf asked.

Benkei snorted. "You like being naked?"

"Excuse me?"

"Brue house rules—if you're here on Sunday then you are naked. It's a family tradition that goes back to Big Daddy. Eris told you about Big Daddy, right?"

Ranulf and Lucien nodded.

"Well, Sunday is God's day and Big Daddy said we should be the way God intended us to be on his day."

"Naked?"

Eris, Benkei, and Cherish nodded.

Cherish added, "But only if you're in the house. Gordon added that stipulation since he didn't like his women parading around for the world to see."

"And Mr. Brue wanted us here for Sunday dinner?" Ranulf found the whole idea amusing. He looked at Eris who looked completely embarrassed.

"You can tell a lot about a man when he's naked." A man Ranulf assumed was Gordon Brue exited the house. He held his hand out to Lucien, "I'm Gordon."

"Lucien."

The handshake switched to Ranulf. "Nice to meet you. I'm Ranulf."

Nothing strange came from Gordon either.

"I have a bone to pick with you two," Gordon said.

"Oh, Daddy, don't start," Eris whined.

"Yes, Gordon. Leave it alone already. It's over and done with," Cherish said in a tone that matched her daughter's.

"If they are going to accompany my daughter who is wearing clothes I designed and made, they will not trash those clothes by wearing mismatching outfits."

"Mismatching?" Lucien asked.

Eris spoke over her father, "Where's the computer? Alphie will be home any minute. I need to fix it before she gets here."

Cherish laughed and pinched Eris's cheek. "There's nothing wrong with the computer. You know I don't like messing with that infernal machine. I let your father handle all that stuff."

"But you said…" Eris sagged. "You said that to get me out here, didn't you?"

"Can you think of a better way to get you out here so quickly?"

Eris pointed at Benkei. "You could have just said Benkei was home after five years. That would have done it. I might have even gotten here quicker. I also wouldn't have been yelled at by Alphie."

"But this way was more fun." Cherish tilted her head to the side with a cute smile. "Besides, I love getting Mariko's blood pressure up. She's such a cold fish all the time. A little excitement every now and then does her good."

Ranulf couldn't stop himself from saying, "You remind me of one of my business associates. She loves setting people off too."

Cherish shrugged. "We all need a hobby."

"Funny. She says the same thing." He smiled when Cherish laughed. When he looked at Eris to judge her reaction to how well he got along with her mother, his smile faded. She looked haunted again.

What was wrong? It couldn't be something he or Lucien had done. They had barely spoken all morning. But, something was bothering Eris in a big way.

"Good. Kaylie is here, and she brought my babies," Cherish said.

Everyone turned toward the minivan that parked at the curb.

Kaylie got out of the front passenger seat and yelled, "I don't want to talk about it anymore. Drop it before I drop you." She slammed the door and stalked up the driveway. "Hi, Benkei," she snapped.

"Hey." Benkei looked a little surprised.

"Where's Last Mommy?"

"Taking a nap. Go wake her lazy ass up. Mariko should be home soon, and lunch is almost ready," Cherish said.

Kaylie nodded sharply and went into the house.

"Yikes," Benkei said in Kaylie's wake. "What did I miss?"

Eris said, "If it's what I think, don't even ask." She looked at the rest of the people piling out of the car.

They all looked a little drawn and tense to Ranulf's eyes.

"The redhead with his hair in a ponytail is Paul. The other redhead is Stephen, his identical twin. And the one with black hair is Marcos, their cousin by marriage," Eris said. "You already met the kids."

Ranulf and Lucien nodded.

Marcos carried Olivia away from the car while Paul and Stephen attended to Emil and David. Even across the distance of the front porch to the curb Ranulf could feel it—Marcos's power. Very like the children's and Kaylie's powers but much older and powerful. Seeing Marcos explained away Olivia, who had to be a quickening of the bloodlines for a very ancient race that had mixed with humans a little too long.

Ranulf looked at Lucien. The man shrugged with a small shake of his head. Ranulf agreed with the sentiment. They had fallen in love with a woman that had a very unique family.

Minnie jumped out of the van and ran to Ranulf. She grabbed his hand and smiled up at him. "Hello, Mr. Ranulf."

Ranulf gave the little girl's hand a squeeze. "Hello, Minnie. How are you?"

"I'm good. You?"

"The same."

She smiled wider.

"What the hell? What about me?" Benkei snapped.

Minnie stuck her tongue out at him and moved closer to Ranulf.

"Oh, I see how it is." Benkei grabbed Eris. "Then I'm taking Eris."

"Mommy!" Minnie dropped Ranulf's hand and ran to Benkei and Eris.

Benkei fended her off with one hand and held Eris back. "Oh no you don't. You wanted Ranulf. Go for it. That means Eris is mine."

"That's not fair," Minnie yelled.

"Welcome to life." Benkei stuck his tongue out at her.

Cherish shook her head at the two. "Children, let's behave while we're in public and the neighbors can see us."

The roar of a motorcycle engine drowned out all conversation. All eyes turned to the driveway as a sports bike carrying two riders pulled up.

"Looks like my last born is here, but what's that he's dragging in with him?" Gordon asked.

Ranulf didn't need a handshake to feel the power radiating off of the motorcycle operator. His rider dismounted, ripped off his helmet, and ran to Benkei.

"Ben-ben!"

Like Eris, the boy jumped on Benkei and hugged him tight. Benkei returned the boy's hug and affection.

Eris said, "That would be Declan."

"I'd guessed as much," Lucien said.

The man still sitting on the motorcycle slipped off his helmet. A cascade of silver hair flowed down his back. Eris gasped, and the man winked at her.

"Deckie-honey, who is that?" Cherish asked.

Declan beckoned to his friend. When the man joined him, he said, "This is Jarl."

"About time you brought home a sugar daddy who doesn't look like he's about to drop dead," Gordon grumbled, holding out his hand.

"Nice to meet you, sir," Jarl said as he shook Gordon's hand.

Cherish pushed Gordon aside and hugged Jarl the way she had Ranulf and Lucien before. The man didn't hesitate in hugging her back. He even kissed her neck. She pulled away with a surprised squeak. "Fresh."

"I couldn't help it. Beautiful women make me want to kiss them," Jarl said with a wink.

Gordon pulled Cherish behind him. "Yeah, and this beautiful woman is taken. Get your own."

"I did, but she didn't want to come." Jarl grinned as his gaze sidled over to Ranulf and Lucien. "I'm glad I did though." He held out his hand to them.

Ranulf debated not shaking his hand, but decided he couldn't avoid it without seeming strange. He shielded himself the best he could before taking the man's hand. That didn't stop Jarl from testing the shield.

"Nice to meet you," Ranulf gritted out between his teeth, tightening his grip as a warning.

"Likewise." Jarl winked. "This should be interesting."

Ranulf knew the gathering would be more than interesting if Jarl didn't watch himself.

Chapter Twenty-five

Lucien looked at all of the people milling before the house. "It's getting crowded."

Cherish said, "Yes it is. Let's take this inside. Mariko should be here soon." She herded everyone into the house. "Benkei, go check on the meat."

"I was cooking the meat," Gordon said.

"Like I said, *Benkei*, go check on the meat. Gordon, you go talk to that daughter of yours and tell her not to ruin my family reunion." Cherish gave her husband a warning look when he would have talked back.

Gordon grumbled something under his breath as he went up the stairs.

Benkei headed for the back of the house. "Yo, Ranulf, Lucien, why don't you join me for some man time?"

Eris grabbed Lucien and Ranulf before they could follow. "Not going to happen."

"Don't get your panties in a bunch. I'm not going to do anything to them." He grinned at her. "Except warn them to run while they can." He cackled in an exaggerated manner.

Lucien patted Eris's hand. "I want to hear what he has to say. I promise he won't run us off."

She looked like she would argue but released them. "I'll be in the family room with the kids."

He nodded and followed Benkei through the house and out of the back door.

Lucien thought it would just be him, Ranulf and Benkei, but they had two additions.

Jarl grinned at them. "I want to play too."

Minnie grabbed Ranulf's hand once more with a defiant look.

Benkei pointed the barbeque tongs at her. "Get your little ass back in the house before I serve you to everyone."

"You don't scare me," Minnie said, moving closer to Ranulf.

"Do I?" Jarl asked. When Minnie looked at him, his face split into a ghoulish grin of sharp teeth and a serpentine tongue.

The little girl screamed and ran back to the house.

Benkei shook his head. "Why did you do that?"

"Don't worry. She won't be able to tell anyone about it." Jarl looked between them. "I'm more interested in finding out what I've married into, as it were."

"Likewise," Ranulf said.

Benkei pointed to his chest. "I'm a *shinigami*." He pointed to Jarl. "You're a demon." He gestured to Ranulf and Lucien. "And you two are…complicated." His joking façade dropped. "That explains a lot though. I always wondered why Thanus sent me."

"Sent you?" Ranulf asked.

"Did Eris tell you about her accident?"

"We've heard."

Benkei held out his hand. "You want to see it?"

Lucien didn't want to see it, but morbid curiosity compelled him to take Benkei's hand. Ranulf put his hand over both of theirs. Jarl cupped his hand around the bottom. It was an intrusion, but one Lucien couldn't dismiss without raising a fuss that the house and neighbors might hear.

The backyard faded from view, and they were hovering over a car wreck. Two SUVs had a compact car sandwiched between them like a crushed soda can. There was no way the person inside the compact could have survived. But, Eris lay on a stretcher beside the wreck with paramedics checking her.

Benkei's voice filtered into the scene from far away. "This is what it looked like before I stepped in and fixed it."

The scene changed.

Suddenly the crushed compact had a body inside it. That body was Eris. She half hanged out of the windshield with blood seeping from several wounds. Fluids from the car mingled with her blood on the ground around the car.

Lucien jerked away. "Enough," he rasped.

Ranulf nodded in a jerky manner. "I agree," he whispered, releasing Benkei as well.

"Thanus could have chosen any of his *shinigami* to attend that scene and fix it so she survived. He sent me because she's my sister. Even if I weren't allowed to save her, I would have still wanted to be with her in her last moments. At first, I thought that was why he'd called me." Benkei shook his head. "It surprised the hell out of me when he told me to save her. I never knew *why* he sent anyone at all until now." Benkei looked at them both in turn. "What's going on?"

"Nothing detrimental, I assure you," Ranulf said. "We simply wish to be with her."

"Please. Nothing with *them* is simple."

Lucien said, "I agree. The same could be said for this family. I thought Kaylie was a fluke, but you and…" He trailed off and glanced at Jarl.

Benkei nodded. "Yeah. We're a weird lot, it seems. I didn't know about Kaylie until after I bit it and became a *shinigami*. Weird to think she and her mom were keeping that secret all of this time."

"When did you die?" Jarl asked.

"Six years ago while in the Middle East. My whole unit was taken out in a sneak attack. It was a massacre that no one survived. My last thoughts were of how devastated everyone would be when they got the news. Thanus reached out and brought back me and two others. He gave us the choice of serving him or remaining dead." Benkei shrugged. "To the world at large and my family, I'm some PTSD-stricken army dude who couldn't suck it up and deal so he resigned his army commission and went into private security."

Lucien shook his head. "Eris doesn't think that about you. Whenever she speaks of you, it's with love."

Ranulf nodded in agreement.

Benkei smiled a little. "I don't regret my decision. I met Mary, my wife, because of it. She's the *shinigami* who trained me. She's also the reason I've been away from home for the last five years. She and Alphie don't get along."

Jarl asked, "Oh? A little mother-in-law-that-hates-her-son's-wife situation going on?"

"Something like that. Mary is Chinese." Benkei shook his head. "It was the old Japanese-Chinese rivalry all over again. Alphie flipped out when she saw Mary, which is hilarious since it's Mary who should have been pissed. I never told her my mother is Japanese since I knew about her past. Mary had been killed by Japanese soldiers during World War Two after they had raped her repeatedly."

"Harsh," Jarl said.

"I told Alphie she needed to get over it or she would never see me again." Benkei gestured to the yard. "Five years later, I'm here to test the waters. I'm going to be around for a while. I don't want to waste the little time I have with my mother being pissed with her."

"Understandably," Lucien said.

"At times like these, immortality sucks," Jarl said. He turned back to the house. "Well, I need to see what my bitch is up to."

"What did you say?" Benkei snapped.

"You heard me, deathling. Declan is my bitch, and he'll admit it in front of all of you if I ask him." Jarl's grin turned menacing. "I'll leave his ass here if he doesn't."

"Man, don't start that shit here. Not in front of our parents and the kids."

"As you wish, this time." Jarl gave them a mock salute and re-entered the house.

"Fucking demons get on my damn nerves," Benkei said under his breath.

"The angels aren't much better," Ranulf said.

"Same thing," Lucien said.

All three men nodded.

Benkei faced them with a somber look. "Just tell me whatever this is, it won't hurt Eris. I didn't save her to be worked over."

Lucien felt the all too familiar feeling of slipping out of his body.

I handle this, a voice said inside Lucien's mind.

Lucien did the mental equivalent of stepping back with his hands up. He watched as an outside observer as his body straightened, lifting his chin up several notches. In a deep voice not his own, he said, "You know better, *shinigami*."

Benkei's eyes widened before he ducked his head. "Sorry, sir. I meant no disrespect."

"She's your sister. Your concern is understandable. Know that your worries are unnecessary."

Benkei nodded quickly.

"Good."

Thank you, Lucien. I intrude no further in this matter.

Lucien felt control of his body returning to him. As always with the transfer, he sagged with a little sigh. It was an involuntary action that he and Ranulf both did, as though their bodies were relieved that they were in control again.

Ranulf said with a raised eyebrow, "That's not like him."

"Let's hope he doesn't do it again," Lucien bit out. He gave himself a shake, mentally and physically. "It wasn't even my turn this time."

"Is the meat ready yet?" Eris called from the house. "We're hungry."

"Coming," Benkei yelled back.

"Benkei!"

The high-pitched scream made all three men face the house. A tall Japanese woman sprinted toward Benkei with her arms out.

Ranulf and Lucien moved out of her way.

She hugged Benkei tight, saying his name over and over.

Lucien jerked his head toward the house. Ranulf nodded, and they walked away.

Mother and son had some things to work out. Lunch would have to wait a little bit.

They joined Eris at the door. She looked up at them expectantly.

Lucien pulled her close and kissed her lips. He then released her so Ranulf could do the same.

Behind them, the kids made grossed out noises.

Gordon snapped, "What are you three doing in front of these impressionable children?"

"Nothing, Daddy," Eris said.

"It better stay that way." He shot all three of them a warning look.

Kaylie came up beside the man and held out Olivia. "Look, Daddy, a baby."

Gordon took Olivia and fawned over her as he walked away.

"I owe you," Eris said.

"Nah, I owed you. Thanks for looking after the kids." Kaylie looked at Lucien and Ranulf as well. "Sorry for dumping them on you without warning."

"No problem. They are good kids."

Kaylie chuckled as she moved closer to Ranulf. "Watch out. Minnie has a crush on you. All she talks about is you and how she's going to visit Eris all the time just to see you."

"Used to be a time she just wanted to visit me," Eris grumbled. "My baby is growing up and discovering boys."

"Now if we could keep her from beating them to death, life would be happy."

Eris hugged her sister's shoulders. "How's the situation?"

"I'm going to talk to Alphie after dinner."

"Good. Then I won't mention it again."

Kaylie nodded and went back to the living room and her children.

Lucien placed a hand on Eris's shoulder. She looked up at him. He noticed her haunted look despite responding to his kiss only moments ago. "What's wrong with you today? I'd think you'd be happy to see your brother after so long apart."

"He told you about Mary and Alphie's falling out?" she asked.

"Yes."

"I am happy to see him. It's just…" She shook her head. "It's nothing."

"That's the same thing you said before we started dating," Ranulf said. "Your nothing turned out to be something. What is it?"

"*Now* really isn't the time."

"Granted. We'll talk when we get home. Okay? No dodging." Lucien made her look at up at him. "I mean it."

"I should say the same to you."

"What does that mean?"

Eris pulled away from him and went into the living room.

Lucien looked at Ranulf who shook his head. "What happened after I left last night?"

Ranulf shrugged. "She was fine. This is something new."

"We're getting to the bottom of this as soon as we get home." Lucien wouldn't let Eris put them off. Something had her upset. He'd only seen her look at him with an expression of betrayal one time before. That time was justified. He hadn't done anything for Eris to give him that look now.

Chapter Twenty-six

Eris put the car in park and looked at the garage light. The sun had set hours ago. Everyone had long since gone home. "They are never going to let me live this down. They are going to say I ditched work to go on a date."

"You had no way of knowing your mother wouldn't let us leave after eating," Ranulf said.

"I should have guessed. My Mommy is notorious for her hostage-taking abilities." Eris sighed. "I wish she had just told me Benkei was home. I would have come out. Seeing him after so long made my year, and it's only just started."

"Yes. Except for our presence, you seemed completely happy and at ease," Lucien said.

She stiffened.

"We need to talk." Lucien exited the car, walked around, and opened the driver's side door.

"It can wait. I didn't think we'd be there for so long." She pulled on the door, but Lucien wouldn't release it.

"Now."

She finally looked up at him. There was no arguing with the stern look on his face. She got out of the car but didn't move away from it. Folding her arms across her chest to keep her hands warm, she faced Lucien and Ranulf. "Well?"

"Inside." Lucien gestured to the house.

"We can talk here."

"No, we can't." He grabbed her upper arm and propelled her toward the house. "I don't know what happened, but you're not getting out of explaining your attitude over the last few hours."

"My attitude doesn't need explaining." She tried to jerk out of his grasp, but his hold stayed firm. "Stop man-handling me like I'm some kid."

"Stop acting like a child and I will," Lucien snapped.

Ranulf held the door for them and then closed it after they passed. He eased her out of her jacket though she tried to keep it.

Lucien asked, "What is wrong with you? Why are you mad at us?"

"Or is it only one of us?" Ranulf asked, looking pointedly at Lucien.

"What's that look mean? I haven't spoken to her since last night." Lucien stabbed his finger in Ranulf's direction. "You're the one I should be questioning. What did you do after I left?"

Ranulf shrugged. "A little joking around. Nothing for Eris to be mad about."

"I'll bet."

"I'm standing right here," Eris snapped. Both men looked at her. She put her hands on her hips and glared at them.

"We are listening," Lucien said.

Ranulf crossed his arms.

Eris looked between them. They didn't act guilty. Maybe she'd misunderstood and took the conversation out of context.

But what other context could there be? Lucien and Ranulf had clearly been fighting over telling her something important.

She sighed and let her hands drop to her sides.

"Well?" Ranulf asked.

The words wouldn't come. She didn't want to ask. Some part of her knew the answer, if they gave her one, would change everything.

"Eris? What happened?" Lucien reached for her.

She let him hug her.

He said, "I don't like seeing you this upset and not knowing the reason why."

If she said it, everything would shatter. She didn't want to lose Lucien's warmth.

She gripped his sides.

In response, Lucien's hold tightened. "What's wrong?" he whispered.

"I don't want to lose you," she said.

"The only one you have to worry about losing is Ranulf to Minnie."

"Hey!" Ranulf yelled.

At the same time, Eris jerked out his arms and said, "I'm serious."

Lucien's joking attitude vanished. "You will never lose us."

The emphasis he put on the word *you* confused her. What did it mean? Lucien and Ranulf always said cryptic things.

Ranulf joined them. He leaned into Eris and brushed her lips with his. "Short of death, you are never getting rid of us. I promise you that."

"But..." She trailed off, looking between them.

"But what?"

It was a misunderstanding. Eavesdropping always got people in trouble. She hadn't heard the whole conversation. They could have been talking about anything.

To distract herself from thinking about what that anything could be, she kissed Ranulf again. He blinked at her before gathering her close and deepening the kiss.

Lucien laid soft kisses on her neck as he rubbed his hands under her shirt.

She gave in. So long as she didn't think about it, it would go away.

A throat cleared, and a flowery voice said, "My, my, is this the reason neither of you cared to keep my meeting today?"

Eris yelped but wasn't given much time to react as both men shielded her from the intruder. She peered over their shoulders.

The woman was tall and leggy with pixie-cut red hair. The no-nonsense vibe of her business pant suit gave her the air of someone not to be messed with or left waiting.

"Genevieve, we're sorry about this afternoon, however, more pressing matters presented themselves," Ranulf said.

"So I see," she said in a knowing manner. "I'm not sure how *pressing* her is more important than meeting me though."

Lucien straightened with his chin in the air. "You may be annoyed we missed our appointment with you, but that's no reason to be rude. I felt this afternoon spent with Eris was more important than your little drama."

Eris frowned at Lucien's back. Why was he talking in such a deep voice? It was uncharacteristic, but she had heard it the night before. Did that mean he was tense?

Genevieve snapped, "Is that what you see this as? A little drama?"

Eris shrank back at the woman's vehemence. She looked back at the door. Could she beat a hasty retreat before the fireworks started?

Better yet. Was this the *she* Lucien and Ranulf had been talking about earlier?

Ranulf said in a normal tone, "Yes. Little drama. Why do we have to put up with so many meetings? Just pick one and be done."

"Don't you dare talk to me like that, you little peon." Genevieve pointed at Ranulf and then snapped her gaze to Lucien. "Why is she more important than me? I'm your—"

"You are my annoyance is what you are," Lucien snapped. "The four you have is enough, Genevieve."

"Are you just saying that or..." She trailed off then sighed. "Fine. I won't bother you any longer. You're right. Four is enough. If you'll excuse me."

The woman's heels clicked out her annoyance as she stalked toward the front door. The men kept themselves between her and Eris.

The door slammed hard enough to shake the table next to it. Eris waited for the sound of tires peeling out of the drive to reach her ears but none came.

Lucien sagged a little then sighed. He looked back at Eris. "Are you okay?"

"She's your what, Lucien? What was she going to say?" Eris asked, stepping back from him. "God, please tell me you're not married."

"No, Eris! I wouldn't do that to you." He reached for her, but she dodged. He let his hand drop. "Genevieve is the sister of our benefactor."

"Lucien," Ranulf snapped.

Eris frowned. "Benefactor? You're independently wealthy. What the hell do you need a benefactor for?"

Ranulf said, "We weren't always independently wealthy. Our benefactor made our current lifestyle possible. In return for his help, we aid him and his siblings at times. Genevieve chief amongst them recently."

Lucien grunted.

Eris looked between Ranulf and Lucien. They were hiding something. All of her earlier fears returned. With them came the ability to ask a very pertinent question. "Is she the woman you were talking about earlier?"

Both men exchanged a look. Lucien asked, "Earlier?"

"Yes. I overheard you two talking about some woman coming back. Was that Genevieve? Who is she really? Who are you waiting for?"

"We aren't waiting for anyone," Ranulf said, reaching for her.

She knocked his hand away. "I know what I heard. There's something you're keeping from me, or *someone*. I want answers."

"To?"

"Everything!"

"Okay." Ranulf rested his chin on his fist. "Pi is three point one four. The sky appears blue despite space being black because of the ozone layer. The moon isn't made of cheese. Plants give off oxygen. Paper is made of—"

"What the hell are you talking about?"

"You said you wanted answers to everything. I'm going in an order that's logical to me." He grinned.

Eris bared her teeth at him. "I don't know why I thought you would take this seriously." She turned to leave, but Lucien blocked her way. "Move."

"Ignore him," Lucien said. "He's an ass. I've told you that before."

"Are you going to tell me the truth?"

"There is no one else but you."

"Bullshit!"

She tried to shove past him, but he grabbed her and held her in place. When he would have kissed her, she turned away and pushed at him. "Don't you dare. This won't be solved with a kiss. You owe me some kind of explanation."

His hold remained firm. "There is no other woman in our lives. None. You have to believe that."

"I don't."

"Does anyone else find it ironic that she's jealous of another woman when she's dating two men?" Ranulf asked with a chuckle.

"Shut up!" Lucien and Eris yelled at the same time.

She glared at Lucien. "Let go of me or I'll scream."

He dropped his hold quickly and even took a few steps back.

As far as threats go, she hadn't thought that one would have much effect. Yet, Lucien looked like she'd threatened him with bodily harm and could actually pull it off.

"Who is she?" she asked.

"No—"

"Someone from our past," Lucien said, interrupting Ranulf.

Eris looked over her shoulder at Ranulf and then back at Lucien. "And?"

"She's from our past. That's where she'll stay."

"Why? You said you were expecting her to return."

"For years," Ranulf whispered.

She looked at him again. "What do you mean?"

"She's been gone for years, Eris."

"And you're waiting for her. Why? If you're waiting for her then why do you want to date me?"

Lucien laughed in a mirthless manner. "You're joking, right? We haven't seen her in all this time. No word, no sign. We don't even know if she's alive."

"You're hoping she is though."

"Yes. But not for the reasons you think." He met her gaze. "We...I want to apologize to her. Truly apologize for all that I did."

There was true pain in his words. Eris could almost touch it if she reached out to him. Suddenly, Lucien seemed weighted with a horrible burden. "What happened?" she whispered.

Her nature wouldn't allow her not to try and comfort him despite being angry with him. She reached out to touch his arm, but he sidestepped away from her, shaking his head.

"That's not something I will talk about under any circumstances. I don't care what you threaten me with. That's between me and her." He sighed. "If she ever decides to return."

She looked back at Ranulf, whose joking attitude had disappeared. He looked almost as strained as Lucien. "You two have shared a woman once before? You didn't say that."

"Because that wasn't dating," Ranulf said. "That was sex in the purest sense of the word."

"So, she left?"

"Yes."

"And now I have to put up with the fallout."

A shadow of Ranulf's usual rueful smile returned. "Yes." He looked at her. "There is no middle for us, Eris. No grey area. We'd rather abstain than take a chance of making the same mistake."

She moved to him. When she reached for him, he didn't move away. She rested her hand on his arm. "You should have just told me."

He snorted. "Uh-huh. Because rational is your middle name, right?"

"Actually, it's Kelly, but that's beside the point. I thought you two were using me as a gap fill. I still think you are. You're biding your time. What happens if she does come back? Where does that leave me?"

"We don't know," Lucien said. "We have no way of predicting the future. She may never come back."

"But you want her to, so you can apologize." She watched Lucien. "Is that it?"

"She won't want more. I'm sure of that."

"If she did, you'd jump at that chance though." She turned her gaze back to Ranulf. "Where does that leave me? Why should I wait around for the inevitable?"

They didn't answer.

"Is she the reason neither of you is married? You've been waiting all this time hoping she'd come back?"

She thought they wouldn't answer again. In a quiet voice, Lucien said, "There have been many women I wanted to spoil, many I wanted to fuck, but never one I wanted to marry." He lifted his head and met her gaze. "Before you."

"Excuse me?"

Ranulf said, "Getting married, committing to one woman, felt too much like giving up."

Eris crossed her arms. "The consummate playboy."

"No, picky as hell. I didn't want to settle when I knew better was out there and it was only a matter of waiting." He lifted her hand to his lips.

She frowned at him. "Me?"

"Do you see any other woman in this room?" He pulled her into his arms. "I want nothing more than to have a legitimate and legal claim to you that is binding under God and law." He jerked his head to the side. "Lucien can tag along as well."

"Thanks for that afterthought," Lucien grumbled. He joined them and kissed Eris's other hand. "His flippant behavior aside, I feel the same, Eris."

"And what about that other woman whose name you have yet to tell me?"

Lucien caressed her cheek. "She is part of our past. While I want to apologize to her, it is you I love."

She let her mouth fall open.

Ranulf pushed her jaw closed with one finger and then placed a kiss on her prone lips. "I wanted to say it first so it had more impact but—" he kissed her again, "—I love you, Eris."

"What's her name?"

Lucien threw his hands up in the air. "We declare we love you and yet you still harp on something that isn't important."

"If it isn't important then just tell me."

Ranulf said, "It's not important. Why do you care?"

She put her hands on her hips. "We could do this all night."

"Or, we could go to bed, get some rest and start fresh in the morning."

"Do you take anything seriously?"

Ranulf shrugged. "Not if I can help it." He kissed her again. "Stop thinking about her. We're with you."

"Really?"

They both nodded.

"Prove it. Sleep with me."

Both men started spouting denials and excuses at the same time.

With an annoyed noise, she rolled her eyes. "I don't even understand why I'm still here. Good night." She did an about face and headed for the front door.

She squeaked when one of them picked her up and tossed her over his shoulder. Since Ranulf was grinning at her, she knew Lucien carried her.

"Put me down," she said in a calm voice.

"In a minute." Lucien carried her up the stairs, into her bedroom and dumped her on the bed. "There."

"You think this is going to keep me here?" She scooted to the edge of the bed.

Ranulf blocked her path. "We could tie you down. In fact, that idea holds a lot of interest for me."

"At least then you might actually do something," she grumbled.

Lucien said, "You want us to sleep with you, then you'll get your wish."

Ranulf looked up in surprise. "Lucien?"

He shook his head. "Sleeping is all we'll do though."

Eris said, "That's not what I meant and you know it."

"That's what I meant, and that's all you'll get."

"Why? I'm *not* her. Why are you punishing me for your mistakes with her?"

Lucien edged Ranulf out of the way and bent over her. In a low voice he said, "What makes you think this is *your* punishment?" He cupped her cheek. "Sleeping next to you and not having you is my idea of slow torture."

"You don't have to torture yourself," she whispered.

"After the faire," Ranulf said.

She looked at him.

"The faire is in a few weeks. After the faire, I will gladly ravage your body until you beg me to stop, and even then, I may not." He grinned in a devilish manner.

Lucien said, "I echo that sentiment."

"Until then, consider us your personal sheet warmers."

She wasn't sure she trusted that. "You mean it? After the faire, you'll stop putting me off and dodging?"

They nodded.

"Can I have that in writing?"

Ranulf looked around. He went to the nearby desk, and Lucien followed him. They pored over a piece of paper for ten minutes and then brought it back to her.

She took it, read it, and then laughed. They'd literally put in writing that they would ravage her without thought of time, location or circumstance until none of them had the will to walk or move, after the faire had ended. Until then, they would retain their platonic relationship with bed privileges.

"Fine. Fine," she said, holding her hand out for the pen. "I'm taking you to court if you renege."

They both signed it and then handed it back to her. Not having any place to put it, she folded it and put it in her pocket. "Now what?"

"Sleep," Lucien said with a weary sigh. "I'm exhausted. No woman has ever run me as ragged as you without even trying."

"Sorry I'm such a pain. I try to leave, but you won't let me."

Ranulf kissed her quickly. "I happen to like your little tortures." He walked toward the door. "I'm going to get changed and I'll be right back. Don't try to leave."

"She'll be here. I'll change after," Lucien said, standing sentry at the door.

Eris said, "You don't have to guard me."

Both men snorted and that made her laugh. Okay, so she had a bad habit of running from her problems. It hadn't failed her yet.

She looked up at Lucien, and he watched her. "What?"

"I'm sorry," he whispered.

"No, I probably overreacted. But you two brought this on yourselves. You're both too damn secretive."

He took a breath but didn't say anything. Instead, he shook his head. "Did you want to dress up for the faire?"

"Of course."

"We have a room of clothes. I can show it to you tomorrow. Pick whatever you want to wear."

"Do you two dress up?"

"Not usually," Ranulf said, entering the room. "But we will since you are." He jerked his thumb to the door, and Lucien left. He looked back at her. "Aren't you going to change?"

"I don't—" She stopped when he held a shirt draped over a basket of toiletries out to her.

"This isn't the night you usually stay over, so I took the liberty of gathering some things for you."

"Why does it feel like you were planning this?"

He winked at her. "If I had, there would have been candles and mood music and a severe lack of argumentative words."

She ducked her head. "Sorry."

"Don't be. You're cute when you jump to conclusions." He kissed the top of her head. "Go get ready for bed."

"I told you to stop treating me like a kid."

He winked at her.

She stood. "You better be here when I come out."

"Try to get me to leave." He crawled onto the bed. "Go to the bathroom and change. Or..." His gaze traveled up her body in a suggestive manner.

"Or?"

"Or, you could do a striptease."

"Wouldn't that make your night uncomfortable?"

"It'd be worth it."

She shook her head at him and walked to her bathroom.

The relationship had moved forward, somewhat. The agreement was as binding for her as it was for them. She knew they were serious about not having sex until after the faire.

She only hoped more issues didn't crop up.

Chapter Twenty-seven

"Lucien," Eris whispered, tickling his ear.

He swatted at her hand.

She leaned across him and blew on his ear while inching her hand over his hip. "Lucien," she said in a soft sing-song.

He caught her wrist just as she was about to caress the very noticeable tent his lower body made with the covers. He grumbled, "Stop being a tease."

"You told me to wake you before I left to go swimming."

"Then shake my shoulder." He yanked her hand, which made her fall on top of him. "Good morning."

"Is it?"

He kissed her as his answer. She smiled against his mouth.

Next to them Ranulf mumbled something incoherent and turned on his side. Both of them looked at him and then exchanged a smile. Eris righted herself so Lucien could get out of bed.

She said in a soft voice, "Don't forget, I'm running out to my dad's shop at lunch so he can give me my dress for the faire."

"I remember. Why was he redoing it again?"

"Not redoing, modifying. He didn't like the way it looked and said he would fix it for me for free. I couldn't pass up the chance."

"Why the sudden generosity?"

"He has—"

"Could you two shut up? It's too early to be discussing anything," Ranulf said then threw himself into a new position and covered his head with his pillow.

Eris stuck her tongue out at his back then continued in a softer voice. "He's almost famous because of my dress's red carpet debut, and he got a new rich client because of it. She's hired him to do her wedding."

"Tell him I said congratulations," Lucien said.

"Get out!" Ranulf threw a pillow in their direction. It sailed past Eris with room to spare and landed on the floor with a plop.

"This is my room," Eris said with her hands on her hips.

"I don't care. It's too early. Go away if you're going and shut the hell up while you're at it."

"Grump."

"Bite me."

She was about to head over to Ranulf's side of the bed and do just as he'd suggested, but Lucien grabbed her arm. He stood and pulled her out of the room.

She called back, "I'll see you at the faire, Ranulf."

He growled then stuffed his head under the pillow again.

Lucien closed the bedroom door.

She asked, "Does he always have such a lovely morning personality?"

"He's never liked morning. You should be used to it after all these weeks." Lucien placed a quick peck on her lips. "I have to get going. Thank you for waking me. We'll see you at two, correct?"

She nodded. "You sure you don't want me to just meet you there. Aren't you and Ranulf supposed to do some sort of opening ceremony?"

"It's called an opening ceremony, but it has never been exactly at opening. It's at our discretion when we do it. So, this year we'd rather wait and have you at our side."

"Fine. I'll come back here and then we can go to the faire grounds together."

"Thank you." He kissed her one last time then headed for his room.

Eris appreciated the way his butt flexed beneath his boxer briefs until it was out of sight then she went for her morning swim. By the time she finished, Ranulf would be awake, in a marginally better mood and waiting for her in the kitchen with breakfast.

That had been the routine for the last few weeks. The three of them rotated which room they slept in, but every morning Eris got up early to go swimming while Ranulf grumbled if she chanced to wake him and Lucien roused himself to do some business.

None of her co-workers commented, but she was sure they knew her overtime sleeping arrangements had taken on a more permanent status.

She smiled to herself. The day of the faire had finally arrived. She, Lucien, and Ranulf would be doing much more than sleeping when they went to bed that night.

Anticipation made her wish for the end of the day to show up sooner.

* * * *

Eris unzipped the dress bag and stared. "Dad, this isn't the dress I gave you."

"Can't fool you. No, it's not. I had the girls embroider the pattern from the other dress onto that one once it was finished."

"This isn't the same pattern."

Gordon shrugged. "I embellished a little. It looks better now and more authentic for the time period."

"It's gorgeous, Daddy. Thank you."

"I know. Go get dressed. Don't forget to forego the bra and undies."

She gave her father her best shocked expression.

"You're going to a ren faire wearing a period dress. You'll do it right." He held out a length of linen. "If you must, you can bind your chest with this."

"I'm not binding nothing. That hurts, and it isn't healthy. Did women really do that?"

"Small boobs were the thing."

She palmed her ample bosom. "Not anymore."

"Then hang, but no bra."

She snatched the cloth from him. "It's too cold to go around without panties."

"No."

"What if I wear a thong?"

He crossed his arms. "A thong is just the same as wearing nothing."

"Fine. Fine."

She grinned to herself as she went to the dressing room. It would probably be best if she didn't mention her plans with Lucien and Ranulf after the faire. Her dad might decide to give her a chastity belt—medieval-style.

After stripping and wrapping her chest, she slipped off her panties and added them to her clothing pile. She called, "I guess I shouldn't tell you I shaved…everything. I took a bath this morning too." She pulled on the chemise then the tunic.

"You are a disgrace to the entire ren fairing community, you know that? Why would you shave or take a bath for that matter?"

"Because I don't like being hairy or dirty."

"I guess since no one will see it, I can't complain too much."

Except Lucien and Ranulf, she thought. It took all of her willpower to stop herself from saying that aloud.

After a quick glance in the mirror, she opened the dressing room door. "Well?"

"You look beautiful, baby girl," Gordon said with an edge of awe.

"You're not just saying that?"

"If those men you've been shacking up with don't appreciate the gorgeousness that is you then you have my permission to call your brothers and uncles to go beat them."

Eris hugged her father. "Thank you, Daddy. That's sweet, but I'm sure Lucien and Ranulf will love it."

"Before you rush off—" Gordon retrieved a wide, flat box from the table behind him. He held it out to her. "Lucien ordered this a while back, but I was too swamped to do it service. I told him the same, but he said whenever I had time. Well, I had time and it's finished." He handed her the box. "He didn't give me much of a description. I figured since he's such a medieval nut that he wanted it in that style, so I used some historical books as a reference. I'd like you to deliver it to him."

"Historical books? What is it? Can I open it?"

Gordon gave her a look to show how stupid that question was. "Do you normally open deliveries? And so help me, you better say no, missy."

"No, Dad, I don't open deliveries. Though I think I'd get special privileges since the customer is my boyfriend."

"Don't make me take the box back and then have to call that man and explain why he has to come get it when it would have made more sense to send it home with you. I'll do it and blame you, I swear, I will. Afterwards, I'll call Mariko and complain."

"Now that's just evil and you know it."

"It'll keep you from peeking, won't it?"

"Fine. I won't peek." She held the box off to the side and gave Gordon a kiss on the cheek. "I gotta get going."

"Business cards! In case someone asks who made your dress."

She didn't even argue. She held out her hand for the cards and tucked them into her purse. The dress didn't have pockets so she'd have to stuff the cards up the sleeves of her chemise. But, she'd do that once she met up with Lucien and Ranulf at the mansion.

The box containing Lucien's order distracted her all the way home. She glanced at it and smoothed her hand over the lid several times, but kept her word. She didn't peek. Besides, Lucien would probably show her.

Lucien and Ranulf were wearing a groove into the foyer tile when she arrived. She smiled at them. "I'm sorry I'm back later than I said I would be, but Daddy just had to regale me with the battle story of the latest monster bride."

She laid the box aside and held out her arms. "How do I look?" She twirled around and ended in a curtsy.

Silence met her display when there should have been words of praise and declarations of renewed love. Her guess was they were speechless because of the picture she presented. She lifted her head.

Lucien and Ranulf both stared at her with twin looks of horror instead of love. There was no mistaking their expressions for anything else.

"That's not one of the dresses you chose," Lucien whispered in a hoarse voice.

"No, it's not. Daddy took it upon himself to make one he thought was more historically accurate. I knew he said he would take the zipper out of the other one, but I didn't know he'd planned to make an all new dress until I got there." She moved closer to them, and their looks of horror didn't change. Lucien even backed up a little. "What's wrong? You don't like it?"

"It's beautiful. You're beautiful," Ranulf said. His words were the compliment she'd wanted, but his tone almost made it an insult.

"Okay, so you think I'm beautiful, but that doesn't explain why you're looking at me like I've sprouted fanged teeth and an extra head." She put her hands on her hips and waited for an explanation.

What she got was Lucien and Ranulf trying their hardest to smile but failing miserably. The whole situation brought tears to her eyes. She turned away quickly before any of them fell. The box she'd put off to the side caught her eye.

"Daddy finished your order, Lucien. It's in the box. I'll, uh, I'll call him and tell him you hated the dress." She ran out the front door.

"Eris!" Both men yelled for her, and their voices blended into one.

She didn't stop running and wouldn't stop running. The dress was the most gorgeous thing she'd ever seen. They acted like she'd come home wearing crap, literally.

It made no sense. She thought they would love the dress since they were such medieval fanatics.

"I don't understand them at all. They're both idiots."

Saying that didn't make the hurt go away.

* * * *

"What's in the box?" Ranulf asked in a dejected tone. He looked at the open front door and couldn't understand why he hadn't chased after Eris and tried to reason with her. It's what he did when his and Lucien's cryptic behavior upset her.

But this time...

He shook his head. The shock of that dress—He'd hoped to never see it again, ever, and yet, for things to work out as they should, seeing it again was inevitable.

Lucien retrieved the box and opened it. He lifted the item inside for Ranulf to see. "Another piece of a puzzle we don't want to put together."

The strength of his legs gave out, and Ranulf fell to the floor. He stared at the billowing black cape, not believing his eyes. "You? You're the one who gave her *that* cloak. It was you?"

"When she mentioned she'd always wanted one, I decided to have one made. I left the choice of material and everything to Gordon's discretion since he knows his daughter's taste." Lucien let his arms drop. The material of the cape pooled around his feet. "I didn't know he'd make *this*. I'd never give her...this is a nightmare."

"One we should have seen coming. The faire has started. We knew this would happen eventually."

"I wanted it to happen later, not the first day."

"You didn't want it to happen at all, no more than I did." Ranulf's words made him regain a bit of his composure. He stood and walked to Lucien's side. He put his hand on the man's shoulder.

Lucien dropped his head. His whole body radiated defeat.

Ranulf whispered, "You know you must. We've prepared for this."

"We've prepared. We've planned. Everything was set and known." Lucien looked at Ranulf.

The heartbreak in the man's eyes mirrored what Ranulf felt.

Lucien asked, "What happens afterwards? What do we do when she returns?"

"Pray," Ranulf whispered. "We pray."

"That won't be enough." Lucien shoved the cape at Ranulf. His movements were stiff as he climbed the stairs.

Ranulf looked at the cape crumbled in his fist. "Why couldn't we have even one day?"

* * * *

Lucien entered his room and closed the door after him. Without thought to his movements or looking at his surroundings, he moved toward the headboard of his bed.

He pushed a series of knots in the intricate woodwork, and a tiny drawer opened. It took some internal coaching before he reached within for the drawer's contents.

The gold ring held a healthy-sized oval-shaped sapphire. A tiny braided chain connected the ring to a cuff wristband made of interconnected leaves. It was a delicate piece of craftsmanship his father had made for his mother.

The woman had cried over it when it was presented to her and had never been seen without it. On her death bed, she made Lucien promise he'd never let the ring leave his possession unless he planned to give it to the woman he loved—the woman who would stay by his side forever.

He'd promised without hesitation. He knew, at the time, that no woman would ever mean so much to him. No woman would ever stir within him what had existed between his parents.

No woman until Eris.

Lucien edged to the dresser and fell onto the bench situated near it. He stared at the ring. It was the last piece of the puzzle. He wanted to throw it away, to destroy it, to do anything except give it to Eris.

He looked at his expression in the mirror atop the dresser. "Don't make me," he rasped.

What stared back at him was himself, but his eyes were deep black pools.

"Why?" he asked.

"Don't," his reflection said in a deep voice.

"If I don't give her the ring then she will never meet Ranulf and me. We won't live through time to see her again."

"You answer your own dilemma."

Lucien dropped his head onto his hands. The ring scraped the skin of his forehead. "I caused her so much pain."

"The pain is necessary or else you will never be. However, the choice remains yours."

He lifted his head and looked at his reflection. His eyes were normal again. He looked at the ring. "I'm sorry. I'm so sorry. Please, forgive me."

Chapter Twenty-eight

Eris sat against a tree staring at nothing and hugging her arms. March or not, it was freezing outside. Someone needed to inform Mother Nature that spring had started.

She wanted to go back to the house and get a coat, but the thought of facing Lucien and Ranulf kept her frozen in place, more so than the weather. Moving around would help raise her temperature. As much as she'd like to use the chaos of the faire to forget her unfortunate encounter and warm up, she didn't know how to get there.

She knew the general direction of where the faire was held. She also knew the general direction of Ireland and had as much hope of finding that locale on foot as she did the other.

"Eris!"

She jerked around at the sound of Lucien's voice.

"Eris!"

Ranulf's voice. They called out to her, but she couldn't summon up the will to answer.

She stood when their calls drew closer. The men entered the clearing and stopped. They stared at her, and she stared back.

"Thank God. We thought you might be hurt and unable to answer," Ranulf said.

"Why would you care if I was?" she asked.

"Eris, we reacted badly, and there's no excuse. The dress is beautifully made, and you look stunning in it."

"Congratulations. How long did you practice saying that to yourself before it sounded genuine?"

Ranulf nodded. "I deserve that. But you must understand our—"

"She wore a dress very similar to that one," Lucien whispered.

"She?" He met her gaze, and the answer was there.

The woman Eris knew held a place in Lucien's and Ranulf's hearts that she could never touch. Eris looked down at the dress with horror of her own.

How?

Her father couldn't have copied the dress. It wasn't possible.

"I should change," she whispered.

Ranulf said, "No. The day is almost gone. It's a fluke that none of us could have predicted. We're sorry our initial reactions upset you, but we're over that now." He held his hand out to her. "Let's go enjoy the rest of the day."

"But, are you sure? There were other dresses."

Lucien took her hand in his. She felt him slip something on her finger and she looked at him then her hand. He slid the cuff on her wrist then whispered, "It belonged to my mother. I had planned to give it to you at some point. I thought today best so as to make up for my insensitivity earlier."

"It's…this is too special. Are you sure?"

Lucien nodded.

She hugged him. His return hug took her breath away. Just when she thought she'd have to ask for air, Lucien's hold loosened, and he let her go. His look was sad, sadder than she'd ever seen from him before.

"Are you sure you don't want me to change?" she asked, cupping his cheek.

"Never. You're fine just the way you are," he whispered.

She got the feeling he didn't mean her dress but decided to drop the subject. Strong arms circled her waist from behind, and she leaned back against Ranulf. He laid a kiss on the curve of her neck.

"I'm sorry," he mumbled. He squeezed her waist then let her go.

"Let's get to the faire." She took Ranulf's hand then Lucien's, and they walked in silence.

Both men seemed subdued, almost depressed. Eris knew it wasn't her imagination. The joy of that morning was gone, but she decided not to bring attention to it. Lucien and Ranulf were pretending to be okay for her sake. She'd play along.

They reached the faire grounds, and Eris realized she'd been closer than she thought. The jostling, happy crowd lifted her spirits somewhat. "What should we do first?" she asked.

Lucien said, "I'm in the mood to spar."

"Likewise. With any luck Clayton decided to make an appearance. I would sorely love to beat him," Ranulf said.

"Now that I would pay to see," Eris said. "By all means, let's go and see if Stupid showed up itching for a fight."

Luck was on their side. Not only had Clayton shown, but he stood in the sparring ring, bragging about how he'd beaten all comers.

Ranulf asked, "Would you like to go first or should I?"

"Rock, paper, scissors for it," Eris said. She didn't think the men would do it and then laughed when they did.

Lucien won best three out of four. He entered the ring and disarmed Clayton in under a minute. Of course, Clayton complained about not being ready and demanded a do-over.

His do-over ended in much the same manner. Rather than do a third, Lucien surrendered the floor to Ranulf, who disarmed Clayton two seconds after the referee called a start to the match.

Eris watched Clayton stalk off the field toward the faire grounds entrance. "I should feel sorry for him."

"Do you?" Lucien asked.

"Nah. The smug, superior feeling of watching him get beaten so easily won't back down and let the sympathy take hold."

Ranulf said, "Good." He faced the crowd. "Any others wish to face us this day?"

No one stepped forward. He returned the sword he'd used to the pile and left the field.

"Maybe you two should spar with each other. The crowd seems a bit disappointed that it's over," Eris said, glancing at the people who had gathered.

"Not a bad suggestion. What do you say, Lucien? In the mood to lose?"

"No. I'm in the mood to win," Lucien said, entering the field. He picked up two swords and tossed one to Ranulf. Before the referee called a start, he held up his hand and turned to the crowd, which had gotten considerably bigger in the last few seconds.

He said in a loud voice, "Good day to you, our guests. I am Lucien Riordan—" clapping erupted and he waited for it to die down "—and this is Ranulf Styr."

Ranulf bowed with flourish. "We welcome you to our property and hope you enjoy these ten days of merriment as we travel back to an era of pageantry, knights and danger."

Lucien continued, "This beautiful lady before us is Eris Brue."

Eris looked at him with surprise, but he only smiled at her. She faced the crowd and curtsied then waved.

"As a real start to the festivities and this event, Lucien and I plan to spar for her favor," Ranulf said.

The crowd roared with excitement. Eris looked at Ranulf to see if he was joking. He didn't look like it. She beckoned him closer and whispered, "What?"

"I'm only playing to the crowd. Polyamory was not a broadcasted affair in the Middle Ages. And it's none of their business that you are with us both." He kissed her cheek then stepped back.

Eris shrugged and pulled a ribbon from her hair. She waved it above her head for the crowd to see.

Ranulf faced Lucien with his sword at the ready. The referee called a start to the match then practically dove over the fence dividing the crowd from the field.

Neither man moved, but the crowd continued cheering.

Lucien said in a low voice, "I owe you."

"You do, but you know you can't collect now."

"I think I can." Lucien lunged forward.

Eris didn't know what their words meant and had to cover her ears when their swords clashed. She'd watched them spar many times before, but this time looked different.

They weren't sparring. They were truly fighting one another. Several times Eris covered her eyes only to peek through her fingers. When she thought one would win, the other gained ground.

She covered her mouth and gasped when Lucien stepped into Ranulf's downward swing. Though she wanted to cover her eyes, her hands wouldn't move. Everything slowed around her as she watched the sword come down toward Lucien's neck.

At the same time, Lucien stabbed his sword toward Ranulf's stomach. Both blades hit their targets, though Lucien's sword found its mark and protruded out of Ranulf's back a few seconds before Ranulf's sword cleaved

Lucien's shoulder in half. Eris stared at the sight of both the men she loved mortally wounded.

She tore her gaze away and buried her face in her hands. Slowly, the sounds of the crowd returned to her.

They cheered still.

"That's the first time you've beaten me," Ranulf said with laughter in his voice.

He was laughing?

Eris looked at them and couldn't comprehend it. There was no blood, on the men or the swords. Lucien stood unharmed while Ranulf lay on his back.

Several hands pushed at Eris. She didn't know what the people around her wanted. She looked back at them to tell them to leave her alone.

"Give your favor to Lucien. He's won," said one of the men who urged her forward.

She entered the ring and walked toward the men. They looked at her, and their jovial attitudes faded. Ranulf picked himself up off of the ground and rushed to her side with Lucien beside him.

"What's wrong, Eris? Did we scare you?" Ranulf asked.

She touched Ranulf's stomach where the blade had pierced him. His tunic wasn't cut and neither was he.

"Eris?" Lucien asked.

She turned to him and touched his neck. The flesh showed no sign of abuse, yet only moments before she could have sworn she'd have to trade her green dress for a black one.

The relief that both men were okay sapped all her of strength. She sagged against Lucien. He lifted her against his chest and carried her away. The crowd seemed to like the display because they whistled and howled.

Ranulf led the way to a storage tent and cleared a spot. Lucien sat Eris down and framed her face with his hands. "You've seen us spar before, Eris. What's wrong?"

"I thought you'd killed each other."

"What?" Lucien looked back at Ranulf then returned his gaze to Eris.

"I saw it. I know I saw it." She touched his neck again. Like when she had checked Ranulf earlier, there was no wound and never had been. She reached for Ranulf. He walked forward. When he was near enough, she yanked open his tunic and stared at his stomach.

Again, no wound.

"We're unharmed," Lucien said.

"I know what I saw," she yelled.

Ranulf pulled free of her hands only to hug her tight. "Calm down, Eris. It's okay. We aren't hurt. We can't hurt each other."

"But—"

He pulled away and kissed her lips. "We're sorry we scared you, but neither of us is hurt. I promise you that. You've seen for yourself. Okay?"

She nodded.

Lucien stepped forward and retrieved her from Ranulf. He kissed her softly then said, "I do believe I won your favor, my lady."

Eris smiled at him. He held out his arm, and she tied the ribbon above his bicep. "I have a request."

"Name it."

"No more violence."

Both men nodded. Ranulf said, "We'll do our best."

"Good. I'm hungry, and you both are sweaty."

"Which would you like us to take care of first?"

"Sweat first, please. You stink." She held her nose with a look of disgust.

"We have a change of clothes at the house. Though, if we were to be true to the era, we would stay in these clothes," Lucien said as he lifted her down from the table and they left the tent.

"If you don't want me to ditch you, you'll get cleaned up like the rules of *this* era say," Eris said.

"As my lady wishes," both men said in unison.

Ranulf flagged down a squire who went to fetch a golf cart for them.

"That's not keeping with the era either," Eris said.

"I'm exhausted after that match. I deserve to rest," Ranulf said.

The squire drove up at the same time another squire ran toward them. "Ranulf, Lucien, there's some trouble with an exhibit. Both men say they paid for the same slot," the running squire blurted out when he slid to a stop.

Before either man could answer, the walkie-talkies attached to both squires' hips crackled. A male voice said, "Attention, squires, if any of you see Lucien, tell him he's needed back at the house for an important call from Japan. I repeat, Lucien has an important call from Japan."

The squire in the golf cart unclipped his walkie-talkie and said, "I've got him. He's coming back now." He clipped the walkie-talkie back in its holder. "Sir?"

Ranulf said, "I'll see about the exhibit. You go see what Mizukinawa wants now."

Eris looked between both men, unsure whom she should stay with. Then she remembered something she'd forgotten. "Business cards," she said. "I need to get my dad's business cards."

"Where are they?" Lucien asked.

"It's just easier if I go with you." She hopped onto the backseat and waved to Ranulf as they pulled away.

The golf cart zipped back to the house faster than Eris thought a golf cart should go. She was happy to get off of it when it arrived at the front door. She vowed to make Lucien walk back.

Lucien held the door for her. She entered and looked down when the floor was softer than usual. A pool of black cloth lay beneath her feet. She stepped off of it and picked up an edge. "What's this?"

"That is yours. I forgot about it completely with the...I had forgotten about it."

She held the cloth between her arms. "I repeat, what is it?"

Lucien took it from her.

"Sir, your phone call," Leon said. He stood in the doorway of the office holding a cordless phone.

"Give me a minute, Leon. Mizukinawa can wait." Lucien draped the cloth around Eris's shoulders then turned her so he could button the clasp. "There. Do you know what it is now?"

Eris knew exactly what it was. She hugged the cloth and did a little twirl. "This is what you had my father make?"

"Yes."

"And it's mine?"

"Yes."

"Oh, Lucien, I love it. Thank you." She kissed him. "Thank you." She kissed him again. "Thank you."

Lucien held her to the last kiss. He didn't release her until she was breathless. She held his arms to keep herself steady.

"It's almost after the faire, Eris. Remember our agreement," he said in a husky voice.

"Did you mean the end of the first day or the last?"

He kissed her one last time then walked toward the office.

Eris twirled around a few more times, feeling the cape billow out around her. Out of all the things Lucien and Ranulf had given her over the last few months, she loved the cape the most. And it was the perfect gift for the cold temperature of the day.

She crept toward the office and peeked at Lucien. He stood talking on the phone with his back to her, drumming his fingers against the desk. Rather than interrupt his call, she retreated and went to her room for a quick potty break and mirror check.

Lucien still wasn't finished when she came back downstairs. Her stomach growled, and she headed for the kitchen. Liselle was probably off because of the faire, but the woman always had snacks handy.

True enough, there were some oatmeal raisin cookies in a glass dish with a note attached. She opened the note then smiled. "For Eris," she read. "Thanks, Liselle."

Five cookies later, Eris went to check on Lucien again. He didn't look any closer to ending the call than he had almost twenty minutes ago. She looked at the wall clock then back at the office. Ranulf was probably wondering what had happened to them.

She found Leon in the den flipping channels. He saw her and stood. She waved him back down. "When Lucien gets off the phone, let him know that I walked back."

"You don't want to use the golf cart?"

Her stomach rolled at the suggestion. "That's okay. I need to walk off the cookies I just ate. You'll let him know?"

"Of course. Be careful. It gets dark in the trees."

"I'll be okay. Thanks." She peeked in on Lucien one last time then left.

The squire watched her walk away but didn't offer to give her a ride. She was happy she didn't have to explain her need to walk to the man. She only hoped he wasn't regularly employed as a chauffeur or else she felt sorry for his employers.

She'd been walking ten minutes before she stopped. "Shit. I forgot the cards." She looked back at the way she'd come. A few more minutes and she'd be at the faire. Once she found Ranulf she could have him call the house, but by the time Lucien got the message he might be on his way back since she wasn't sure where Ranulf was.

"Forget it. I'll just hope the person who asks has pen and paper handy."

She faced the faire once more, took two steps and then fell down a deep dark hole with a strangled scream.

Chapter Twenty-nine

Lucien had had enough. He yelled in Japanese, "Mizukinawa, stop wasting my time and get the hell off my phone. You know you want to sign it. Just do it already and be done, woman."

"You have some nerve talking to me like that, Riordan."

"Fine. Don't sign it. I couldn't care less either way."

"You—"

He slammed the phone on its cradle and walked away. "Her however-many-greats grandfather wasn't that annoying or stubborn," he grumbled to himself.

The phone rang just as he crossed the threshold, but he ignored it.

Leon came out of the den.

"Let it ring," Lucien said through his teeth. He looked around. "Where's Eris?"

"She went back already some fifteen minutes ago."

That meant she'd be with Ranulf. Lucien looked down at himself. The smell of sweat still clung to him. He could probably get away with simply changing his clothes since the scent was mostly there.

"Lucien! What the hell is taking you so long?" Ranulf jogged toward him. "Why are you still in that? I thought you were changing and that was the hold up. Well, actually, I thought you had dragged Eris into the shower with you."

"She's not with you?" Lucien asked, his blood freezing.

Ranulf opened his mouth to answer but no sound came out. Horror then understanding crossed his face. He ran out the way he'd come. Lucien followed close behind him.

They hit the tree line running. "Eris!" Lucien bellowed at the top of his lungs.

"Eris, answer us!" Ranulf sounded understandably frantic.

Lucien stopped and turned in a circle. A sense of the inevitable settled around him.

"Eris!" Ranulf continued running past Lucien then returned. "Why have you stopped?"

"She can't hear us. Not through time," Lucien whispered.

"You don't know that's where she's gone. You don't know that for sure."

"I gave her the cloak."

Ranulf grabbed Lucien's shirt and shook him. "Why, damn you, why?"

"Why did you leave it on the floor where she could find it and ask about its purpose?" Lucien knocked Ranulf's hands away. "What was I supposed to do?"

"The hole. We need to find that damn hole."

"It's in England."

Ranulf backhanded Lucien then shook him again. "Snap out of it, man. She may be gone, but she's coming back. We need to find that damned hole so we can help when she does."

"We should have known. We should have known it would happen soon. She saw the true fight."

That statement seemed to make Ranulf deflate. He released Lucien. "How? Why?"

Lucien thought back on the earlier match against Ranulf. His sword embedded in Ranulf's stomach mere moments before Ranulf's sword cleaved his shoulder. The win was his though both wounds were mortal. Or, they would have been mortal if the laws of mortality applied to them.

But the audience hadn't seen the carnage. Instead, they saw Lucien bat away Ranulf's sword with his own then body check Ranulf to the ground. A completely harmless end to a fake battle.

Eris had been the exception, and what she witnessed had shaken her badly. Lucien had no explanation why she had seen it and said as much. "It doesn't matter. We should have taken it as a sign that *his* powers were in effect and known he would take her."

"What would knowing have done? He acted to separate us—that argument, that phone call. Both were merely distractions so he could get her alone."

Lucien looked toward the faire then the house. Eris had walked that very path before she found a portal through time. The way she'd left would be how she returned. He knew that. "We have to find that hole."

Ranulf nodded and then went the opposite direction from Lucien.

* * * *

Eris brushed the dirt and leaves from her cloak then rubbed her arms. Nothing was broken. She was a bit bruised, but the pain was ignorable. Her more pressing problem was finding a way out of the hole in which she'd fallen.

She looked up then around. There was nothing to grab hold of and no way she could jump for the edge. Whoever had dug the hole made sure their quarry wouldn't get free easily. Though, what they'd planned to catch with such a deep hole, she had no clue. She was just happy the person hadn't put something detrimental at the bottom, like spikes.

She took a deep breath then yelled as loudly as she could, "Help! Anybody! I need help!"

After a few moments of silence, she tried again. She repeated her cry ten more times, stopping to listen between each, before her throat got raw. It didn't make sense that no one heard her. Then again, the noise from the faire could probably drown out anything.

Lucien and Ranulf should have been looking for her though. Unless they thought she was lost in the crowds of the faire. She should have stayed put and waited for Lucien to finish his call. Or, she should have taken the golf cart back. It had been stupid to walk.

The sound of something heavy striking the ground pulled Eris out of her funk. She yelled again, hoping the people would hear her. Dirt at the edge of the hole rained around her, and she pulled her hood to keep it out of her hair. Several men crowded the mouth of the hole and looked down at her.

"Can you help me out, please?" she asked.

"It's a poacher's hole," one of the men said.

"Get her out of it."

Though he wasn't at the edge like the others, Eris would recognize Lucien's voice anywhere. Two men braced a third as he reached into the hole. She grabbed his hand, and the men pulled her up and out. She thanked them profusely as she brushed the dirt from herself and the cloak once more.

"Lucien, thank God you found me. I almost screamed myself hoarse hoping someone would hear me. Where did that hole come from?"

"Do I know you, woman?"

"It's me. Eris." She pushed back her hood and smiled up at him.

The men around her pulled their swords. She looked around then back at Lucien for an explanation but came face-to-face with his sword as well. "Okay, you guys are taking this faire way too seriously," she said with a nervous laugh.

"Who are you, woman? Why are you in my forest?" Lucien asked.

"If this is a joke, I'm not enjoying it." She pushed the edge of his sword away. Lucien almost cut through her hand when he moved it back. She jerked away in time to keep from being injured. "Watch it. You almost cut me."

He shoved the sword under her chin, the point digging into her neck. "I'll do more than that if you don't answer my questions, woman."

She wanted to smile and laugh off the joke, but it felt too real. The sword at her throat felt real too. She wanted to back up but was too scared to move.

"Answer me!"

"Best to do as he says." Ranulf reined his horse closer to her.

His was the only sword not drawn against her. She wanted to take that as a good sign, but he stared at her with the same eyes as Lucien. They didn't seem to recognize her.

Where was she?

The trees were the same, but Lucien and Ranulf were dressed differently. They were also on horseback with ten other men. Something strange had happened while she was in that hole.

Either Lucien and Ranulf had devised an elaborate but tacky prank for her benefit, or…

It had to be a joke. Time travel was impossible. Wasn't it? And even if it were possible, why would Lucien and Ranulf be there?

She might be dreaming. That was a good explanation. She'd taken a nasty fall. Maybe she was dreaming that she'd woken up and was being held at sword point.

The sword biting into her skin seemed like proof enough that she was indeed awake. She looked up at Lucien. He wasn't the man she knew. His hard, angry look seemed out of place. He'd never looked angry when he looked at her—remorseful and sad sometimes, but never angry. Then she noticed the length of his hair. It brushed his shoulders when it should be nothing but peach fuzz atop his head. And, his beard and mustache were gone—shaved clean. He almost looked like a different man.

She probably would have taken him for someone else if she hadn't heard him speak.

A man on a golden mare said, "A search of her would turn up more than her words, Lucien. She may have a weapon and is only waiting for you to drop your guard."

Lucien removed his sword from her throat and sheathed it. "Good point, Hugh. Strip her."

Eris didn't wait for anyone to act on the command. She ran.

"Catch her!"

"She's a fast one."

The men pursued her on horseback.

She dodged into a denser part of the forest to slow them down. Several of the men cursed then dismounted and chased her. She didn't look back, but kept her eyes on her path instead.

Something or someone snagged her cloak. She was pulled up short until she unsnapped the clasp. It came loose, and she continued running.

This was a bad dream. Please let it be a nightmare she would wake from any second.

Unfortunately, her wish went unfulfilled. The forest thinned, and a man on horseback waited for her. She ran into him—rather his horse—and would have changed course, but the other men caught up with her.

They pulled at her clothing, laughing and jeering as they disrobed her. Eris fought them as best she could, but there were too many. They knocked her to the ground.

One of the men moved his hand between her legs, and she kicked him in the face. He reeled back, holding his nose. She tried to get away, but the other men held her.

"She's a wildcat, this one, Lucien. Best to give her to me to break. She'll tell you all once I'm done with her."

The man reached for her breasts, but his hand didn't make contact. Ranulf came up behind him and used the back of the man's shirt to throw him off of her. One look made the other men jump away.

She got off of the ground and was ready to bolt, but Ranulf grabbed her wrist and wouldn't let her go. He pulled her against him and wrapped her in her discarded cloak. She looked up at him in confusion.

He still looked at her without recognition and a little suspicion.

"She has no weapon, Lucien," Ranulf said. "What do you do with her now?"

Lucien approached them. He grabbed Eris's chin, turning her this way and that. "A Moor on my land. Either she's a runaway slave or..." He narrowed his eyes, watching her, probably for a reaction that would give her away.

Eris tried to keep her face blank even as she panicked internally. There had been black slaves in the medieval era? No one ever told her that, not that she had ever been in a conversation where the topic came up. She knew all about American slavery and harbored no delusions that medieval slavery would be much better.

In fact, she hoped the *"or"* Lucien mentioned was a better option. She didn't want to be someone's slave.

Lucien looked at her closer. "She probably belongs to the sultan, but why would he send her? We passed his test. Killing me or you is a waste of time and resources."

"Only the sultan knows his mind. Recreating his thoughts is a headache waiting to happen." Ranulf looked down at Eris.

Sultan? Now there was a sultan?

She wanted so badly to ask what was going on but thought it best not to add to the conversation. Anything she said would probably get her in more trouble, though she didn't know if it could get worse. Runaway slave or sultan's agent—both options sounded like she wouldn't be alive much longer.

Lucien snapped, "Answer me, woman! Who are you? Who sent you?"

She shook her head.

"I know you understand me."

His statement made her realize something very important. Lucien wasn't speaking English, not any English she knew. It was more Germanic and resembled the language she'd learned about back in college in her History of the English Language class. Stranger still, she understood every word. How? Middle and modern English were wholly separate languages.

Lucien, unaware of her confusion, barked, "I also know you have knowledge of me. You gave yourself away already."

"Eris," she whispered, hoping that satisfied him while she came to terms with her new discovery.

"What?"

His near yell made her flinch back against Ranulf. She opened her mouth a few times before she managed to mutter, "My name is Eris."

"And? Who sent you?"

"Or did you run away?" Ranulf asked.

Lucien sneered at him. "Don't be simple. She happens to run away to my lands and knows me on sight. You as well." He turned his incredulous look on her. "She was sent."

"No, I wasn't," Eris said, forgetting that she probably shouldn't be arguing with Lucien.

"Be silent!" Lucien roared.

She ducked her head, ready to cover it if Lucien resorted to hitting her. The man before her definitely wasn't the Lucien she knew. Her Lucien very rarely raised his voice. In fact, she could remember very few instances where she had seen him angry.

One of the men called, "Give her to me, Lucien. I'll get her to tell you what you want."

Eris looked up quickly but didn't know who had spoken. It didn't matter. All of the men were equally dangerous. The only one who had protected her and shown any amount of decency was Ranulf.

She looked up at him.

He met her gaze. There was no recognition. There wasn't even sympathy. So it surprised her when he said, "Give her to me."

"What?" Lucien asked.

"You heard me well enough." Ranulf lifted his gaze to Lucien's. "Give her to me. Make her my problem."

"She's bewitched you. Release her." Lucien grabbed Eris, hauled her away from Ranulf, and then threw her to the ground.

She landed in a pool of black cloth, which she clutched at to make sure no part of her bare body could be seen.

Lucien drew his sword. "She is either a spy or a runaway slave. Either is a death sentence."

Eris's cry of denial mingled with Ranulf's command for Lucien to stop. She watched the sword descend toward her and threw up her hands to protect herself as best she could.

The blow didn't come. A surprised gasp greeted her ears seconds before she was grabbed again and yanked to her feet.

"Where did you get this?" Lucien roared. He didn't give her time to answer, but instead shoved her hand in Ranulf's face. "This is proof she is the sultan's."

Eris didn't know what he was talking about. The only thing on her hand was the ring Lucien—*her* Lucien—had given her before they went to the faire.

She tried to pull out of Lucien's grasp. "That was a gift."

"From the sultan!"

"No!"

"Who then? How else would you come to be in possession of a ring the sultan stole from me?"

She almost told him the truth. Logic made her keep her mouth shut. Not only would he not believe her, he might think she was a witch for talking about time travel and have her burned at the stake. Given his current anger, he might do it whether she was a witch or not.

It was a no-win situation.

Lucien undid the clasp of the bracelet and pulled the ring from her hand. It caught on her knuckle, ripping a jagged line to the tip of her fingernail.

She cried out. Pulling against his grasp did no good as his hold was firm. She looked around for something that would help. Her gaze landed on Ranulf.

He wouldn't though. He didn't know her.

Neither man knew her. The whole situation brought tears to her eyes.

"Please. I don't know any sultan," she said in a near frantic voice. She continued pulling against him.

One man called, "Kill her and be done, Lucien. There are other things to do this night."

"You've the right of it." Lucien released her.

She fell to the ground again. When she looked up, his sword was poised, ready to strike once more.

"I claim my boon." Ranulf grasped the blade of Lucien's sword and held it.

Lucien snapped, "No, you don't."

"Then kill her, but you must maim me to do it. Is that how you repay a debt?"

Eris didn't know what debt, but she was happy for it. Lucien looked like he was actually weighing the situation for the pros and cons.

He made an angered noise and loosened his hold on the sword.

Ranulf released the blade. "She is mine to deal with then."

"Your boon was that I spare her life. I've done that."

"So you feel her life is equal to yours."

Lucien looked like he would punch Ranulf for that. He turned his angered look on her. She shrank back and shook her head. He whipped around. "Fine. Keep her then."

Ranulf said, "She is my problem."

"She is a pawn of the sultan. Why he sent her is a mystery, but he did send her."

Ranulf crossed his arms over his chest. "Prove it."

"I have already." Lucien waved the ring at Ranulf. "There is no explanation except that for her to have this ring."

"That is flimsy at best. Thievery was common in the palace. Who's to say the girl didn't get it that way?"

"You expect me to believe she's a thief?"

"Just as you expect me to believe her a spy, or worse, an assassin."

Lucien charged forward. He grabbed Ranulf by the collar, but his assault ended there.

Ranulf said, "My boon is to make her my problem. *If* you find proof that links her to the sultan, then I will give her to you. Agreed?"

"You will regret this," Lucien said between his teeth. He released Ranulf and went back to his horse. "Ride." He mounted and left the clearing.

The other men followed after him. Each one gave Ranulf a look a loathing.

Eris looked up at Ranulf.

"Don't think this reprieve is to your benefit, girl. Lucien need only present me with proof and I'll kill you myself." He pulled her to her feet. "Until then, you will not leave my sight."

She nodded. Though she wouldn't tell him, she didn't want to leave his sight. It had already been proven twice that near him was the safest place to be.

Until she figured out a way home, she planned to keep Ranulf between her and all danger. That included Lucien.

Chapter Thirty

Lucien lived in a fortress.

Eris saw a lot of similarities between Lucien's medieval keep and his present-day mansion. Dense forests surrounded the keep on all sides, but the tree line stopped well away from the wall that surrounded the perimeter, just like the mansion. No one would be able to use the surrounding foliage as cover if they planned a sneak attack.

Of course, the gate had guards, but she doubted any of them would be asking for her name and then checking it against a prepared list. The guards did glare at her though when Ranulf's horse passed.

She tried to make herself look as small and harmless as possible.

"Our women aren't good enough. Now he brings back theirs," someone in the crowd of onlookers grumbled.

Eris looked around, but she couldn't tell who made the statement.

Were they talking about Ranulf?

He stopped the horse, dismounted, and then helped her down. She stayed close to his side, almost hugging him, because getting too far away might make someone think she was fair game.

He led the horse, and her, to the stable. She thought he would call for an attendant. Instead, he walked all the way to the farthest stable and proceeded to unsaddle and groom his horse.

Maybe he preferred doing it himself. That made sense except no one in the stable acknowledged him. A few others brought their horses to the stable and one of the boys ran forward with a greeting and took charge of one man's horse. They even looked happy to do it. Why hadn't they done that for Ranulf?

"Do you know how to care for a horse?"

She stared at him, not knowing where that question came from.

"Well?"

"No," she whispered. "This is my first time near a horse."

The animal in question pushed his nose into her shoulder. The gesture made her injured hand throb. She'd wrapped a small edge of the cloak around it to soak up the blood and keep away whatever germs were prevalent in this medieval age. Lucien wouldn't have to worry about killing her if an infection got to her first.

The horse didn't like her ignoring him. He rubbed his nose against her and pushed at her more. With her uninjured hand, she patted the top of the horse's head. She was a little unsure how to touch a horse. Did horses like being scratched like a dog? If not, would it bite her?

"Your first time, and yet Zeus is taken with you. That is rare. He hates everyone except me."

"Is that why you're taking care of him and not someone else?" That question just slipped out. She was prepared to apologize, but Ranulf didn't look angry.

"What can you do?" he asked.

Tons is what she wanted to say. Just find her someone with a computer and she could wow him with her programming skills—two seconds before they burned her at the stake for witchcraft. She only had one talent that might actually be of use. "I can sew."

Ranulf snorted. "You must think me truly daft to believe I would give you something as easily concealed as a needle."

"You asked," she mumbled.

He straightened, and she ducked her head quickly, ready to run for it if he turned violent. "Prove it."

The Ranulf of the past was a skeptic. That sucked for her. She hadn't touched a needle and thread in years. The last time she'd sewn anything was over a year ago. Even then, she'd used a machine.

"Does your silence mean you can't?"

"I can." She met his gaze. "What do you want me to sew?"

"I would like another dress like the one you wore. No doubt Lucien has given yours to some deserving lady. You will need clothing of your own unless you plan to wear that cloak from now on." He watched her closely.

"I can't. I didn't make that dress."

"You admit you lied."

"I can sew, but another made that dress. It was given to me."

"Given? The sultan must have prized you above all others to give you such a fine garment *and* Lucien's ring."

"I don't know any sultan."

He grabbed her chin and held her so she couldn't look away. "Neither are you a slave. Your body does not have the marks of a slave. One with a defiant nature such as yours would have intimate knowledge of the lash." He moved closer to her. "Though you try to hide it, I can see it. You have known privilege. Your eyes mark you as a woman who is used to being obeyed."

She looked down quickly. How could he tell so much about her just from her eyes? She thought she looked plenty scared and unassuming.

He released her. "Don't waste your time pretending to be meek now. I have seen through that ruse. In time, I will see through the others as well. Your true purpose here will be revealed."

"I have no purpose." Except to get some clothing and then go home. She'd even forego the clothing if she could just go home.

"Come." He left the stable. He didn't even turn back to make sure she followed him.

But then, he didn't really have to. She scrambled after him and mirrored his steps. When people came in sight, she moved even closer to him. The urge to grab his hand, to draw some comfort from his closeness, almost overwhelmed her.

Her Ranulf would have laughed and hugged her. This Ranulf would probably think she was trying to kill him if she touched him. She settled for walking as close to him as she could without tripping up both of them.

They entered the main room of the keep. Eris looked around. Yet again, Lucien's tastes had spanned time. Weapons decorated every wall. The walls not covered in weapons held long tapestries.

She could almost pretend it was his mansion, except the mansion didn't have dozens of people milling around. It also didn't have rushes on the floor.

She was a little surprised though. The room didn't reek. There was a slight odor, but it didn't smell that bad so long as she ignored the body odor—and it was hard to ignore. The keep itself smelled overwhelmingly like lavender. She expected the smell of excrement and rotting food and had hoped her sense of smell would deaden quickly.

Maybe history had it wrong and the people of the Middle Ages weren't that—a woman walked past and the overwhelming stench of period filled Eris's nostrils. She coughed as her eyes watered.

Nope, history hadn't been wrong. There was just something off about Lucien's keep, something besides her.

"You took so long, I thought she'd killed you and run," Lucien said, walking over to them.

Eris made sure Ranulf was firmly between her and Lucien. Ranulf smirked at her over his shoulder.

"You think I would protect you from him, do you?"

She didn't say anything.

He faced Lucien once more. "I had to see to Zeus."

"Just tell one of the stable boys to do it. You spoil that horse."

"And they would abuse him." He grabbed Eris's cloak.

She immediately squeaked and tightened her hold. He didn't pull it off of her though. He simply held it.

"I'll take her to my room," he said.

Lucien made a knowing noise as he looked her up and down.

Ranulf tugged at her cloak and started walking.

She followed him to keep him from taking her cloak away and leaving her naked. She had no choice but to half jog because his pace was so fast. He led her through the common room to the staircase at the back of the room. A woman they passed held Eris's stolen dress. Ranulf was right, Lucien had given it away.

If she were ever to get home would she need it? And if so, how would she get it back? A better question would be how she would get back the ring if she also needed that.

It was all too much. Time travel to medieval era, presumably England. Ranulf and Lucien alive and as young as when she met them in the present. Well, not completely. They looked a bit older, a little rougher. She got the impression neither man smiled much.

Ranulf opened a door and pushed her into the room. He then entered, closed the door after him, and faced her. "You will remain here when not with me. If you try to escape, you will be killed on sight. Lucien will make sure of that."

She nodded.

"I'm glad we understand each other." He moved toward her. "Give me your hand."

She held it out to him.

"The other hand."

Since she had it balled into her cloak, she had to loosen her hold to unwrap her hand. The cloak settled around her. So long as a freak wind didn't show up or Ranulf didn't yank it open, she should be okay.

She held out her bleeding hand to him.

He took it and examined the wound. "Not too deep."

"No," she whispered.

"Come." He pulled her to a small table. "Sit."

She lowered herself onto the stool. Ranulf pulled out a small wooden box. Next, he took out a jar and a roll of cloth. He then washed and bandaged her hand.

It surprised her that he washed her hand. Didn't medieval medical practices include dirt, urine, and leeches? Not that she wanted those things, but it was what she expected.

He repacked his supplies once he finished. "Who are you?"

She blinked at him. Hadn't they covered this already? "Eris."

Did he want her last name too? Would it matter? Did they even have last names in medieval times? Why hadn't she paid more attention in history class?

He asked, "Who sent you?"

"No one."

"Why are you here?"

"I'm lost."

He raised an eyebrow. "Oh? On your way to where?"

"Far away."

"Does far away have a name?"

Yeah, two thousand-ten. She couldn't say that though. "I don't know it."

He snorted. "More lies. No matter. The truth will reveal itself in time."

Ranulf placed the wooden box of medical supplies back on its shelf. He looked her over one last time and then left the room. The lock clicked loudly, reinforcing her prisoner-status.

She was happy he had locked the door. That meant no one could get to her. Maybe that was the reason he put her in his room to begin with.

Whatever Ranulf had put on her hand soothed the pain. She could focus on something else, like how had she ended up back in time? Lucien and Ranulf as well?

Or, an even better question—had they known she'd travel back?

They had to have.

And what about when she returns?

Everything will change when she comes back.

Lucien had uttered those words. She'd thought they had been talking about another woman. Lucien and Ranulf had always been talking about her. They had met her long ago, long, long ago and then re-met her when she showed up at the mansion to catalog their comic collection.

Suddenly their weird behavior toward her made sense. All their cryptic statements took on a new meaning.

She tried to remember everything they ever said that she'd found strange.

One thing above all others stuck out—the way they had dodged being intimate with her. At the time it was beyond frustrating, but would it become important somehow?

Women of the past had used their virginity as currency.

But what was she supposed to be buying? And from whom?

There was no way she would approach Lucien. Ranulf was the safer and more rational of the two. But what did she say?

It was probably best she do nothing and let them lead the show. Hopefully she wouldn't squish an ant and change the entire course of history. But then, she'd already done this once, according to Lucien and Ranulf.

Was history immutable? Had she fallen back in time because she was supposed to and nothing that occurred while in the past would change anything in the future…present?

All of her questions had her head spinning. She paced around the room, trying to organize her thoughts. A focus would help.

Instead of playing what-if, she went back to thinking about everything Lucien and Ranulf ever said to her.

Her pacing froze, and her heart rate sped up when one memory in particular took hold.

Lucien had apologized.

He'd apologized with such sorrow and remorse. That was an apology he wanted to utter to her…once she returned.

Why? What had—*would* he do?

Since he was waiting for her to return so he could apologize, that meant whatever he did—would do, was something she survived—would survive.

He didn't kill her. He *wouldn't* kill her. Either Ranulf or something else kept him from it. But what else could it be?

The phrase "there are fates worse than death" made her hug her arms. She hoped and prayed whatever Lucien did wasn't something that would make her hate him. She didn't want to hate him.

All she could see was his face when he'd apologized. She knew that she might not have a choice in the matter. Hating him might be the only option left to her.

She sat heavily on the bed and let her head fall onto her arms. "Why is this happening to us?" she whispered.

Unfortunately, no answer was forthcoming.

Chapter Thirty-one

"That was quick," Lucien said in amusement.

Ranulf closed Lucien's bedroom door behind him and faced Lucien. "I didn't bed her, if that's what you mean."

"You have some sense, at least."

"I hope I have more than some, or you're a fool for making me your steward."

Lucien walked to the window. He looked at the tree line, scanning for any movement. Any at all. That little Moor had friends, and they were waiting for the opportunity to attack.

He wouldn't give it to them. His guards were on high alert.

"She's not of the sultan," Ranulf said.

"Stop thinking with your dick. This keep has plenty of women. Use one of them, if you must, and give her over to me."

"When you give me proof."

Lucien glared over his shoulder at his longtime friend. If it hadn't been for that infernal boon, Lucien would know all of that woman's secrets and plans. Ranulf always chose the most inconvenient times to interfere.

He asked, "Who do you think she is if not one of the sultan's women?"

Ranulf joined Lucien at the window. "I cannot begin to guess. She is no one's slave. That I know for a certainty. That one hasn't known the hardships of servitude."

"You questioned her, I know. What did she say?"

"Nothing definitive."

Lucien grunted. "She may not be the one sent to kill us, but she is part of a plot." He scanned the tree line again. "They are out there waiting for her signal." He pinned Ranulf with a look. "Where is she?"

"My room."

"Alone?"

Lucien didn't give Ranulf time to answer. He raced out of his room and down the hallway to Ranulf's, who stopped Lucien before he could kick the door down. Lucien could only glare as the man retrieved his keys, unlocked the door, and opened it for Lucien to enter.

The girl contained within yelped and dodged behind the bed. He advanced toward her. "You will tell me what I want to know, woman." He reached for her.

"Lucien," Ranulf said in a flat voice.

He stopped.

"She is my problem. Remember that."

It would be so easy to reach out and snap the conniving wench's neck. Ranulf was too far away to stop him.

He straightened and stepped back. "You're a fool to leave her in your room unattended. There is no telling what mischief she will cause."

"None so far as I can see. You overreact."

"Put her in the dungeon where she belongs."

Ranulf said, "No."

Lucien wanted to argue with the man. It would be a waste of breath. He took another step back, glaring at the woman as he went. She stared at him with wide, scared eyes. It was an act, and it didn't fool him.

He said, "I can wait. She'll prove who she is before too long. Then, she is my problem."

"As agreed," Ranulf said.

Lucien looked the girl over one last time and left the room. Ranulf didn't follow him. Instead, the man closed and locked his door.

Ranulf was wrong. Lucien only hoped Ranulf wasn't dead wrong. He would ensure she died a slow and painful death if her actions resulted in Ranulf's death.

The man may annoy the hell out of Lucien with his incessant nagging about things that didn't matter, but Lucien knew him to be an asset. He trusted no one more than he trusted Ranulf. No one else had earned the right.

He returned to his room and slammed the door. The chore of finding proof Ranulf wouldn't dismiss had Lucien angrier than finding the girl in the first place.

He hadn't seen a Moor since escaping the sultan's lands. He never wanted to see another. The few years following his return from the crusades after the fall of Jaffa had even faded his memory of his experiences somewhat.

One look at her and it had all come back with crystal clarity.

"Damn her," he said through clenched teeth.

His gaze fell on his mother's ring. It was stained with that woman's blood.

He doused it with water once he'd gotten back to his room. The blood remained. He'd even chanced holding it in the fire, hoping the blood would melt away before it ruined the ring. Still the blood remained. Just thinking that the blood was permanent had him ready to kick down Ranulf's door so he could throw the woman out of the window for her insult.

He picked up his mother's ring. After the sultan had bragged of melting it down to make jewelry for his concubines, Lucien thought he'd never see it again. The only reason he carried it with him during the holy war was because he hadn't trusted the safety of his keep in his absence.

Many lords had lost their lands while serving the king in the crusades. It wouldn't have mattered if he'd become one of them. Lucien hadn't cared about anything except keeping his mother's ring safe. But, his security measures had only ensured its theft.

Now that he had it back, nothing would take it from him again. No woman was worthy.

* * * *

Ranulf shook his head as he locked the door after Lucien.

Rustling made him look over his shoulder.

Eris crept out from behind the bed. Her eyes were wide with terror. She looked as though she would say something but held herself back.

It was that aspect of her personality that had him doubting Lucien. She had smiled so genuinely when they pulled her from the hole. Nothing in her manner had spoken of fear or subterfuge.

She'd even said his and Lucien's names in a familiar manner. As though she knew them and that acquaintance was a good one.

That alone had motivated him to intercede and save her life. If it was a trick, it was a good one. But he didn't think it was. Her face was much too open for her to be a spy.

"Who are you?" he asked.

"Eris."

"Not your name. Who are you?" he snapped.

She ducked behind the bed again and watched him like a cornered rabbit watched a fox.

That fear was genuine.

He cursed under his breath as he turned away from her. Lucien couldn't prove the sultan had sent her. Ranulf couldn't prove the sultan hadn't. Neither could Ranulf keep her locked in his room forever.

A thought occurred to him and he faced Eris once more. She continued watching him.

He held his hand out to her. "Come here, Eris."

She hesitated. Her scared look turned to one of uncertainty.

Little by little she inched forward. He got the distinct impression if he made a loud noise, she'd run and hide again. While tempting, since he could use a good laugh, he refrained.

She stood before him, and he regarded her.

"Such strange hair." He rolled one of the braid-like strands between his fingers. But it wasn't braided. It looked more like the hair was purposefully tangled. "Does your hair do this naturally?"

"No."

"You do not speak more than is necessary, do you?" He tilted her chin up so she looked at him. "One would almost think you are watching your words."

That spark of defiance entered her eyes again.

No, his little burden had been no one's slave. With her attitude, Ranulf doubted she had belonged to the sultan either. The sultan had demanded nothing but abject obedience from all those around him, especially his women. The slightest hint of defiance led to a painful punishment and sometimes death.

"Take it off." He tugged at her cloak. Not enough to strip it off of her but so she knew what he meant. Though there was little else left for her to remove.

Eris clutched at the cloak and stepped back from him. She didn't say it aloud, but her whole body radiated a negative response to his request.

"You act as though I am giving you a choice."

She took another step back rather than obey his command.

He jerked forward, pretending to lunge at her. As he predicted, she retreated quickly but had forgotten the bed was behind her and fell onto it. The billowing cloak tangled around her legs as she tried to scramble off of the bed.

Ranulf decided her being trapped in the cloak worked to his advantage. He fisted his hand in fabric, trapping her further.

Eris stopped trying to get free of the cloak and started trying to get free of him. She flailed her legs wildly and squirmed. Her hands pushed at the cloak, but she couldn't seem to find the opening.

He grabbed one of her ankles when her foot hit his chest. The entire situation amused him. Depending on the outcome of his hunch, he might feel the need to avail himself of his energetic captive.

Trapping the ankle he'd caught beneath his knee, he grabbed her other leg.

"Release me," Eris yelled. "Let go."

It was the first forceful thing she'd said. Ranulf had been right. She was someone who was used to being obeyed.

Not this time. He loosed his hold on her cloak so he could slide his hand up the inside of her leg. It was faster than trying to part the cloak. It also incited Eris to struggle more.

"Don't. Please don't."

Ignoring her, he focused on his task. Either he was right or Lucien was. He reached the place where her thighs met. There was no hair. Her breasts proclaimed her mature, so she must have shaved it. The sultan had preferred his women shaved.

Ranulf didn't let that distract him or sway his opinion. Many of the women in the East shaved.

He slipped one finger past her nether lips.

Her struggles stopped and her whole body stiffened.

That made his job easier. He forced his finger as high as it would go. A small barrier stopped his progress.

His hunch had been right. She was a virgin. That meant she couldn't belong to the sultan. The old lecher considered deflowering virgins a hobby. Ranulf should know. He'd interfered with that particular pastime and had paid the price.

He eased his finger from her depths and backed away from her.

Eris jumped to a sitting position, freed her hand, and smacked him.

Her actions surprised more than hurt him. That and her look of complete betrayal confounded and amused him at the same time. She'd forgotten to be scared in favor of being indignant. He'd finally glimpsed her true nature.

He smirked at her.

"Ranulf?"

His name on her lips was a mere whisper uttered in confusion with a tinge of hope. She searched his gaze. It was like she was looking for something in his eyes. He reached for her cheek. She didn't look scared or flinch from his touch.

"Who am I to you?" he asked in a soft voice.

That broke the spell. She pulled away from him and huddled into her cloak once more.

He straightened. "No matter, little Eris. I now know what you aren't." She looked up at him again. "In time, you will tell me what you are."

"Time," she muttered and then shook her head.

Nothing about the woman before him made sense. She knew him, Lucien as well. Ranulf didn't doubt that. But there had been no point when they would have met.

Even if they had met, he wouldn't have forgotten her.

He went to his closet and rifled through it until he found a tunic. A maiden in a hurry to be away from him had left her clothing. That was a frequent occurrence with him. They all found him alluring and mysterious until they were with him. After which, none would look at him.

The tunic clutched in his hand, he turned back to Eris. She watched him and even drew back when he moved toward her.

He held out the tunic. "There is no undergarment. This will have to do until you make something. If you can."

"I can." She snatched the tunic from him.

He'd insulted her. Pride was a luxury of the nobility. She couldn't be so lofty of an individual though. He would admit she was no one's servant, but a titled lady was a little farfetched, even for him.

"Are you hungry?" he asked.

"No."

Stress and fear dulled the heartiest of appetites. He asked instead, "When did you last eat?"

For some reason his question made her laugh—a short harsh sound with very little humor in it.

"I'll take that to mean some time ago."

"I'm not hungry."

He didn't acknowledge she'd spoken as he left the room. He secured the door and walked toward the stairs. As he neared Lucien's room, he slowed his pace.

Lucien might not believe Eris was a virgin if Ranulf simply told him. Lucien had to find out things for himself, and in his own way, before he believed them. The man could be amazingly stubborn in that way.

Ranulf continued walking.

Even if Lucien discovered Eris was a virgin, would that be enough to convince the man she wasn't a pawn of the sultan?

No, Ranulf needed to know who she truly was or else he'd never convince Lucien.

He entered the kitchen. Everyone within stopped and looked at him.

"Carry on," he said.

They obeyed him slowly. Their eyes followed his every move.

He was used to that. Everyone thought he was irrational because of the many changes he'd instituted once he and Lucien had returned to the keep— changing the rushes on a regular basis rather than covering the old with new, mixing lavender with the rushes to deter fleas, stopping the men and women from simply discarding their scraps on the floor for the dogs, and other such things. No one thanked him for their better health as a result of his changes. Doing so would be to admit Ranulf wasn't a devil in disguise.

"That little heathen is perfect for his perverted appetites," a woman whispered.

The girl she'd whispered to nodded. "He learned them in her country. Better that he practice them on her."

Ranulf didn't know if the women meant for him to hear their words. He ignored them. Acknowledging their words with anger would only encourage them.

He gathered some food items and then headed for the storage room. There was cloth there and other supplies Eris would need to sew.

He had no doubt that she could.

"And what do you do with all that?"

Ranulf pushed past Hugh, who thought to block him. Hugh was too short and not nearly strong enough to stand against Ranulf, yet he continually tried.

"Does Lucien know you have taken these things?"

"If he doesn't, will you tell him?" Ranulf grabbed a few more items.

"Of course. He needs to know you are wasting our resources."

"It is I who is in charge of these resources. Lucien left their use to my discretion. Like all other aspects of his household." Ranulf pinned the man with a look. "Perhaps it's time I change the duties of those who have too much free time."

The man walked away quickly.

Ranulf glared around the room. Everyone busied themselves with something or other. He knew they all hoped for the day when he would be punished for the crimes they imagined he committed. That day wouldn't be soon.

If not for his oath of loyalty to Lucien, he'd leave the keep and all their accusations.

Ranulf returned to his room. Eris sat on the bed, staring at some strands of string she seemed to be braiding.

He placed the food and sewing materials on the bed beside her and then pulled the string from her hands. She didn't try to keep it. He looked at the design in fascination.

It was not braided but knotted. He ran his fingers over her handiwork. "What is this?"

"A rope braid." She shrugged.

Her indifference at the talent he held amazed him. With three different colored strings, she'd managed to make a band as long as his hand with a repeating diamond pattern.

He turned it over. The string looked familiar. "Where did this string come from?"

She pointed at the closet.

Ranulf handed it back to her. He then lifted her chin so she looked at him. "That is the last thing you will find. We will deal much better together that way. Understand?"

"Yes."

"Good." He stepped back. With a gesture to the things he'd brought, he said, "There is bread and some dried meat for you to eat. I've brought needle and thread as well as the cloth."

"Thank you."

She ignored the food and the cloth in favor of returning to her project with the string.

Ranulf simply watched her. He couldn't and wouldn't force her to eat. She seemed content at the moment. Strangely enough, that put him at ease. Lucien was right—she'd bewitched him.

Chapter Thirty-two

Eris jerked awake when Ranulf's arm tightened around her waist. She waited.

Ranulf continued breathing evenly as he held her close. He was still sleeping. Eris wished she could say the same.

Sleep was an ever elusive entity for her. She kept expecting to wake with a knife at her throat, so she never truly slept.

Sunlight streamed through the far window. There was no point trying to go back to her version of sleep when Lucien would arrive soon. It had become his morning routine to check on Ranulf to ensure the man was still alive.

After nearly three weeks, Lucien should have realized Ranulf was in no danger, but Lucien persisted.

She eased from beneath Ranulf's arm. The very second she left the warmth of his body and the blankets her temperature dropped, and she started shaking. She hugged her arms as she reached for her cloak.

A side effect of her trip through time was her inability to get and stay warm. Her body couldn't retain heat. She'd almost set her cloak on fire one day because she'd gotten too close to the hearth and hadn't noticed a cinder bounce onto the edge of the cloth. With all of the treatments the cloth had undergone for waterproofing and wrinkle-resistance and the like, it would have gone up like a Roman candle if Ranulf hadn't seen the danger in time to keep anything bad from happening.

Her cloak helped keep her warm, but the only time she felt truly warm was when Ranulf held her at night. Though it wasn't like she'd given him much choice. He'd told her, after their first night together, that she had latched onto him in the night and wouldn't let go. That news had totally embarrassed her, but he'd found it amusing. He'd obliged her need for warmth by simply starting out the night holding her.

She could almost pretend she was in the present once more. But, her imagination wasn't that good and such a delusion would only depress her when reality re-instated itself.

A loc tendril fell into her line of sight. She brushed it aside. That was another strange thing—her hair. It hadn't grown. It looked as pristine as when she'd had it done the day before the faire. She'd even washed it a few times. Every time it reverted back as though she'd never touched it. It wasn't even fuzzy.

While not having to worry about her hair was a blessing, it not growing at all still worried her. A small sigh left her as she headed to the hearth. Careful of her cloak, she stoked the fire. The warm glow was welcome. Once she could feel her hands again, she filled a nearby kettle with water and set it over the fire to boil. Next she retrieved Ranulf's mug, which greatly resembled his latte mug in the present both in size and in coloring.

Ranulf groaned.

Eris looked back at him. He struggled with the covers and then finally kicked them off.

"It's too hot," he mumbled before rolling onto his side. After five seconds in that position, he rolled onto his other side and patted the spot she'd vacated. "Eris, return to bed."

"Lucien will be here soon."

"I care not. It's too hot without you. I wish to sleep longer." He reached out in her direction, but she stayed near the fire. "Eris." There was an edge of warning in his voice.

She was about to deny him again when the banging started. The door wobbled with the force put behind the blows. Lucien had arrived, and as was his custom, he pounded on the door as hard as he could.

"Why does he persist?" Ranulf grumbled before stuffing his head under his pillow.

Eris took the key ring off its hook near the fireplace and went to the door. She twisted the lock and then walked back to the fire, replacing the keys.

Lucien swung open the door and glared around the room. Eris stayed perfectly still when his gaze landed on her. "Ranulf."

"Leave," Ranulf bit out.

Lucien crossed his arms.

The room descended into silence. Only the rumbling of the boiling water could be heard.

"Blue."

Eris jumped. She looked at Ranulf. "Excuse me?"

"Blue, yellow, orange, a dash of red, and no sugar."

She looked at the shelf near the fireplace that held colored jars containing Ranulf-only-knew-what. She'd learned that Ranulf was the resident physician and apothecary of the keep. His room was filled with various jars of powders and liquids—some he kept under lock and key and others left where ever he placed them last. He even had a small garden in the darkest part of his room where he grew plants that didn't take well to sunlight.

He never volunteered the names of what the colored jars contained, and she never asked. He simply named the colors and the amounts and she mixed them. She pulled down the ones he named and scooped about a teaspoon of each powder. She reached for one jar and then stopped. "No green this time?"

"Is that what I drank yesterday?"

"Yes."

"No. It made me jittery."

She shrugged. A strong herbal smell rose from the concoction when she poured hot water over it. She wasn't altogether sure she wanted to know what Ranulf was drinking since it had the ability of waking him fully, whereas a latte mug full of espresso barely fazed him. Her only guess as to why he hadn't continued drinking the same in the present was because some of the powders were derived from illegal substances. But that was just a theory.

She stirred the mixture and then walked the mug over to Ranulf. Lucien's gaze followed her every movement.

Ranulf took the cup and drank deeply.

Lucien said, "My worry of you being poisoned seems more and more absurd as the days pass. It wouldn't surprise me if you were immune to poisons after drinking that foul smelling potion of yours every morning."

"I am immune to most poisons," Ranulf said. "But that is a skill my father honed within me while I was a child."

Eris found that bit of knowledge interesting. She wanted to ask him to elaborate but kept her mouth shut so Lucien's attention wouldn't return to her.

Ranulf said, "I am immune to all that is within this room, however. So, you needn't come pounding on my door any longer."

"Are you immune to being stabbed as well?" Lucien bit out. He glared at Eris as he asked the question. "The girl might take advantage of your inability to wake."

"In all the years that you have known me, have you ever seen me succumb to an attack whilst I slept?"

Lucien rubbed his bare chin—something Eris still couldn't get used to—in thought. "If my memory serves, you are more lethal if attacked in sleep."

"Exactly. Leave off waking me so early when there is no need."

"You sleep too much," Lucien snapped.

Eris hid a giggle behind her hand.

Both men looked at her. She turned back to the fire quickly.

"Eris, make another and bring me a cloth for my face," Ranulf said, holding out his mug.

She filled a nearby basin with water and then grabbed a towel before she walked to the bed. Once she'd set the items on the bedside table, she took the mug.

"Put in a dash of green this time," Ranulf said in a low voice.

She nodded.

"At least she can be trained," Lucien grumbled.

Ranulf asked, "Jealous?"

Lucien grunted.

Eris half filled Ranulf's cup when she repeated the early mixture of powders, including green. He never finished two full cups, and she didn't want to be wasteful since she'd seen the work he put into preparing each of the powders.

Ranulf joined her at the fire. He threw the contents of the basin out of the nearby window and then placed the bowl where it belonged. She handed him his cup.

The fire popped. The sound made Eris jump. At the same time, Ranulf pulled her back a few steps. She mumbled a thank you and checked her cloak to make sure nothing was about to catch fire.

"Tunic," Ranulf said between sips.

She looked in Lucien's direction. He stood next to the chair where she'd left Ranulf's tunic. Not wanting Lucien to lash out at her, she tried to stay as far away from him as she could.

Ranulf said, "Eris."

She nodded as she walked forward.

Lucien watched her, but he didn't move.

She snatched up the tunic and rushed back to Ranulf's side, putting him between her and Lucien.

Ranulf took the tunic from her and handed her his mug. "What is this?" He unfolded the tunic and stared at it. He looked at Eris. "Where did you get this?"

"I made it. You should recognize the cloth. You gave it to me."

He looked at the tunic again, running his fingers over the embroidery.

She said, "It's incomplete."

He looked at her.

She gestured to the tunic. "The design on the sleeves is incomplete. I had to stop so I could finish your belt." She returned to the bed for the belt she had stashed under her pillow. Hiding it had been the only way to keep Ranulf from trying to take it before she finished.

He'd been so amazed at her friendship bracelet. She thought nothing of it since most of the girls back in high school could do it, some of the boys too.

He'd asked for a longer, wider version to be used for a belt. She had no problem with the request. There was nothing else to fill her time once he locked her in his room and went about doing whatever medieval men did to fill the day. Having a project kept her from being bored.

When the tedium of making the belt had gotten to her, she'd switched to Ranulf's tunic. It had surprised her how quickly her sewing came back. She guessed it was like riding a bicycle, not something she'd forget.

"I've never seen stitching like this." Ranulf looked closely at the seams of the tunic. He even tugged at the fabric, probably to test the strength of the sewing.

Lucien snapped, "You're a fool to give her needles."

"She's had them all this time and this is all she could think to do with them." Ranulf slipped the tunic over his head and then held his hand out for the belt. "I think I want another."

"Belt?" She looked at the pile of thread he'd unearthed for her project. She'd only found a few strands here and there when she'd done her initial search but Ranulf had several spools. He even had a spool of spun gold.

"Tunic," he said.

"There's no more fabric."

"I'll bring you more." He tied his belt and then faced Lucien. "Did you want one?"

Lucien bared his teeth.

"No?" He shrugged and turned back to her. "Busy yourself until I return with the cloth."

She nodded.

The men left.

She waited for the click of the lock and their footsteps to sound far away before she moved. As had become her habit, she tested the door.

It held.

Medieval locks probably weren't that sophisticated, but she didn't know the first or last thing about lock picking.

She indulged a moment of self pity. Almost three weeks. In that time Lucien hadn't been able to find a way to prove she was an agent of the sultan, not that he would, and Ranulf had elevated her to servant status even though he still kept her locked in his room.

Her saving grace was that Ranulf hadn't taken advantage of her position.

She looked at the bed.

Lucien and Ranulf, the ones from her time, said their past relationship with her—even though she hadn't known they were talking about her—had been all about sex. She couldn't see how. Lucien looked like he'd just as soon strangle her than take her to bed.

Ranulf seemed interested but never did more than hold her at night. If their relationship was supposed to turn sexual, she couldn't see how.

The lock clicked.

Eris swung around.

Ranulf entered. He held his hand out to her. "Come."

"Why?" She stepped back. He didn't look angry or like he wanted her dead. What was with the sudden change in routine?

"I think I give you too much freedom that you think you can question me. Come now. And bring your sewing supplies."

Now she was really confused. She didn't question him again but gathered her things and walked to him.

"Must you continue wearing this?" He picked up an edge of the cloak. "It is autumn and hardly so cold that you need it."

She didn't answer but looked at him with one eyebrow raised.

He laughed. "Of course. What am I thinking? You could probably be standing at the threshold of Hell and still complain of cold."

"I'm not that bad," she mumbled.

It was his turn to look at her incredulously.

"I'm not."

He stepped back so she could leave the room and then closed and locked the door behind her.

"Why lock it? I'm going with you."

"Lucien allows your stay in my room rather than the dungeon only because he knows my room is the most secure." He walked away.

Eris wanted to ask for an explanation but the hostility radiating from the people they passed froze her voice. Like the last time they'd walked together through the keep, she stayed as close to Ranulf as she could get without tripping them both.

Everyone whispered as they passed.

Ranulf led her to a tree and pointed at the ground. "Stay here."

There was a basket with cloth sitting next to a blanket spread over the ground. Had he brought her to the courtyard for a change of scenery, maybe? She wouldn't ask that aloud.

She moved her cloak out of the way and knelt near the basket. Her gaze strayed to the gates. There were too many people between her and the gate but part of her dared to hope.

"You can try, if you like." Ranulf's look was amused, like he'd known what she was thinking.

"I'm not stupid."

"Neither am I. There are plenty of men who will stop you if you try to run. Do not think to abuse this freedom, or you'll never have it again."

"Why give it to me at all?"

He gestured to his tunic. "A reward."

"Leave the girl," Lucien barked.

Ranulf looked her over. He took a breath, probably to say something more, but only nodded. He walked away.

Instead of starting the task Ranulf implied with the basket of cloth, she watched Lucien and Ranulf speaking to a man who looked like a merchant.

She took a few deep breaths, enjoying the fresh air even as it chilled her skin. Except for trips to the bathing room, Eris had not left Ranulf's room since her arrival, so she wouldn't complain about a little discomfort. She pulled her cloak closer and then turned to her task. After laying out her supplies, she chose a length of dark blue cloth. Tunics were an easy pattern. Sewing the first one hadn't taken her long. The embroidery was a bit more time consuming. She hoped Ranulf would return the tunic he currently wore so she could finish the pattern.

"Lord Lucien, would you care to show them a true warrior's skill?" one of the men called. He hefted his sword when Lucien looked at him.

Several of the men cheered the suggestion.

Lucien called back, "I wouldn't want to embarrass you."

"Match me, then," Ranulf said. He clapped Lucien on the back. "You've been itching to put me in my place since my little burden arrived."

They glanced at her.

"You're right. I have." Lucien made his way to the practice area. "It's a pity you don't have Corpse Maker with you."

Ranulf lifted two swords and tossed one to Lucien. "I would never draw Corpse Maker against you. That sword is meant for killing my enemies, not practice."

Several people stopped what they were doing to watch Lucien and Ranulf. Eris didn't blame them. One of her favorite past times was watching them spar.

"My money is on Lucien," said the man standing near her.

His companion said something she couldn't catch.

Eris smirked but kept her thoughts to herself. Ranulf would win. He always won. He'd only lost once that she knew of.

She continued sewing, using the tip of her finger as a guide, as she watched the match.

Lucien and Ranulf didn't have the same fluid grace as they did in the present, but she hadn't expected them to. It would probably take them a few years to achieve that level of skill.

A small frown creased her brow. Something was wrong with Ranulf. She couldn't be sure, but it looked like he was hesitating. No one else said anything so she thought it might just be her.

The match didn't last long. The victor was Lucien.

Eris was so stunned she stopped sewing.

"Congratulations on a battle well met," Ranulf said. He clasped arms with Lucien.

"Keep at it. One day you will best me."

Both men laughed. They left the middle of the crowd, headed in her direction. She packed up her supplies and gathered the basket against her side. Lucien glared at her as they got closer but she kept her gaze firmly on Ranulf.

He nodded to her as they passed. She fell into step behind them.

Lucien glanced back at her every few steps, but she didn't look at him. She only knew he was looking at her because she saw his body twisting.

"Do you expect her to do something?" Ranulf asked.

"Much more than you." Lucien broke stride with Ranulf. He gave her one last suspicious look and then walked away.

Eris stopped walking as she stared after him. She jumped in surprise when Ranulf's hand brushed her cheek.

He said, "Such a sad expression. What is it for?"

She pulled away from him and shook her head.

He smiled. "You can't be upset to see him leave. You're scared of him." He searched her face. "And yet, I've seen you look at him with such regret. Was it he you thought would be your protector?"

"I didn't think of anything. There is no plan," she whispered. Continually assuring him of her innocence was getting old. It was as much a part of their daily routine as Lucien banging on the door in the morning.

"So you say and yet I know you're hiding something."

"Why did you let Lucien win?"

Ranulf jerked. He took a breath as though he would say something but snapped his mouth shut. Instead he turned and continued back to the keep. "I have other tasks to see to this day. You will finish your sewing in my chamber."

"Now it's your turn to hide things." She clutched the basket and stopped when he swung back to face her. His expression told her she'd made him angry.

"You do not know of what you speak, so be silent." He glared at her until she bowed her head.

They continued to his room.

She entered and put her basket on the floor. Just as Ranulf was leaving once more, she said, "I do."

He stopped and looked at her. "What did you say?"

She met his gaze. "I do know what I'm talking about. You threw that match."

Ranulf slammed the door as he faced her.

She didn't let the return of his anger deter her. "You weaken him by pretending your skills are less than his."

He stalked toward her, but she stood her ground. The constant suspicion had worn her down. She was ready to tell the truth and let fate have her.

"Who are you?"

"Eris."

"You have said that many times already. Who—"

"Brue."

"What?"

"My name is Eris Brue. I was born in nineteen eighty-two."

Ranulf frowned at her.

"I've seen you and Lucien spar many times. He's never beaten you. While that does annoy him, he still enjoys the match."

"You're crazed. Or have mistaken us for others."

She snorted. "I wish you were the Ranulf I know. I'd actually sleep better at night knowing you wouldn't be thinking about killing me."

"I am no magical creature or practitioner of magic that I would live until any year in the nineteens."

"Up until I fell back through time, I didn't even know you had. And I'm sure I'd have been skeptical, like you are now, if you'd told me." She watched him for some kind of reaction. The only thing she saw was pity.

She wished she knew some tidbit about Ranulf that would prove her words beyond doubt. Her father's business cards would have made great evidence if she'd remembered to grab them. Then again, she might have lost them when the men had stripped her.

Well, she'd given it her best shot. She shrugged. At least she tried. She turned back to the basket she'd dropped.

Ranulf laughed.

She faced him once more.

"To think we would remain friends for centuries instead of decades and not kill each other." He laughed more.

Did he believe her?

She said, "I'm sure you've wanted to. You can't be with someone for that long and not want to."

"Your words hold more truth than you know," he said in a sober voice. "And you? You have yet to explain your relationship to us. Are we close that you would have an opportunity to see Lucien and me spar on more than one occasion?"

She closed her mouth.

"You are comfortable in my arms at night. I assume that is a position that is familiar to you." He watched her closely.

It didn't matter. She knew how to keep her face blank.

"And yet you are a virgin still. I know myself well enough to know I wouldn't let a woman enter my bed without pleasure being involved."

"That's not true. You haven't touched me…much."

"That's different. Lucien won't take my word. Your maidenhead must remain intact for when it enters his mind to check."

So that was why he hadn't done anything. Well, she was happy for the reprieve and hoped no one clued Lucien into the idea of checking. But Ranulf's other statement concerned her. She moved closer to him. "Lucien does trust you."

"Lucien trusts no one, least of all me."

"You're steward of his keep."

"Charity because I lost my title, and he felt he owed it to me."

"Why did you lose your title? What did you do?"

"I saved his life."

"Don't people normally get rewards for something like that?"

He made a shooing motion. "I'll not talk about that so leave off asking."

"That's not fair."

He grinned at her. "Really now? You'd know much about that subject, wouldn't you?"

"That's different," she said, looking away from him. She pulled her chin away when he would have turned her head back. "Telling you too much about the future might change something. But, your situation with Lucien is the past."

"And like you, telling my story may change something."

"What?"

"To answer that I would have to tell you my story. I have no intention of doing that."

They stared at each other.

Eris asked, "You truly believe me then?"

He snorted. "Something so fantastical can't possibly be true."

"But, you just said—"

"I keep my original opinion. You are not an enemy." He opened the door once more and that ended the conversation. "I will return later."

She watched the door close and wanted to throw something at it.

He didn't believe her. She'd taken a chance telling him the truth and he thought she was crazy. The up side was that he hadn't immediately called her a witch and tried to have her burned.

The only way he'd stop thinking she was a threat was to make him believe the truth. Except for her cloak, she had nothing that she'd arrived with. Not that any of it was particularly special to her time.

"Should have told him I was from Venus," she mumbled.

Chapter Thirty-three

Ranulf chuckled to himself. He'd been doing the same thing at odd intervals the whole day. He'd have to thank Eris for keeping him in such a jovial mood.

He couldn't stop thinking about what she'd told him. The more he thought about it, the more absurd it sounded.

Time travel.

Nineteen eighty.

The concept of such a far off date defied all logic. That was what made her story that much more interesting. She could have picked any time. Why the nineteen hundreds?

"Should I even ask what has kept you so amused?"

Ranulf looked at Lucien. In contrast to him, Lucien had stayed in a foul mood all day. It seemed like the more Ranulf had chuckled to himself the more annoyed Lucien became.

It occurred to Ranulf to simply tell Lucien of Eris's wild tale.

"I..."

He stopped. He found Eris's story amusing, but Lucien didn't have his sense of humor. Ranulf actually doubted Lucien had any sense of humor at all.

"Ranulf?"

"I doubt you want to hear about anything my burden has done that I found funny."

Lucien's face clouded more. "You're right. I don't."

While there was no way what Eris had told him was true, Ranulf didn't think he should repeat her words. Some might think it justification to do her harm. Lucien was included in that number.

"It's too bad your incessant good cheer didn't infect the others of the keep." Lucien looked around.

Ranulf didn't bother. He could feel the hatred without having to look.

Lucien chuckled under his breath. "Ah, bath day. It is always good to see my people united in their hatred of a common theme."

"They should be done with it already. I have done the same these past four years. I will not suddenly stop. They have benefited."

"They won't thank you."

Ranulf knew that all too well already. He also knew the bath was just a convenient excuse. If not that then the people of the keep would find another reason to hate him more than they already did.

"How does your burden handle your habit?" Lucien asked.

Ranulf touched his scalp with a grimace of pain. "Well. She's no stranger to bathing."

"Of course she isn't. The sultan likes his women clean and smelling sweet. You told me that."

"I think I shall bring her to the common room after the evening meal," Ranulf said quickly. The conversation had taken a dangerous turn. He wanted Lucien to forget the idea of Eris being from the sultan.

The only other way to prove she was not a threat was to continue indulging Lucien's need to wake him every morning. That small sacrifice— annoying as it may be to Ranulf—allowed Lucien to witness Eris's docile and accommodating nature. There was no malice in her actions. She was eager to be helpful in any way she could. Such an attitude could not be faked for such a prolonged period, especially not on a woman as expressive as Eris.

"Are you trying to provoke me?" Lucien snapped. "It was bad enough you brought her out to the courtyard earlier. Leave her locked away. Or better still, give her to Mason. He could find my proof in little time."

Ranulf's face hardened. He hated Mason. He hated the fact that Lucien employed the man. "I do not understand how you can stomach the likes of him after all that we endured."

"I should say the same of you about her."

"She is different."

"So is he. He does what I cannot—*will* not do." Lucien's fist clenched at his sides. "He is necessary."

Ranulf wouldn't voice an opinion on that matter one way or the other. He saw the necessity of Mason, but his skin crawled at the thought of sharing a shelter with the man.

He said, "I go to my bath. I shall see you at the evening meal."

"Leave her locked away."

Ranulf ignored Lucien's words. Except for annoying Lucien, there was no harm to bringing her to the common room. Her mood had improved after the short excursion to the courtyard.

He unlocked and entered his room. Eris already had several of his bathing soaps and oils—his own recipes—in a basket awaiting his return.

She stood. "Ready?"

He touched his scalp again and winced.

"Stop being such a baby. It doesn't hurt that much." She grabbed the basket and walked to the door.

Ranulf stepped back so she could pass him and then pulled the door shut. "I think you do it purposefully as a form of retaliation."

"I think you just like to whine." She smiled up at him.

Her banter was said with an edge of caution as though she would apologize quickly if he took offense. He laughed, and Eris instantly relaxed. The woman was constantly on edge, awaiting attack. Her uneasiness made him uneasy at times. That was another reason he knew she was not what Lucien thought. A spy or assassin would work to make Ranulf feel relaxed so he would let down his guard.

He led the way to the bathing room. No, Eris was no assassin. A distraction for another to attack them, maybe, but the attack wouldn't come from her.

Ranulf was more worried about the people of the keep doing him harm than her. They entered the bathing room and his gaze went immediately to the tub that sat in the middle of the room, steam billowing from its depths. Ranulf would guess, as always, the people who had fetched the water had filled the tub with boiling water without adding any cold to cool it down.

"Are they trying to boil you alive or do they just not realize a tub full of boiling hot water would really hurt?" Eris set down the basket. She went and touched the water in the tub, jerking back quickly with a tiny yelp. "They got it extra hot today."

"Yes."

"Do they not like you, or do they just not like how many baths you take?"

"Both." He gathered the nearby empty buckets and siphoned off some of the hot water. Normally the servants would take the buckets but they probably thought to annoy him by leaving them. They only aided him.

He set the buckets aside and then went to a smaller tub nearby that was also filled with water. After a quick touch to judge the temperature, he scooped some of the water from the smaller to the larger tub. The water hissed and billows of steam rushed off.

"So, we've got ice cold and boiling hot." She crossed her arms. "What did you do that has them so upset?"

"Many things. Never mind that. Attend me." He stripped down, heedless as to whether Eris was embarrassed or not.

She didn't act embarrassed. In fact, she watched him with avid appreciation. Ranulf was used to that. Women liked watching him and flirting with him. It was always the same until they learned of his tastes in the bedroom. Then, the whispering and censure started.

He sighed as he lowered himself into the water. Eris placed her hands on the top of his head and pushed. Not enough to move him. It was her way of telling him to dunk his head. He complied, tossing his head as he surfaced.

Eris squeaked in dismay and that only made him smile. He glanced back at her. She'd stripped off her chemise and stood wearing the undergarments she'd made for herself. A strange design—at least he thought it was. She'd attached string to a strip of cloth she passed between her legs and then tied neat little bows at both hips. More string was tied behind her neck and supported the cloth that covered her breasts.

It had to be uncomfortable. He wanted nothing better than to pull the string and relieve her shoulders of the burden.

"I can't wash your hair with you facing me, unless you *want* soap in your eyes," she said.

He faced front and tensed.

"Relax. You act like I'm hurting you."

She applied a little of the soap and started scrubbing his scalp. He swore she used her nails. Nothing else could account for the pain.

Through gritted teeth, he said, "You are."

"You big baby." She lessened the pressure. "There. Is that better?"

"Marginally."

"I think you're just tender-headed."

"If you know that then stop abusing me."

"You're the one who told me to wash your hair and you keep letting me do it. I think the lord doth protest too much."

"What?"

"Never mind." She pushed at his head.

He dunked himself again. This time he didn't swing his head when he surfaced.

Eris soaped his hair once more. He didn't understand why she washed it twice, and he couldn't get her to stop.

"Ranulf."

"Yes?"

Eris smiled as he gritted his teeth. That only made her want to scrub harder. It wasn't like the man had a dirty scalp. He was surprisingly clean, which confused her.

"Why do you take so many baths? This is the third one this week."

"Are you complaining that I do not smell?"

"I appreciate it, but it doesn't hold with the era. People in the Middle Ages didn't bathe all the time, which is weird since the Romans did. How civilization deteriorated like that, I'll never know."

"I cannot guess either."

She waited, but he didn't answer her question. After rinsing the soap off of his head, she said, "Lucien doesn't bathe as often as you."

"Ah, but you are wrong. Lucien is more fastidious than even me. He simply doesn't bathe in the keep."

"He doesn't want people to know."

"No."

"But you don't care?"

Ranulf sighed. He tapped his shoulder.

She placed her hands there and started kneading. While she massaged his shoulders, he washed the rest of his body.

He said, "The people of this keep benefit from my many baths though they do not think so. Because they do not want to waste the water and the effort, many of them use it after me."

Eris made a face but kept her opinion to herself. "Why do you do it?"

"Since I know you will not leave off this subject, I'll tell you. It has to do with how Lucien and I met."

At last, she cheered silently.

"I was branded a traitor."

"Huh?"

What did that have to do with bathing or Lucien?

"You heard me."

"You're not a traitor. Betrayal isn't in your nature."

He glanced back at her. "You're so sure, are you?"

She gave him the best stubborn look she could muster. Ranulf could never betray anyone, and she refused to entertain the idea that he had. She didn't care what time period it was. Ranulf was Ranulf.

"Is this faith of yours based on knowing my future self?"

"First, you say you don't believe me and then you ask me questions like that. Which is it?"

He said nothing.

She nodded. "Ranulf is many things, but a liar isn't one of them."

"I could have changed over the course of a few centuries."

"You were accused of betrayal. What happened next?"

"I think I like your defense of me, and you're right. I didn't betray anyone, but I was forced to make it seem like I had." He sighed. "I and my knights were captured."

"By the sultan."

"No, the sultan's maternal uncle. He took a liking to me."

Eris didn't think she wanted to hear the story after all. She almost asked him to stop.

Almost, except the story was an important part of both Ranulf's and Lucien's pasts. She needed to hear it, no matter how painful.

"He wanted me to entertain him for the night—" Ranulf clenched his hands where they rested on the rim of the tub, "—in exchange for all our lives and our freedom."

That's just what she hadn't wanted to hear.

She asked in a shaky voice, "I thought same sex relations were against their laws." Was that the case in the old Middle East? She knew it was in the present one.

"Laws do not apply to the favored brother of the sultana, the sultan's mother. She made sure no one could touch her brother, not even her son, or even think of betraying his tastes." He expelled an annoyed breath. "The sultana even used her influence over the harem and sent him girls to keep up appearances for the court. Everyone knew it was a lie, but none were stupid enough to accuse him."

"You went to him."

"To save my men—yes. I thought it a small sacrifice so long as we lived."

"He set you all free then." She tried to hold back the hopeful quality in her voice.

Ranulf growled. "He freed my men but kept me. The prince enjoyed my prowess."

"You were the *top*?"

She didn't know why her whole body sagged as relief swept over her when he nodded. The thought of Ranulf beneath some man hadn't set well with her. That he'd been forced at all didn't make her happy either, but at least he'd been the top.

"I pretended the prince was a woman. My imagination served me so well the prince determined he would keep me. Over a week passed before my men saw me again. When they did, the prince had me dressed as one of his courtiers. He made me denounce my duties as a knight of England before my men or else he'd have them all killed."

She gripped his shoulders.

"For almost a year, I served the prince when he called."

"Upon threat of death."

"I would have welcomed death," Ranulf snapped, facing her.

She jerked away from him lest he lash out at her.

"Death doesn't scare me. The prince wouldn't have settled for such an easy punishment. I saw the men who had tried defying or betraying his secret. They were eunuchs and some had their tongues cut out. They were made to service him in the ways left to them. And he used them to vent his rage when disgust at his own desires reached its peak." He shook his head. "Death would have been preferable. Not having that option, I performed my duty and kept the prince satisfied." He spat the last word like a curse.

Eris edged toward him. She slid her hand down his arm and took his hand in both of hers. Bringing it to her cheek, she whispered, "I'm sorry. I'm sorry." She closed her eyes, trying to forget the look of angry disgust etched on his face. "Stop. You don't need to tell me. This is too private."

He jerked her hand, pulling her into the tub with him. "It's too late for that, little Eris."

She winced when he griped her hand.

"The prince's favorite game was parading me through the harem. The days when I pleased him especially well meant I could have one of the harem's occupants. Of course, the prince watched. He liked interrupting and taking the girl's place so he could have my release."

A faraway look entered Ranulf's eyes. He seemed to be reliving his past even as he told her about it. She wished she hadn't pried. She thought Ranulf and Lucien had met at a joust or something similar.

"The sultan tolerated my use of the harem grudgingly. A new girl, a virgin, entered the harem, and the sultana gifted her to me to be her first instead of her son. The sultan was furious because initiating virgins was a favored hobby he cherished." His gaze focused on her. "That is why I do not believe you belong to him."

Thank God for small favors then. No wonder Lucien and Ranulf of her time had been so adamant about not having sex. It wasn't that she gave it to one of them in barter for her life—or whatever—but that she had it at all.

She said, "I take it the sultan took revenge somehow."

Ranulf smirked. "That's putting it lightly. He drugged me, bound me, and threw me into the prison of his other palace far from his uncle and mother. I think his intention was to leave me there to rot."

"Obviously you didn't."

"The prince loved giving me gifts of jewels and other trinkets. I kept some of those baubles within my clothing at all times as thieves were prevalent in the palace. A few well-placed bribes and my jailers gave me more and better food. That dungeon is where I met Lucien."

That explained how he'd started the story at least.

"He'd been there only a month, but the environment and lack of proper food had taken its toll on him and his men. The sultan thought to see me in a like condition when he finally returned some weeks later. I'm sure my jailers were punished."

"You don't know?"

He shook his head. "The sultan gave us our freedom the same day he visited the dungeon. He even said we could keep it if we could make it to the next city."

"But? There has to be a but."

"I already said Lucien and his men were in a bad way. The sultan gave us one water skin for twelve men and shoved us into the desert only a few hours before noon." He stroked her cheek. "I can see from your expression that you understand the consequences of such an action."

"I've never been to the desert, but I know what can happen if exposed to the heat for prolonged amounts of time."

"Yes, and it happened to us. The water didn't last long. Men died as they walked. Lucien only survived because I dragged him along with me and fed him my blood when the thirst became too much for him."

"You made it to the next town and the sultan let you go, right?"

"We made it to the city, and the sultan wasn't happy to see us. He chased us back into the desert. A nomadic tribe with no love for the sultan and an eye for the few fine jewels I had left aided us. We traveled with them for several months while Lucien recuperated.

"I bathe as often as I do because of my time with the prince and the nomadic tribe. Though the nomads used sand more often than they used water. Lucien developed the same habit. I learned much more about medicine from the nomads. The lavender, for instance. I insist upon it being mixed with the rushes because it repels fleas. The men of the keep hate the smell."

She laughed a little, trying to lift the somber mood his story had caused. "I bet. They probably complain that they smell like a bunch of women."

"Yes."

"Why would you say you were branded a traitor if you saved Lucien's life and brought him home?"

"My men returned with the tale of my betrayal. The king stripped me of my lands and title. I was to be put to death if anyone ever laid eyes upon me again. Only Lucien's intervention has kept me alive. I entered his keep as a penniless knight. The king will not allow me to gain any wealth or property."

Eris was about to ask more questions when Ranulf shifted. He pulled her to his chest as he stood.

How long had they been sitting in the bath talking?

Ranulf released her, stepped out of the tub, and then lifted her out. "Let us return to my room before we continue this conversation." He dressed.

Eris did as well and then followed him out of the room.

The glares of the people around them made more sense. She knew they weren't directed solely at her. But, Ranulf had made his own situation worse when he rescued her.

As soon as they were safely in his room, she asked, "Does Lucien know all of what happened to you?"

"No. It will remain that way."

"But why? He's your friend. He deserves to know."

Ranulf presented her with his back as he warmed himself at the fire.

She asked, "You'd let him think you only dragged him out of the desert so you wouldn't be killed when you returned to England?"

"Lucien knows what he must. I saved his life, and he saved mine. That should have made us even, but he didn't see it that way. Rather than have him be indebted for life I told him to give me one boon. When I called upon it, his debt to me would be repaid."

She stared at him. "That wasn't…you used that to…Ranulf, why?"

He faced her. "Something about you makes me act contrary to how I should. I am truly beginning to believe you have bewitched me."

"I'm not a witch," she said quickly.

"My conscience would rest easier if you were." He crossed to her side so he could frame her face with his hands. "Then I could explain away this overwhelming need to keep you safe despite all logic and good sense."

Whatever his reasons, she didn't care, so long as she lived to see her home again.

He released her. "Dry yourself and get dressed. We go to the common room tonight."

"We do?"

He grinned at her.

Chapter Thirty-four

"Three days, Lucien. For three days he has flaunted her around the keep."

Lucien drank and listened, but his gaze was only for the girl that caused the irritation of his table companions. He watched them together every night Ranulf brought her to the common room.

He watched that woman make Ranulf laugh. The man joked constantly, but his amusement was always cynical and perverse. There was genuine humor in his manner when speaking with Eris.

Another man said, "He is taunting you. He knows you will not foreswear yourself."

"I will not," Lucien said. It had never crossed his mind. He'd given Ranulf his word and wouldn't break it.

"Can you not see this for what it is, my lord?" Hugh, a man known for taking advantage of every opportunity that showed him favor, moved closer to Lucien. "Look how friendly they are with each other. It's hard to believe the girl only came to this keep a month ago and already she's won over your fiercest warrior."

Lucien made a non-committal noise. He continued drinking as he stared at Eris and Ranulf. They *were* close, unnaturally so.

"It's almost as though they know each other from a previous meeting."

Hugh had voiced Lucien's own thoughts, but he didn't say so. The man didn't need any input from Lucien to continue the conversation.

"You have to see what is happening here, Lucien." Hugh gripped Lucien's upper arm.

That finally got Lucien to look away from Ranulf and Eris and give Hugh his full attention.

However, Hugh mistook Lucien's reaction as interest when Lucien only wanted the man to release him.

Hugh leaned closer, gripping Lucien's arm. "This is a plot of some kind. Ranulf never takes a woman in his confidence. I've heard the women talking about his prowess in bed but never repeat performances, and yet that Moor has retained her position this entire time." Hugh lowered his voice. "You have to know the girl is from the sultan, and Ranulf was her way of fulfilling the mission he charged her with."

"It's plausible."

"It's true. Can't you see that? Ranulf was a favored man in the sultan's court for one whole year. He didn't get as high as he did unless his allegiances changed. He's been lying in wait all this time for the sultan to enact a plan using *that* girl."

The sense of Hugh's statements angered Lucien even more than he already was. He couldn't deny the logic. He also couldn't deny that those very same thoughts had crossed his mind more than once after seeing how easy Ranulf was with his *prisoner*.

Hugh leaned in closer. "You must stop them before they have time to act."

"Leave off whispering in my ear before I begin to think your tastes run toward men." Lucien shoved the man away hard enough that Hugh stumbled and his chair tipped over.

The man sprawled but quickly righted himself. In a loud voice, he said, "Will you wait to be near your death before you see what most of us already know? Don't be a fool."

Lucien erupted from his seat. Hugh dodged back but not fast enough. Lucien slammed the man into the nearby wall with his arm lodged against Hugh's windpipe.

All sound in the hall stopped.

Lucien said in a low voice, "The only fool I see is the one who would call me such to my face."

"Peace, my lord. Peace," the man croaked.

He released Hugh. The man rubbed his throat as he walked quickly away. Lucien turned back to his chair only to notice all attention on him, including that of Ranulf and Eris. He spared them only a glance and then quit the room as well.

Hugh's words followed him. Lucien trusted Ranulf. He had no reason to doubt the man's loyalty.

Admittedly Ranulf had acted strangely since the girl had come to the keep, but that had a plausible explanation. Lucien didn't know what it was but was sure it existed.

He prowled his room. Hugh's words dogged his every step.

What if the man was right? It would explain Ranulf's strange behavior toward the girl when Ranulf had never shown more than a momentary interest in any woman before.

And yet, Ranulf had jumped to Eris's aid almost immediately. He treated her with care instead of as a prisoner.

Lucien made an annoyed sound. The more he let the thoughts whirl in his mind the angrier he became.

Footsteps outside of his room brought his pacing to a halt.

Eris's voice filtered through his door. "You can't!"

Her tone surprised Lucien.

Did Ranulf normally allow her to speak to him in such a manner? Such behavior only proved Lucien's suspicions of the girl being more than what she seemed and Ranulf knowing what that more was but not telling Lucien.

"Ranulf, listen to me," Eris said in a scared voice.

"I hear you just fine."

"Don't go."

Lucien stared hard at the door.

"I have to. It's the king's order."

"What about me?"

Whatever Ranulf's answer was, Lucien interrupted it when he yanked open his door. Eris dodged quickly behind Ranulf and peeked at Lucien from her position there.

Lucien ignored her and looked at Ranulf. "What is the king's order?"

Ranulf held up a letter. "It arrived directly after you left the hall. The king is ill. His physicians aren't able to help. He's heard of my skills and has summoned me."

"It's a trap."

The man chuckled. "You think everything is a trap." Ranulf glanced over his shoulder, looking at Eris. "I am leaving Eris here."

"What?" Eris yelled.

Ranulf said, "I hold you to your vow, Lucien, even though I'll be absent." He turned his gaze back to Lucien. "I want no harm to come to her."

Lucien bared his teeth at that request. Even though it annoyed him, he wouldn't go back on his word. "You know me better than that."

Ranulf nodded and continued on to his room. Eris stood staring after Ranulf with a horrified look. She glanced at Lucien, and he glared at her in return.

She took a step back from him then ran after Ranulf.

Lucien watched her flee. Ranulf was leaving to attend the king, and he would leave Eris in Lucien's care.

He smiled.

He would keep his word. No harm would come to the girl. But, she would tell him all before Ranulf's return. Lucien would shove the proof in Ranulf's face then wring the woman's neck.

Maybe then thoughts of her would stop plaguing him.

* * * *

Eris paced Ranulf as he gathered his belongings. She tried to get in his way, but he dodged around her. "Ranulf! You can't leave me here by myself. You can't."

"I must. Taking you to court is not an option."

"Why not?"

He stopped and cupped her cheek. "You are too distracting. There is a worry that the king will take a liking to you and demand you stay at his side. As well, I will not able to split my attention between why I'm summoned and protecting you."

"What about protecting me here?"

"Lucien will do that."

"Have you lost your mind? You don't leave the fox to guard the hen house, Ranulf."

He stopped his motions and laughed.

"It's not funny."

"I must mention that analogy to Lucien."

She finally managed to get in Ranulf's way and made him stop. "Don't leave me here with him. Please. I don't care what he's promised. The second you leave something will happen. I know it."

"You travel through time *and* see the future?"

"Please."

"You claim to know us, and yet you doubt Lucien's oath. That only proves you don't know us at all."

"I do—"

"Lucien will never betray a trust once given. He may not like it, but he will protect you until I return." He moved around her and continued his packing.

"This Lucien is different," she whispered.

Ranulf stopped and looked back at her.

She hugged her arms. "This Lucien is angry all the time."

"And the one from your time isn't?"

"Not that I've ever seen. I saw you, the Ranulf from my time, get angry a few times, but never Lucien. He's not like that."

"I envy them," Ranulf said in a low voice.

She looked at him in confusion.

He returned to her and put his hands on her shoulders. "To have such devotion and unerring faith. I begin to understand your relationship with them though I had my suspicions before."

"We're friends."

"Oh, I don't doubt you're friends with Lucien, but the way you hold me at night says you are more than friends with me, despite remaining a virgin."

She looked away from him.

"If you would love the future version of me then you have to love this version as well, Eris. Whatever he became doesn't matter because he started with me."

"People change."

"You said I hadn't. Not very much."

"Lucien is different." She hugged her arms tighter. "Very different."

"Something must have happened to change him."

Of that Eris had no doubt. She also didn't doubt that whatever had changed him was somehow related to the reason he wanted to apologize to her.

Chapter Thirty-five

Eris rolled inside of her cocoon. With a little inner coaching and a lot of effort, she made herself push back the covers so she could see out.

The sun was rising, finally.

She'd just had the worst night's sleep ever. Not even being dumped back in time and sleeping next to an earlier version of Ranulf who was dubious about whether or not he should kill her had affected her sleep as badly as Ranulf not being there at all.

Every sound woke her. Footsteps that came too close to Ranulf's door had her ready to bolt toward the closet and hide. She had almost considered sleeping there but had been too scared to move.

She felt like a kid afraid of the monster under the bed that would grab her if she dangled her feet over the edge. In fact, she hadn't left the bed since Ranulf's departure.

The idea had occurred to her to simply stay there for the rest of the day. Except...

She sighed and pushed back the covers. Anxiety had a way of working up an appetite.

Ranulf had left some dried fruit and meat as well as flat bread. It was enough to see her through one day, three if she only ate once a day. But she'd have to venture from the room to get more food eventually.

It was also the day Ranulf usually took a bath. She harbored no misconceptions that the keep folk would still prepare the bath. More than likely, the keep would start reverting to the stereotypical medieval dwelling, complete with the smells.

Ranulf's room at least would remain clean. It wasn't like she had much else to do.

She looked at the door when someone's footsteps neared it. The person stopped. She tensed and held her breath, ready to run if need be.

Whoever it was walked away.

Eris sighed. She only hoped everyone in the keep forgot her presence. If not then she hoped Lucien didn't forget his promise.

* * * *

Lucien walked away from Ranulf's room. He didn't know what that girl did in the room alone. Whatever her preoccupation, she did it quietly.

He was a fool to leave her alone. Ranulf's room held too many potential weapons. Lucien's first thought once Ranulf had departed was to lock her in the dungeon. The idea had carried him as far as his doorway where he'd stopped and rethought his decision.

He couldn't keep his promise to Ranulf if he put the girl in the dungeon because Mason, the dungeon master, would surely abuse her despite being ordered otherwise.

No, it was best she stay in Ranulf's room.

He'd walked to Ranulf's room without being conscious of doing so. It was a morning habit. With Ranulf gone, there was no more need to continue verifying his continued health.

The girl could rot for all he cared. He walked back to the stairs. There were many things that needed his attention. Worrying about that girl wasn't one of them.

He decided to visit the courtyard before attending the chores Ranulf had abandoned in his haste to serve the king. Lucien only hoped he was wrong about the summons being a trap.

"What happened to Frederick?"

The voice stopped Lucien before he rounded the corner.

Another man answered, "Lucien. Last night he caught Frederick beating Sally again. Damn near beat the man to death."

Lucien jerked his head in a curt nod. He had, and he'd do it again. He'd warned Frederick to keep his hands off of his wife. The woman almost died the last time Frederick laid hands on her, and they had five children to worry about.

The first man said, "He wasn't like that before his stay in the cursed lands. He came back with some weird notions. Sally is Frederick's wife. If he wants to beat the woman, that's his right."

"It's as strange as his protection of the other one—that little Moorish bitch. I thought Ranulf's absence would mean we could finally be rid of her. Everyone knows she's a spy or an assassin or both, but no one will touch her so long as Lucien protects her in Ranulf's stead."

"Ranulf's away at the palace attending the king. And Lucien hates that little bitch the same as everyone else in the keep. That makes her fair game."

Lucien stiffened.

"What about Lucien?"

"A little poke won't get his attention. So long as we don't mark the girl, he won't know."

Both men chuckled.

"It's early yet. No one will miss us if we take a short break."

The men laughed and moved toward Lucien.

He practically jumped back up the stairs in his haste to get to Eris before the men did. He burst into Ranulf's room, and she screamed at the sight of him. He didn't care.

"Come." He held his hand out to her.

She backed into a corner of the room and shook her head at him.

"I don't have time for your stupidity, woman." He stalked toward her.

"Stay away from me."

"Little idiot." He grabbed her around the waist and threw her over his shoulder. She fought him, but he held her.

He walked out of the door and Lucien came face-to-face with the two men who'd spoken earlier. The men looked at him in surprise.

"What?" he snapped.

They stepped back, shaking their heads.

"Get back to your duties." Lucien passed them, Eris still flailing on his shoulder. He carried her to his room and dumped her on the bed. She scrambled off the other side, looking for a place to hide.

"You're not leaving this room," he said. He left without waiting for her reply.

* * * *

Eris stared after Lucien in shock. She thought he'd come to take advantage of her vulnerable state since Ranulf wasn't there protecting her. He only dumped her and left.

She looked around his room. His room looked just like Ranulf's, but the tapestries were different.

His reasoning behind bringing her there was unknown, though she had one guess. She knew it was inevitable. Hiding in Ranulf's room and hoping everyone forgot about her was only a temporary and flimsy fix to a much bigger problem.

Eris yelped when the bedroom door flew open.

Lucien came in carrying an armload of clothes and her sewing basket. He stopped at the bed and dumped it all. "Keep yourself busy until I return." He left.

Eris heard the telltale sound of a lock turning. He'd made her a prisoner again. She looked at the clothes he'd left then shrugged. "Beats being bored, I guess."

The pile consisted of tunics and leggings in various states of disrepair. Most of it was quick fixes. She picked up the nearest article of clothing and started her work.

The mending didn't take long. Rather than count the holes in the ceiling, she searched Lucien's room. She didn't know what she was looking for—possibly something to explain this version of Lucien—but the activity kept the boredom at bay.

Poking around in the corner between the bed and the wall turned up a small rectangular wooden box. It almost resembled a shoe box, except shoes didn't come in boxes yet.

There was a lock on the outside. She looked at her needle and then she shrugged. Why not try? She had nothing else better to do, and picking the lock might be easier than she thought.

After some random jiggling of a needle inside the lock, she managed to open it. She didn't know what she expected to find. What would Lucien keep locked up and hidden? His mother's ring maybe?

If that was the locale of the ring, she could take it and find a way into the forest and back to her hole. The ring had been the last thing Lucien gave her right before she left. Well, that and the cloak, but the cloak had originated with her father so she doubted it had anything to do with her trip. Logic dictated the ring was the culprit.

She opened the lid but found no ring. There were only papers. She picked up one and then another.

"Drawings? Why would Lucien lock away drawings?"

They were good too. There were several birds and a few flowers. The drawings were close. Not as detailed as some nature and still-life drawings she'd seen in the past, but definitely better than most of the art that would come out of the Middle Ages. Whoever the artist, that person had embraced realism before it had even become an –ism.

"What are you doing?" Lucien asked in a low, cold voice.

The drawings had so distracted her that she hadn't heard Lucien enter the room. She wanted to ask about the artist of the pictures, but his red-faced, angry look choked the words in her throat.

He snatched the drawings from her and took the box. After examining the lock and the contents, he asked, "How did you open this? Only my key should open this. Why are you searching my room?"

With each question, his voice grew louder and angrier. Eris huddled in on herself, preparing for the beating she knew was coming.

Lucien growled, but he didn't hit her. He replaced the drawings in the box and relocked it, jiggling the box lid to test that the lock held. He then faced Eris. "If you touch this box again, you will regret it. My drawings are not for you to look at."

"*You* drew those?" she asked.

"You sound so surprised. Yes, I drew them."

"They're beautifully done. I didn't think…" She trailed off before she insulted him without meaning to. "I didn't know you could draw."

"And who would have told you that I could? Not even Ranulf knows of this." He replaced the box where she'd gotten it from then faced her.

She waited.

"I am not Ranulf. Your stay in this room is a luxury I will strip from you should you continue annoying me."

"I'm sorry," she whispered, looking down.

Lucien grabbed her chin and made her look at him. "I don't believe this innocent act of yours. Keeping you close will reveal your flaws. When that happens, vow or no vow, you will die."

He released her and left the room.

Eris stared at the closed, locked door.

The next few weeks would be a trial. Why had Lucien even moved her from Ranulf's room? He could have simply kept her locked up there and not have to deal with her.

She looked at the bed. No way she would sleep there. Lucien might be a jumpy sleeper. If she hugged him during the night, he might think she was trying to strangle him or something.

A quick search of the room turned up nothing more than a bench and lots of floor space. She had no intention of sleeping on the floor. Lucien's room wasn't as clean as Ranulf's, and she wouldn't chance her health just to avoid a misunderstanding.

The chances of getting him to sleep on the floor were nonexistent.

She looked at the bed again. There had to be a way to make sure she didn't end up hugging him in her sleep. The Lucien from her time wouldn't have minded but this one would.

Chapter Thirty-six

Lucien stared at the moon. He had walked the entirety of his keep from top to bottom and then back to the top. The journey had taken less time than he thought it would. Once ended, he was still faced with the same problem he'd had when he started walking—Eris.

She waited in his room, more than likely on his bed. The little wench would have the nerve to do just that. He should have told her to sleep on the floor.

He entered his room and immediately scanned the entire interior. Seeing nothing out of the ordinary, he entered and closed the door after him.

Eris lay on the bed, just as he thought she would. He locked the door and then went to the bed. The girl had wrapped herself in her cloak and slept on the thinnest sliver of the bed she could manage. If he nudged her, she would fall on the floor.

A small shiver shook her body, and she clutched at the cloak more.

"Little idiot," Lucien grumbled under his breath. He pulled the blanket from the end of the bed and spread it over her.

Eris made a little squeaking noise then her whole body loosened as she relaxed under the blanket.

Lucien walked around to the opposite side of the bed. He undressed, dropping his clothes where he stood, and got under the blanket. He was on the edge of sleep when Eris shifted. He stiffened in anticipation of what she would do.

She reached toward him. Instead of stabbing a knife in his back, she grabbed the edge of the covers near his neck and yanked. He didn't understand her goal until the entire blanket was wrapped around her, leaving him in the cold.

He lay there, bared to the chill air, and wondered why he found the entire situation amusing rather than annoying. The brazen little wench had stolen his covers. He glanced at her. And what's more, she looked pleased with herself that she had.

Did Ranulf have to endure the same?

It didn't matter what she'd done with Ranulf. She wouldn't be doing it with him. He grabbed the blanket and pulled.

Eris whimpered.

He stopped pulling, and she resituated the blanket around herself once more. Her pleased expression returned. Lucien let her savor her victory for half a minute before he pulled the blanket.

Again, she whimpered. He didn't let that stop him. He situated the blanket over himself once more and presented Eris with his back. She tugged at the blanket, but he had a firm hold.

She finally stopped.

Lucien thought she'd fallen into full sleep once more. Instead, she reached toward him again. Her hand landed on his back. He jerked as her ice-cold fingers brushed his skin. The woman was frozen.

She patted his back a few times and then shifted so she was pressed against him. A small sigh left her lips, and she relaxed.

Meanwhile, Lucien was wide awake in more ways than one. Thoughts of sleep fled as his lower body sprang to attention. Eris shifted, pressing herself against him and forcing one of her legs between his.

He tried moving away but stopped when her sounds of protest returned. He wondered if Ranulf slept in like manner every night. It would explain why the man was in his bed more often than anywhere else.

Lucien looked over his shoulder at Eris. She looked pleased with herself again. Whatever she dreamt about, whomever she thought she held, the doing of it had made her happy. But, sleep wouldn't come to him so long as she was coiled around him like creeping ivy.

His only saving grace was Eris didn't sleep nude like he did. He closed his eyes. Sleep would come if he simply ignored her.

Eris proved a trial to him even in her sleep. Every few minutes she rubbed her cheek against him and dragged her foot along his calf.

"You would tempt a saint, woman," he rasped.

"Lucien?"

He jerked his eyes open. Eris had sat up and stared at him. She didn't look fully awake. Confusion marred her features. She touched his hair and then frowned.

"Not him," she whispered then turned away from him. She balled in on herself and went back to sleep.

That wasn't what he wanted to hear. Not from her. It didn't matter if he wasn't Ranulf. She was in *his* bed. Her presence had made him hard and heavy, and by damn, she'd do something about it.

He rose up on his knees then pulled Eris beneath him. She woke with the same confused look in her eyes.

"Don't scream."

She nodded.

He removed her clothing. She didn't protest his actions. When he reached between her legs, she opened for him and pressed her hips upwards, eager for his touch.

Lucien knew she must still be partially asleep and dreaming Ranulf touched her. He didn't care.

He kissed one taut nipple then sucked it into his mouth. She hugged his head, and her hips moved in time with his fingers. When he settled his weight between her legs, she hugged him tighter and said his name in a whispering sigh.

His name, not Ranulf's. She knew it was him, and she responded with a matching hunger, not fear.

He surged into her, then stopped.

Eris cried out in pain, digging her nails into his neck.

"A virgin," he whispered. He eased back.

Eris jerked visibly and made a wounded puppy noise as he left her body.

The evidence of her innocence coated his arousal, which hadn't diminished in the face of his utter confusion.

"You are a virgin. How?"

Eris blinked at him a few times.

"Answer me, woman."

"Lucien?" She moved to a sitting position, wincing as she went. Her confusion grew as she touched between her legs then peered at the blood on her fingers. "I thought I was dreaming," she whispered.

"You belong to the sultan. You can't be a virgin." He looked down at the proof once more then back to her. "Why are you a virgin?" he bellowed.

"Why are you yelling at me? You just raped me and now I'm getting yelled at!" She looked around and snatched up her cloak from where he'd discarded it.

"You were enticing me."

"I was asleep!"

"The hell you were. No one does what you did in their sleep."

She stopped trying to cover herself and stared at him. "What did I do?"

Lucien snapped his mouth shut when he would have answered. Eris had truly been asleep. Her confusion was not an act. All the things she'd done were to warm herself. It was he who'd taken advantage of the situation.

But, damn it, he'd thought she was awake. She'd looked at him and answered him.

He shoved his hand through his hair and cursed under his breath. In a grumbling voice, he said, "A virgin wouldn't have been in the sultan's harem. Who are you? Why are you here?"

She looked away.

"What are you hiding?"

"If I told you, I wouldn't be hiding it, would I?" She gasped and slapped her hand over her mouth. Her gaze went to him. She looked ready to bolt.

Lucien struggled to find some explanation for her because the one he'd clung to for the past month was wrong. He stared at her as she stared at him. "Have you run away? Is that why you won't tell me?"

Her continued silence frustrated him.

"Does Ranulf know?"

She looked down.

"You tell Ranulf but you will not tell me. Why? Whatever it is caused him to trust you. It might have caused me the same."

"He knew I was a virgin," she whispered.

Lucien jerked. "For how long?"

"Since the first night. He checked."

"He never told me."

She shook her head.

Ranulf had known and hadn't told him. Why? What was gained by letting Lucien continue to think Eris was a threat? Why hadn't Ranulf told him before leaving to attend the king? Ranulf had to have known such news would ensure Eris would be treated better.

Lucien jerked on his clothes with angry movements. "Get dressed."

Eris moved slowly, but she obeyed. Her hands shook as she tied her breast covering in place. The sight shamed Lucien. He faced the fire.

If only Ranulf had told him, Eris's pain could have been avoided. Virgin or not, Lucien still wanted to know who she was.

Her sigh made him face her once more. She'd lain down again, wrapped in her cloak. Her intention was to sleep but he had other plans.

"Eris."

She looked at him.

He slung a satchel that sat near the door over his shoulder. "Come."

"Huh?" She sat up once more.

He held his hand out to her.

She shrank back. "Where are you taking me?"

"Stop questioning everything I do, woman, and come." Lucien grabbed her wrist, hauled her to her feet, and dragged her out of the room in his wake. She followed him docilely enough. He was happy for that.

Everyone had already retired, so he had to saddle his own horse. Once done, he put her on the saddle then mounted behind her and turned the horse toward the forest.

Eris asked, "Where are we going?"

"I preferred your silence. Return to it."

He waited for her to say more, but she didn't. The woman had no problems obeying, at least. The heat of her body and her smell made his body react. He spurred the horse faster to cover his state.

A cave loomed ahead. Lucien slowed. He dismounted and tethered the horse to a nearby tree then reached for Eris. Her tears made him pause. He hadn't known she was crying.

She sniffed, and her shoulders shook.

"Are you in pain?" Had their brief encounter hurt her that badly? The horse ride probably hadn't helped.

"Why do you care if you're only going to kill me?" she whispered. Her tears came harder, and she buried her face in her hands. "I don't want to die."

Lucien shook his head. To her it probably seemed as though he'd brought her out there to kill her. He looked at the cavern. It did present itself as an ominous locale.

He knew better.

Ignoring her frightened cry, he plucked her from the horse. Doubting she would walk on her own, he carried her.

The cavern was dark, but he knew its paths well. He didn't need light. In the darkness there were only the sounds of his footsteps and Eris's tears.

A glowing ahead of them made Lucien smile. He jostled Eris and said, "Look."

He didn't know if she obeyed, but she did sniff.

They entered a hollowed out area where the rocks of the ceiling and walls glowed all on their own, shimmering off of the pool of water contained within. It was Lucien's favorite place. He and Ranulf had found it one day when they'd gotten lost in the caverns. Once they'd found their way out, they had purposefully ventured in again to find the glowing grotto.

After a time, Ranulf and Lucien made the caverns their place to meet should anything ever go wrong or they simply wished to be away from everything.

"I know not why the rocks glow, but they do," Lucien said.

"Phosphorous," Eris whispered.

"What?" He looked down at her, but she stared around with wide eyes. He couldn't see her well, but he could see her. She'd stopped crying.

She shook her head and rubbed her sleeve over her eyes. "It's beautiful."

Lucien let her stand on her own. "Aye. And you're the only other person besides Ranulf to see it. It matters not if you tell anyone. No one can find this cavern that easily."

"I won't tell."

"Good." He dropped his satchel and went about building a small fire. The glowing rocks provided some light, but more was better.

Once he could see properly, he looked at Eris. She was busy looking around and touching the walls.

"Why bring me here?" She looked back at him.

"When I leave the keep, you will accompany me. That's how it shall be until Ranulf's return. The men have grown bold in Ranulf's absence. They seem to think I won't mind them abusing you."

"You wouldn't."

"I would."

"You would?"

"Aye, and my reasons are my own, so leave off asking." He stripped off his tunic. Eris immediately put several steps between her and him. "If I want you, woman, that little bit of distance won't keep me from you. Running would only make you lost."

"If?"

He finished stripping and walked into the water. "Come attend me." He was surprised when Eris stripped her dress off and joined him in the water.

"It's warm."

"It's a hot spring." He handed her the soap.

"Hot springs are hot. The water is just warm." She skimmed her hands over the water. "Do you come here to bathe all the time?"

"Aye." He looked over his shoulder at her. She was grinning at his back. "What's so amusing?"

"Nothing." She soaped his back.

He thought he heard her whisper something about a heated pool. It was, but he didn't understand why that was important or amusing. He didn't ask her meaning.

* * * *

Eris calmed. Lucien washed his front, and she his back.

When Ranulf returned, she'd ask him to bring her back to the grotto.

She asked, "Do you want me to wash your hair?"

"Aye."

"You'll have to kneel down then."

Lucien complied, and she stared at him.

He glanced back at her. "Why do you hesitate?"

"You actually…why would you…" She couldn't get the question out so she gestured at him.

"I suspect the sultan did not send you, but someone has." He faced forward once more. "Attack me if you like. When you do, I'll have my proof."

The man would actually leave himself open to attack just so he could prove his suppositions. He already admitted she wasn't whom he originally thought, but he was still convinced she meant him harm. She wouldn't hurt him, but his actions were too reckless.

Then again, she'd already seen Lucien be reckless. He'd stepped into Ranulf's attack at the faire so he could be the victor, though no one had seen that version of events except her. She would have thought her imagination was playing with her if not for her little trip back through time. Now she wondered if she really had seen the men kill each other, and then time had somehow re-aligned when she closed her eyes and changed to a different outcome that everyone else had seen.

Only the Lucien and Ranulf of her time knew the answer to that question. She pushed thoughts of the future out of her head lest she get homesick. She returned to the present and the Lucien before her.

With careful movements so he wouldn't think she was attacking him, she soaped his head and scrubbed his scalp. He didn't make a sound. He didn't even wince.

She said, "You're taking this better than Ranulf. Either you have a thick scalp or you're good at hiding pain."

"Both."

"Am I hurting you?"

"No."

"Maybe Ranulf is just a big baby then. I didn't think I was scrubbing that hard. He says he's gotten used to it, but I still catch him wincing." She was about to tap his shoulder like she did Ranulf but stopped herself. "I'm finished."

He ducked below the water. While he rinsed off, she waded farther into the water. The bottom dropped off, and she treaded water.

Lucien said, "Careful. There is no bottom near there."

"Thanks, I found that out already."

"You can swim?"

"Yes. Can you?"

"Aye." He frowned at her, a question in his eyes, but he didn't voice it.

She moved herself away. She hadn't been swimming since she got to the past. It wasn't like she needed much exercise since she barely ate anything for fear of getting sick.

Still, the water felt good. She went a little farther out. Lucien didn't protest. He probably felt the cave was enough of a deterrent for her not to run, so she swam away.

The spring was quite large. Not as big as the Olympic-sized pool she'd utilized for the last few months before falling through time, but a good size. She got so caught up in swimming laps that she didn't realize Lucien was beside her until his shoulder touched hers.

She slowed her pace and looked at him. He was breathing quickly. That little bit of exercise was nothing for her. She hadn't even been going her regular speed.

"You swim well."

"Yes." She swam back toward shore and left the water.

"Who taught you how to swim? You made it look effortless."

She stopped herself from telling him there was no effort involved since he might get insulted. In fact, she didn't answer him at all. She busied herself brushing off the excess water so she could get dressed.

Lucien grabbed her arm and forced her to face him. "I grow tired of you ignoring my questions."

She stared at the scar on his chest.

He made an angered noise and released her. "Keep your secrets then."

Once he dressed, he doused the fire and walked away. It took Eris a second to realize he was leaving. She chased after him. It got darker and darker. She was forced to grab his tunic so she could keep track of him.

Lucien didn't acknowledge her action or slow his pace. Only a short time ago, he probably would have threatened her for touching him. And, he never would have let her walk behind him in a dark cavern. So much had changed in only one day. She hoped that was a good thing.

Chapter Thirty-seven

Lucien was more fastidious, just as Ranulf said, and he liked having a set routine. Once Lucien got used to the slight deviation she represented, he stopped snapping at her as much. He changed to the occasional gruff command and grunting.

Eris had accompanied Lucien to the phosphorous grotto every day for the last twenty. Every morning, a few hours before sunrise, he woke her and they left the keep. The only ones to see them leave were the night guard.

If those guards wondered why Eris accompanied Lucien, they didn't ask. Her role was the same for Lucien as it had been for Ranulf. She helped Lucien bathe. They didn't talk much, mostly because the only topic that interested him was who she truly was. She was still convinced he wouldn't take it as well as Ranulf had.

Once the bathing was finished, Lucien dried himself at the fire while Eris swam laps. She was thankful for the exercise, and it didn't seem like Lucien minded. He sat and watched until she finished without saying anything to hurry her along.

She remembered the Lucien from her time had said watching her swim was one of his favorite pastimes. That must have originated with their trips to the grotto.

"Eris."

She faced him, the water splashing around her at her sudden movement.

"It's time." Lucien went about dousing the fire and gathering his things.

Eris waded to shore and dried herself quickly. After so many days, she knew Lucien wouldn't just leave her, but the possibility always kept her moving quickly just in case she was wrong.

Lucien started walking to the exit. Eris caught up with him and grabbed his tunic. He quickened his pace, leading her through the maze that she still found confusing. If she could see, that might help, but she doubted it.

Just when the darkness and twisting and turning had started to get to her, the cool night air brushed her cheeks. Moonlight shined through the mouth of the cavern, showing the way. Eris released Lucien, and he moved away. After securing his satchel, he put her on the horse and then mounted behind her. As every day before, they would return to the keep well before anyone woke for the day.

"Have you finished my tunic?"

Eris jerked in surprise at the question. The horse whinnied and tossed its head. She mumbled an apology.

"Eris."

"Almost. I'm adding your crest to the sleeve. It's a lot more intricate than I originally thought."

He grunted.

It wasn't like Lucien to talk to her. She usually dozed on the way back because swimming in the warm water did a good job of relaxing her. As soon as they got back to the keep, they'd both return to bed.

Eris didn't know how Lucien could go to sleep, wake half way through the night, go bathe, and then return for a few more hours of sleep. It seemed a bit much just to maintain appearances.

"Lucien?"

He grunted again.

"Why doesn't Ranulf use the cavern? He wouldn't have to worry about the people of the keep trying to boil him alive if he did."

"Ranulf lives to make life difficult for others. He finds amusement in the anger he causes."

She didn't doubt that. "If you bathed at the keep too, everyone would stop being so mad at him."

"No, they would simply think me more crazed than he for bathing everyday as opposed to every other day like him."

She smiled in the darkness. He'd hear no complaints from her. She appreciated her bed mate not smelling like something had died on him.

* * * *

Lucien awaited more questions. Eris remained silent. Her posture deteriorated until she leaned back against him. She'd fallen asleep. His only acknowledgment of her actions was to shift so he held the reins in one hand and stabilized her with the other.

They'd both come a long way in a short amount of time. If Lucien hadn't seen the note from the king himself, he'd accuse Ranulf of concocting the whole scenario simply so Lucien could become accustomed to Eris and stop seeing her as a threat.

It was true he didn't see her as much of a threat any longer. Well, not in any way that could be truly detrimental. She was a threat to his peace of mind, however. Sleeping next to her while she curled around him for warmth was torture.

He glanced down at her when she mumbled in her sleep. Their first encounter had been their last. The woman tempted him sorely, but his mistake had cooled his lust.

Cooled, not extinguished.

He sighed. Ranulf should return soon, and then Eris's temptation would be removed.

The guards waved to Lucien as he guided his horse through the gate and to the stables. Eris startled when he stopped the horse.

"Are you awake?"

She nodded.

He snorted softly and helped her dismount. Her version of awake resembled Ranulf's. They functioned and even carried on conversations, but neither was truly aware. In her semi-unconscious state, Eris had enough sense to stay in one place while he attended his horse.

She was asleep on her feet when he returned. Rather than try and wake her, he lifted her against his chest.

"I can walk," she said in a sleepy voice.

He ignored her. It was tempting to dump her on Ranulf's bed so he could actually rest. Knowing there were those waiting for him to be just that careless stayed the idea.

"The man takes his time purposefully," he grumbled.

"Who?"

"Cease feigning wakefulness."

"Huh?"

"Sleep," he snapped.

She smiled and snuggled against him.

He was happy to reach his room so he could put her down. She curled into a ball. He knew from experience that she'd curl around him as soon as he lay on the bed with her. The woman seemed incapable of generating her own heat.

"Damned annoying."

She shivered, and he sighed.

He stripped and lay on the bed. There was only a few seconds delay before Eris's cold hand patted his arm. He sighed again. Eris scooted over to him and wrapped around his side with her head buried against his arm and one of her legs draped over his.

Goose bumps rose all over his arms as her cold skin contacted his. Trying to pull away from her would do no good as the woman had a death grip once she found a heat source. There was also the possibility that she would shift position to one even more trying to his senses.

The memory of her lying atop him when he woke two nights ago came to mind. The woman had actually crawled onto him and trapped one of his legs between hers. One of her hands had perched dangerously close to his manhood, which had started to stiffen when he realized how the sleeping arrangements had changed.

He'd managed to extricate himself without waking her, but it had taught him a lesson about Eris and her desire to stay warm. One last sigh preceded Lucien pulling the blanket around them both. He closed his eyes and wished for sleep, knowing it would hover but not truly come to him while a certain female rubbed her breasts against his side.

* * * *

Eris jerked upright. "Lucien!"

"Yes?"

Her gaze landed on him where he stooped near the fire. She could only stare at him.

She'd dreamt of his fight with Ranulf, the one where they'd stabbed each other. Only this time the men didn't laugh it off. They both lay in a pool of their own blood, dying. She could only stand and stare.

"Eris?" Lucien straightened. "You are having nightmares of me now? I thought you had grown past your fear."

She shook her head. "It's nothing." She looked around the sunlit room. "It's morning already?"

"Morning?" He shook his head with a pitying laugh. "It is noon time."

"Noon? I slept all that time?"

"My schedule does not agree with you. Perhaps I should go to the caverns without you."

"That won't help. I wouldn't be able to sleep until you came back."

"Aye, you'd probably freeze without me here to heat you."

She shrugged. "You're warm, but that's not why. Someone might try to get in while you're gone."

"It proves your sorry state when you think of me as your savior." He met her gaze. "Even after what I did."

"What you...oh." She waved that away. "That's different."

"Is it?"

"Of course it is. You stopped when you realized I was a virgin. Any other man would have kept going regardless. Hell, any other man would have taken advantage now that my virginity is gone."

"You are too trusting."

"With you, it's not hard."

"And yet a short time ago, you feared me."

She looked down. In a soft voice, she said, "Not you. I've never been afraid of you, Lucien. Just your temper." She stroked the scar on her finger, the one Lucien made when he ripped his mother's ring from her hand. "You used to glare at me from the doorway of Ranulf's room."

"Ah."

"Did you think I would try to sneak out if you came farther into the room?"

Lucien grinned. It was the first time she'd seen him wear that expression—past or future. "Do you think me addled?"

"What? No."

"Infirm?"

"Of course not."

"Ah, so you feel I am crazed then?"

She shook her head, not sure where he was going with his questions. "I never thought any of that."

"Then why do you believe I, or any sane man, would approach Ranulf after rousing him from his slumber?" He quirked an eyebrow at her.

She covered her mouth as she laughed.

"You are the only one I know of who has not suffered after waking him."

"I don't wake him. You do."

"No," he said, shaking his head. "He is awake once I arrive or else he wouldn't be lucid enough to answer and he would attack me."

She shook her head. "I don't...I mean, he wakes up when I leave the bed. Usually complaining that it's too hot."

"I empathize."

"I'm not that bad. And, Ranulf wouldn't attack you."

"He would, as a reflex. We were not speaking in jest at that time. Ranulf is more lethal when roused from sleep. He likes his rest and is somewhat incoherent when first waking. Those who tried to take advantage of his perceived weakness paid the highest price."

She looked at him in surprise. "He really killed them?"

"You doubt it? Ranulf is not a man to trifle with and neither am I."

She felt the mood shift and knew what was coming. Every day, like with Ranulf, Lucien questioned her, but she had no answers she was willing to give him. She sighed and looked down at the blanket.

"Will you remain in bed all day?"

That wasn't the question she was expecting. She looked up at him and he watched her. He didn't look upset or act annoyed. "Yes." She lay down quickly and pulled the covers over her head.

Lucien laughed.

It was a good sound, and she enjoyed hearing it. She peeked out at him. "May I?"

"Why ask? You've decided for yourself." He looked down at her after walking to the bedside. "I take it you won't finish my tunic this day."

She sat up again. "I'll finish it, if you—"

He pushed her back down when she would have left the bed. "Rest."

"You're sure?"

He tucked the covers around her. "I only wish I could indulge in such luxuries."

"Why can't you?"

"Sleep during the day? I have no ailment."

"You don't have to be sick to want to stay in bed."

"No, only lazy." He turned away.

She caught his hand before he could get too far. When he looked back at her, she smiled. "So be lazy. You're the lord of the keep. You're allowed to be lazy when you feel like it. It's not like anyone can say anything to you."

"Are you cold, Eris? Is that why you think to tempt to bed?"

"A little."

He laughed.

"Well?" She tugged at his hand.

Lucien pulled away from her. She thought he'd walk away. Instead, he untied his belt and then lay beside her. "Only for a short time."

Eris moved so she lay against his side. "Warm."

"'Tis you who is cold."

They lapsed into silence. Eris listened to Lucien's heartbeat. It would have lulled her to sleep if she'd been tired. After sleeping half the day away, that wasn't the case.

She picked at a loose thread in Lucien's tunic. She'd fix it later. When she returned to her time, she'd have to remember to thank her father for teaching her how to sew. Her usefulness to Ranulf and Lucien would have been short-lived, and who knows what they would have done to her if not for that talent.

"Lucien?"

He grunted.

"Who taught you to draw?"

He stiffened beneath her hand. "Woman, I warned you to leave that box be."

"I haven't touched it. That doesn't mean I'll forget what I saw."

"You should," he snapped, sitting up.

Eris grabbed his arm. "Why? They were beautiful and so lifelike. You have a gift to be able to draw so well."

He didn't face her, but he didn't pull away either. "A knight has no need of drawing."

"Who told you that?"

"My father. He felt I wasted time. That if I wanted to draw, I should have become a priest and joined a monastery rather than learning the blade and becoming a knight. He even threatened to give his title to another if I persisted."

"The drawings looked recent."

"They are." He pulled away from her and retrieved his belt. "My father is dead, and his title is mine."

"You still hide it though, like you hide everything else, even from Ranulf. Doesn't it tire you out, hiding like that all the time with no one to confide in or talk to?"

"I should ask you the same." He looked over his shoulder at her.

She looked down at the bed, but she nodded. "It does."

"Then tell me who you are."

"I can't."

"Did you tell Ranulf?"

She nodded. "He says he doesn't believe me but then talks to me like he does. It's confusing. I know you won't believe me at all, so why bother?"

"Do you compliment my intelligence or insult my honor?"

Shifting so she sat on her knees, she met his gaze. "Can't we stay like this? I like it like this. You're not angry with me anymore."

"No, we cannot stay like this," he snapped as he stood. "It confounds me how Ranulf could lay with you all this time and not touch you. Virgin you may have been, but you must have tested his self-control greatly, just as you test mine."

"I'm not trying to test anything. I don't even know why you hold back. I'm your prisoner. Ranulf didn't touch me because he wanted you to have no doubts about my innocence. You have it. What's stopping you?"

"I need no weeping woman beneath me. Unwilling partners have never interested me." He looked her up and down.

"Unwilling?"

"I tire of this topic. Ranulf will return soon, and you will become his burden once more." He walked away with an annoyed sound.

Eris left the bed and followed him. She pulled up short when Lucien opened the door and Ranulf stood on the other side. The man looked mildly surprised as he lowered his hand. He must have been about to knock.

Ranulf looked over Lucien and then switched his gaze to Eris. "You are both whole. That is good."

Lucien shoved past Ranulf. "Take her back to your room since you've returned." He stalked down the hallway toward the stairs.

"Yes, my trip was a good one, and the king is well thanks to my knowledge and efforts," Ranulf said to Lucien's back.

Eris said, "That's good."

He faced her. "Are you truly well?"

She nodded. "Lucien kept his word."

Ranulf looked around the room. "You have resided here? I thought he would lock you in my room, or worse, the dungeon."

"I think he wanted to put me in the dungeon but moved me here instead. He said it would be easier to watch me for mischief."

"Was there mischief?" He looked her over.

Was he asking if she had done anything or Lucien? She shook her head. "Besides me stealing the covers, none."

Ranulf laughed. "Yes, the nightly battle for warmth is one I have missed. I'm surprised Lucien tolerated your sleeping behavior without—" he paused and made a thinking noise, "—acting upon it."

Again he searched her face, but she stayed looking wide-eyed and innocent.

"Eris?"

"Yes?"

He moved closer to her. "Should I check again or will you simply tell me?"

Heat encompassed her, enabling her to keep her independently warm for the first time in weeks. It was tempting to stay silent and let Ranulf check. Perhaps the doing of which would lead to more—more heat, more trust, just more.

The loss of her virginity and the resulting absence of malice from Lucien had her feeling a little bold.

"Is that an invitation?" He touched her cheek.

She said, "Lucien checked."

"He knows you to be a virgin?"

She nodded, not bothering to correct Ranulf's tense usage. A little bold didn't mean ready to find out what would happen if she no longer had it. Ranulf already admitted he only refrained from touching her because of her virginity. Keeping up the pretense of having it seemed best in her mind for the time being.

"So the king is healthy and pleased then?" she asked in a bid to change the subject.

"That he is."

It was Eris's turn to search his face for clues. "Did anything happen while you were there?"

"I attended the king. When not in his presence, I was relegated to my room." He rubbed his thumb over her cheek. "I now know how you must feel, though your situation is much more improved as compared to my own. Did you tell Lucien your story? Is that how you won his favor?"

"I didn't win his favor."

"You slept here, did you not? That indicates a certain amount of trust."

"No. Lucien said if I attacked him then that would be his proof and justification for him to kill me."

Ranulf laughed. "Yes, Lucien is a shrewd tactician if not a little foolish at times. I dread to think of the mess he'd have made of his life without me here to help him."

That sounded like the Ranulf from her time.

Rather than let herself be confused, she pulled away and faced Lucien's room. Ranulf's return meant she'd no longer share quarters with Lucien. It was probably too much to hope either man would let her have a room of her own.

"I know Lucien wants me out of his room, but where do I go now that you're back?" she asked.

"To my bed, of course. I've said already that I have missed you next to me. I could barely sleep."

She jumped when he touched her side. He slid his hand forward and teased the spot near her belly button.

He lowered his head so his lips were near her ear. "Though sleep is not what fills my thoughts at this moment." He inched his hand lower. "Lucien has his proof therefore my need to remain noble and celibate is at an end."

When she would have moved away, Ranulf's hold tightened. He pulled her back against him. She let him hold her close, enjoying the feel of him even if it was the wrong version, but kept herself on alert. "Ranulf, I—"

"Ranulf!" Lucien entered the room. "You have duties to attend."

Eris pulled away, thankful for the save. She faced Lucien, who didn't look happy.

Ranulf said, "I have only returned. You have managed all this time without me. Whatever there is to be done can wait." He glanced back at Eris.

"If you've enough energy to bed a woman then you have enough energy to work," Lucien snapped.

"Alas, your logic isn't flawed." Ranulf shrugged. "If I must." He reached out and pulled Eris to his side. "I shall see you tonight. Until then, return to my room." He reached out and folded her fingers around the key to his room.

She nodded, at a loss as to how else she should react.

He released her and left with Lucien.

It took Eris a moment to realize the door was open. She peeked out, but the hallway was clear.

If it were night, she would have chanced trying to get to the woods and her time-transporting hole in the ground. Trying such a feat in daylight was too stupid even to consider.

She returned to Lucien's room. His tunic needed to be finished. While she did that, she'd find a way to put off Ranulf. She wasn't sure she was ready to start the physical-only relationship the Ranulf and Lucien of her time had warned her about.

Chapter Thirty-eight

"Is this a habit you developed while attending Lucien?" Ranulf rubbed between his fingers the towel Eris had donned and regarded the cloth with disdain.

She lied. "Yes. It seemed appropriate."

"You needn't be so shy with me." He tugged at it.

Eris stopped washing his hair and held the towel. There was no way she would stand around in her underwear while Ranulf was naked and horny. His state had been very obvious when he'd undressed. He hadn't even tried to hide it.

"There is no need to be nervous. I will make your first time memorable."

Her first time was already memorable, but she didn't say that. She stepped back from the tub, but Ranulf continued holding the towel.

He shifted so he faced her.

She asked, "Aren't you tired after your long journey and all the work Lucien had you do?"

"You are not wrong," he said then sighed and released her towel. "I'm sure my performance would not be at its best in my current state."

Eris sagged internally with relief. That was one bullet dodged. She returned to washing his hair.

"I did not miss your abuse of my scalp."

She scrubbed a little harder. Ranulf grunted, and she smiled. "Lucien never complained. He said it felt good, and I washed his hair every night."

"You've seen the grotto then."

She nodded as she tapped his shoulder. When he surfaced after rinsing his head, she said, "It's gorgeous. The water feels good too."

"We shall visit there again."

"Thank you."

Ranulf stood.

Eris removed her towel and handed it to him. He dried himself while she dressed once more.

"You will not bathe?"

"I did this morning with Lucien."

Ranulf looked thoughtful but said nothing.

They returned to Ranulf's room. He immediately fell onto his bed with a tired sigh. "I do not think I truly slept the entire time I attended the king. Those around me had been conspiring to do away with me without alerting the king. The mood of the castle was the same as the night the sultan had me taken to the dungeons."

Eris crawled onto the bed next to him. "You're fine, and you're home." She lay with her shoulders propped against the headboard then pulled Ranulf over so her stomach cushioned his head. "Sleep. No one will harm you. No one in this keep is that stupid or crazy."

Ranulf laughed.

She threaded her fingers through his hair over and over. A weird inclination made her start humming softly.

"You can be gentle," Ranulf muttered in a sleepy voice. He sighed, and his whole body seemed to sink into the bed.

Eris continued her ministrations until she put herself to sleep.

* * * *

Lucien looked at his bed in annoyance. He hadn't been able to sleep. The reason why irritated him. He bit out a curse and turned to retrieve his satchel. All he needed was a bath.

He stalked over to the chair where the satchel lay. He reached for it, intending to grab it as he walked past, but he stubbed his toe against the chair leg. Another curse left his lips as pain shot up his abused appendage.

He grabbed the satchel then stopped. A thought made him look at the bed again. Eris's absence reminded him that he would have no entertainment while at the grotto. He had never needed it before, but that was before.

He retrieved his box of art from its hiding place. Drawing tended to calm his nerves so he would take the box with him. He opened the satchel.

Before he could shove the box inside, it flipped out of his fingers and hit his already wounded big toe.

The urge to kick the box was tamped down. He picked it up, shoved it in his satchel, and then stalked to the bedroom door.

He knew the reason for his abnormal clumsiness and knowing only made him angrier. Changes to his routine always disoriented him for a short time, causing him to make stupid mistakes.

Leaving Ranulf in his room with Eris earlier that day had redefined stupid. If Lucien hadn't returned, who knows what Ranulf would have done, and in Lucien's room no less.

Seeing Eris in Ranulf's arms had made Lucien feel almost as angry as when he'd caught Frederick beating his wife. Lucien wanted to beat Ranulf the same way he had Fredrick. Knowing jealousy caused Lucien's anger made him even more irate.

Eris was Ranulf's problem. Lucien was happy to be rid of her. Though it had eluded him at first, her absence meant he'd finally be able to sleep without disturbance.

He hoped.

He closed his door. As he turned to face the steps, he stopped. Someone waited in the shadows. Lucien put his hand on his dagger.

"Lucien." Eris stepped forward into the light.

"Eris?" He straightened, though he kept his hand on his dagger. "What are you about?"

She held up her small satchel. "It's bath time."

"You must truly feel yourself safe and above suspicion if you think you can sneak up on me without consequences."

Her smile faded, and her face took on an all too familiar look of fear. She worked her lips on what Lucien knew would be denials of guilt. He didn't want to hear it.

"I didn't...I only—"

"Ranulf has returned. You've no more need to accompany me." He looked down the hallway at Ranulf's door and then back at her.

"Who...Who will wash your hair and your back if I don't go?" She moved closer to him with a hopeful look.

Lucien couldn't help the smile that curved his lips. His good cheer translated instantly to Eris. Her whole being relaxed, and she smiled with him. "Come then," he said.

She followed silently. Having her behind him, walking almost close enough that they should both trip but didn't, helped calm his earlier bad mood. It confounded him how her presence had become so familiar to him in such a short amount of time, but he didn't question it.

He also didn't question why he enjoyed the feel of her sitting before him as they rode to the cavern. In her usual fashion, she settled back against him and dozed. Lucien inhaled her scent.

His indulgence stirred his lower body. Normally he would shift so Eris wouldn't feel his arousal at her nearness, not that she'd be conscious enough to notice. Instead, he tightened his arm around her waist, pulling her more against him.

Eris startled slightly with a tiny mew. She looked around. "Are we there?"

"Almost. Go back to sleep."

She nodded and relaxed once more.

How easily he could take advantage of her position—move her dress and lift her onto his need then let the horse's movements fulfill them both.

Lucien stayed his lust as he had many times before. Or rather, he stayed the impulse. His lust would take considerable more time and concentration. Soaking in the hot spring would help.

The cavern came into view. He stopped the horse at the tree near the entrance. The animal whinnied, and Eris woke once more.

"Are you awake enough to walk?"

She nodded as he lowered her to the ground. Hiding a yawn behind her hand, she said, "I'm awake."

He snorted. "I've heard that before."

"Huh?"

"Come." He waited for her to grab his tunic and then led her through the maze to the glowing grotto.

"You never get lost," Eris said in a sleepy voice.

"I would be a rare type of fool to lose myself on a path I've walked hundreds, if not thousands, of times."

"But you never use a torch, and it's so dark."

"Torches leave a scorched trail along the roof of the caves. Ranulf and I want no one to be able to follow should we need to use these caverns as a hiding spot."

"That makes sense."

He would have looked back at her but, as she had said, it was too dark to see. The path, once learned, was familiar and never changed, so he had no need for a guiding light.

Though he couldn't see her, Lucien still found himself glancing back at Eris. "Ranulf knows the way here as well as I. Why accompany me?"

She clutched his tunic.

"Eris?"

"If you don't want me here, you should have said so at the keep. I wouldn't have come."

"That wasn't my..." He trailed off with a muted sound of frustration. "I finally understand your purpose in coming to my keep."

"Huh?" She stopped walking and released his tunic.

Lucien whipped out his hand, catching her wrist before she could run and get lost. He knew the path to the grotto but trying to find her in the cavern's labyrinth would take time and a torch, both of which he didn't have.

Eris squeaked when he pulled her close to him. He said, "You came here to annoy me. What's more, you do your job well."

"I'm not trying to annoy you."

"That is why you are so good at it."

"What are you talking about?"

He continued down the path, pulling her in his wake. "The night is ending while I deal with you. If you must annoy me, do it while washing my hair."

"Yes, Lucien."

Her answer, delivered in such a meek voice, made him smile. He released her once the grotto was in sight.

He'd built the fire and was undressing when Eris spoke again. "Lucien, do you mind that I'm here?"

"Of course I mind. Your presence is a constant distraction to many of the members of my keep, including myself."

"I meant here, now, not the keep."

He turned and met her gaze. She looked unsure.

"I do not see why you would willingly follow me here."

She bowed her head, and her shoulders sagged. "Oh."

"However, I do not mind your company. Not any longer."

Her thankful smile caught him off guard. She looked so relieved. The woman before him couldn't be the same who had cowered behind Ranulf whenever Lucien chanced to get too close to her.

"Then I'll keep coming with you." She added a nod to that statement.

"I didn't give you permission for that."

"You said you don't mind."

"That is not permission to continue."

Eris ignored him and undressed.

The girl had some nerve. A few weeks ago, she wouldn't have dared speak to him in such a manner. In fact, not even a few days ago.

Lucien let the subject drop and walked into the water. Ranulf's return meant Eris might decide waking in the middle of the night was too bothersome. She only had trouble breaking the habit and that was why she'd accompanied him. Only that explanation made sense to him.

He knelt when Eris tapped his shoulder. Her fingers kneading his scalp seemed to push away all troublesome thoughts. He'd be hard pressed to duplicate her ministrations if she did decide to forego bathing with him.

Too soon, she finished washing his hair. He rinsed off. When he resurfaced, she made quick work of washing his back before swimming away.

Her swimming was a talent that confounded him more than any other. What would a desert-born woman know of swimming? It was possible that some of the women in the cursed land could swim, but not with Eris's skill. She was quick, sleek, and made the act of swimming from the back wall of the grotto to the shore look effortless. He'd tried several times to pace her and had only exhausted himself. Eris barely looked winded when she finished.

What father would train their daughter to swim like that? And for what purpose? And why to swim and not to ride? Eris was a woman not accustomed to horses. It wasn't only Lucien's earlier paranoia of being stabbed in the back that had prompted him to seat her before him when they rode to the cavern, but also the knowledge that Eris would try very hard to ride *him* if she were seated behind him.

He chuckled at the memory of the one time she'd ridden behind him. She had inched ever closer until she hung from his back. He'd stopped the horse and changed her position so she sat before him with his arm firmly around her waist. She appeared much more at ease. They'd ridden that way ever since.

The memory of her legs almost wrapped around his waist and her breasts pressed to his back…

He shook his head violently and left the water.

Eris would be swimming for a while longer. He planned to draw instead of watching her as he normally did. He so engrossed himself in his latest creation that he didn't hear Eris approach him.

She said, "That's beautiful. You have real talent if you can do that from memory."

Lucien watched her sit next to him and peer over his arm. His first instinct was to hide his work, only Eris's open appreciation kept him still. "The hawk caught my eye this morning."

"You must have been staring hard to get this level of detail."

"I saw him for only a moment."

Eris met his gaze with surprise on her face. "Really? That's amazing."

Her words shouldn't make him feel so pleased, but they did.

"Are you that good with people?"

"No." He looked down at his drawing. "Faces elude me."

Eris moved so she sat across from him. "Draw me."

"Why?"

"Maybe I can point out what's wrong and that'll help you fix it."

"I know what's wrong. This is a waste of time." He shoved the supplies back into the box.

Eris grabbed his hand before he could return the box to the satchel. He looked at her. "Please?"

"Fine," he bit out.

She resumed her position and even dared to smile at him as he tried to copy her image to the paper. When he finished, he didn't want her to see. The image was not very close.

Eris leaned over him, as she had done before, and stared.

"I am better with animals," he mumbled.

"The proportions are off."

"Proportions?"

She reached out. "May I?"

He handed her the paper and the quill then watched as she drew an oval with a cross in the center.

"There." She handed it back to him. "Draw me again using this—" she pointed to the horizontal line, "—as the place where my eyes and the tops of my ears should go. And this line—" she pointed to the vertical, "—where my nose and the middle of my lips should go."

Lucien doubted a cross would help him since his father always claimed his art was a blasphemy. He didn't argue though. He drew Eris once more and was amazed at how following the cross she'd drawn helped.

She looked at the results and nodded. "Much better."

"Where did you learn this technique?"

"A very patient woman who wouldn't give up even though I have absolutely no talent." She took the paper and quill from him once more. She drew three more ovals and then a cross in each but it was positioned differently for each oval—one had the cross off-center and slightly curved, the next had the cross curving to match the line of the oval, and the last had the cross lower to the bottom of the oval instead of halfway like the first.

She handed it back to him. "Always draw the eyes on the horizontal line and line up the center of the face with the vertical one."

He did as she bade, using her as a model. For each oval, she turned in a different direction. For the last oval with the cross more near the bottom, she bowed her head.

Each drawing came much closer to emulating the real woman than any he'd ever drawn before. Only his animal drawings had ever looked true to life.

"Amazing," he whispered.

"Yes, you are." She smiled at him.

He almost found himself trapped in the admiration he saw in her eyes. Someone found merit in his drawings. It was a new experience for him. Not only had she found merit, but she helped him improve.

"Lucien?"

"Yes?"

"Should we get back?"

Her question jerked him out of his fanciful thoughts. He replaced his drawings in the box and packed the rest of his belongings.

Eris gathered her few things.

He couldn't help but watch her.

The mystery she presented had grown more complicated. What surprised him was the knowledge that he was starting to no longer care.

Chapter Thirty-nine

Eris snipped the thread then held out the finished tunic so she could admire the embroidery. She'd outdone herself with Lucien's crest. The first two times had turned out...rough. That was a nice way of putting it. The hawk was easy, but the shield and the emblem on the shield the hawk grasped had thwarted her every attempt to copy it.

She'd wanted to skip the emblem on the shield but learned that was the crest for Lucien's distant cousin. That received an annoyed sigh and some grumbling when he'd told her.

A suggestion from her to simply take off the crest and put something else had been strongly vetoed. Her third tunic and several discarded practice sessions later saw success.

Lucien would probably be annoyed the perfected crest adorned the sleeve of a new tunic for Ranulf. She planned to add the crest onto the tunic she'd finished for Lucien so wasn't worried about his reaction to Ranulf's.

"Why are you shut away when you can come to the courtyard?" Ranulf entered the room and walked to where she sat near the window.

Eris held out the tunic to him as her answer.

"You still manage to impress me with your skill. Lucien will enjoy this."

"I doubt it, since it's for you."

Ranulf looked from the tunic to her. "Me?"

"I worked on tunics for you and Lucien while you were away. I just decided to finish this one first as a welcome home gift."

She stood and stretched with her arms over her head and her back arched.

"You could just as easily have finished this outside. There is more light." He moved closer to her. "Though your choice of locale seems more prudent as time passes." He stroked her stomach, letting his fingers trail under her breasts.

She lowered her arms, but Ranulf didn't stop touching her.

Could he feel her heartbeat had quickened?

He said, "I awoke last night, and you were gone."

Eris nodded, watching his hand as he teased the area above her belly button. He seemed to like that spot. "I went with Lucien to attend his bath."

"Why?"

"Habit, I guess." She glanced at him then turned her attention back to his hand.

Ranulf didn't look happy with her. "It is a habit you can break then. You've no more need to bother him."

"He said I wasn't."

"Lucien values his time alone."

She nodded again, not wanting to argue.

Ranulf turned her and then lifted her chin so she looked at him. "At the very least, it is good he no longer suspects you. Did he hurt you when he checked for your virginity? Is that why you seem skittish around me?"

"I'm not skittish."

"You are. He hurt you, didn't he?" A harsh edge entered his voice.

"Not much. I was asleep. He was angry that you hadn't told him since you knew. Frankly, so was I."

"This way left no room for doubt." Ranulf searched her gaze. "Did Lucien demand service other than attending his bath?"

"You mean sex, right?"

His look hardened.

"No. Lucien never touched me."

"Good." He released her. "I didn't want you abused while I was away."

"I wasn't."

"Good." His normal good humor returned. "You are merely nervous then."

She nodded.

He cupped her cheek again. "There is no need, Eris."

Banging on the door drew their attention to Lucien, who stood looking annoyed. "Why, when I find you absent, are you near Eris?"

"The scenery is better here. You cannot fault me."

Eris didn't think Lucien appreciated Ranulf's answer. Lucien looked even more annoyed when Ranulf ran his thumb over Eris's lips. She didn't know Ranulf's game was but wished he wouldn't put her in the middle.

Ranulf caressed Eris's cheek as he removed his hand. "Tonight."

She nodded.

He returned her nod.

"What is tonight?" Lucien asked.

Ranulf didn't answer the question and switched out his current tunic for the one Eris had finished. "Your work is without flaw, as usual."

"Thank you," Eris whispered. She looked behind him at Lucien.

Ranulf followed her gaze. "She did a fine job copying your crest. I'm sure yours is just as fine."

Lucien moved closer so he could see Eris's handiwork. "She has outdone herself." He stood back. "If you're done preening, we have to return."

"You lead, and I follow." Ranulf smirked at Lucien's back then glanced back at Eris. She only shook her head at him and then returned to her chair.

* * * *

Eris watched Ranulf as he finished preparing some herbs he'd mixed while in the common room earlier. He'd given every indication that tonight would be their first time.

"Eris, stop staring at me like that. I will not attack you."

"You said you would."

He laughed and shook his head. "What I plan to do to you will not be an attack." He glanced over his shoulder at her.

Heat rushed to her cheeks and dried out her lips. She licked them, and Ranulf's gaze followed her tongue's progress. He shifted on his seat. That small movement caused her to jump.

"Definitely skittish." He held out his hand. "Once you experience my touch, you will no longer fear it."

"I'm not afraid."

"Yes, you are." He beckoned to her. "Come to me."

She crossed to him and let him pull her so she stood between his legs.

"Simply stand."

She nodded.

Ranulf moved his hands under her dress. He didn't do any of the things she thought he might. He simply rested his hands on her waist. "You don't eat enough."

She ate all she planned to of medieval food and was happy it hadn't made her sick. Also, she didn't have much of an appetite. She attributed that to the same something that kept her in a constant state of cold. Since she didn't think Ranulf wanted a reply to his statement, she kept quiet.

He slid his hands over her hips and down her legs then back up again. The journey took his hands to her breasts. He cupped them. "I dislike this cloth you wear. It is not a binding, for which I am thankful, but what purpose does it serve?"

"Support. It feels weird to simply hang." She sucked in a breath when he touched her nipples.

He teased her for a moment before untying the bra. Pulling it free, he let it fall then returned his hands to her bare skin.

She pressed against his touch.

Ranulf smiled up at her. "Perhaps I mistook skittishness for anticipation."

She bent forward slightly. Ranulf curved his hands around her back and pulled her forward.

Her lips met his. The kiss wasn't a chaste one. And though below her, he still dominated the kiss. He pushed his tongue past her lips.

She moved closer to him, and his hands slid down her back. He cupped her behind. A tingle spread over her body when he pushed aside her panties.

Bringing her closer, he curved his hand through her legs from behind and touched her heated flesh. She couldn't help the tiny mew she uttered. Ranulf stroked his fingers over her bottom lips.

He teased, or was he testing? Whatever it was, he wasn't doing what she wanted. She wanted to feel him inside of her.

Her non-existent telepathy must have been working because Ranulf eased a single finger inside of her. She gasped against his mouth and clutched his shoulders. Her reaction seemed to urge him along because he pumped his finger faster.

She moved closer to him, straddling his legs and opening herself more to his touch. All of her earlier worries fled as pleasure took hold. She gathered Ranulf close, and she rode his finger.

"Eager," he whispered, adding another finger.

The feel of his fingers was good, but she wanted more. Her hands remembered holding Ranulf's arousal so many months ago. She wanted— *needed* to feel him inside of her.

She fumbled with his tunic, trying to pull it out of her way.

Ranulf added another finger inside of her.

She gasped, and her momentary task of disrobing him was forgotten.

His other hand curved around her behind and squeezed. She didn't mind. In fact, it only made her move against him faster.

He sprinkled little kisses across her neck. All the while the hand clutching her behind kneaded. One of his fingers brushed her rear opening, but she ignored it. The touch returned, more deliberate as the pad of finger swirled around the spot.

Eris lifted a little. Ranulf seemed to take the hint and retreated, moving his hand back to the small of her back and pressing her against the hand between her legs.

She decided to try moving his tunic once more.

"Stand up." Ranulf punctuated the command with a particularly deep thrust of his fingers.

Her legs wouldn't obey her at first, but she managed to get to her feet. Ranulf followed but he went to one knee. He kissed her thigh through her dress and then laid his head against her stomach and inhaled.

"I want you ready," he rasped.

"I am."

She was so ready she felt like she would explode.

"Show me." He pushed at her dress.

She lifted it out of the way.

Ranulf kissed her stomach and then her thigh. She thought she'd feel his tongue inside of her along with his fingers. Instead, his other hand returned to her behind. Bolder this time, he applied a little pressure and then retreated only to do it again. She squeaked when the tip of his finger entered her. "Ranulf?"

He jerked back, releasing her all at once.

"What's wrong?"

She reached for him, but he stood quickly and moved away. "I have only just remembered an errand. I shall return shortly. Retire without me."

He didn't give her a chance to reply. She flinched when the door slammed behind him.

What had just happened?

The atmosphere had been good. Ranulf had been in to it. Something spooked him. But, what?

She couldn't even begin to guess.

"Retire," she whispered then snorted. "He's joking, right?" There was no way she'd get to sleep. Ranulf's attention had her hyper sensitive. The feel of her dress brushing her skin as she breathed was even too much.

Going solo was out of the question. The experience would be lacking, especially without something that vibrated at varying rates of speed.

She sighed. "I want to go home."

Chapter Forty

Eris glanced at Ranulf before she closed the door. Like last time, he hadn't stirred when she left the bed. She didn't know why she felt guilty. It wasn't like going with Lucien was anything bad. She'd done the same for the last few weeks. That night was no different, even though Ranulf had said she should stop.

If the topic came up, she'd tell him she'd gotten used to bathing on a daily basis and going with Lucien ensured the continuation of that habit.

That was it.

Bathing. Nothing else. Nothing that should make her feel guilty.

She turned and jumped with a startled gasp.

Lucien smiled at her.

She said, "You scared me."

"You're late. I thought you would not come this night."

"I said I would continue so long as you let me."

He nodded and led the way.

Eris waited until they were well away from the keep before asking, "Are you angry about the tunic?"

"Ranulf's?"

She nodded.

"Annoyed, not angry. You have improved."

"I'll have yours finished soon."

He made a noncommittal noise. She lapsed into silence.

Lucien tightened his hold around her waist. She glanced back at him, but he didn't say anything. He looked like he was thinking about something. She didn't want to disturb him so she faced front and stared at the woods.

She must have nodded off because the next thing she knew Lucien was dismounting. He kept a steadying hand on her waist so she wouldn't fall.

"Are you awake?"

She nodded then yawned.

He smirked at her as he lifted her from the horse.

"I am awake," she said in a firm voice.

His smirk got bigger and was accompanied by a light snort.

She decided not to force the issue.

Lucien led the way with her in tow. After a few moments in the darkness, he reached back and grabbed her hand. He asked in a gruff voice, "Is there ever a time when you are not cold?"

"Only when I sleep."

His grip tightened.

"Oh, and when we're here. But that's only when I'm in the water."

They lapsed into silence once more. Eris didn't know why Lucien had grabbed her hand. His behavior since Ranulf's return was becoming more and more erratic.

He released her when they reached the grotto. Eris missed the heat immediately. She stripped and entered the water.

Lucien followed after he'd built the fire. His bath didn't take long, as usual. Eris swam a few laps but didn't feel like doing her normal routine.

"You've normally finished five laps by this time."

She turned around and looked at Lucien. He was busy drawing.

"Did your night plans with Ranulf tire you?" he asked.

So he suspected. Was that the reason he was acting so strange? Could he be jealous? If he was the Lucien of her time, she wouldn't even need to ask. The answer would be yes. The medieval Lucien was a little harder to read and predict.

She said, "I'm not tired. I just don't really feel like swimming today."

"It's a shame you didn't bring your sewing. You could have finished my tunic."

There was an edge to his voice.

"You *are* angry."

"I said I am not." He stopped drawing and looked at her. "Am I not allowed to be annoyed about my second receiving something I should have gotten first?"

"Okay, so my timing was off. I was working on yours and his at the same time and decided to finish Ranulf's first."

He returned to his drawing. "Next time let him wait."

"Grump." She sliced her hand through the water, sending a wide arc toward Lucien.

He roared when it hit him, and Eris laughed. Her laughter turned to a yelp when Lucien bounded into the water after her.

"You'll pay for that," he said, reaching for her.

She dove under the water, but Lucien caught her foot. Kicking her legs to gain her freedom did no good. Lucien pulled her back and trapped her in his arms with her back to his chest.

They were both breathing hard. Lucien shifted so he held her with one arm. That freed his other hand so he could turn her head and meet her gaze. "You ruined my picture."

"Sorry."

"You got me wet."

"You weren't completely dry, and your tunic needed to be washed, anyway."

"Imp."

She grinned.

Lucien stared at her. His humor faded as his gaze roamed over her.

She frowned at him. "Is something on my face?"

"You should be with Ranulf," he whispered.

"He's asleep. Did you want me to stay there?"

He released her chin and hugged her tight. "Why do I miss your presence in my bed?"

"I'm not stealing all your heat. Maybe you're too hot."

He snorted. "That may be part of it." He dropped his head to her shoulder and inhaled deeply. "He had you this night."

"No."

"I heard his words and saw how you reacted."

"Nothing happened."

"I would count myself as lucky and blessed if the man had gone impotent. But, I doubt that is what happened."

"No. He thinks I'm still a virgin and skittish because of it."

"You are a virgin."

"No, you took care of that."

"I didn't, not completely. But I shall now." Lucien swung her into his arms and carried her out of the water. He laid her on the blankets near the fire then covered her body with his.

"Lucien?"

His mouth descended to hers. The kiss surprised her, but it wasn't unwelcome. She curved her hands around his neck and returned his kiss.

He didn't have the technique of his future self. The kiss was hesitant. She was about to take it over when he pulled back.

He whispered, "Don't cry."

"What do you—?"

"This time."

She snapped her mouth shut and stared at him with wide-eyed surprise. His worried expression said all she needed to know.

Cupping his face with her hands, she said in a measured tone. "I'm awake. I know when I am, where I am, and who I'm with."

She ignored his confused expression. She had said *when* for her own benefit, not his. It was important for her that she knew which version touched her. Though the same man, time had changed him. She needed to get to know *this* Lucien.

"I won't cry." She pressed a light kiss to his lips. "Well, I might, if you decide not to touch me."

Lucien's eyes darkened.

She would have said more to assure him, but his mouth descended and stole the words and her sense. His hesitation had vanished, replaced with a very obvious hunger. She could only receive his kiss as he left her no room to respond.

He pushed his hand down her side, feeling his way between her legs. Despite his urgency, his fingers entered her slowly, as though testing. She was more than ready to receive him. That simple touch somewhat soothed the ache deep inside her.

She pressed upwards when he curled his fingers inside her. He rubbed upwards, not pumping, in a circular motion. She almost screamed. Instead she clutched at his neck and ground her hips against his hand.

"You like that," he whispered, pulling away from the kiss and looking down at her.

She could only nod.

"And this?"

He changed the motion of his fingers, retreating and then pushing his fingers to her depths. Over and over at a measured pace.

She panted, unable to answer his question or remember what he'd asked.

When he touched the pad of his thumb to her nub, she arched beneath him with a sucked-in breath. Her whole body tensed as her release washed over her.

Lucien continued teasing her nub, holding her in the orgasm, as he removed his fingers and replaced them with something longer and more solid. She moved beneath him, inviting all of him in, all the way.

He gritted his teeth as he started to move.

She didn't want him to leave her so she wrapped her legs around his waist and held him tight.

Lucien chuckled as he tried to loosen her hold. She only held him tighter.

"I need to move for you to have more pleasure, Eris." He rotated his hips and applied just the right pressure to her nub that acted as a combination lock.

Her legs fell open, and she pressed upwards, wanting more of him.

He pulled back. When he returned, he pressed deep inside of her and rocked his hips. The sensation had her teetering on the edge of another orgasm. She held it back, barely. Savoring Lucien's feel for as long as he could last won out over release.

The only coherent thought Eris could muster was to wonder where Lucien had learned to move. He pulled out at an angle and returned at a different angle. Or, he tilted his hips back as his entered and then leaned his hips forward as he exited.

All his movements ensured his arousal touched every part of the inside of her body. Her battle to hold out, to feel all that Lucien could do, was lost. She threw her head back and called his name as her body convulsed with her release.

He hugged her tight, burying himself as far within her as he could go, and shuddered. Warmth spread into her and, like all heat, she accepted it greedily.

Everything got still and grew quiet. The only sound was their breathing.

Eris closed her eyes. She focused on Lucien's heartbeat. Fast and steady. She knew her own heart matched his pace. As they lay there, Lucien still buried deep inside of her, she listened to his heart return to a normal speed. The steady thump-thump calmed the frenzy.

She sighed.

* * * *

Lucien looked down when Eris relaxed completely. He smiled. She'd fallen asleep, and she was smiling. Just a slight curve of her lips—a look of utter satisfaction.

Careful not to wake her, he eased out of her body. Leaving her warmth without returning was a Herculean task. He was ready to taste more of her. If he'd known how her responses would excite his blood, he would have bedded her the very first night he laid eyes on her.

He stroked her cheek. She sighed and turned into his hand.

"Who are you?" he whispered.

Her only response was to murmur his name.

He moved so he lay on his side and gathered her close. She snuggled against him then returned to restful slumber.

Thoughts of who she could be danced around his mind as he stared at the ceiling and stroked Eris's arm lazily where it rested across his stomach.

They would have to leave soon. He glanced at her. He hated to wake her. But, wake her he must. It was long past when they should have returned to the keep.

He slipped from her hold, got on his haunches, and then lifted her. She curled against him with a happy murmur. It sounded as though she said his name again, but he couldn't tell.

Lucien walked into the water until it reached his chest. Eris blinked a few times and looked up at him. He asked in a soft voice, "Are you awake?"

"Yes."

"Are you sure?"

She nodded.

He released her legs. She clutched at him with a startled gasp. Her reaction tugged a smile from his lips. "Be easy. I have you."

She looked at him. Confusion—a sure sign she wasn't fully coherent—still marred her features. She loosened her hold and let her hands slide down until they rested against his chest.

His body reacted, and Lucien knew their return would be delayed even longer.

Eris seemed to sense his intention—or she felt the hardening of his arousal—because she turned her face upwards to receive his kiss.

He bent forward but stopped before his lips touched hers. The hairs on the back of his neck stood on end as heat that wasn't from the water swept up his back.

"I should have asked *how* Lucien had checked for your virginity," Ranulf said with a low growl.

Eris jerked back and looked around Lucien's body. "Ranulf."

She tried to get around him, but Lucien held her. The overwhelming urge to shield her nakedness from Ranulf couldn't be denied.

Ranulf said, "I did not see to your need so you turned to Lucien."

Eris shook her head. "Ranulf, please. That's not what happened."

"How could it be anything else when I find you like this?"

She tugged against Lucien's hold and looked up at him with pleading eyes. He ignored the look.

"That's not—"

Lucien said, "If you had come only a little earlier, there would be no doubt and no need for explanation. I merely claimed that which you left me, as you intended."

"I intended for you to check!" Ranulf stalked closer to the water's edge but didn't enter. "She is mine."

"You can own no property and gain no fortune, Ranulf," Lucien said. "Unless the king rescinded that decree whilst you attended him, you merely oversee that which I own."

"Bastard," Ranulf spat. "By your own oath, you gave her to me."

"I gave her life to you until I found proof. She is not who I suspected, and thus her life is no longer in danger. She is mine to do with as I see fit."

Lucien purposefully held Eris closer. A smug smile curved his lips as Ranulf fisted his hands at his side. The man would have to enter the water to get at Lucien, if that was his intention.

Lucien said, "I thank you for interceding and keeping her alive, else I would have missed the pleasure she gives."

Ranulf glared at them both.

Lucien felt Eris shiver, but he kept his gaze on Ranulf. Would the man attack?

Ranulf looked one last time at Eris. He said in a low voice, "My father's mistake will not be my own." Then he turned and left.

Eris looked up at Lucien. "His father's?"

He shook his head. "I know not. Ranulf has never spoken of his family."

"We should go after him."

"Why?"

She stared at him in shock.

"His jealousy will abate in time when he comes to terms with my claim."

"Claim? I'm not property."

Lucien captured her chin between his fingers and made her meet his gaze. "What are you then?"

She stared at his eyes.

He could see a battle within her gaze. She wanted to speak to him, but something held her back. His grip on her chin tightened. "The time when I would tolerate your silence is at an end."

"The truth?"

He stiffened.

"The truth then," she said with a small nod.

He released her and stepped back.

"My name is Eris Brue. I come from a land that, at this point in time, has no name you'd recognize. Heck, I wouldn't even recognize it."

"What are you talking about?"

"I'm from the future—the year twenty-ten." She watched him. "Two thousand and ten."

"I know my numbers," he snapped.

"I met you and Ranulf in that time."

"Did you?"

"We're friends."

He nodded. "Is that why you had my mother's ring then?"

She touched the scar on her ring finger. "You...the Lucien of my time gave it to me. He'd actually just given it to me a few hours before I stumbled back through time. I think it may have caused the whole thing."

"Ah."

No wonder Ranulf trusted Eris wasn't a threat. She was crazed.

Two thousand and ten. Such an absurd and impossible number. He wondered why she'd chosen it. The more he thought about her words the more amused he became until he started laughing.

Lucien threw back his head and laughed. His whole body shook. The sound echoed in the grotto and made him laugh harder.

Eris said nothing as she watched him.

He finally calmed, taking several deep breaths. "Two thousand." He chuckled. "I think Ranulf is addled if he believed such a tale."

"It's true."

"Judgment day shall come before any day in the two thousands. And you say you will meet Ranulf and I then. How? We are not magical beings."

"I don't know."

"You don't know because your tale is just that—a tale."

She jumped when he reached for her again. He didn't do more than cup her cheek.

"Yet, I see in your eyes you believe your nonsense." He released her with a slow nod. "Ranulf is right. You are no threat. Only crazed."

"I'm not crazy."

Lucien walked toward the fire. He doused it then went about dressing and gathering his things.

"I'm not!"

He didn't care how many times she said it or how loudly. No other explanation made sense. She believed all that she told him, and he knew it couldn't possibly be true.

A quick glance at her almost made him laugh again. She looked indignant with her arms crossed over her ample chest. He let his gaze roam over her and remembered Ranulf had interrupted before Lucien could have Eris a second time.

She made an angry noise and rushed to get dressed, shooting him a look that plainly said for him to stay away.

He wondered how her passion would change if tempered with anger.

The oncoming dawn curbed his curiosity. He needed rest.

"Come then, my little time traveler." Lucien beckoned to her.

She regarded him and looked like she would balk.

He waited to see what she would do.

With an annoyed sound, she walked over to him. He got the impression she wanted to hit him. He turned his back to her and walked out of the grotto, anxious to test whether she would assault him or not.

She took hold of his tunic, grumbling under her breath the entire time.

Her irritation only made him chuckle. His amusement made her irritation worse, which only made him laugh more.

Two thousand and ten.

He snorted and shook his head.

Impossible.

Chapter Forty-one

Eris glanced at Lucien as she eased into her cloak. He slept peacefully and undisturbed. Unlike the night before when she snuck away from Ranulf, she knew exactly where her sudden feeling of guilt originated.

She should be worried about her growing ability to sneak from one man's bed without awakening him to see another. Lucien had only mumbled incoherently and rolled onto his back when she'd slipped out of his arms.

She continually glanced back at him as she made her way to the door.

Lucien remained oblivious.

All of her steps were the loudest she'd ever heard. Even the door when she opened it made more noise than usual. She was sure the thundering of her heart would rouse Lucien whereas all the other noise hadn't.

If he woke and found her headed in Ranulf's direction, he wouldn't be pleased in the least and nowhere near as amused as he had been that morning. Thinking back on that still annoyed her.

She pushed that thought aside and focused on getting out of the room without waking Lucien. No explanation for her actions would be good enough for him. Pointing out the irony of his anger when he hadn't seen a problem with her sneaking away from Ranulf to see him would only make matters worse.

She closed the door as softly as she could and then waited. Lucien didn't come bounding through the door after her. That had to mean he was still sleeping. She waited a little longer just to be sure.

With a silent sigh, she faced down the hall toward Ranulf's room. He wouldn't be there. It was bath day. The sour mood of the keep's inhabitants was testament to that.

Their less than amicable attitude was even more magnified because of the irritation obvious between Ranulf and Lucien. Neither man had tried hiding their annoyance with one another. The people of the keep had clearly taken Lucien's side without even knowing—she hoped they didn't know—what the men argued about.

Alas, she was the cause. It wasn't ego that made her think that. History was repeating itself, though this time around the men didn't know sharing her was an option. She wasn't even sure she should bring it up.

Before she even tried to think of how to approach *that* subject, she had to set things straight with Ranulf.

She made sure her cloak covered all of her as she walked. Only her undergarments covered her beneath its folds. She hadn't wanted to chance getting dressed fully and waking Lucien.

Hopefully, her talk with Ranulf wouldn't take long, and she could return before Lucien awoke for their nightly trip to the glowing grotto.

She placed her hand on the door to the bathing room and then stopped. A loud curse and muted splash greeted her ears.

Ranulf was definitely there, and he was angry. She took a bracing breath and pushed the door open.

She didn't get two steps before a sponge came sailing in her direction. It flew past her shoulder and into the hallway.

"Get out!"

Eris stood her ground. She met Ranulf's gaze and waited to see what he would do next. He hadn't wanted to hit her with that sponge or else he would have. He'd missed purposefully, probably thinking he would scare her.

"Ranulf—"

"Why do you remain? Leave!"

She entered and closed the door behind her so his voice wouldn't carry.

"You belong to Lucien. Go to him for your needs."

"That's not why I'm here."

"You like attending my bath so much, then?"

She moved closer to him but stayed out of arm's reach. "I didn't know Lucien would do what he did. He never showed any indication he saw me as anything more than an annoyance."

"I should believe that?"

"It's the truth."

He made a derisive noise and rolled his eyes. "Yes, we know you are so good at speaking the truth."

"I have never lied to you, Ranulf."

"You say you are from the future. What is that, if not a lie?"

"It's the truth," she said with an annoyed gesture. "I am from the future. A future where you, Lucien, and I are friends."

Okay, so that was a kind of lie. They had started out as friends. Minus their sleeping arrangements and the occasional kiss, their relationship could be seen as a type of friendship. A very intimate type of friendship. But, that lie kept Ranulf and Lucien from delving too much into the relationship the three of them had planned to have.

Assuming she ever returned. As the months crept by, she was beginning to wonder if she ever would.

"Such a sad expression cannot be because you miss me. You have Lucien to comfort you now."

"I do miss you," she whispered. "I miss both of you."

Tears threatened to come pouring out of her eyes as a wave of homesickness hit her. She hadn't felt the like since her first days in the past. She turned away, prepared to leave her talk with Ranulf for another day.

Something caught her cloak. She looked back.

Ranulf held it in his fist. A knowing look graced his features. "Did you think to gain my sympathy and, when that failed, to entice me instead?" He looked pointedly at her body.

She looked down at her underwear, which was on display for Ranulf, then gasped. "I forgot," she squeaked as she yanked at her cloak.

He didn't release it. In fact, he tightened his hold. "You actually take me for a fool that I would believe you forgot such a blatant display?" He gathered the cloak to him, using it as a tether to bring her to his side.

She didn't fight him, mostly because she would need her cloak once she returned to Lucien. He would notice its absence immediately if she didn't have it since she was never without it.

Once she was close to him, Ranulf reached up and unclasped the cloak. He tossed it over his shoulder even as she tried to keep it near. "Your seduction will not work if you do not display what is offered."

"That's not why I came here. I wanted you to know the truth of what happened."

Ranulf's hand smoothed over her hip. "I know the truth. He's had what was supposed to be mine." He untied the string at her hip. "He was to check only." Pushing the cloth out his way, he cupped her.

She stared at him. Thoughts of trying to convince him there was no intentional wrong-doing fled as the heat from his fingers suffused her body from the point between her thighs.

"And you." One finger trailed between her lower lips. "You opened for him and let him rut between your legs so as to ensure your safety."

"That's not—" She bit her lip as he purposefully moved his finger over her nub. "I wanted him."

She yelped.

Ranulf had clenched his hand, digging his fingers into her skin. He glared up at her. "I left you scared and trembling. You couldn't stand to be near him. It was I you clung to."

She nodded.

"You admit you took advantage of the situation, using what little knowledge you have of sex to entice me." His hold loosened, and he resumed teasing her. "Did you enjoy it?"

She nodded without hesitation. Why lie? Ranulf was already angry.

"Good. You will enjoy this as well." He rose and stepped out of the tub. The whole while, he stroked his fingers inside of her.

With his free hand, he untied the other string of her panties and pulled the cloth off of her. He then untied her bra, tossing that away as well.

Eris stared up at him.

"Is that anticipation I see? How easily you've become a bitch in heat. Will any man satisfy you now? Were you even really a virgin?"

She reached out to him, but he caught her wrist before she could touch him. "Ranulf, please."

The purpose of her plea eluded her. She wanted so much in that moment. For him to continue touching her topped the list easily.

She moved closer to him, and he frowned down at her. It didn't matter how it looked to him. She knew what the future held.

She laid a kiss on his chest.

"Eris?"

"Please."

Ranulf hooked his finger inside of her and pulled her as close as she could get. She panted at the sensation. He cupped her cheek with his free hand, turning her face up to him.

She whispered again, "Please."

Ranulf lowered his lips to hers.

She felt no anger in his kiss, only need. She clutched at his shoulders and moved her hips against his hand.

He pushed her away. "Fine. You wish to be a bitch in heat, then I will treat you like one."

With a hand on her shoulder, he whipped her around so her back was to him. "Bend over."

She looked back at him with a worried expression. He didn't mean to do anal, did he? She was prepared and ready for sex but not like that.

"Down," he barked, pushing at her shoulder.

She braced herself on the edge of the tub.

Ranulf urged her legs farther apart then spread her wide. "Such a sight. Glistening and dripping with anticipation for any man that cares to have you."

She shook her head. Not any man. She knew that her body only reacted for Ranulf and Lucien.

"No use denying it now. Your body betrays you."

Something blunt and thick prodded her entrance. She sucked in a breath.

Ranulf thrust forward and seated himself within her fully.

Eris let loose a small cry of satisfaction. Her arms shook, protesting her weight. She folded her arms and rested her head against them.

He moved. Over and over, he drove to the depths of her body, grunting with each thrust.

She panted his name and wiggled her hips.

"Such an eager little wanton. Perhaps you want something more."

His meaning confused her until she felt his finger push into her rear. Her mouth opened, but no sound came out. The sensation, the pleasure of having him touch her there while his hard flesh drove into her took her breath away.

Would it feel even better if he used his arousal instead? Would she lose herself in pleasure if Lucien were there while Ranulf claimed her rear? She wanted to find out.

Just the thought of it made her come.

She called Ranulf's name as her body reached its release.

Ranulf slammed into her one last time then spilled himself. His breath came hard, and he leaned into her.

Eris tried to look back at him, but she couldn't move.

He pulled out of her, and she sagged to her knees. Semen and her body's fluids pooled beneath her.

"Clean yourself up and go back to Lucien. He should be waking soon for his nightly jaunt to the grotto."

She looked at him. Soon? How much time had passed?

He smirked. "Better still. Go back like that. Let Lucien see you for what you truly are."

"Ranulf, I didn't—" She stopped when he left the room without a backward glance.

Her words had fallen on deaf ears, and sex had accomplished nothing. He was still angry with her and Lucien.

She struggled to her feet. Once she was sure she was steady, she stepped into the tub and cleaned herself. It wasn't shame that prompted her actions but a need to head off a fight she knew would happen if Lucien found out she and Ranulf had had sex.

No solution as to how to fix their problem came to mind. She almost wondered if her Ranulf and Lucien had been plagued with such thoughts while they were seducing her.

She shook her head. Compared to her current situation, the future versions of Ranulf and Lucien had had it easy. And there were two of them against one of her. The tables had turned. One wrong move on her part, and she wouldn't have either man. Not only that, but she might land in even more trouble if her efforts angered Lucien.

Donning her cloak, she rushed back to Lucien's room. Maybe a good swim in the grotto would help her figure out the situation. She pulled her cloak tighter and walked faster. How long had she been gone? Was Lucien awake and wondering where she'd gone?

She stopped at the door and listened. All was silent. Lucien hadn't started his preparations to leave. Holding her breath and praying for silence, she pulled open the door and entered the room. She immediately looked at the bed.

Lucien slept.

She went to her clothes, dropped her cloak and started dressing. If Lucien caught her, she could tell him she woke first and decided to get ready. She stuffed the panties she'd worn on her visit to Ranulf in her bag. As an afterthought she added a few more pairs so she could give the excuse of washing her clothes.

Lucien stirred. "Eris?"

"I'm ready when you are," she said, forcing humor in her voice.

He looked at her for a long while before he smiled. "You are eager this night. Good."

She only nodded and edged to the door to wait for him. A thought made her sniff her skin. Did she smell like Ranulf? Would Lucien notice as they rode together?

There was no smell she could discern. Hopefully, Lucien wouldn't find anything amiss with her either.

Chapter Forty-two

Lucien watched Eris.

Watching Eris had become a hobby of sorts for him. It seemed to be all he ever did when she was near him. For that reason alone, he appreciated her self-confinement to his room. She was no longer a prisoner kept under lock and key, but she professed a liking for her confinement. That night, however, she decided to sew near the big fire in the common room.

The light of the flame framed her in a halo of light that could only be described as equal parts angelic and carnal. She shimmered with an ethereal glow whenever she moved. But the firelight also reminded him of how the shadows cast by the grotto fire had danced off of her bare skin when she'd writhed with pleasure beneath him.

He shifted to relieve the ache of his sudden and quite hard arousal.

No woman before Eris had ever made him react in such an immediate manner. He shouldn't desire her as much as he did. All he had to do was catch the whisper of her voice or see an edge of cloth from that blasted cloak she stayed swathed in and he was ready to take her then and there.

Eris responded and matched his lust every time. On that topic he had no complaint. But the past week she'd been distracted. He'd also noticed her gaze following Ranulf whenever the man chanced to be in the same room with her.

Ranulf and Lucien had reached an understanding of mutual annoyance that Lucien was sure the entire keep had noticed. They were cool to each other whenever they chanced to converse and generally avoided each other if circumstances didn't require they interact.

Lucien was sure everything would return to normal once Ranulf moved past his jealousy. The better man had won, as always whenever they matched each other.

Then why did his entire being go on alert when Eris watched Ranulf leave the common room?

He was about to blame paranoia and return to his musings about Eris swathed in firelight and nothing else, except Eris wouldn't sit still and cooperate. She gathered her sewing into the basket beside her chair as though preparing to leave.

In fact, she did.

Lucien almost called out to her, but stopped. He placed aside his drink and followed her instead.

Actually, his intention wasn't to follow her. Their destinations happened to be similar—his room—and he didn't feel the need to bring her attention to his presence behind her since she hadn't noticed.

He stopped at the top of the stairs, letting the darkness mask him. A precautionary measure only. He wasn't hiding. Eris might become frightened if he appeared behind her without warning. He'd wait a bit and then enter the room.

Or so he thought.

Eris exited the room, looking one way and then the other. She didn't seem to see him. Her lips moved, but he couldn't hear her words. She nodded to herself and then walked down the hallway toward Ranulf's room.

A coincidence. Many things were down that hallway. Many things, but nothing that should or would interest Eris except Ranulf's room.

Lucien turned away.

It was nothing. Eris probably wished a word with him in private. Ranulf had been her savior for many weeks before Lucien. She probably only missed their friendship. Or perhaps she had left something in Ranulf's room and needed to retrieve it.

He walked down the stairs.

Eris wouldn't betray him. She appreciated his attention and good humor toward her. He knew for a certainty she would do nothing to jeopardize either.

Why then did he turn back after reaching the bottom of the stairs?

Lucien made himself maintain a normal pace as he climbed the stairs once more. Or he tried.

He was overreacting to absurd imaginings. Eris had probably already returned to his room. He'd find her there and then feel foolish for doubting her.

Preparing himself to feel foolish, he opened his bedroom door.

Eris wasn't there.

He paced the length of the room, making sure he hadn't overlooked her. His eyes hadn't deceived him. She wasn't there.

He waited.

She would return in a moment.

He crossed and uncrossed his arms several times while he waited. Glaring at the door didn't make Eris walk through it.

He cursed under his breath as he stormed out of the room and down to Ranulf's.

* * * *

Eris stepped out of Lucien's room. She looked down one way and then the other. When she didn't see anyone, not that she'd expected to, she breathed a sigh.

Finding opportunities to speak to Ranulf alone had been hard. She'd thought to meet him after Lucien had fallen asleep, like she had the other time. The first night, Lucien had come to bed late and only dozed until it was time to leave for the grotto.

The next night, Lucien awoke as soon as she moved. A complaint of cold and needing her cloak had led to being hugged for the rest of the night with no hope of escaping without waking him.

She'd thought changing her time of escape until after the trip to the grotto would help.

It didn't.

Lucien had a tendency of becoming amorous once they returned, regardless of the fact that they'd had sex in the grotto beforehand.

The sex was great, and she didn't mind in the least as Lucien was a passionate lover. But she still needed to set things straight with Ranulf. She wouldn't feel right until she did.

"Let's just hope he'll listen this time," she whispered to herself.

She faced his room and walked quickly. Lucien had stayed in the common room, but she didn't know for how long. Time was definitely a factor.

Ranulf had just opened his door when she reached it. He stopped and stared at her.

"Ranulf, we need to—"

"Leave unless you want me to give you more of the same as last time."

She didn't move. She couldn't. Her body flushed hot as his threat brought back all of the delicious sensations their one and only time had brought her.

In a breathy voice, she said, "We need to talk."

"What could we possibly have to speak about?" He didn't wait for an answer and instead tried walking past her.

She got in his way. "Please, Ranulf. I only want to explain."

"Why should you? Your actions are obvious and understandable. Lucien has more power. He is a better protector for you."

"He's not you," she whispered.

Ranulf's angered look lessened. He stared at her for a few breaths.

"Please."

She felt a moment of joy when Ranulf stepped back so she could enter his room. He closed the door after her.

"Are you naked this time?"

She looked down at her cloak. In answer to his question, she lifted her arms. She had her usual chemise beneath it. The idea of visiting Ranulf naked, or even in her underwear, hadn't occurred to her because she truly wished to speak with him.

Ranulf sighed. "More's the pity." He snaked his arm around her waist and pulled her close. "Though, I do so enjoy untying you."

He kissed her before she could say anything.

As much as she wanted to push him away, the feel of his lips was a pleasure she'd missed. She wound her arms around his neck.

He squeezed her behind, and she jerked. Nothing would be accomplished if she let things play out the same as last time.

She pushed away from him and was a little surprised he let her go. After a few calming breaths, she looked at up at him.

His guarded look of annoyance surprised her. "You think I'm a deviant as well."

"What?"

He reached for, but she backed up a step, knowing her self-control could only take so much.

"You avoid my touch," he said.

"No. I want to talk."

"Women like you aren't for conversation. You serve one purpose." He reached for her again, and again she moved back. "Did you find it so disgusting? You seemed plenty sated at the time."

Eris felt heat rise up her neck. "I never had...that was..."

"Disgusting."

"What?"

"Say it! The very idea of doing that again repulses you."

He didn't give her a chance to reply before he stalked away from her to the window. "He ruined me. I never had such urges before him."

"Him?" Eris whispered. Ranulf was clearly upset and angry. She didn't want to agitate him further with questions, but the change in subject had her a little confused.

"The prince. Ever since..." He clenched his fist and hit the wall.

Eris jumped at the sound.

"I cannot be with a woman unless I touch her there. It is disgusting to want that. Men do not interest me. That is *not* why I do it. So, why? Why am I plagued with *that* desire?"

She blinked at him. A pitying expression softened her features, and she shook her head. "Ranulf." She crossed the room and touched his back. He didn't pull away from her. "Liking anal sex doesn't mean you like men."

"What would you know?" He pushed away from her.

She caught his arm before he moved too far away, and he looked back at her. "I know that what you did haunts my dreams."

"More like plagues your nightmares."

She lifted his hand to her cheek. "I think about you doing that while I'm with Lucien. I imagine how it would feel if you used..." She trailed off and let her gaze slide to his lower body. She shivered and her breathing quickened. That wasn't why she'd come to Ranulf's room, but it was fast replacing her original motive.

"You..." He shook his head. "You enjoyed it?"

"God, yes."

His eyes darkened with lust, and he rubbed his thumb over her lips.

She dropped his hand and stepped back.

"Eris?"

"I should go. I didn't mean..." She shook her head. Why was holding a simple conversation so hard all of a sudden? "Lucien must have returned to his room by now. He'll wonder where I've gone."

Ranulf caught her against him. He lowered his lips to hers, ignoring her attempts to get away.

The kiss melted her resolve. When she felt his hand gathering the cloth of her chemise, she helped him. She pulled at the dress until she held it bundled in her arms, leaving her lower body exposed.

Ranulf smiled against her lips. He untied her panties then slipped his fingers into her center.

Her moan escaped into his throat. She was about to lift her leg against his hip when Ranulf started walking.

He maneuvered her back to the bed and made her sit. That only drove his fingers deeper.

"Lie back," he said in a husky voice.

She let herself fall.

Ranulf trailed his fingers from her depths to her rear. Using her own fluids as lubricant, he pushed two fingers deep inside her puckered opening.

Eris's back arched off the bed, and she gasped. Her hips moved against his fingers with a mind of their own. She couldn't stop even if she wanted to. Though she'd only known the sensation once, having it again impressed upon her how much she missed it.

"You do enjoy it."

She couldn't answer him.

Ranulf bent over her and licked at her center.

Eris almost screamed. She released her dress and clutched at Ranulf's head.

Something banged, but the origin of the sound didn't register. She cried out a denial when Ranulf left her. Then, she saw why.

Lucien had grabbed Ranulf and thrown him. Ranulf lay sprawled, glaring up at Lucien.

"You dare!" Lucien roared.

Ranulf said, "Me? It is I who should say that. She was my burden."

"Then you should have claimed her."

"I left her intact to prove her innocence." Ranulf got to his feet. "You were only supposed to check, not take it."

"When she was offering it so sweetly, how could I resist? No man could." Lucien looked Ranulf up and down. "No man that desires women alone could."

Eris yelled, "Lucien!"

Ranulf punched Lucien in the face. The other man responded in kind.

Eris looked around the room for something that could stop the fight. A pitcher of water caught her eye. She rushed for it, tested the water to make sure it wasn't hot, and then ran as close to the men as she dared.

"Ranulf! Lucien! Stop this!"

Neither man listened. The sickening sound of fists meeting flesh made her wince.

She threw the contents of the pitcher in a wide arc, splashing both men.

The water seemed to surprise them enough that they both stopped and looked at her. All three of them were breathing hard. Ranulf's cheek was cut while Lucien's right eyebrow bled freely.

"Please stop. I don't want you two fighting." She put the pitcher on the ground and walked near them. "You two are friends, and that friendship is important."

"Friends do not betray one another," Lucien spat.

Ranulf snapped, "I could say the same."

"She belongs to me."

"She *wants* me."

When neither of them backed down from the glaring match, their angered gazes turned to her. She stepped back quickly. "I didn't mean for this to happen."

"What did you think would happen when you continually go from me to him?" Lucien yelled.

"I didn't."

"Then I dreamed the scene I interrupted."

"No. I…" She stopped and looked at Ranulf. "I wanted to talk, to make sure Ranulf understood what had truly happened."

"You couldn't satisfy her so she came to me," Ranulf said in a smug tone.

Eris jumped between them when Lucien would have hit Ranulf. He stopped. She was happy for that since she hadn't been sure if he would.

"You protect *him*?" Lucien yelled.

"I'm protecting both of you. I don't want you to fight. There's no need." She reached out to him, but he jerked away. "You two share so much else, why am I any different?"

Lucien cursed then stalked out of the room.

Okay. That wasn't what she thought would happen. It's not like she expected Lucien to stop being angry immediately in favor of a threesome. But she hadn't expected him to just leave either.

She looked at Ranulf.

He rubbed his jaw. "Both of us sharing you."

"Can you think of any other way to keep you two from killing each other, thus having the whole keep blame me and then string me up in the nearest tree?"

Ranulf cupped her cheek. "They wouldn't hang you, little Eris."

"Says you."

He kissed her lips, wincing a little as he did. "They burn witches." He kissed her again. "Because that is surely what you are that you could have me considering your idea."

"I don't want you two fighting. Not because of me. Your friendship is too important." She met his gaze. "You need to tell him all that happened to you."

"It sounded as though you already had."

"I wouldn't betray your trust like that."

"Haven't you already by sleeping with Lucien?"

She looked down. "I didn't tell him anything," she whispered. "I keep your secrets and his."

"His? What secrets could Lucien possibly have that I don't know about?"

She pulled away from Ranulf.

"Eris?"

"I need to find Lucien."

He caught her arm. "Stay here. I'll find him."

"Ranulf—"

"And we'll talk. Assuming he wants to talk."

"Please don't hurt him too badly."

He grinned as he kissed her. "Why ever not? If I do, he can't perform and then you are all mine." He kissed her again and then walked away.

Chapter Forty-three

Ranulf found Lucien in the grotto.

"Leave," Lucien snapped before Ranulf could speak.

"You will hear me."

"Take her. I care not."

Ranulf laughed at such a blatant lie. "If you didn't care then you wouldn't have interrupted us, and Eris would still be moaning beneath me and panting my name."

As he expected, Lucien swung at him. The man missed because Ranulf dodged. "I came to talk, not fight."

Lucien continued glaring at him.

Ranulf didn't care. He recited his whole sorry tale to Lucien's angered visage. When he finished, he asked, "What would you have done in my place?"

"Killed myself," Lucien snapped.

"A coward's death, but perhaps I should have. Then we'd both be dead."

Lucien jerked back.

Ranulf nodded. "My shame led to your survival. Remember that, Lucien."

"So you desire men now?"

"As much as I desire having my balls chopped off and fed to me."

"The women of the keep whisper of your...tastes."

"So that was where you heard it."

"Where else?"

"I thought Eris had broken confidence with me."

Lucien snorted. "That girl knows how to keep her tongue even if what she says when she does finally speak is so fanciful no one but a fool would believe her."

"So she's told you of her origins?"

"You cannot seriously believe she is from the future?"

"Give me more credit than that, old friend. She is hiding a great secret, and it is buried in that fantasy of traveling from a distant future. But I know the truth is no danger to either of us."

Lucien nodded with a tired sigh. "Two thousand and ten. I cannot even imagine such a year."

"Neither can I. And the very idea that we survive such a great span *together* is even more impossible."

"Agreed."

"She said you have a secret to tell as well." Ranulf crossed his arms when Lucien glared at him.

In a grumbling manner, Lucien said, "I draw."

"And?"

"There is no and. That is all. I draw."

Ranulf laughed. "That is not a secret worthy of standing up to my own."

"A knight—a lord shouldn't do such things."

"According to whom?"

"My father."

"Your father is dead."

Lucien nodded.

"Do you have talent?"

"According to Eris." Lucien eyed Ranulf. "You can't have her."

"Hah! Only moments ago you said I could."

"I changed my mind."

"Then we are at an impasse unless we do as she suggested."

"Share her? One night she is in your bed and the next night she is in mine." He shook his head and sliced his hand across the air. "No. It's sheer stupidity to even consider it. We'd only trade one argument for another."

"And if we share her at one time?"

"Both of us simultaneously?"

Ranulf nodded once.

Lucien looked thoughtful. He met Ranulf's gaze. "If you touch me, I'll kill you and have Eris over your corpse."

"Fair enough, and to you the same. Not that the idea hadn't occurred simply so I could have her all to myself."

"Likewise."

"Shall we return to have what was offered then?"

* * * *

Eris had paced the length of Ranulf's room so many times she'd lost count. It was the most exercise she'd had in a long while, outside of her swimming.

She wanted to go after Lucien and Ranulf so badly, but she had no clue where they were. And, she didn't even know if the gate guards would let her leave the keep's grounds—if Ranulf and Lucien had gone to the grotto—to search for them.

She'd been stupid to let Ranulf go without her. He and Lucien were probably beating each other to death again. She'd be flattered except she didn't want them fighting. Their fights were more deadly in the past than the future.

The door to the room opened. Eris whirled and found Ranulf standing there.

"Ranulf?" She looked at him hopefully.

He entered the room, and Lucien followed. They both watched her. She recognized the look in their eyes. She'd seen it many times from the Lucien and Ranulf of her time.

Her heart rate increased.

Ranulf closed the door.

Lucien said, "Undress."

She looked between them as she untied her cloak and let it drop. Gathering the material of her chemise, she pulled it over her head.

"Wait," Ranulf said.

She stopped.

"Changed your mind?" Lucien asked in a knowing manner.

"Not at all. I simply enjoy doing this part myself." He pulled loose each of the knots that held Eris's underwear.

She looked away when Ranulf's gaze became too much. Instead, she looked at Lucien. His expression confused her. He didn't look angry or jealous. He didn't look happy either.

Ranulf slid his hand between her breasts, down her stomach and then he cupped between her legs. Leaning into her, he asked, "Shall we continue from earlier?" He pressed his fingers into her center before she could answer.

She inhaled loudly and clutched at his upper arms. All the while she kept her gaze locked with Lucien's.

He moved toward them, and she reached for him. When he took her hand, she pulled him close.

Ranulf moved to the side and around to Eris's back. He removed his fingers only long enough to reposition his hand. Even that small interruption was too much.

Lucien held her chin while he lowered his lips to hers. He palmed her breast with his other hand.

"You should feel this," Ranulf whispered against Eris's neck. He nibbled at her ear lobe while he spread her lower lips wide.

Lucien's hand joined Ranulf's between her legs. He slipped two fingers into the opening Ranulf had made for him. Ranulf moved his fingers to her rear.

She mewed and clutched Lucien's shoulders.

Ranulf urged her leg onto Lucien's hip. She wanted nothing more than to lie down as her legs threatened to give out at any second.

They only used their fingers, and her body was close to release. She gasped when Ranulf tried inserting a third finger. But her gasp was one of pain. She twisted and tried to pull away.

He hooked his fingers inside her, holding her in place. "Calm yourself, Eris. I am merely preparing you."

She wet her lips and stared up at Lucien. He offered no salvation or sympathy. She'd known what was coming. That didn't change the fact that it would hurt.

Lucien said, "Perhaps something to ease the way." He released her and walked to Ranulf's medicine rack. "I saw a jar here that should help."

"Why would you be looking through my salves?" Ranulf asked that question while resuming the movement of his fingers and massaging Eris's breasts with his free hand.

Lucien glanced back at Ranulf with a pointed look but said nothing.

"Ah. Of course." Ranulf nodded.

Eris half turned and looked at Ranulf for some explanation.

"Merely something to keep you out of trouble."

"Huh?"

He kissed her lips but didn't elaborate on the silent understanding.

"Here." Lucien held up the jar he'd found.

"What is it?" Eris asked.

Ranulf said, "Animal fat. That will do nicely." He reached for it.

At the same time, Eris pulled away from him, putting some distance between her and the men. "That's disgusting. You're not using that on me. No way and you can't make me."

Lucien said, "In fact, we can make you do a great many things."

She stared at him with wide eyes.

"We won't, however." Ranulf joined Lucien at the medicine rack and did another search. "We shall use this instead."

He walked the jar over to her. She was ready to run if need be. The scent of roses wafted under her nose and that made her pause.

"Rose oil," Ranulf said.

"Now I object." Lucien walked over to them, bringing the jar of animal fat with him. "We will all smell like a bunch of court ladies. My men think me strange enough already." He hefted the jar. "The fat is better."

"I'm not using that. End of discussion," Eris said.

Lucien's lip quirked on a half smile. "You think because we currently desire you that you can dictate to us?"

"Using the fat might make me sick," she said in a cautious voice. There was no *might* about it. Animal fat in any orifice, especially animal fat from the Middle Ages, would indeed make her sick. She'd survived several months with barely a sniffle. She wanted to keep it that way.

Staying healthy also meant not angering Lucien. A little kiss and tickle and she'd momentarily forgotten which version she was dealing with.

Lucien said, "Your argument is unsound. The rose oil—"

Ranulf put his hand on Lucien's shoulder. "It is I who will bear the brunt of the smell because of how I will use it. What little happens to touch your skin will be washed away when you take your nightly trip to the glowing grotto."

Lucien nodded. "True enough."

Eris only relaxed when Lucien replaced the jar he held. Hopefully the topic of it would never return.

Rustling clothing made her face Ranulf, who had stripped completely. He held his hand out to her as he backed toward the bed. She took it and let him pull her to him.

"Now then." He kissed her lips. "I've waited long enough."

She wanted to echo his sentiment but didn't.

He pointed to the bed. "On your knees."

Anticipation made her a little shaky. She crawled onto the bed on all fours with her behind facing Ranulf. He smoothed his hand over one cheek and kissed the other.

"Yes, I've waited much too long," he said in a low voice.

Lucien said, "I have wondered about your control until this point."

Ranulf only grunted.

Eris jerked when the cool rose oil coating Ranulf's fingers came into contact with her puckered flesh.

Ranulf kissed the small of her back. "Forgive me, little Eris. I know how susceptible you are to cold. It will heat soon."

Soon was almost instantaneous as her entire body was engulfed in heat. She pressed against Ranulf's fingers, moving her hips and using her body to beg for more.

A finger under her chin coaxed her gaze into traveling the length of Lucien's naked body to his eyes. He'd undressed while Ranulf had her distracted, not that she minded.

She reached for his arousal, but he caught her hand.

"There is time for that later. Sit up."

With slow motions so she didn't dislodge Ranulf's fingers, she sat back on her legs.

"Up," Lucien said. "And spread your legs."

She rose up so her weight was on her knees instead of her legs and waited for the next command.

Lucien moved in close to her with one of his knees between her legs. He guided her down with one hand while the other opened her wide for his waiting need.

She started to move almost immediately.

Ranulf chuckled and kissed her shoulder. "Not yet, Eris. Wait for me."

His fingers retreated and were replaced with something thick and hard. Eris knew what it was and knew pain would come with it.

She stared into Lucien's eyes.

Little by little, Ranulf seated himself within her. The rose oil eased the way but didn't help with Ranulf's girth and length. She wasn't sure she wanted to do anal again. The finger play had been fun, but in no way had it prepared her for what came next.

Once he was fully sheathed, Ranulf shifted so one of his knees sat beside Lucien's between her legs. Nestled between them, all thoughts of being cold fled.

The twin intrusion made her inner muscles clench. Both men groaned appreciatively.

Lucien moved so he retreated from her while Ranulf pressed upwards. As Lucien returned, Ranulf eased back. Neither man spoke, but somehow they knew the rhythm. Eris just enjoyed the ride.

She let her head fall back onto Ranulf's shoulder, which thrust her breasts toward Lucien's waiting lips. He suckled greedily at one nipple and then the other.

It almost felt like Ranulf was left out, until she felt his fingers caressing her nub. All of the sensations drowned her senses, and she climaxed with her mouth wide open. Where she should be screaming, there was only silence.

Neither man seemed to have noticed she'd orgasmed, or they simply didn't care, because their movements and teasing didn't stop. She wasn't sure if she could continue as another climax built within her.

She wanted to beg for a short pause so she could gather her senses. The words that left her mouth were their names. That only spurred them into moving faster.

Then she did scream.

She clutched both the men's thighs on either side of her, digging her nails into their skin, and let loose a scream she knew everyone in the keep must have heard.

Her vocalization must have been all they needed as Lucien and Ranulf both surged into her with labored grunts. Lucien jerked a few times while Ranulf panted against her shoulder.

She stared up at the ceiling and wondered why she could see stars indoors.

Chapter Forty-four

Eris couldn't remember what had happened after they all had their release. She did know she was cozy and warm between Lucien and Ranulf and both men slept. She'd been asleep until only a moment ago but hadn't remembered when she'd lay down, or what had woken her, for that matter.

Everything still had a fuzzy, glowing feeling around it. If the Ranulf and Lucien of the past made her feel so euphoric, their older—and more well-versed—counterparts would probably have her thinking she'd reached nirvana and enlightenment. She couldn't wait to find out.

She snuggled closer to Ranulf since she faced him. His arms closed around her, and she realized he was awake. His hold tightened when her gaze met his. She figured he planned to take advantage of Lucien being asleep to be intimate with her without a third.

He kissed her forehead. She raised her head so his next kiss would touch her lips.

He obliged her. The bed shifted as he moved her closer and draped a leg over her hips. She smiled against his lips.

Ranulf rubbed his knee up her side, and she shifted beneath him, moving her hips in invitation.

His sudden jerk surprised her. The bed jiggled and there was a thump a few seconds before Lucien roared. He loomed over them with the promise of pain shining in his eyes and rushes sticking to his bare chest. "You'll pay for that."

Eris took in Ranulf's mischievous grin. What she'd thought was part of their foreplay had been Ranulf kicking Lucien out of the bed.

"I never agreed to sharing my bed." Ranulf stroked his hand over her hip.

She startled with a tiny intake of breath when his fingers entered her.

Lucien glared at Ranulf. Eris thought another fight was about to start. Instead Lucien jerked on his tunic, gathered the rest of his belongings, and stalked out of the room. He even made sure he slammed the door hard enough that it shook in its frame.

"Now then..." Ranulf trailed off as he turned her head back so her lips met his.

Eris allowed the kiss but ultimately pulled back. As much as she wanted a repeat performance, her body was sore. She needed to distract him before things went too far. "Ranulf."

"Yes?" He ducked his head and kissed each of her nipples before latching onto one.

"What did you mean when you said you didn't want to be like your father?"

He stopped all movement.

"Ranulf?"

"I will not speak on that subject." He pulled back so he looked down at her.

She could see the topic had annoyed him, but it had worked at turning his attention from sex, maybe a little too well. However, she knew the topic had to be important and needed to be broached. "I think we should."

"Leave off."

"You told me about the sultan's uncle. How is this worse?"

"It is not important or as damning, so leave it be."

"Then why bring it up at all? And will you use it as an argument again?"

He rolled away from her and left the bed.

"Ranulf, please. I only want to understand—"

"Go to Lucien for the remainder of this night. I've no more need of you."

Eris jerked back, not liking his words or the way he said them. "Excuse me?"

"There is nothing wrong with your hearing. Leave my bed and occupy Lucien's. I will call when I need you next."

She blinked her eyes rapidly as the meaning of his words washed over her.

He was treating her like a whore. Was that how he saw her? She'd thought having both men cooperating with her in the middle meant their relationship was on track.

Then why did it feel like she'd taken a giant leap in the wrong direction?

Ranulf tossed her chemise at her and then her cloak. Both garments brushed her face before falling to her lap. Each felt like a slap—the hand of reality waking her from her dreamland.

That was sex in the truest sense of the word.

Those had been Ranulf's words of warning.

She jerked on her clothing and didn't leave the bed until she was completely covered. Not that it mattered since Ranulf wouldn't even look at her. He'd moved to the far end of the room and busied himself mixing some herbs.

She walked out of the room without a background glance.

The short trek to Lucien's room gave her enough time to get herself into quite a funk. She didn't bother knocking when she reached Lucien's room. She shoved the door open, slammed it behind her and then stalked to the bed.

"Back so soon?"

She stopped herself from telling him to shut up. Instead, she gave him her back.

"I thought Ranulf ousted me so he could have you again. Surely he was not so quick."

Eris didn't want to talk about Ranulf. She cocooned herself in her cloak with her head covered and lay down so she could go back to sleep, assuming she stopped being mad long enough to actually fall asleep. It didn't seem likely.

Lucien rustled behind her. She was determined to ignore him.

"Come, Eris."

She shook her head, even if he couldn't see the motion.

"I said come. The grotto awaits us."

She could hear him getting annoyed with her. Every part of her argued that she should get up and follow him like usual. The small childish part seemed to be in control though. She stayed in her cocoon to see what Lucien would do next.

He touched her shoulder.

"Lucien, I'm tired," she said in a measured tone.

"You can sleep as we ride, like you usually do."

"Ranulf takes his bath tomorrow—"

"And yet tonight is when you reek. I'll not have you in my bed smelling of another man's seed and sex." He dragged her off of the bed, put his shoulder to her stomach and carried her out of the room.

She only sighed and let him do it. Fighting would do her no good. It wasn't like she could run to Ranulf. He had no more need of her.

Just thinking the words made her gnash her teeth. She wanted to curse a blue streak and hit something, or someone. Even as angry as she was, she kept herself from venting that anger on Lucien. She confined her outrage to angry noises made under her breath.

"Are you in pain?"

"Do you care?"

Lucien stopped and lowered her to her feet. "Eris?"

She looked up into his concerned face. Did he, at least, see her as something more than a convenient lay? She wanted to ask. Instead she let her anger dissolve in the air and said, "I'm tired."

"As well you should be." He grinned and urged her to start walking.

Lucien's horse awaited their arrival already saddled. The page who stood next to the horse said, "You're late this night, my lord."

"Other matters had my attention." He glanced at Eris then looked at the boy. "Off to bed with you."

The boy nodded and ran back to the stable.

Eris frowned at the boy's back. "You always saddle your own horse."

"That I do. However, he makes sure my saddle is ready and takes charge of it when I return." He looked up at the sky. "He is right. We are late."

He lifted her onto the saddle sideways and then mounted behind her. With one arm firmly clamped around her middle, he spurred the horse forward.

Eris looked up at him several times as they rode. She'd always faced front so never had the chance to see Lucien as he rode.

"Continue staring and I'll have you here and now whether you are sore or not." He glanced down at her.

"On top of the horse?" He couldn't be serious.

"Care for a demonstration?" He inched her cloak and skirt up with the tips of his fingers.

She swatted at his hand. "No. That's mean to the horse."

Lucien laughed. "Sleep, my little innocent." He laid her head against his chest and held her there until she relaxed.

She'd lied about being tired but soon found the sound of Lucien's heartbeat lulling her to sleep.

Warmth spread over her body. She sighed.

"Eris?"

She made a questioning noise, not wanting to answer and leave sleep just yet.

Lucien's hands wandered over her body.

"Not on the horse," she mumbled.

He chuckled and laid a kiss on her shoulder.

A soft splashing noise made her open her eyes. The walls of the glowing grotto greeted her. She looked around in surprise. They were in the water. She really had been tired if she hadn't noticed Lucien carrying her into the water without waking her.

He cupped her breasts.

Not only had he carried her, but undressed her first. She faced him.

"Are you awake?"

She nodded, and he stroked her cheek.

"Are you sure?"

"Yes," she whispered.

A small smile curved her lips when Lucien kissed her hands. He was being so gentle with her, a huge difference from how they began when she first arrived. She'd thought the incident with Ranulf would land her back where she started.

She searched his gaze for some sign of his thoughts. Not finding anything, she finally asked, "You're not angry?"

"No longer. Ranulf and I overreacted. We are both possessive, so it was to be expected." He cupped her chin and held her as he kissed her lips. "There is no reason we cannot share."

"None." She made an appreciative noise when he trailed his hand down her body.

"And your obvious enjoyment of our attention will make this addition to the services you already render us not so much of a burden."

That woke her. "Services?" She pulled back slightly. Again, reality smacked her in the face. First Ranulf and now Lucien had both referred to her as…

Her earlier anger tried to reassert itself, but a deep sadness overwhelmed her first. "Lucien, I…"

She what? Nothing she could possibly say would change the situation she'd made for herself. The Lucien before her didn't want emotion. He wanted her body.

"Eris?"

"Never mind," she whispered.

He continued touching her. She even reacted, but it almost felt as though she were outside her body looking in, watching from a distance rather than participating.

…Sex in the purest sense of the word…

Ranulf's words echoed through time, haunting her.

Chapter Forty-five

Eris jerked awake with a scared gasp. Someone was touching her. She pushed at the hand between her legs as she tried to get away.

"Eris."

Ranulf's calm voice stilled her struggles. She stared at him for a second before she truly saw him. "Ranulf?"

"Yes."

He moved his hand, sliding it between her rear cheeks. She winced as he slid the pad of two fingers over her opening.

"Sore?"

"A little." She understated her condition only because certain parts of her body knew of the pleasure to come and didn't want Ranulf to stop.

"Then I'll go slowly." He moved away only to return a second later.

Roses greeted her nose, and her body reacted instantly. A tingling burned between her legs. She could feel moisture rushing to greet whatever part Ranulf cared to touch her with.

The last thing she wanted was to develop a Pavlovian response to the smell of roses. Telling Ranulf that wouldn't help since Pavlov hadn't even been born yet, thus the reference to his discovery would be lost.

Though it didn't matter since thinking took a backseat to pleasure when Ranulf slid one finger deep inside her rear. She bucked against his fingers.

He only had to touch her thigh for her legs to fall open, inviting him to do more.

He chuckled. "So eager now. Naughty as well. Did you know I would be here and that is why left off your coverings?"

If he expected an answer, he would be disappointed since Eris had lost the ability to speak when his mouth descended to her nether lips. She made little mewing noises as she panted and clutched at Ranulf's hair.

"I should have known," Lucien said from the doorway. He closed the door behind him and crossed his arms.

Eris looked at him. He shook his head with amusement and approached the bed. Gone was the anger that had greeted her and Ranulf the first time Lucien caught them together so many days ago. Neither man even showed surprise if they interrupted each other.

Ranulf didn't stop or show any other indication that he'd heard Lucien. But the man wouldn't be ignored.

Lucien thumped Ranulf on the back of the head.

"I'm busy," Ranulf grumbled.

The vibrations of his voice almost sent Eris over the edge.

"Busy was what you were earlier. This is recreation at the expense of your work."

Eris knew what was coming despite Lucien trying to urge Ranulf to leave her. She watched Lucien move along the bedside so he stood over her.

He smoothed his hand over her forehead and said, "I understand, however."

That was the only warning before Lucien pulled her chemise over her head, tossed it aside, and latched his mouth onto one of her breasts. She arched beneath him.

Lucien gathered her close and shifted her, to Ranulf's annoyance. The man made an angered noise at being interrupted. Eris also was a little upset at Ranulf's mouth leaving. His fingers still moved inside her rear, but the pleasure was halved.

Lucien moved her until she sat astride him and he buried himself deep inside her. "So warm and ready. Thank you, Ranulf."

"That was not my intention." Ranulf kissed Eris's shoulder. He whispered in her ear, "Ready?"

She nodded.

Ranulf removed his fingers. The blunt head of his arousal pressed against her opening. She couldn't help tensing as the soreness returned.

"Relax," Ranulf whispered. He laid another kiss on her shoulder.

She nodded but couldn't seem to make her body obey.

Lucien rubbed his finger over her nub and shifted so his need caressed within her, making her whole body turn liquid. His little motions were enough to make her stop tensing and welcome Ranulf properly.

Ranulf sighed and murmured a thank you. His gratitude was probably to Lucien, not to her, but she didn't care.

The men moved, and the world turned into one large pleasurable sensation. Panting their names in turn was all she was capable of. Her climax came on a satisfied scream that the men echoed.

Ranulf leaned against her back as she sagged onto Lucien.

"I think next time you will be on the bottom," Lucien grumbled. He rolled them both to the side and extricated himself from the tangle of bodies.

Eris missed having him within her. She reached for him.

Lucien kissed her hand then released her. He turned his gaze to Ranulf. "Up. Now. You've had your fun."

Ranulf rolled away as well. He straightened his clothes as he walked to the door.

Eris watched them leave. She thought she heard the lock click but wasn't sure. It didn't matter if they had locked the door. That only guaranteed her continued privacy.

She moved to her side and stared out of the window. It hadn't even been a week and she already lost count of how many times they had sex.

A yawn snuck past her lips.

She needed to get some sleep. Every time she had been close to sleep Ranulf or Lucien or both had woken her for sex.

She just needed a little nap.

* * * *

Eris slumped forward. Before she could fall, Ranulf reached out and steadied her. He couldn't help the smug pride that caused him to grin. It would seem he and Lucien had exhausted her over the last few days. So much so that she had fallen asleep mid-stitch.

He took the sewing from her then shook her shoulder. "Eris."

She jerked awake and looked at him in confusion.

"Return to my room and sleep."

His words didn't seem to register. He stood and pulled her to her feet.

"Ranulf?"

He faced her toward the stairs. "Go to my bed."

She nodded and walked away. Her steps were slow, but Ranulf was sure she'd go straight to his room without stopping.

He looked at Lucien. His friend wore the same smug look.

Ranulf made his way to Lucien's side and said, "Perhaps we should let her sleep this night."

"You are right. I have never seen her so tired."

"A whore's job is pleasuring men, not sleeping," said Hugh, who sat a few chairs away.

Ranulf bit back the words he would have said. Hugh wasn't worth the effort.

"A whore's job is also to pleasure multiple men of which the keep has many."

And that was the end of Ranulf's patience. He started to say something to put Hugh in his place but Lucien said, "Any man who cares to challenge me for her may step forward." He looked around.

All the men at the table shook their heads.

"That's what I thought." He took a sip of his drink. "When I tire of her, then you can have her. Any man who touches her before that time will rue the day."

Hugh said, "All except Ranulf."

Lucien nodded.

Ranulf stood as though Lucien's motion were a cue. He smirked at the group and walked toward the stairs.

Without Eris in the common room, it held no interest for him. It hadn't always been that way. Eris's entrance into his life had changed many things.

He made his way to his room and stared at her from the doorway. She'd gone straight from the common room to his bed without even bothering to remove her cloak, or get beneath the covers.

He and Lucien really had exhausted her. There was no help for it. His desire for her had only grown with having her. If Lucien ever did tire of her, Ranulf alone would have her because he would never allow any other to touch her. That he allowed Lucien still surprised him.

Ranulf shifted Eris out of her cloak. She protested in her usual manner, but he won the tug-of-war, and she curled into a shivering ball. Her actions made him chuckle. He got beneath the covers, and Eris immediately clung to him.

He gathered her close, and she burrowed against him with a thankful sigh. She even whispered his name.

He'd missed that. Simply holding her in the night. There was something so soothing about her presence. Though he had gained her body, Ranulf felt he'd lost something in the trade.

It was in Eris's eyes. She looked resigned, almost sad, whenever he touched her. He thought it was his imagination. He only heard satisfaction in her voice, and her body welcomed him.

Still, something about her eyes had changed.

Whatever that something was, he wanted it back. He tightened his hold.

* * * *

Eris woke and found Ranulf asleep beside her. He hadn't woken her for sex. Was he not feeling well?

That question surprised her. When had she started seeing a lack of sex as a sign of sickness?

She rolled her eyes. Probably when the men stopped letting her get a moment's rest when they could be having sex instead.

She looked at Ranulf. He had gone to sleep without waking her. Did that mean he wanted her to rest? That thought wasn't very far-fetched. Lucien and Ranulf weren't completely unfeeling toward her.

During all their time together, she thought she'd felt more than lust being sated. It had to be her imagination. They never lingered once they finished. If either man had left money on the bedside table, it wouldn't have surprised her. It wouldn't have hurt her either.

It took a little while, and she had to overcome a few days of denial, but she finally knew her rank in the grand scheme. Knowing her place made her numb.

She left Ranulf's bed and went to the window. The sun had just set. Ranulf had retired early. More than likely because she was too exhausted to see to his needs.

A tiny flash from the woods caught her attention. She frowned and looked out over the woods. The flash occurred again, but not in the same spot. She had to search for it the third time. Whatever was flashing was definitely moving.

She moved to the bed. "Ranulf."

He grumbled in his sleep and turned to his side.

Eris didn't care how grumpy he got. Something weird was happening in Lucien's forest. She'd stared out over the trees many times over the last few months and had never seen anything shiny.

"Ranulf, wake up."

"No. Return to bed." He beckoned to her.

She rushed back to the window instead. The shiny moving thing was steadily getting closer. A small shiver coursed over her body and, for once, it wasn't from the cold. A sense of foreboding swept over her.

She returned to the bed. "Ranulf, please. There's something in the woods."

Ranulf sat up, clear-eyed and alert. She'd never seen the like. He didn't even look tired.

He bound off the bed and rushed to the window. "Show me."

She moved in close beside him. There was no movement. It was a tense minute before the thing in the woods shined again. She pointed. "Did you see it?"

"No." He looked, even squinted.

"It shines and then moves closer and shines again."

"Where did you first see it?"

She pointed farther into the woods. "There. It hasn't moved that far, but it is definitely getting closer."

Ranulf continued staring. Finally he shook his head. "I see nothing."

Eris looked up at him, and he met her gaze. She didn't see disbelief. That was a good sign.

He said, "Retrieve Lucien. I'll go to the parapets. Perhaps the sentries have seen it."

"Wouldn't they sound an alarm?"

"Not unless they felt it was a threat. It may only be someone lost." He guided her away from the window. "Bring Lucien to me."

She nodded and grabbed her cloak on her way out of the door.

She headed for Lucien's room. Of course he wasn't there. That meant he had to be in the common room still.

Great.

She looked across his room at his window. She couldn't even see the trees from where she stood, let alone the shining thing. Maybe it was nothing or a lost person as Ranulf had said.

Her gut told her it wasn't nothing. The longer she stood trying to avoid seeking out Lucien, the more that sense of dread consumed her.

She rushed out of the room and down the stairs. Thankfully Lucien sat at his normal spot. She headed for him quickly.

"Eris, awake I see." He toasted her. "Where is Ranulf?"

She ignored his question. "I need you."

The men at the table laughed in a knowing manner and nudged each other.

One man called, "Perhaps she wishes to be made tired once more, my lord."

The men laughed louder.

Eris didn't even want to know. She moved closer to Lucien. "Please."

His smile faltered only a little.

Did he sense her unease? Whatever he saw in her face got him moving. He set aside his drink and preceded her out of the room and up the stairs. The men continued to joke behind them.

"What is this?" Lucien asked, glancing back at her.

"I hope it's nothing." She looked up the stairs. "I saw something in the woods. Ranulf has gone to the parapets. He said to retrieve you."

Lucien opened his mouth and then closed it. He turned away and led her to the walkway that spanned the outside perimeter of the keep. Several men clustered around Ranulf, all of them peering at the woods.

Lucien nudged the men aside and stood next to Ranulf. "Have you figured out what it is?"

"None of us have seen it." Ranulf glanced back at Eris.

She pushed into the cluster and scanned the treetops.

Nothing.

She looked around, but couldn't find it. "Are we above Ranulf's room?"

Ranulf pointed a few feet away. She moved to that spot and looked out. She almost missed it. The thing in the woods shined. And like all of the other times, it was closer than it had been the last time she'd seen it.

"There!" She pointed.

Lucien and the others looked, but it would be too late. The thing only shined for a second and then was gone until it shined again.

She tried to predict where it would appear next.

Ranulf beckoned behind him. "Wesley, do you see anything?"

"No." The man shook his head.

"It's there." Eris knew her voice sounded whining. She'd stamp her foot if she thought it would make the men believe her.

She pointed again. "There. Don't you see that?"

"There is nothing," Lucien said.

"Wait." Wesley crowded in close to Eris and followed the direction of her finger. He leaned far enough over the ledge that Eris thought he might fall. "Something is moving in the woods."

"An animal, more than likely," one man said in a dismissive tone.

Wesley shook his head. "No. Whatever it is, it's definitely moving toward the keep." He looked back at Eris with a confused look. "How did you see that? I can barely see it."

She shrugged. They couldn't see the shining so citing it would do no good even if it was as plain as day.

Ranulf cut between her and Wesley, taking the man's spot. "I still don't see it, but if Wesley says it's there, then we have to trust his eyes." He looked back across Eris.

Lucien had moved to the other side of her. His attention was for the woods, but he said in a low voice, "Ricker, take two others and find out who our guest is." He looked back at Ricker. "Do it carefully."

Ricker nodded and left the parapets.

Eris watched the man leave and looked back at Lucien. Finally she looked at the woods. What if it really was nothing? No one else seemed to see the shining except her.

The shiny moving thing winked at her again.

Ranulf put a hand on her head. She looked up at him, and he tweaked her nose. "There's no need to look so worried. You were right to bring attention to it, though it may be a lost person. Lucien's forest is not one easily navigated."

That sounds familiar, she thought.

Lucien pulled her away from Ranulf. "Let's greet this guest in the common room."

Eris glanced back at Ranulf to see his reaction. He followed them, yawning the whole way. That made her smile. The crisis was averted so he was sleepy again.

Maybe, when they returned to his room, they could sleep together again, without sex. She'd even skip the trip to the glowing grotto for that.

Chapter Forty-six

Eris stared at the "guest" and knew she'd be skipping the trip to the glowing grotto whether she wanted to or not.

Everyone in the common—a number that had grown in the last ten minutes once word spread—stared between Eris and the newcomer. Eris didn't blame them, she was staring too.

The woman had Eris's cloak. The cloak her father had made at Lucien's request. The one Lucien had given her before she fell back through time. And it wasn't a matter of looking like Eris's cloak except for one thing or another. They were exact replicas.

Her father had said he'd referenced some historical books for the design, but even the laws of coincidence had limits.

To make matters worse, the woman was black and had been caught skulking around Lucien's forest. She'd even put up a fight when the men tried to bring her back. Unlike Eris, the woman got to keep her clothing. The men probably hadn't wanted to strip the woman and chance angering Lucien.

Eris looked at him. He had the same look on his face that he'd worn when she first arrived in his forest. That wasn't good.

"Who are you, woman? Why were you in my forest?" Lucien asked in a guttural voice full of repressed anger.

Déjà vu, Eris thought. She would have said it aloud but was too busy trying to fade into the background.

If she could have snuck away, she would have. Ranulf blocked her exit. She knew he did it purposefully since he'd moved her between him and Lucien once the other woman had been presented. He looked almost as angry as Lucien.

"I do not answer to you," the woman spat. Her voice was heavily accented, but understandable.

"I am lord of this keep, and you will answer me, woman!"

The woman looked surprised. "You are Lord Lucien?"

He gave a single nod, and the woman smiled.

She stopped fighting the men who held her and inclined her head. "Forgive me. I did not know. Greetings, great Lord Lucien."

"Answer my question," Lucien barked.

"Of course, my lord. I entered your forest to find you." Her gaze moved to Eris. "I am happy my sister found her way before me."

"Sister?" Eris practically screamed. "Whose? I don't know you."

She looked at Lucien and Ranulf quickly to see if they believed her words.

They didn't look at her.

The woman's smile persisted. "This language is…new. Sisters because we are the same."

"Same color. That's it," Eris said in a frantic voice.

"We are more than that."

"No, we aren't!"

"Silence, both of you!" Lucien grabbed Eris's wrist and dragged her in close. "Know your place."

Fear crept over her. "Lucien, you're hurting me."

His only response was to tighten his hold.

She looked at Ranulf who kept his gaze on the other woman.

Lucien faced her as well. "Who are you, woman?"

The woman pulled away from the men, which caused them to stiffen and touch their sword hilts. She bowed deeply. "Great Lord Lucien, though we did not arrive together as planned, the gift is still the same." She straightened and gestured to Eris. "We are a gift of goodwill and continued health from the sultan."

"The sultan," Lucien whispered.

Eris stared at him. She thought he would yell and rage. His quiet parroting worried her.

"Yes. The sultan sends this as well. A treasured item returned as further proof of his amicable feelings to you." She held out a wrapped bundle she'd kept hidden within her cloak.

The bundle glittered in the torchlight of the common room. Eris had to look away, the light was so bright. She noticed no one else seemed effected by it. In fact, they didn't react at all.

Didn't they see the light? It was the same light that shined in the forest. And like then, they didn't see it. That made no sense.

Ranulf retrieved the bundle. He uncovered it and jerked back with a quick look at Lucien.

"What? Show me," Lucien said.

Ranulf lifted a very familiar ring and bracelet combo—Lucien's mother's ring. The light that had almost blinded her while the ring was covered disappeared. It was a normal ring with no way to give off light. Eris didn't know what that meant.

She did know Ranulf stared at her, watched her, with pure loathing. The look made her stumble back. She couldn't go far because Lucien tightened his hold even more. She could feel the bones of her wrist scraping each other.

The woman said, "The sultan boasted of melting it but only to upset you. He kept it for this moment."

"This moment," Lucien whispered.

His grip tightened to the point that Eris thought he would tear her hand off. She pulled a little to show her discomfort.

He looked at her. Actually, it seemed like he was looking through her, seeing something that wasn't her.

"Lucien—"

"The sultan sent you," he said in a voice dripping ice and quiet as death.

"No!"

"You almost..." He shook his head and growled. "The sultan sent you!"

"I don't know any sultan! Lucien, listen to me. She's lying. She—"

"She called you sister. She has my mother's ring. She has *your* cloak." He released her wrist and snatched the cloak from her shoulders. After checking it, he ripped it in half and then again before throwing it toward the hearth.

It didn't make it to the fire, but the men standing nearby helped get it there. Just as Eris thought, the fabric treatments made the cloak catch and burn to ashes in a matter of seconds. The last of the things that made the trip to the past with her was gone.

"Lies! All lies!" Lucien roared.

She tore her gaze from the fire and watched Lucien. He clenched and unclenched his hands at his sides while glaring at the ring Ranulf held. The situation was getting away from her. She had to make him see reason, bring him back to her before he did something he'd regret through the centuries. Eris knew that moment had come, and she didn't want to find out what could cause Lucien such deep sadness.

She grabbed his arm, but before she could think of a way to plead her case, Lucien backhanded her.

"Don't touch me, you little bitch."

The force of his blow spun her before she hit the ground. Stars burst all around her, and her jaw exploded with pain.

No one had ever slapped her before.

The tears that coursed down her cheeks were an involuntary reaction. Lucien seemed unfazed. He glared down at her, looking as though he wanted to hit her again.

She looked at Ranulf. His expression matched Lucien's.

"I didn't lie," she whispered. "I've only ever told the truth. I knew you upon sight. She didn't. How would I know you and you've never seen me before?"

She looked at both men in turn. Lucien's expression was closed to her. His eyes blazed with hatred. Ranulf turned from her. He looked at the ring he held before leaving the room.

"Ranulf!"

He ignored her.

She looked back at Lucien. "I'm not who she says I am. You know I never lied to you. Not ever."

Lucien clenched his fists at his side. He stood glaring at her. She could see the internal battle that raged in his eyes.

"Take her to Mason." He looked at the other woman. "Take them both."

Mason?

She'd never heard that name before. From Lucien's usage, she guessed she wouldn't like the man after meeting him.

Several pairs of hands grabbed her. They propelled her out of the common room, away from the way she normally exited, to a set of stairs that led down.

She yelled, "Lucien, I never lied to you! Lucien!"

Her words echoed in the corridor, but no one responded.

The other woman made no noise and didn't even struggle. She did glare at Eris, though. She mouthed something, but Eris didn't understand.

Eris faced front. Firelight glowed from a chamber at the bottom of the stairs. The men shoved her ever closer despite her not wanting to go. When she saw the room, she finally realized the source of Lucien's guilt.

Chains, shackles, and various implements of pain and torture hung from every visible wall. In the middle of the room stood a tall, skinny man who wore no shirt and too-loose pants held on his small frame with a belt.

Upon seeing her, the man's face lit up, and he grinned ear to ear. "Is this her? Is she the one?" he said in a voice breathy with anticipation.

One of the men who held her shoved Eris forward. "That's Lucien's whore, Mason. He's given her to you."

"This one as well," another man said, shoving the other woman forward.

The first man pointed at Eris. "Start with her."

"Yes, yes, yes. I want to start with her." Mason looked at all of the men in turn. "Lord Lucien has truly given her to me? Really?"

"Yes, Mason. He said so."

"To keep?"

The men looked at each other. The first said, "He didn't look like he wanted to see her ever again."

Eris's blood pounded in her ears as Mason approached her. She pulled away from him when he grabbed her arm. Despite looking like he couldn't bend a blade a grass, the man was incredibly strong. He held her without showing any effort.

Without looking away from her, he said, "Chain the other one. I want to focus on her. Sweet Eris." He stroked her cheek. "Sweet, sweet Eris."

The men did as Mason bade them and then retreated. It looked like they were running.

Eris said, "You don't want to do this. Lucien didn't mean to send me here. He'll come any second and take me back."

Mason grinned.

"I mean it."

He turned away from her quickly and dragged her in his wake. "I prepared this for you. I knew he'd give you to me eventually. I never let anyone else touch it."

He sounded like a child telling her about the objects in his room. Eris couldn't get over how the man exuded such a childlike aura, and yet...

She stared at the large table with manacles at every edge that stood upright against a wall. It looked brand new and, like Mason had said, never used.

"Just for you."

Eris was about to ask, but the words were yanked from her throat when Mason whipped her forward, slamming her against the table face first. The impact dazed her long enough for Mason to close her wrists in the manacles.

She struggled to no avail. The chains only clanked, mocking her as they held.

He bound her ankles then grabbed the back of her dress and ripped it open.

"Look at that," Mason gushed in excited tones. "So clean. No marks, no scars, so soft. A virgin."

Eris jerked when he smoothed his open palms over her back. She'd almost call it a caress if the man didn't frighten the hell out of her. "Please, stop," she said in a breathy voice. "Ranulf will be here soon. I shouldn't be down here. It's a mistake."

"No mistake. I've been waiting for you all this time. I knew Lucien would come to his senses once he'd had his fill. Now..." He trailed off with a happy sound and laid a kiss on her back. "Now, lovely, you are mine."

"Just wait. Please wait." She looked at the other woman, who stood silent in her chains. Self-preservation told Eris to volunteer the woman and gain herself a reprieve.

"No waiting. Oh no. I've waited long enough. Had I known what lovely untouched skin..." He drew in a shaky breath. "Marring such pretty skin is a crime."

"Yes!"

"No, no. We won't mark this skin."

Eris sagged with relief.

"First, we must prepare it. Then we will mark it."

"Prepare? What does that mean?" Even as she asked the question, she knew she didn't want him to explain.

Something behind her clanked. Mason was moving things around to get to something. She couldn't turn her head far enough to see what. His footsteps rang out on the stones as he returned.

She struggled against the manacles. "Don't do this. Ranulf will be here. Ranulf will—"

A rush of air and a whooshing sound stole her words…and then she screamed.

Chapter Forty-seven

Lucien stormed into Ranulf's room. He slammed the door and then kicked it with a loud curse. "How? How did she get it out of the keep without us noticing and give it to another. She's never been left alone."

"She didn't," Ranulf said.

Lucien stared at the man. "What do you mean? That…that…she had my mother's ring."

Ranulf turned. He held Lucien's mother's ring—one in each hand.

Lucien could only stare. "What? Why are there two?"

"The box you hid in my room was not tampered with."

He nodded. "She searched my rooms, probably looking for the ring. I moved it when you left her under my care."

Staring at two identical rings muddled his thinking. He shook his head to clear his thoughts. "One is a fake."

Ranulf held out both to Lucien. One was marred with blood while the other gleamed. "You would know better than any other which is false."

Lucien grabbed the rings in one hand. He knew the blood-stained one, the one Eris had had with her when she arrived, had to be false. It would explain why he couldn't get it clean.

He pulled his dagger and pried the stone out of the ring. His haste made the jewel catapult away. Ranulf caught it. He frowned at the jewel and held it close to the firelight, peering at it. Lucien kept his attention on his task.

When his father had made the ring for his mother, the man had an inscription carved into the jewel housing. No one knew about the inscription. If the sultan had a copy of the ring made, his craftsman wouldn't have noticed it. Of that, Lucien was sure.

The inscription was there. Lucien quoted, "'For all time.'" He nodded. "This is the true ring. The sultan must have made a copy and given it to the other woman to gain her entry if Eris had failed."

"You haven't checked the other, Lucien."

"Why should I?"

"Humor me."

Lucien put aside the blood-stained ring and pried out the jewel of the other ring. He paused, not believing his eyes. "It can't be!"

Ranulf came over, but not to look at the identical inscription Lucien had found. He took the jewel and returned to the fire, studying it as he had the first.

Lucien looked at one ring and then the other. The inscriptions were exactly the same. Even the tiny X the craftsman had used for the dot of the I was the same.

"How?"

Ranulf looked away from the jewels he held. "Could it be the sultan found the inscription?"

"No!"

"Then, I ask you this—why would the sultan send two assassins and give each a ring? That is stupid, and we know the sultan wasn't a stupid man."

"Get to the point," Lucien said through his teeth.

"Even if the sultan had sent two—one a virgin to fool us and the other an assassin—he wouldn't have given each of them a ring if they were to arrive at the same time."

"You heard the woman. She said Eris became separated from her."

"Or…" Ranulf trailed off and looked at the jewels he held.

Lucien slammed his fist down on the table in front of him. "Say whatever it is you mean to say and be done. You know I hate your riddles."

"Or, both rings are true."

"That's not possible. My father made only one ring."

"It is possible—" Ranulf held out the jewel so Lucien could see what he'd stared at earlier, "—if one was from the future, much like its carrier."

Light from the fire shined through the jewel. Lucien stared at the impossible. Words were etched *inside* the jewel. He snatched it from Ranulf's fingers and rubbed at it, but the words were beyond his reach.

Unless the jewel was held to the light, the etched words were not that visible. He moved closer to the fire. Without the light, someone might actually mistake the words for a blemish within the stone. But it was far more than that. Lucien's coat of arms sat next to Ranulf's mark. Underneath were three words.

Lucien mouthed the words, afraid to utter them aloud. He looked at Ranulf.

"You know that's your coat and my symbol. I might overlook your coat since you inherited it from your father, but there is no way the sultan would know my symbol. I didn't adopt it until after we returned, and I only use it on messages to you so you know they are from me and have not been tampered with."

Lucien shook his head violently. "It isn't true! She cannot be from the future."

"Lucien, you're denying what is right before your eyes." Ranulf pointed at the jewel. "No one of this time could do this. Maybe if they had scratched the message onto a flat edge of the jewel, I would be more skeptical. Those words are *inside*. There is no seam, no possible way for those words to get there without cracking the jewel in the process. It is not marred in any way."

"Witchcraft."

"Yes. Some powerful spell implanted those words and then sent Eris back in *time* with it for us. This is a message from ourselves in the future, where Eris is from."

"It can't be," Lucien whispered. He dropped the jewel and grasped the two rings, staring at them and looking for the flaw that would declare one false. "It defies all logic."

"Which is why it is true. The proof is here." Ranulf picked up the jewel Lucien had dropped and looked at it again. "Even I, the one who humored her words more than believed them, cannot deny this."

Ranulf's words sank in along with the message within the jewel. In Lucien's search for an explanation that made sense, Ranulf's fit better than any other.

He looked at the man. "Does the other jewel—"

"No. It is flawless." Ranulf held it out to him.

Lucien believed his friend so didn't bother looking. If this were a trick of the sultan's, he would have made sure both jewels were identical. Such a feat should have cracked the jewel. Some means other than those available in this age had etched that message, possibly put there by his future self for him so he wouldn't hurt Eris.

"God, forgive me, because she won't." Lucien dropped his head into his hands.

"Eris was not terribly hurt by your abuse. No more so than—"

"I gave her to Mason."

"What?" Ranulf yelled. He didn't wait for an answer but ran out of the room.

Lucien looked down at the rings one last time then ran after Ranulf. Not much time had passed since he'd given the order for Eris and the other woman to be delivered to Mason. The man probably hadn't even started yet.

They ran into the common room, but a crowd of people stopped them cold.

"Ho, there, Lucien."

"Kern? What do you do here?" Lucien stared at his nearest neighbor in confusion. They shared a border marked by the edge of the forest.

"It would seem you are a popular man, Lucien. Just now, your men told me the tale of capturing a Moor woman in your forest."

"Yes. What of it?"

"And just yesterday—" he signaled the men behind him, "—I caught another."

"What?" Lucien yelled.

He watched one of Kern's men carry a large wrapped bundle forward. The man dumped the person in the bundle onto the floor. She was bound and gagged, and dead.

Kern said, "She put up quite a struggle when we captured her. Even tried escaping several times. The last time just this afternoon. She ingested some sort of poison as we traveled here. We didn't know she carried it."

A ringing started in Lucien's ears.

"She had these." Kern signaled another man who brought forth a dagger, a corked vial, and a black cloak.

Ranulf took the vial. He uncorked it and sniffed. "Poison. Very potent."

Lucien's stomach started hurting as he stared at the cloak. "No," he whispered.

"What?" Kern asked.

"Why bring her to us?" Ranulf asked.

"That's what she wanted. She screamed over and over about belonging to Lucien."

"I do not know her." Lucien could only stare at the cloak.

Kern grinned. "Ah, but your men say you are practically drowning in these little Moorish whores. I bring another for your collection. The sultan must have truly liked you to send three of his women. Or he truly wanted you dead."

"He didn't send three." Lucien tore his gaze from the cloak and shoved past Kern.

"Lucien, what of this one?" Kern called.

He didn't answer. He had to get to Mason.

Three girls when there should be only two. Two rings when there should be only one. The only explanation that made sense was the one he hadn't wanted to be true.

Female screams and the sound of a whip echoed up the stairwell.

"Mason!" Lucien bellowed over the noise.

The whipping stopped.

Lucien and Ranulf spilled into the room.

Mason watched them, looking pleased. "My lord, I am so happy to see you and honored by this visit. Did you want to watch?" He gestured to his victim.

Lucien prepared himself, but it wasn't needed. Eris wasn't the one Mason had been beating. He looked around. "Where is she?"

"Eris?"

Hearing her name on the man's lips made Lucien clench his hands. "Where is she?"

Mason pointed. "There. I am letting her rest while I entertain this one."

Ranulf pushed past Lucien and went in the direction Mason indicated. Lucien followed.

Both men stumbled to a halt.

Lucien sagged. He was too late.

Eris stood chained to an upright table with her dress back torn open. Her bared skin was bright red from all the blood rushing to the surface. The muscles beneath twitched.

She didn't bleed, and there were no marks.

"Isn't she pretty?" Mason asked from Lucien's shoulder.

Lucien swung around and faced the man.

"I wanted to savor her. She's new to pain. Such pretty sounds she made." Mason grinned, looking like a child who discovered something amazing. He pointed to the table nearest Eris. "I used a new toy."

Lucien stared at the cat-o-nine tails, breathing hard.

Mason said in a proud voice, "Half of the tips are covered in rabbit fur. It keeps the skin from scarring. Keeps her looking new. The pain is no less though. She screamed quite a bit. It was a pretty sound."

Pain of his own erupted behind Lucien's eyes.

"I tried treating the other the same as sweet Eris." Mason jerked his head toward the other woman and curled his lips in disgust. "That one has known the lash. She barely flinched. It took much, much more to bring sound from those lips." He caressed the whip he held.

Lucien's stomach turned as he watched tiny droplets of blood fall from the whip's barbed tip.

"Once Eris is prepared, then I can do so much more." Mason nodded. "You have to prepare them or they break too quickly." He smiled. "Such pretty skin."

Before he realized, Lucien slammed Mason into the nearby wall with his hands around the man's throat. "You will never touch her again! Never!"

Mason looked instantly afraid. "How have I angered you, my lord? The men said you ordered her to me. What did I do wrong?"

The whining quality of the man's voice only made Lucien's anger hotter.

"Lucien!" Ranulf rushed forward and grabbed Lucien from behind, pulling him back.

All the hatred Lucien felt for himself in that moment had a target.

Mason whined, "I'm sorry. I'm sorry. They said Eris was mine. I asked to be sure. They said so." Fat tears rolled down his cheeks. "I'm sorry, Lord Lucien. Don't be angry. I should have asked you directly before touching Eris."

"Stop saying her name!" Lucien tightened his hold but that didn't stop Mason's apologies or crying.

"Release him," Ranulf barked. "It's not his fault."

Lucien stilled.

No, it wasn't Mason's fault. Lucien dropped his hold and turned away. A target but not the one responsible. To see that man, Lucien need only look in a mirror. Instead, he looked at Eris.

She hadn't moved the entire time. He'd question if she were even still alive if he didn't see her shoulders shaking and her sides expanding and contracting as she breathed. Was she asleep?

"Down," Eris croaked, answering his question.

She didn't move except to utter that word.

Lucien's hands shook. He tried to walk forward, but he couldn't.

Ranulf did instead. He retrieved the keys and undid Eris's bonds, feet first. She sagged into his arms once he undid her wrists. "Eris?"

"Let go."

"What? No. You're hurt."

She lifted her head and looked at him. Ranulf stiffened. She said in a slow, measured tone, "Let go."

Ranulf released her slowly, aiding her to sit as her legs didn't support her.

"Get away from me."

He stepped back.

Lucien walked to Ranulf's side. "Eris, I...I'm sorry."

She jerked her head up. Her eyes sparkled with her anger and tears as she looked at him. "Sorry? You're sorry?"

He nodded stiffly.

A humorless laugh passed her lips. "Well, that just makes it all better now, doesn't it?" A violent shiver shook her body and caused her to suck in a pained breath.

"You're cold," Ranulf said. He looked around the room.

Mason rushed up with a blanket.

Ranulf took it and walked it to Eris.

She snatched it away from him before he could put it around her shoulders. But, she didn't wrap it around herself. She only clenched a small edge in her fist as she glared at Lucien.

He dropped her gaze. "I acted in anger."

"I don't care. Stop talking."

Ranulf moved forward.

"Don't!"

Lucien looked up and saw Ranulf frozen in place as Eris struggled to her feet. Her breath came in labored puffs, and she gritted her teeth. Once upright she tried to wrap the blanket around her shoulders. Her arms shook too badly to accomplish the feat.

Mason inched forward. He touched the blanket, but Eris said nothing. He took it from her and then placed it around her shoulders. She hissed through her teeth, and the man jumped with a quick glance at Lucien.

He could say nothing. She allowed Mason, the man who had beaten her, to help but refused Ranulf's help. That told Lucien more than any words could.

Eris looked at Mason and nodded. He backed away, mumbling apologies.

Clutching at the blanket and shivering, she took one step. A sigh escaped her lips. She took one more step, wobbled a little and then righted herself.

Watching her struggle to walk tortured Lucien like nothing else could. He wanted to help her but knew she'd only hurt herself more trying to get away from him. That knowledge kept him rooted to his spot as he watched Eris inch past toward the stairs.

Ranulf followed her step for step, hovering in case she fell.

Lucien let them get a good distance away before he turned and followed.

Mason trailed after them looking anxious. "What of the other, my lord?" He twisted his hands and looked ready to run if need be.

Lucien wanted to ignore the man's question but Eris stopped walking. She didn't look at him but he knew she waited for his answer.

Ranulf looked at Lucien and then walked over to the other woman. She spat in his direction.

"I want none of your sympathy."

"I don't offer it," Ranulf said in a flat voice. "The sultan sent you."

"No. He did not have to. I volunteered for the honor. You should have died in the desert. You besmirched his honor, made him look foolish and weak before his men. You deserve nothing less than death for your impudence." The woman spat toward Ranulf again. "If that little bitch had not ruined the plan, I would have succeeded."

"Eris doesn't belong to the sultan. The woman who would have partnered you was killed earlier in the day by our neighbors who captured her."

The woman looked surprised. She looked from Ranulf to Eris and back. "This is a trick. You think to gain secrets after confusing me."

"Her body is upstairs. Would you care to see it?" Ranulf didn't wait for the woman to answer. "You came here to kill us, but you would have died as well."

"I care not. Dying for my sultan is the highest honor. I will be revered in the afterlife for my sacrifice."

Ranulf nodded and walked away. He returned to his spot behind Eris but said over his shoulder, "Have her." He looked back at Mason. "When you finish, kill her."

Mason's look of glee returned. Lucien turned away from it.

Eris started walking once more, and the men followed.

In the common room, everyone waited. Eris looked at no one as she traversed the length of the room to the stairs on the other side. All was silent during her slow trek.

Lucien had just reached the threshold leading to the stairs when Kern called, "Lucien, what of this one?"

He looked back at the man. "You killed her. You dispose of her." He looked at his men, who watched him. "Give Lord Kern escort off my land."

They nodded to him, and Lucien continued away from them. He didn't get far. Eris had stopped to rest, so Ranulf had stopped as well. The man knelt on the stairs and waited.

She still shivered and clutched at the blanket even though it caused her to hiss in pain as the blanket rubbed her back.

With one hand against the wall and the other fisted in the blanket, Eris started up the stairs once more. She bypassed his room. But, he hadn't thought she would stay there.

Ranulf walked ahead and opened the door for his room. Eris said nothing as she passed him. She went to the bed and sat gingerly.

"Why did you change your mind?" she whispered, looking at Lucien.

Her words were soft, but Lucien attributed that to her voice paining her. Her expression was thunderous, and he knew she would yell at him if she could without hurting herself more.

Ranulf walked forward. He slowed when Eris looked ready to bolt and held out his hand. "This."

Eris watched him as she took the jewel and looked at it. "Is this a bribe?"

"It's the jewel from my mother's ring," Lucien said, finally finding his tongue.

"Oh." She tossed it aside. "I don't want it."

Ranulf retrieved it and held it before Eris's face so the light shined through, making the inscription visible.

Eris looked at the inscription then them. "What does it say?"

"You can't read it?" Ranulf asked.

"Sorry, no. I may speak Middle English—and I don't know why—but I can't read it."

"Eris speaks truth." Lucien stumbled over her name as he spoke to the floor. "That is what it says."

She took the jewel from Ranulf and held it up. Her whole arm shook with the effort. "This is your crest, right? What's this other symbol?"

"My mark," Ranulf said.

"A message from the future so you two don't mistakenly kill me. Too bad you didn't find it before I got hurt." She stood, walked to the window and threw the jewel.

"No," Lucien said, but knew it was too late. "What if you need my mother's ring in order to return?"

"What if I believed you cared?" She faced him. "Now I know why. I thought it was you taking my virginity that made you so guilty. I forgave you for that almost immediately and couldn't understand why you carried it all those years."

"I don't understand."

She moved toward him. Lucien stood rigid when she stopped one step from him. Good sense told him not to, but he met her gaze. He regretted it instantly. All he saw was hatred.

"I told you the truth. I gave my innocence as proof. I resided with you, served you, and never did anything that could even remotely be confused as threatening. Yet all it took were the words of an unknown woman for you to turn on me." She inhaled shakily a few times. "I don't care how you say it or *when* you say it. You don't deserve forgiveness."

He nodded.

"I'm glad you understand now. So, asking the me that doesn't know you for true forgiveness is a waste of your breath." She turned away and returned to the bed. "Like talking to you now is a waste of mine."

Lucien looked at Ranulf. The other man shook his head.

"I'll retrieve the jewel," Lucien whispered.

It took all of his willpower to walk out of the room instead of running.

Betrayal had coursed through his body when he thought Eris had duped him, made a fool of him. That emotion had turned to anger the more he thought of all they'd shared.

He'd lashed out.

Lucien looked down at his hand. The one he used when he hit Eris. He would cut off that hand and offer it to her if he thought she would forgive him.

No amount of his pain would be compensation enough for hers.

She'd never known servitude. Her attitude, no matter how meek she pretended to be, was testament to that. Her skin, as Mason pointed out, was clean of any signs of abuse. A surety that she'd never been beaten for the defiance he'd glimpsed on more than one occasion. She'd spoken her mind as though it were her right.

All of those things were his proof, and he'd ignored them for what had come easiest.

Eris was right. He didn't deserve forgiveness.

Chapter Forty-eight

"Eris, Lucien acted in anger of a supposed betrayal. He made a mistake," Ranulf said from his place near the fire.

He moved there after Lucien had left and started mixing herbs with some water. Eris figured he probably was making her something for the pain. She'd tell him to shove it but didn't want to suffer just to hurt him. Walking the entire way from the dungeon to his room had been enough pain for her. Pride had to take a backseat to sense.

She stared at him, but he didn't meet her gaze. "Tell me you aren't asking for his forgiveness after I just said he doesn't deserve it."

He looked surprised, possibly because of her tone.

She was done playing. They knew the truth and finally believed it. That meant she could be herself and speak without fear. What more could they do to her?

Ranulf nodded and returned to his task. "Of course. That was wrong."

"What are you doing?"

"A drink for your pain. It will allow you to rest." He set the pot of water and herbs into the fire and then walked to the bed. "You're shivering. Let me help you beneath the covers so you can get warm."

"Don't even think of touching me."

He stopped.

"How could you?"

"I didn't know he'd sent you to Mason. I would have intervened, though I should have known. I was angry. I ignored the consequences of leaving him."

She shook her head at him. "How could you stand there and lie to my face and make me believe this would last?"

"What do you mean?"

"All of it was a set-up. You made me think you cared so I would stupidly go along without questioning you. If I got too close to the truth, you simply distracted me."

"Eris, what are you—"

"Is your precious immortality so important to you that you don't care who you step over or on to get it?"

"I'm not immortal." His face showed his worry. He probably thought she cracked.

She was fine. And she knew the man in front of her wasn't the version who should be hearing her words, but he was close enough and would probably remember. Or would it be too insignificant in the grand scheme of living forever?

It didn't matter. Saying the words made her feel a little better. She pinned him with a look. "My part in this is officially over. Send me home."

"Eris, I'm not him. I don't understand any of this. I would never send an innocent to such as this simply to prolong my life. You know that of me."

"I don't know anything about you. Nothing at all."

"That's not true. You know me better—"

"Shut up!" Her command winded her and caused her pain.

Ranulf snapped his mouth shut.

A thought occurred to her. It almost made her smile, but, it seemed, the muscles of her back were connected to those in her face.

She said, "Tell me about your father."

"Eris, is this really the time?"

"You don't get to say no."

He opened and closed his mouth several times and then nodded. After a small sigh, he said, "I am a foundling, or that was what I was led to believe most of my life. The man who raised me was an apothecary, hence my herbal knowledge. He made sure I received training as a knight as well." He stopped.

To Eris's eyes, it looked like Ranulf was stalling. She shifted, knowing she'd cause herself pain. That little bit of movement made her suck the air through her teeth and wince.

Ranulf closed his eyes. "The man I knew to be my father subjected me to the most rigorous knight training he could. No man could beat me. Except, the fall of my eighteenth year, I matched a knight on the jousting field that came close. It was a good match. We lifted our helms to congratulate each other, and I saw my eyes staring back at me."

"Your real father."

He nodded. "I would have liked to think it was a coincidence only, but our looks were too similar for there to be any other explanation."

"Did he abandon you?"

"He was not given that chance. My mother did away with me to hide her shame at having lain with one of her lord and husband's knights. She thought to pass me off as her husband's, but I was born with black hair and amber eyes, unlike my brown-haired, blue-eyed siblings. My sire had marked me in a way no one would ignore. She proclaimed that the child she bore was stillborn while sending me away with the man who had attended the birth. I guess I should be thankful she didn't kill me."

When he looked over his shoulder, she followed his gaze to the sword hanging above the fireplace.

"Corpse Maker. My true father's blade. He gave it to me after the tournament. He said it should never be drawn unless in battle, so there it hangs, not used since my time in the cursed lands." He looked back at her. "He couldn't claim me. His infatuation with the lord's wife cooled after some years, and he eventually married and had legitimate children. To claim me would be to reveal my origins and bring danger to his family."

"So what does that have to do with us?"

Ranulf walked away. She thought he was running from the topic and was about to call him on it, but he went to the fire to retrieve her drink.

He brought the cup back to the bed though he didn't give it to her. She looked at him in question.

"I vowed not to be with a woman who would not be with me alone," he said in a low voice.

A bark of laughter left Eris's lips and was promptly followed by a hiss of pain. She indulged her mirth even as her aching body protested. It felt good to laugh with actual humor.

"Of course you find my resolve laughable given our current...the relationship we shared."

"That's funny too, but not what I'm laughing about." She took the tea from him and sipped at it.

She remembered relating a similar vow to the Ranulf of her time and how funny he'd found it. He truly had been laughing with her, albeit a few centuries later.

Fate had a twisted sense of humor to make two people who had both vowed to be monogamous end up in a polyamorous relationship with each other.

"Well?"

She raised a questioning eyebrow at him. "Well what?"

"Will you not tell me what about my statement amused you when I do not see how wishing for a faithful woman is a laughing matter?"

His tone grew more and more annoyed as he spoke. Eris put aside her tea before she threw it at him. Emotions were high. She'd started the topic as a distraction—something to make it feel like there was nothing out of the ordinary, and yet, her throbbing back was a constant reminder.

She said, "You say that like I'm not."

He opened his mouth and then closed it.

"No, Ranulf. Say it."

"You know your behavior better than I."

"Oh yes. Lest we forget I've been your and Lucien's willing whore these past few weeks. I'm surprised you even let my lowly self sully your bed, or does guilt motivate you?"

His hands twitched at his sides. He looked like he wanted to grab her. She would almost feel sorry for him if she hadn't used up her pity quotient on herself.

"Why both, Eris?"

"You didn't ask that while we were in bed together."

"I'm asking now. You were mine alone. Why turn to Lucien?"

She cocked her head to the side. "I'm sorry. Did I bind myself to you and forget?"

"Your meaning is unclear."

"Did we get married and you forgot to tell me?"

"No."

"Then explain to me how I wasn't loyal when my loyalty was never requested. I am your prisoner—completely at your mercy. Or, did tonight's beating escape your notice?"

"And my future version? What of him?"

"You aren't him."

"You have betrayed him. He and I may be one in the same so your time with me could be overlooked, but your dalliance with Lucien is a betrayal to your relationship."

She smirked, mildly amused at his choice of words. "What relationship? I told you, the Ranulf in the future and I are friends, nothing more. Lucien as well."

Ranulf looked unsure.

"Besides, if I in any way resemble your mother, it's you and Lucien who put me in that position since I was merely acting in my best interest to ensure I survived the two of you until I return to my time." She blinked at him. "Obviously turning myself into a servant and giving both of you my body whenever it pleased you to take it wasn't enough."

She snorted. "I even warned you both about that bitch in Lucien's forest. Did anyone bother to wonder why I would bring attention to someone whose very presence would possibly get me killed?"

"No. It didn't occur to me," Ranulf whispered.

"No, it didn't. All you saw was my skin color. All you heard were her lies." She yawned. "I just want to go home. Everything is strange here. Something is wrong with me. I can never get warm. My hair hasn't grown in all these months. I understand and can speak with you though I've never spoken this language before."

Whatever Ranulf had given her was working. She barely felt the pain in her back.

Ranulf moved slowly. He helped her stand, and she didn't protest. Once he moved the blankets out of the way, he helped her lay on her side and then covered her. "Sleep, Eris. No one will hurt you anymore."

"I want to go home. Send me home," she whispered in a voice heavy with sleep.

She didn't hear his reply if he had one.

* * * *

Ranulf closed the door quietly and then leaned his head against it.

"How is she?" Lucien asked from behind him.

Ranulf faced Lucien. "Distant."

Lucien cursed.

"Not in the way you think, though it is present. She refers to her time more openly as though speaking of it will transport her there."

"Of course she wishes to be there rather than here after what I..." He trailed off and looked at his hand.

Ranulf followed his gaze. The bruise that hand had created marred the lower half of Eris's jaw. It was the only outward evidence of her mistreatment.

"Did you find the jewel?"

Lucien nodded. "It didn't go far." He looked at the jewel, staring into its depths even though he couldn't possibly see the inscription within without light shining through it. "We must send her back to her own time. We have to find a way."

"Has guilt addled your brain? Why would you betray yourself in such a way?"

Lucien looked away from the jewel and stared at Ranulf. "What betrayal?"

"She has proclaimed her relationship with our future selves is merely friendship, but even you must see that is a lie or a gross understatement of the situation. She came readily to us, as though being with both was more natural than one or the other."

"Your point?"

"If you return her to her time now, she will hate you—the you in that time."

"Holding her here will not endear her to me either."

Ranulf placed his hand on Lucien's shoulder. "That's where you're wrong, my friend. You can earn her forgiveness. Once you have it, then you can send her home. The following centuries will be easier if you know she will not forsake you after this adventure."

Lucien snorted and knocked Ranulf's hand away. "It is you who makes no sense. Her hatred means you alone can have her. I would think you would take that opportunity and leave me to my folly."

"It is not only you she disdains."

"Maybe so, but her feeling for you is annoyance, an emotion that will wane in time. Hatred can last forever." Lucien turned away. "Despite what you say, I leave to find a way of returning her to her home."

"Don't, Lucien. Give yourself time."

"My friend, time is the one thing I do not want. Though, it seems, I am to be cursed with it."

Lucien walked to the stairs. Ranulf could think of no way to stop the man.

While Ranulf agreed Eris didn't belong in their time, they couldn't send her back yet. She was hurt and angry. As such, she would never be with their future selves.

Ranulf knew that was why he would seek out immortality, Lucien as well. He'd never wanted to extend his life. Even when his father had told him the stories of potions that may prolong a man's life into forever, Ranulf had thought that stupid. One lifetime was enough for any man.

Unless that man loved a woman from a far flung future time. A time to which she would eventually return.

Ranulf had every intention of following her. He would make her love him, a task made that much easier if he kept her in the past until she forgave him.

He looked at his door. "You will," he vowed softly.

Chapter Forty-nine

Eris looked over her shoulder as Ranulf entered the room.

"I would think you wouldn't want to look at the forest any longer," he said.

She shrugged and turned back to the view. "The trees aren't to blame for what passes through them."

"True enough."

She knew he was staring at her. That's all he did when they were in the same room together, which was every night. Despite repeatedly telling him to leave, Ranulf stayed his ground. He'd spent the last two weeks sleeping on a nearby chair, which obviously was uncomfortable for him, but he didn't complain.

His presence had helped her on more than one occasion when nightmares had roused her screaming from a dead sleep. Ranulf had held her until her grasp of reality reasserted itself. Then, without her prompting, he'd return to his chair.

He never hinted at returning to his bed, not even when she'd spent an entire night shaking from the cold her body couldn't seem to shake off. He had merely stoked the fire as high as it would go and then returned to his chair.

"Is it fixed?" she asked.

"Yes. It's still covered in your blood."

She stroked the first wound Lucien had given her. It was nothing but a small jagged scar. She touched the second. Her jaw healed faster than she thought it would. There were no remnants of the abuse she suffered, only her memories.

"Where is it?"

"Lucien has it." Ranulf joined her at the window. "Are you so sure that is all you need to return? Your cloak is gone, and your dress left with the lady who took it when she returned to her uncle's keep."

"He'll want it back."

She jumped with surprise when Ranulf touched her shoulder.

"You know the story behind that ring, don't you?"

"I don't want to know." She tried to pull away, but he held her. "Let go."

Ranulf ignored her words and turned her so she faced him. "Lucien was only supposed to give that ring—"

"I don't care."

"Yes, you do." He tightened his hold. "That ring was never to leave his possession unless given to a woman with whom he wanted to spend forever—a woman he loves. That was the promise his mother made him give on her deathbed. Lucien never breaks a vow once given. That was why it almost killed him when the sultan took it and said he melted it."

She shoved his hands away. "Why is it so important to you that I forgive him? What do you gain from that?"

"This isn't about what I gain. It's about what you'll lose if you return to your time with this anger for him."

"You make it sound like I'm being petty. He had me beaten. Beaten!"

"I know that."

"The only reason I didn't fare worse was because Mason wanted to *savor* me." She shuddered at the revulsion that memory, that word, caused her. "He deserves every bit of the anger I care to throw his way."

"And me? What makes my involvement so different than Lucien's? I left you to him when I knew what he would do."

Eris walked to the fire—one of her two favorite spots. Favored only because staying warm was all but an impossibility for her. Her cloak had kept her warm when not in bed or near a fire. She never thought that strange until Ranulf tried replacing her cloak—A disaster as she seemed to freeze all the faster.

It was like her cloak had held the warmth of her time. Lucien destroyed it along with any hope she had of ever being warm so long as she stayed in the past.

"Answer me, Eris. Why do I deserve forgiveness when Lucien doesn't?"

"You don't. Neither of you do. None of this would have happened to me if I had never met you."

"Hold. I will not carry the burden of blame for my future self. I refuse. I didn't send you to this time. He did."

She faced him. "You are him!"

"Not according to you." He shook his head at her. "According to you, we are different. It cannot be both. I cannot be him when you are angry and then not be him when you are happy. We are the same. He is who I will become. If you hate me then you hate him."

"I don't hate him," she whispered. "I don't hate him. Why? Why don't I hate him? This is his fault. This is your fault. You knew what would happen to me. You should have told me to run."

"No, I would never do that."

"Of course not. Then your precious immortality would be in jeopardy."

"I am not immortal!" He held out his arms from his sides. "Look at me. I have aged every day from the time of my birth until now. So far as I know, I will die one day."

"But you didn't."

"Why?"

She opened her mouth and then stopped herself when she realized what she was about to say. Instead she shook her head. "Stop it."

"Say it, Eris."

"No."

"Say it!"

"Because of me."

He smiled without humor. "Because of you I sought a way to become immortal. Now tell me why?"

Memories flooded through her. A day of misunderstandings and accusations when she thought she'd lose both men to an unknown woman and that had scared her to death.

"Forgiveness."

Ranulf jerked back. "What?"

"They told me for forgiveness. You'll wait all those centuries for me to take this trip and then return just to ask for my forgiveness."

"No, that isn't the reason why."

"Yes, it is. You told me so yourself. You and Lucien. Which means I never gave it before leaving."

"You and I both know Lucien and I wouldn't suffer through centuries of time simply for forgiveness. Stop being simple, Eris."

"I'm not."

Ranulf searched her gaze. Could he tell she was hiding something? While it was true the Ranulf and Lucien of the future wanted her forgiveness, that wasn't the only reason they had given her. She wouldn't utter the second.

"Fine." He nodded. "If I would live all that time just to gain your forgiveness then I should do something that would warrant needing it."

Eris stepped back quickly. "What do you mean? What are you going to do?"

He grabbed her arm and propelled her toward the door. "This." He shoved her through it and then closed it in her face.

"Ranulf?"

The door lock clicked.

She knocked. "Ranulf?"

He didn't answer, and she heard no movement.

"Stop playing."

Still nothing.

"This isn't funny. Let me in." She banged her fists against the door. "Ranulf!"

Down the hall, a door opened. She faced the man who stared at her.

She couldn't stay in the hall. The mood of the people was hostile since the other woman's visit. Ranulf had told her as much, and she'd stayed secluded in his room during her recovery because of it.

But Ranulf wouldn't just leave her…

She stared at the door. He'd said he would do something for which she had to forgive him. Leaving her in the hall while she was attacked definitely counted.

While she didn't want to believe it of him, she knew Ranulf had a temper that rivaled Lucien's.

She ran toward Lucien's room. It was the only other place she could go. It took her three tries before she finally knocked.

There was no answer.

She tried the knob, but the door was locked.

Could Lucien be in the common room?

Even if he was, she couldn't go down there.

But it was so late. Why wouldn't he be in his room resting before his trip to the glowing grotto?

Maybe he was sleeping and had locked his door so he wouldn't be disturbed.

She knocked again and then called, "Lucien."

The lock clicked, and the door opened with a very confused Lucien standing on the other side. "Eris?"

She walked into his room and straight to the fire.

"Why are you here?"

"Ranulf has kicked me out of his room. Since neither of you have seen fit to give me a room of my own, here I am." She didn't look at him as she spoke.

She didn't know what Lucien would do. They hadn't seen each other, let alone spoken, during her entire recovery.

"I shall sleep elsewhere then."

"What?" She looked at him.

He looked tired. Had he been sleeping like she thought?

A quick glance at the bed showed it hadn't been slept on recently.

Lucien said, "You do not want to be near me. I will not make you suffer my presence because Ranulf has a whim."

She frowned at him. Something was wrong. He seemed like he was being crushed under a heavy weight that had him dragging.

Weary. That was the word she wanted. Lucien looked weary—tired physically and mentally and withdrawn.

Was that what guilt had done to him? Was that why Ranulf wanted her to forgive him? Lucien and Ranulf were good friends, and no friend would want to watch another suffer like Lucien.

"Stay."

She uttered the word before she'd realized.

Lucien looked back at her.

"You don't have to leave. This is your room. I'm the one who's out of place."

God help her, now *she* was feeling guilty. He'd caused her tremendous pain but holding the grudge and seeing the effects was making her feel guilty.

She knew why.

And just like with Ranulf, she refused to utter it or even give it much thought. It was a betrayal to how she currently felt. His actions hurt her, and yet…

"I just need to be close to the fire," she said and turned back to the warmth of the flames.

"Ranulf said your inability to stay warm had grown worse."

She nodded.

"Returning you to your time might help."

She looked at him in surprise. "What?"

He retrieved the ring, the one from her time, from the bedside table and held it out to her. "I'll take you to the hole and send you back."

She couldn't believe her ears. "How do you know where it is?"

"I placed a sentry there after you were pulled from it. I thought whoever you were meant to meet would show up there, and I would have my proof, but no one ever came."

"Except that one woman."

He stiffened but shook his head. "My men did not capture her near the hole or headed toward it. Her destination was the keep. The sentry I placed told me no one has ventured near the hole, not even hunters. There is no explanation of how it came to be there, and the person or persons who dug it have not come to check on it in all this time."

"A nine-foot hole doesn't just suddenly appear."

"You did."

She opened her mouth then closed it. "You mean it? You're not yanking, uh, playing a prank? You'll send me back?"

"When have you ever known me to play pranks?" he asked with a sad smile.

She faced him, hugging her arms, and asked in a small voice, "You're willing to send me back with your mother's ring?"

"It may be my mother's ring, but not the one of this time. I have that back now. There is no harm in giving you this one. If I gave it to you in the future then it is you who should have it."

Ranulf's explanation about the true meaning of the ring echoed in her mind. The Lucien of her time had said he always meant to give it to her. How far back did always span? Did that mean he'd loved her since—?

She stopped the thought.

It didn't matter about the vow he'd given his mother. He'd given her that ring to send her back in time. And giving it back would return her home.

He didn't approach her, only waited.

Eris searched his eyes. She took one step toward him and then another until she stood before him. Her gaze never left his as she reached for the ring. When it was in her hand, she whispered, "Thank you."

"Come," he said and turned away.

Chapter Fifty

At first, Eris held the ring, but nothing happened. She tried putting it on, and still nothing happened. The chill night air made her shiver.

"Lucien?"

He peered over the edge of the hole.

"I don't think it'll send me back."

"Is there not some incantation you must speak?"

"No. I didn't do anything except fall down here. Granted, I didn't fall this time, but I figured just being here would do it." She walked to the wall and reached upwards.

Lucien grabbed her wrists and lifted her out of the hole. Once her feet were on solid ground, he let her go and stepped back. "Perhaps you must go back at sunrise since you arrived here at sunset."

"There's a thought."

"We will try again in the morning then."

Eris watched Lucien walk back to the horse. For the first time, he somewhat resembled the Lucien from her time.

It was the guilt.

Knowing he was that way because he regretted what he'd done made her feel a little better. It also explained why his future version had so desperately wanted her to forgive him.

They were simple words to say and doing so would probably assuage a little of her own guilt. She didn't utter them, mostly because she wouldn't mean them.

"Eris?"

Lucien held his hand out to her. They'd arrived on the same horse because Eris didn't know how to ride. She could almost mistake the outing for their usual if the atmosphere between them wasn't so tense.

She hadn't gone back to the glowing grotto and only bathed when Ranulf did. Without being asked, she'd lapsed back into the habit of washing his hair. Ranulf hadn't questioned it or complained about how hard she scrubbed.

But she missed bath day since Ranulf kicked her out of his room.

As a matter of fact, she hadn't performed any of her other old habits since her abuse. No sewing or mixing morning drinks or anything else. But of all the things she'd grown accustomed to doing, she missed the grotto the most.

She joined Lucien at the horse and let him lift her onto the saddle. He mounted behind her. Before he could turn the horse back to the keep, she covered his hands. He jerked, making the horse sidestep and whinny in complaint.

"Lucien…" She started to look back and then stopped.

"Eris?"

"How close are we to the glowing grotto?"

"Not far."

"Can we go there?"

"If you wish."

She relaxed. "Thank you."

She felt him nod.

They lapsed back into silence. Eris was about to fall asleep when Lucien stopped the horse. He hadn't been joking. That trip took hardly any time at all. They could have walked.

Like with every visit, Eris held onto Lucien as he guided her through the maze.

There were blankets and other supplies in the cave, including Lucien's box of drawings. She looked at it all and then him.

He busied himself building a fire and seemed to ignore the obvious question on her face.

She finally said, "You've been sleeping here, haven't you?"

"Yes."

Her guilt grew just a little with that admission.

"Had you arrived at my room a little later, you would have missed me."

"I'm sure Ranulf was aware of that."

"As am I."

He held out a small sack to her. "There is soap if you like."

"What about you?"

"I'll bathe later."

She almost asked about his hair but stopped herself.

Lucien sat with his back to the water and pulled out some drawings. She wanted to see what he'd worked on while shut up in the grotto, but refrained. Things couldn't be like they were. Not even if she wanted them to be.

She stripped completely and entered the water. After a quick scrub down, she swam laps. The water felt wonderful. Her stiff muscles welcomed the exercise.

After ten laps, she floated and stared at Lucien's back. He was concentrating hard on whatever he was drawing.

She made a splashing noise, and he stiffened, covering his drawing quickly. That made her smile. He expected her to splash him. "Lucien?"

He started to turn toward her and then stopped as though remembering why he'd given her his back in the first place. "Yes?"

"Why haven't you ever gotten married?"

"Did you ever ask my future self that question?"

"Yes. I asked him and Ranulf."

"What did he say?"

She paused so she could remember accurately and answer without giving anything important away. "Ranulf said it would be too much like admitting defeat. I didn't know what he meant and still don't. When I asked for clarification, he said he just didn't have the inclination."

"What of me?"

"*He* said he'd never met a woman he wanted as his wife."

"Then I will not change my thinking in that regard in the future to come. Good."

"Do you have any children?"

"If I do, the women who bore them have not come forward."

Eris was about to ask another question when footsteps distracted her. She sank farther into the water. Lucien turned toward the entrance of the grotto and put his hand near his sword.

Ranulf jogged in and stopped. He looked at Lucien and then around Lucien. "Where is Eris?"

"Over here," she called, waving her hand.

Ranulf looked her over without shame. The water covered her, but his scrutiny was still a little unnerving. "Why are you two here?"

Lucien said, "Eris wanted to come."

"The gate sentry said you left a little after sunset and have been gone all this time."

Eris waited for Lucien to explain about the botched attempt at sending her home. He said nothing. In fact, he looked a little uncomfortable. Ranulf met her gaze.

She asked, "Why don't you tell him you tried to send me home, Lucien?"

"You what?" Ranulf yelled. "Without telling me?"

"Yes," Lucien said.

"You had no right."

"He had every right to try and send me home. It's what I want. Why are you so pissed about it?" Eris walked out of the water, not caring if the men saw her naked or not. It wouldn't be the first time. She hurried to the fire.

Lucien handed her articles of clothing so she could dress faster. All the while she shivered. Once she finished dressing, he wrapped a blanket around her shoulders as she crouched at the fire.

Ranulf walked over and knelt beside her. "I agree this is not your place, but I was not ready for you to return."

She stopped rubbing her hands together and looked at Ranulf. "*You're not ready? You?* Who gives a damn about you? I want to go home where I can be sure some idiot's whim won't land me in a torture chamber covered in pain." She stopped and thought about her statement.

It was a partial truth, since walking through a poorly lit alley at night in her time would garner the same results. But, she wouldn't tell Lucien and Ranulf that. Besides, she'd rather go back to the danger she knew than stay in the danger she didn't.

"Why do you even care?" she asked. "You banished me from your room."

"Only to force you to speak with Lucien."

"You succeeded. Congrats." She inched closer to the fire.

Lucien pulled her back to her original position and then stamped out the edge of the blanket that had caught fire. "Perhaps you should stay in the water until we leave."

She shook her head. "Nothing helps. Not for long. It's always so cold."

"You were warm in our arms." Ranulf met her gaze without flinching or guilt. "You could return."

"Yes. Home. I need to go home. I never had this problem in my time. Being in the past is freezing me from the inside out, but for some stupid reason you don't seem to care about that, do you?"

"I do care."

"Then find some way to send me home. Why is that so hard?" She stood and put the fire between.

Lucien said, "Sunrise approaches. We can try again."

"No." Ranulf straightened. When he tried to go to Eris, she moved so they stayed apart. He stopped and looked at her across the fire. "Eris, you cannot return with this hatred. I won't let you. I won't betray myself in such a way."

"If you had believed me, truly believed me from the beginning, that wouldn't be a problem now."

"You can't possibly have expected us to believe such a story without proof."

She jerked up her hand. Lucien's mother's ring rested there. She'd forgotten to take it off when she'd started bathing. "You had it."

"We didn't know that, and neither did you. Not until it was too late."

"I don't care!" She looked between Ranulf and Lucien. "I want to go home. I don't belong here. I don't belong with or *to* you. I've had enough." She paced a little, staying near the fire yet needing to vent in some physical way. "I'm tired. I'm tired of being scared. I'm tired of being cold. I'm tired of all of this and you, both of you. Why anyone would want to live in or wish to visit this God forsaken time is beyond me."

"Is your time so much better?" Lucien asked quietly.

She snapped, "Yes."

"You're lying," Ranulf said. "I can tell when you're lying."

"Obviously you can't, or we wouldn't be having this conversation."

Lucien said, "Not lying. Holding something back." He looked at Ranulf and the man nodded in agreement.

She sighed. "My time is better for me. I was born there, raised there, and by God, it's where I want to die. Not here. I want to be around people who know me, care about me, and love me."

Ranulf walked toward her with a hand raised in a calming gesture. She stayed put and let him approach. He stopped a few steps away from her.

"Eris, I do care about you. That should be obvious. When I thought you had tricked me…tricked *us*, the pain I felt—"

"Oh, don't even start talking to me about pain," she said. "Pain is what I felt when Lucien nearly crushed my wrist. Pain is nearly having my jaw broken when Lucien hit me. Pain is watching two men I thought I could trust throw me to the wolves without even giving me a chance to explain or hear my words when I tried."

"We know all that happened. You don't have to repeat it." Lucien's eyes pleaded with her to stop.

She met his gaze. "Pain is knowing without a doubt that any second one of you would come and stop Mason *before* he started and then realizing you wouldn't. You don't care about me. I don't even know how you can tell me that lie when you meet me in my time. Then again, you will have centuries to practice lying with a straight face."

"It's not a lie." Ranulf grabbed her arms and made her face him.

Heat from his hands radiated throughout her body from that simple contact. It was the warmest she'd been in days. It angered her to admit that Ranulf was right. She was warm when they held her.

No cold had touched her while she'd ridden with Lucien to the hole and then the grotto.

"I care about you, Eris. I care *for* you. Why else would I have shared you with Lucien if I didn't care for you?"

She shrugged. "You were horny."

"That's not…" He ended with an annoyed growl. "You wanted us both. I couldn't deny such a request and see you unhappy. Even while held in my arms, you looked at him."

"And you looked at him when in mine," Lucien said.

"I didn't just kick you out of my room so you would speak to Lucien. That excuse was convenient." Ranulf moved his hands so he cupped her cheeks. "I cannot have you beside me and not touch you. I made you leave out of self-preservation so I wouldn't jeopardize my chance at forgiveness."

"Why do you even want forgiveness? You may know the truth, but that hasn't changed anything. I'm still your prisoner." She pulled out of his hold, instantly missing his heat. "Prisoners don't get rights of refusal."

"Eris—"

"Enough, Ranulf." Lucien guided Eris around the fire with a gentle hand. When she was away from Ranulf, he returned and went about dousing the fire. "Sunrise approaches. We have to leave if we don't want to miss it."

"Have you not listened to a word I've said?" Ranulf yelled. "You cannot let her leave like this. Why live through time only to say goodbye? That is madness."

Lucien gathered his belongings into a neat pile and then walked to the grotto entrance. Eris followed him, taking hold of his tunic just before they passed the threshold.

"Lucien!"

Ranulf's shout echoed off the walls and chased them through the tunnels. Lucien didn't stop or falter.

"Though you may not want to hear or believe it," Lucien said in a soft voice, "I do regret what I have done. I am sorry."

"If sorry solved the problems of the world, we wouldn't need prisons." Her voice was as soft as his and just as emotionally charged.

No more was said.

Ranulf caught up with them halfway through the maze. Eris could feel his anger and was happy he didn't voice any of it. They could go around in circles for days, but one fact remained true—she didn't belong there and needed to go home.

* * * *

Alas, Fate didn't agree.

Eris stood once again at the bottom of the hole. Lucien watched her from the hole's edge with Ranulf beside him. If she was to leave him, he wanted to watch it happen.

Except nothing happened.

The sun crested over the trees and spilled light into the hole, but Eris remained. She stood with tears pouring over her cheeks, crying silently. The sight tore at him. He wanted her to return to her time just as badly as she did.

He looked at Ranulf. The man tried hard to hide his satisfaction, but it was obvious.

Eris whispered with a shake of her head, "Why?"

No answer was forthcoming.

Ranulf jumped into the hole. Lucien thought Eris would fight him, but she allowed Ranulf to hold her waist as he lifted her above his head to Lucien's waiting hands. Lucien lifted her out and placed her behind him. He then turned back and gave Ranulf a helping hand out.

Both of them stood and watched Eris for what would come next. Remaining at the hole all day would probably accomplish nothing, but Lucien didn't want to say that aloud.

Eris walked toward the horses.

Ranulf jogged after her. The man really needed to hide his good cheer at her failure to return or another argument would erupt. Lucien was tired of repeating the same words over and over without gaining or losing ground.

Eris rode with Ranulf for the return trip. No one spoke, and the silence didn't bother Lucien in the least. As they neared the keep gates, Eris concealed her arm beneath her blanket, hiding his mother's ring. No one knew she had it, and no one was supposed to know.

A man running from the keep gates called, "Lord Lucien, a messenger arrived whilst you were away. He said his news is urgent."

Lucien dismounted. "Where is he then?"

"Here, my lord." The messenger rushed forward and held out the letter he carried.

Lucien broke the royal seal with apprehension and read the contents. He read the message three more times before he believed what it said. Once he was sure he hadn't misunderstood, he pinned the messenger with a look.

The man took a step back, obviously nervous.

"What is your excuse for the delay of this message?"

"Bandits, my lord. My original mount was stolen along with my money and other valuable belongings, even my crest as a royal messenger. They did not take the message because I had it hidden within my tunic. I had to travel a long ways before I came upon someone who would allow me to borrow a mount with the promise of repayment."

Ranulf neared them and asked, "What does the message say, Lucien? Has the king asked that I return?"

"No. He is rewarding me for having the foresight to bargain for your life and keep you in my employ."

"That is good then. What does he give you? More land?"

"A wife. The king sends his youngest brother's daughter to be my bride." He looked at Eris. "The message says she's to arrive with her escort tomorrow."

"Tomorrow? Why so soon?" Ranulf snatched the message from him and read it. He then pinned the messenger with an angry look. "This message was supposed to be delivered a fortnight ago so we would have time to prepare for the wedding ceremony."

"Even that isn't enough time to prepare," Lucien said.

Ranulf looked at Eris. Slowly all gazes moved to her. She turned from the crowd and walked into the keep without a word to anyone.

"Lord Lucien, what do we do?" a nearby man asked.

Lucien watched Eris disappear from sight before he answered. "Prepare as best we can. Arrange a hunting party. See if you can bring down that big stag some have spotted in the forest. I'll set the women to cleaning."

"Including the Moor?" Hugh asked.

Lucien looked at the man. Those around him backed away.

Hugh didn't look scared. The man even lifted his chin with a defiant look in his eyes. "If our women should slave for the coming of the king's niece, so too should she. There's nothing special about her that she should be pampered. She's nothing but a slave and a whore."

Ranulf sidestepped, putting himself between Lucien and Hugh. It wasn't needed. Lucien was angry, but he wouldn't act on the emotion. Not ever again. Too much had been lost by letting blind rage lead him.

Thinking was needed, not fighting.

He handed the reins of his horse over to the waiting stable boy and walked to the keep. "She has served her purpose and would be of no useful help. You need to worry about catching that stag, Hugh, and leave my whore to me."

Ranulf caught up to Lucien, but neither man spoke. They didn't need to. Lucien was sure they were thinking the same thing.

The king had sent his niece, a knight escort, and one of his advisors to oversee the wedding. Except, there would be no wedding. Lucien knew a trap when he saw one. If the king truly offered his niece, he would have summoned Lucien to the castle for the festivities, not sent the girl to him.

Try as he might to think of all possibilities for the king's show of mistrust when Lucien had been nothing but loyal, he knew of only one— Eris.

Word of her must have reached the king, and those words were not favorable to Lucien. Now, more than ever, he truly wished the hole had sent her back because the coming days would probably bring her more pain.

Chapter Fifty-one

Ranulf sat at Lucien's left hand because the royal advisor Peyton had taken his seat at Lucien's right. It didn't matter on which side he sat, the tension of the room was palpable from all sides and every corner.

"This meal is truly magnificent, my lord." Lady Fleta was the only one who seemed oblivious of the malice circulating the table.

"Thank you, Lady Fleta," Lucien said.

Ranulf congratulated Lucien. The man hid his surprise well. Neither of them had truly expected the king's niece to actually arrive. Ranulf would almost think they were being paranoid if not for the presence of Geoffrey—Lucien's long time rival and the appointed escort of the king's niece.

The whole of the kingdom knew of the hatred Lucien and Geoffrey had for one another. The king had pitted them against each other during tournaments more than once because the man had known both would fight as though the match were real.

Even now, Geoffrey glared at Lucien from his end of the table.

"My lord Lucien, I have heard tales of a girl within your keep that is of much interest," Peyton said with a sly smile.

"Have you?" Lucien asked in a bored manner.

"Oh yes. A Moor. It seems you had several at one point."

"I have only one Moor, your grace. The other was an assassin who is now dead."

"And the third?"

"Lord Kern would know more of her than I."

"Yet she was caught headed to your keep."

"Another assassin, I should think. It would be best to ask Kern about her."

Geoffrey said over Peyton's next words, "In fact, I did. He had much to say on the subject, and he wasn't the only one." His gaze went down the table to Hugh. "The king found all the news coming from your keep quite disturbing, which is why I am here."

The man had a superior look on his face Ranulf knew he wouldn't be wearing if they were faced sword to sword. But Geoffrey had answered a simple question without being asked—Lucien had spies within his keep, and those spies had been spreading lies.

"Where is your Moor, Lucien? I find it strange she isn't serving you." Geoffrey looked around in an exaggerated manner.

Lucien said, "She's served me already this day."

"And Ranulf as well?"

"It pleased me to have her do so. Yes."

"I meant, Lucien, did Ranulf please you as well?"

Ranulf lowered his goblet before he crushed it.

Geoffrey grinned at him in a knowing manner. "Oh, I've heard rumors about you, Ranulf. I thought them utter nonsense until I had a chance to speak with the women of this keep. It seems your tastes have strayed from the fairer sex since your stay in the savage lands."

How easily Ranulf could throw his knife into the offending man's lying throat and silence him. He didn't move. All eyes were on him. How he reacted would be telling.

He made himself relax and even returned Geoffrey's grin for one of his own. "It's strange that only women spoke of my tendencies. Surely if my appetites ran toward men, there would be those who would speak out of such abuse. Or do you think the men of this keep are weak cowards to be taken advantage of?"

All the men at the table turned hostile attention to Geoffrey.

"Unless, of course, you think all the men of this keep prefer the company of other men," Lucien said.

The men grumbled amongst themselves. Some even handled their daggers as though preparing to use them for more than cutting meat from the venison that graced the middle of the table.

Geoffrey said quickly, "Those were not my words."

"Ah, but it was your meaning," Lucien said. "Ranulf does not leave this keep. If he partnered with men, then they would be patrons of this keep. To not speak out would mean they welcomed it, if such were taking place. What other possible meaning could be inferred from such an accusation?"

The grumbling grew louder.

Ranulf had the satisfaction of watching Geoffrey squirm while trying to look like he wasn't. The man was nowhere near shrewd enough to out think both him and Lucien. Anything Geoffrey said would only further damn himself.

"I would like to meet the Moor," Peyton declared.

Lucien nodded. "As you wish. Ranulf, fetch her."

Questioning Lucien's ready acceptance of Peyton's request would only raise suspicions of why Ranulf would want to keep her hidden. He left the table without saying a word, happy to have the chance to leave.

He continued to think of the whole situation as a trap, even with the presence of the king's niece. His time with the sultan's uncle had taught him to pay heed to those primal instincts that warned of danger. At the moment, those instincts told him to take Eris and run.

He opened his bedroom door. Eris stood at the window, staring out over the forest. He knew without asking that she stared at the patch of forest where her hole resided. There was no way to see it through the treetops but still she looked.

"Eris, you've been summoned."

"And if I don't want to go?" She looked back at him.

He beckoned her to him. "I wouldn't have come for you if there was a choice."

"You both said this might be a trap."

"It is a trap. Because of that, I would rather have you near me. Now come."

He breathed an inward sigh of relief when she moved toward him without further argument. It didn't matter what problems she had with him and Lucien. Those problems were secondary when faced with the one at hand.

She reached for her blanket.

"Leave it."

"I'll be cold."

"I know that, and I'm sorry." He let a little grin cross his lips. "That will give you all the more reason to stay near Lucien and me."

Instead of accusing him of taking advantage of the situation or railing at him for making her leave the room with him despite her anger, she looked scared.

"Will I be safe?" she whispered.

Ranulf grabbed her hand and pulled her near. He wanted to kiss her but checked the impulse. "None shall touch you unless they go through Lucien or me first. You have my word."

They left the room and headed back to the feast of the damned.

"Say nothing. Ignore them as best you can. They will try to bait you. Simply remain silent and—" he paused with a sigh, "—forgive us for any insults or lies we may say about you."

She nodded. "Just do what you have to do to keep me safe."

"Always." He kissed her hand and then released her.

As all other times, she melded herself to him as they walked. He could feel the fine shivers of her body and only hoped Eris could endure—both the cold and the coming hardship.

"She's dirty," Lady Fleta said with her lips curled in disgust. "Couldn't you wash her before presenting her to us?"

Lucien said, "That is the color of her skin, my lady, not dirt."

"It must rub off, surely."

"Would you care to try?"

The woman blanched with a look of horror. "Of course not. I wouldn't want to touch her. She might be diseased." Her look of horror grew. "And you might have caught whatever she has from lying with her. What was my uncle thinking giving me to such a lord who consorts with diseased and dirty things?"

Ranulf could feel Eris's anger. He was proud she didn't give voice to it. He resumed his seat, and she stayed pressed to his back.

"Don't let her touch the food or she may taint it," Lady Fleta said.

Lucien said, "Normally Eris does not eat with us, but I could not deny Duke Peyton's request." He glanced at Eris as he spoke.

Lady Fleta snapped, "You've seen her then, your grace. Now send her away."

"Calm yourself, my lady. There's no need for alarm. The girl must be clean or else all of Lucien's keep would be ill. They are healthy. Look for yourself," Peyton said, gesturing to the people at the table.

The woman didn't seem convinced.

"And she is quite lovely and young. I'm sure she performs her duties to Lord Lucien with vigor. Sir Ranulf as well." Peyton looked over Eris with a lecher's eyes.

Ranulf was glad he and Lucien were between Eris and the man.

"So this is the fabled female who has the lord of the keep and his steward dancing attendance upon her as though she were a court-born lady," Geoffrey said. "I expected more. I'm sure the king will be likewise disappointed."

"What do you mean?" Lucien asked.

"Upon my departure, the girl comes with me to be delivered to the king. She is a source of information about the sultan and can prove useful in the coming battles. In fact, the king wonders that you did not offer her to him before now. Like when he requested Ranulf's presence some months ago."

Eris clenched Ranulf's tunic. He was happy her actions were masked since her hands rested below his shoulder blades.

"She has no information, vital or otherwise, or I would have relayed it to the king as soon as it was uttered," Lucien said.

Peyton said, "That is for the king to decide."

"Poor, Lucien. You must relinquish your toy." Geoffrey toasted Lucien in a mocking manner.

"If I must, then I shall escort her to the king myself."

"And leave your lovely bride-to-be alone?" Geoffrey looked over Lady Fleta.

The woman blushed and turned her gaze to her plate, though she continued to steal little glances at Geoffrey.

In fact, the woman had been staring at Geoffrey all night. Ranulf hadn't paid attention to it because he'd been too focused on trying not to kill the man. He recognized the expression from having seen Eris wear it. Lady Fleta's looks were those of a woman longing for her lover.

Lucien's intended bride had already been initiated.

"I'm sure Lady Fleta would like to return to the castle and say her farewells to her family and gather more of her belongings. She brought so few with her," Lucien said.

"We had to travel quickly."

"Yes. So quick, in fact, that you arrived at almost the same time as the king's messenger."

Geoffrey stopped trading glances with Lady Fleta and faced Lucien. He grinned and then laughed. "Ah, I shall miss this banter of ours, Lucien. No other challenges me as you do."

"And that means what?"

"It was no run of misfortune that the messenger arrived a day before us. We planned it that way."

"I had guessed that on my own. Why?"

Geoffrey said, "The king didn't want you to have time to prepare or *hide* anything." He looked at Eris when he said the last. "The king sent me as not only an escort to his niece but a judge of the true situation within your keep walls. I have sent him my assessment, and he has judged you all to be conspirators who have lain in wait until some plan involving her—" he pointed at Eris, "—can be enacted."

Lucien sat back in his chair. "You sent a message to the king and received his reply in only a few hours time? I should like to meet your messenger, for surely the man is a marvel to cover such a distance so quickly."

"Ah, we both know, I sent that message days ago. The king thinks we have resided here for a week already. Plenty of time to deem you a traitor to the crown."

Lucien asked, "And you go along with this, Your Grace?"

Geoffrey said over Peyton's reply, "Seeing as I promised the girl to him during our long return trip, Duke Peyton couldn't help but add his agreement to my opinions."

Neither Lucien nor Ranulf spoke.

Peyton said, "The king is not without mercy. He will spare you, Lord Lucien. He knows you to be loyal and only led astray by those closest to you." He looked pointedly at Ranulf. "You only need turn over Ranulf and the Moor to us, and you can keep your title and properties. It is a simple show of loyalty."

Ranulf knew Lucien wouldn't just hand Eris over.

"So be it," Lucien said.

Eris's gasp was the most audible thing in the room. Ranulf didn't blame her. He would like to think Lucien was merely playing a part, but the man looked serious.

Ranulf asked, "What are you saying, Lucien?"

"I'm saying she is not worth my title." Lucien faced Geoffrey. "She'll be delivered to you tomorrow."

"Why not now?" Geoffrey looked at Lucien with suspicion.

"You truly expect me to surrender such an accomplished bed warmer without a final performance?"

Geoffrey smiled knowingly. "Have her then."

"I didn't need your permission." Lucien stood and grabbed Eris's arm. "Enjoy the rest of your night. I shall."

He pulled her toward the stairs, and she didn't fight. Ranulf didn't wonder. She, like him, was in shock.

Ranulf followed Lucien without excusing himself. They trekked to Lucien's room where he herded them all inside and then shut and locked the door.

Only then did Ranulf speak. "You bastard."

"I'm quite aware of my parentage, unlike you," Lucien snapped. He released Eris, grabbed his satchel and went around his room gathering items here and there and shoving them inside.

"What are you about?" Ranulf asked, inching toward Eris. She moved so he stood between her and Lucien.

Lucien didn't stop his movements as he said, "I'm gathering all things of value. I suggest you return to your room and do the same in what little time we have."

"So you think to bribe the king with us as well as money?"

That stopped Lucien in his tracks. He stared from Ranulf to Eris and back. "Have you gone crazed?"

"I should ask you the same," Ranulf snapped.

"We don't have time for this!" Lucien looked at the door and then back at them. "We need to be away from here and put as much distance between us and this keep as we can in the time my excuse allotted us."

Ranulf asked, "What?"

"Don't be simple! You really think the king sent Geoffrey to take her and you back and that is all? Even before Geoffrey's false report, my title was already forfeit. Geoffrey has even made sure to have my intended bride before me. We are all in danger. I will not stand by and wait for the inevitable."

Eris finally spoke in a soft whisper, "You said I wasn't worth your title."

"You're not. You're worth more, and I mean to see you safely back to your time before Ranulf and I flee this place forever." His look saddened just a little. "If it still does not work, then you will simply run with us until such a time as we can return and try again."

"What about the glowing grotto? You said it was a hiding place."

Ranulf said, "For only a short time. It didn't take Lucien and me long to ascertain the path. Though an idiot he may be, Geoffrey would eventually discover it as well."

He went to the door.

"Where are you going?" Eris asked, chasing after him.

Ranulf held her back with one hand. "Stay here. I must retrieve some things from my room."

"But—"

"Stay." He looked at Lucien one last time before leaving the room.

Everything was happening so fast. Ranulf could barely keep his thoughts going on a coherent path. He walked to his room and entered as though nothing were amiss. Once the door was closed, he ran, gathering all those things of value and items he knew he would need on the journey to come.

He strapped Corpse Maker to his waist and knew the sword would live up to its name that night. There would be no holding back. Not so long as Eris's safety was at stake. Any who glimpsed his blade would carry the image of it with them into the afterlife.

The last thing he grabbed was Lucien's mother's ring—both of them.

He checked the hall to ensure it was empty and then returned to Lucien's room. Eris stood in the middle of the room, holding Lucien's satchel and shivering. Lucien had stoked the fire so high it threatened to leave the hearth and burn all the things around it. Ranulf was sure that was Lucien's intention.

Ranulf said, "I have these, but the blood is gone."

Eris nodded. "It washed away yesterday."

"I cannot tell which is which." He held out the rings.

Lucien rushed over to Ranulf. He looked from one ring to the other and then shook his head. "I cannot either. Let me see the jewels."

"You can only see the inscription if you pry them loose. We don't have time to reset them."

Eris joined them. She grabbed one of the rings and slipped it on her hand. "It's this one."

Both of them stared at her. Lucien asked, "Are you sure?"

She reached for the other ring. Her fingers barely touched it and a bright flash accompanied by a loud pop occurred. Eris pulled back with a hiss of pain and then nodded. "I'm sure."

Ranulf asked, "Did you know it would do that?"

"No, but I thought it might do something. That's what I saw shining in the woods."

"But, how? It was covered and hidden within that woman's cloak." Lucien shook his head. "Never mind. We need to go. Now."

Lucien took the satchel from Eris and then grabbed her hand. He pulled her to the far wall where he pushed at a stone. It slid inwards with a grating noise. There was a loud creak before a hidden door swung open.

"I never thought there would be a day when we would use this door." Ranulf looked at the dark passage.

"Be happy it exists. Now move." Lucien pulled Eris into the passage after him.

Ranulf looked back at the room. One of the many blankets Eris had used to keep herself warm caught his attention. He tossed the blanket near the fire, entered the passage, and then secured the door behind him. In a few moments, a spark from the fire would catch the blanket and the whole room would be engulfed in flames shortly thereafter.

He could think of nothing in the keep he would miss. And no one. The only person he would miss was before him, running for her life and continued freedom. He had every intention of seeing her again once he and Lucien sent her safely back to her home.

Chapter Fifty-two

"I wish I'd had the forethought to have the horses ready," Lucien grumbled.

Eris said, "Too suspicious."

"Agreed." He glanced back at her. "How are you?"

"I'll run all night if I have to."

Ranulf snapped, "Save your breath for running faster."

Eris nodded. She hadn't lied. She would find the energy to run all night and the next day if it kept her away from Peyton and Geoffrey. She wanted so badly to ask how far to the grotto but didn't. Knowing the distance wouldn't make it any shorter.

Something shined in the corner of her eye. She glanced over her shoulder and then gasped. "The keep."

Ranulf put his hand on her back, pushing her forward since she'd slowed. "Keep moving."

"It's on fire."

Lucien said, "We know. Now run."

"Lucien." She didn't know what she could say. He'd torched his home to cover their escape.

"They'll know we've run, and they have horses. Keep focused." Lucien tightened his hold on her hand. "We'll get you home, Eris."

"I'm sorry."

Lucien snorted. "If sorry solved the world's problems then we wouldn't need prisons." He glanced back at her. "You'll get home, and you will see us again."

"I know."

He nodded and faced forward.

"Quiet!" Ranulf pulled Eris to a stop, and she pulled Lucien. He held up a hand.

D. Reneé Bagby

Eris didn't want to stand there. She looked between the men. They were listening to something she couldn't hear.

But she felt it. The ground beneath her feet rumbled.

"Horses," Ranulf whispered.

Lucien pulled Eris into running again. "Worry about the dogs."

She heard the howl after he said it.

"No point hoping they get lost. Run straight," Ranulf said.

Eris didn't know what that meant. She thought they had been running straight. Lucien pulled her tight against his side.

"Follow me close."

"I am."

"Jump."

She only got a two second warning before Lucien jumped a branch. She just cleared it and stumbled. Ranulf slipped his hand around her waist, keeping her on her feet.

"Down."

She ducked without trying to see what she was dodging. Lucien led the way like that, calling warnings only seconds in advance of needing them. Eris didn't have time to worry about her pursuers while trying to keep Lucien's prompts straight.

"Stop." Lucien caught her against his back and held her steady.

Ranulf crowded in close as he peered over Lucien's shoulder. Lucien held up two fingers and pointed in front of him.

Eris's heart rate doubled.

How had Geoffrey's men gotten in front of them? Even on horseback, it should have taken them a while to catch up.

Lucien pushed Eris against Ranulf, who wrapped his arm around her waist while Lucien left the protection of the undergrowth. She almost called out for him to stop.

He went toward the two men on silent feet. They didn't notice him. Eris hoped it stayed that way. He pulled his dagger.

Everything went dark the moment Lucien attacked his targets. Ranulf had covered her eyes. She lifted her hands to his but didn't move his hand or struggle. He hugged her with his other arm.

"Come," Lucien called.

Ranulf kept his hand over her eyes as he guided her forward. He wouldn't let her see the bodies. She didn't mind since that wasn't something she wanted etched into her memory.

Ranulf asked, "Do they have horses?"

"Yes. Give me Eris."

Ranulf's hand left her eyes, and he lifted her to Lucien. She was only given a moment to sit properly before Lucien spurred the horse forward.

"Ranulf." She tried to look back, but Lucien held her so she stayed facing forward.

Lucien said, "He'll catch up to us."

Thundering hooves of a second horse greeted her ears. Ranulf spurred his mount, closing the distance between them.

Once Ranulf was close enough, Lucien kicked his mount faster and called, "We go to the caves first. No doubt someone in the keep has told Geoffrey about the hole."

"You lead. I follow," Ranulf called back.

Eris prayed for no more obstacles. Now that they had horses, they could get to their hiding place faster.

She threaded her fingers through Lucien's. He gripped her hand and laid a kiss on a shoulder.

"You'll be home soon," he whispered.

A sudden sense of dread stopped her words of agreement. It was the same feeling that had struck her when Lucien's mother's ring had winked at her from the forest depths.

But she wasn't sure what the warning meant. Was it danger from the path they took or the path they had taken?

A twig snapped.

Eris pulled back on the reins and, at the same time, yelled, "Stop!"

Both horses skidded to a halt.

"What is it?" Ranulf looked around and then back at Eris.

She looked around as well. She didn't see anything, but something was wrong.

"Eris?" Lucien squeezed her hand.

The feeling persisted.

"Down!" Ranulf leapt across his horse and tackled both Lucien and Eris. They hit the ground in time to watch three arrows whiz through the spots where they had been and lodge in the tree behind them.

The horses spooked and ran.

"How did they get ahead of us?" Ranulf asked in a low, growling voice. He pulled his dagger.

"Geoffrey set a trap knowing we might run." Lucien pulled his dagger as well.

They put Eris between them and waited.

The attack happened quickly. Three men spilled from the darkness with swords drawn. Eris knew Lucien and Ranulf were no match with just daggers. She didn't know why they didn't pull their swords as well.

One attacker swung at Lucien, but his sword hit a branch, slowing his attack enough for Lucien to cut his arm and then bury his dagger in the man's stomach. The other two had similar issues. Their swords caught low hanging branches and tangled in the vines. That made it easier for Lucien and Ranulf to kill all three.

"We're running again." Lucien held his hand out to Eris.

She'd just touched his fingertips when something hit her and pushed her back. A burning sensation spread from her shoulder.

"Eris!" Ranulf ran to her.

She touched her shoulder and then looked in confusion at the arrow piercing her flesh.

Ranulf caught her when her legs buckled. She stared up at him.

Lucien roared, but she couldn't sit up to see why. A second later, someone else screamed in pain.

"How is she?" Lucien jostled Ranulf when he returned. He touched her forehead.

"The arrow did pass all the way through. It missed her heart but it's close. I…I don't want to pull it out." Ranulf's voice sounded scared, and his hands shook where they held her.

Lucien cursed. He looked around quickly. "I know they heard that scream. They're coming for us. The hole is close, and the grotto is just beyond it."

"The hole," Eris said, surprised that her voice sounded so steady considering the growing pain in her shoulder.

Both men looked at her.

"I need to go home. The doctors in my time can fix this easily."

Ranulf gave her a pitying look.

She laughed and shook her head, only to hiss in pain from doing it. His hold tightened. "You still don't believe me after all that's happened."

He didn't speak, and that was answer enough for her. She braced herself, knowing she'd felt worse when in Mason's dungeon, and sat up.

"Eris, stop." Ranulf tried to hold her, but she fended him off.

"The arrow is in my shoulder. The rest of me is fine." She held out her hand to Lucien.

He pulled her to her feet and then steadied her. "Can you run?"

"I damn well better if I want to get home." She touched her shoulder again. Blood dripped down her arm. She needed to get back to her time and to a hospital before she bled to death.

"Eris."

She looked at Ranulf.

He cupped her cheek and searched her gaze. "Tell me you'll live."

"Get me home and I will. This wound would be mortal here. In my time, it's mundane. The cause is unusual, but fixing it is mundane."

A dog howled in the distance.

Ranulf held her gaze for a moment longer. He nodded. "To the hole then."

He put his hand on her wounded shoulder. "Bite down."

Eris didn't ask. She clenched her teeth.

Ranulf snapped off the shaft of the arrow, leaving only an inch or so showing. He watched her.

It took a lot of willpower on her part not to curl up and start crying. They didn't have time for that. She said through her clenched teeth, "You owe me for that."

Ranulf nodded. "Remind me when you see me again." He tore a strip of cloth from his tunic and tied her arm to her side so she wouldn't move it.

"Let's go." Lucien grabbed other her hand. "If you need to stop—"

"You never babied me before. Don't start now." She squeezed his hand. "Run. I'll keep up."

He looked at Ranulf. Both men nodded and then they ran. Eris felt every beat of her heart pushing out more blood. She hoped the hole was close. She also hoped it worked. Her silver lining was that if it didn't work, she'd die of blood loss before Geoffrey could get a hold of her—morbid yet comforting at the same time.

Horses carrying yelling riders sounded around them.

"They're gaining," Ranulf said.

Lucien stopped. He pulled his sword and faced the way they'd come.

Eris frowned at him and then Ranulf when he followed suit. "Lucien, Ranulf, what are you—"

"Eris, run!" Lucien yelled. "Keep straight. The hole is there. Run. We'll slow them down."

"No. We can get there together." She reached for him, but he knocked her hand away. "Please."

Ranulf snorted with a half laugh. "Now who doubts? You know we survive. You wouldn't be here if we hadn't."

She looked at him. Did that mean he really finally believed?

His joking façade dropped, and sadness entered his eyes. "Run, little Eris," he whispered.

"Now!" Lucien yelled.

She jumped back at the anger in his voice. After one last look, she ran. Her shoulder throbbed, and her vision blurred. Everything felt hot and cold at the same time. She wasn't even sure if she was running straight.

Metal striking metal rang out. That only spurred Eris to run faster. She had to survive. She needed to see them again.

A whistling noise made her look back. Several arrows were headed her way. She wouldn't outrun them. She dove to the side heedless of whatever she would land on. It was better than being shot.

Except she didn't land. The ground disappeared, and she screamed as she fell into a deep dark hole.

At least I found it, she thought as she closed her eyes and waited to hit bottom.

* * * *

Lucien pulled his sword from the gut of the man in front of him in time to block another enemy. The man's sword sliced his shoulder, but only his skin. He ignored the wound and the miniscule amount of pain it caused in favor of killing his opponent.

He only had time for a quick glance at Ranulf to ensure the man was still alive before another attacked him. In the distance, Geoffrey sat atop his horse laughing at them.

Lucien wanted to get at him, but too many of Geoffrey's men stood in his way.

He'd just killed his fourth opponent when a woman's scared scream reached his ears.

"Eris," both he and Ranulf said in unison.

Geoffrey made a triumphant noise. "She's mine now."

What happened next confounded Lucien. Ranulf shouted. In a blur of motion and flashing steel, five men died. Lucien had never seen Ranulf move so fast.

He didn't question it. Ranulf's momentary berserker-like rage had cleared the way. He sheathed his sword and ran. Let Geoffrey call him a coward. He needed to know Eris was safe.

"After them!" Geoffrey yelled.

Lucien and Ranulf dodged into the densest part of the forest. It was the long way but would slow their pursuers.

"We never should have left her," Ranulf growled.

"Just run," Lucien snapped.

They reached the hole, and Lucien jumped inside without a question to his own safety. He stayed close to the wall in case Eris was at the bottom. But, she wasn't.

All that was left was a puddle of blood.

"Eris," he rasped.

"Lucien, give her to me. Quickly."

"She isn't here." He returned to the wall and grabbed Ranulf's offered hand. "She returned to her time. We need to get to safety so we can see her there."

Ranulf pulled him from the hole. They ran to the caverns.

"Lay false trails and then meet in the grotto." Lucien didn't wait to see if Ranulf would agree but ran to the right.

He ran down every tunnel at least once before taking the path to the glowing grotto. If Geoffrey and his men found the true path, there would be no escape.

"Ranulf, we need to—"

Lucien ducked a sword aimed at his neck and pulled his own sword as he rolled out of the way. How had Geoffrey known of the grotto? None of Lucien's people knew of the grotto.

He faced his attacker.

"Ranulf?"

Ranulf's face was contorted with the same rage that had overcome him earlier, and that rage was directed at Lucien.

"You said you would never draw Corpse Maker against me," Lucien said, dodging another blow.

Ranulf said nothing as he tried his best to kill Lucien.

Lucien defended against Ranulf because that was all he could do. Anger couldn't have improved Ranulf's skills that much. Had the man been letting him win their matches all those years?

The answer was yes.

Ranulf body-checked Lucien, which threw him off balance. While Lucien tried to regain his footing, Ranulf jabbed his sword forward. Lucien only just managed to twist out of the way, but the sword still sliced his side.

He clutched at the wound. "Why are you doing this?"

"You left her!"

"She has gone back to her time."

"Time travel doesn't exist."

Lucien could only stare. "You say that. *You.* It was *your* words that convinced *me*."

"It is absurd. Time travel cannot exist. Geoffrey has her, and you left her to a fate worse than death."

"Geoffrey's men were behind us, not in front. They cannot have her. She's gone back."

Ranulf froze mid-swing. He jerked then stood straighter. "You're right. She has," he said in a calm and deep voice. Even the rage had left his face. The man's eyes had turned into deep black pools, almost as though they weren't there.

Lucien jerked back. "Ranulf?"

"Yes and no."

Ignoring the pain in his side, Lucien jumped to his feet and leveled his sword at the thing that used to be Ranulf. "What are you?"

"I do not explain at this point in normal flow. I wait."

"Now, demon!"

"I am not a demon."

* * * *

Ranulf edged back toward the grotto opening. "Then what are you?"

He didn't care. He only asked the question as a stall until he could escape. Ranulf wanted to look back to see how far he was from the entrance but refused to take his eyes off Lucien.

"You do not understand me at this point in normal flow. Understanding occurs at a later point."

"What do you want with me?"

"I give you Eris."

Ranulf almost dropped his sword. "What?"

"You wish to see her again. I ensure that you do."

"You will send me to her now."

The thing inhabiting Lucien made his lips curve into a smile that Ranulf had never seen Lucien wear before. "No. You have many centuries to go before you are worthy of her. I give those centuries to you."

* * * *

"Centuries," Lucien whispered. He lowered his sword, still clutching his side. "And you will *give* me that time, make it so I am able to see her again."

"We exchange favors."

That put Lucien on edge. "What favor?"

The thing moved Ranulf's arms out from his sides. "Simply this. I must inhabit a body to interact with you humans. A sad necessity of my existence. Rather than confiscate a body, I have yours at my disposal."

* * * *

"Disposal?"

"Your suspicions are unfounded. I do not harm you."

"I would be a fool to trust that." Ranulf turned and ran.

He didn't need light to know his way.

Or so he thought.

He turned a corner and found himself back in the glowing grotto facing black-eyed Lucien once more.

"You tire yourself. There is no need. Harm is not my intent or you would have never existed."

Ranulf hefted his sword again.

"That does not harm me." Lucien chuckled when Ranulf didn't lower the sword. "Strike me then."

"I will not hurt Lucien to get at you."

"Why not? You have already at this point in normal flow." He lifted the tunic from his side. "I stop the blood so the body lives, thwarting your intention of killing him."

"I was angry…"

* * * *

"He was angry. I understand that because I am as well." Lucien looked at his side. "You can stop the bleeding. Can you heal the wound?"

"I do."

Lucien looked again. All that was left was a scar. He touched it. There was no pain. "How?"

"I speed up your healing. The scar is so you never forget."

"I could never forget this day."

"Reminders are the key to an immortal's memory. You feel surprise at a point in time past this one because of how easy it is for you to forget."

"I won't forget her."

Ranulf smiled. "No. You do not. Your actions of the point before this moment and the guilt from those actions reminds you."

The hope of having the opportunity to see Eris once more was dashed against that simple reality.

Lucien sagged. "Even if you can give me this time, she will not want to see me."

"Are you so sure?"

* * * *

"Yes," Ranulf snapped. "She was obvious with her anger. Even though I tried to dissuade her of it, I think I may have failed. Lucien will not want to live until her time only to be rejected."

He waited for the thing inhabiting Lucien's body to say something. It merely stared at him.

"Do I take your silence to mean I'm wrong?"

"I do not educate normal flow creatures of the workings of time. Live your life and see."

"I would hear Lucien's opinion on this."

"You do." The thing bowed Lucien's head. He sighed and sagged a little before giving himself a good shake.

"Do you think this deal sound?" both asked in unison.

Ranulf frowned at Lucien. "How could you know of the deal? You hosted the creature as it spoke to me."

"No, *you* hosted the creature."

"You both are correct."

Those words came from the water but were spoken in Lucien's voice. Both men exchanged a look before walking to the water's edge. Their reflections awaited them, smiling at their confusion.

Ranulf stared at his black-eyed reflection. He looked at Lucien's reflection and noticed its eyes were the same. They looked at each other.

"What is this?" they asked at the same time.

Both alternated between looking at the water and then each other.

Lucien's reflection said, "There is no trickery. I merely fold time."

"Folded time? What does that mean?" Ranulf asked.

Ranulf's reflection gestured to Lucien's reflection. "I inhabit your bodies in turn and speak. I leave your bodies, turn back normal flow to the point before, and allow you to be aware."

None of it made any sense. How had the demon—or whatever it was—known what he and Lucien would ask or say?

462 D. Reneé Bagby

Ranulf's reflection smiled. "You are new. A small length of normal flow passes to make you believe."

"Time. Is that what you mean?" Lucien sliced his hand through the air. "We will not have the luxury of time if Geoffrey's men find us."

Even as he said the words, the sounds of search filled the caverns. Geoffrey's men and their dogs were getting closer. The false paths wouldn't waylay them long.

"You see Eris at a point far from this one," said Lucien's reflection. "Step forward."

Both reflections gestured to the water in invitation before fading from view.

"We've made a deal with the devil."

Ranulf said, "I care not. I'll become the devil himself if I must. I'll rain horrible destruction if that's what he asks." He walked into the water. "So long as I can see her again, I'll do whatever it takes."

Chapter Fifty-three

Lucien smirked at his desktop. "Do you remember that?"

Ranulf asked, "There is so much to remember. What incident are you speaking of?"

Lucien met Ranulf's gaze. "The day you said you'd become the devil himself if it meant seeing Eris again."

"Yes, I do remember that. I'm glad no one took me up on my offer. Hell has enough problems without me at the helm."

They lapsed into silence once more. Both were exhausted. They had searched every inch of the forest, missing every day of the faire in order to find the hole that had taken Eris.

There was no sign of it. They had been loathed to do it, but Lucien and Ranulf had given up the search. It was the last day of the faire. They could no longer excuse Eris's absence from the lives of her friends and family as being too busy having fun or too exhausted to come to the phone.

Now they sat in their office contemplating whether they should disappear as well.

"Sirs."

"What is it, Leon?" Lucien stared at the computer screen. The blinking cursor had his undivided attention.

"You said to tell you when five-thirty rolled around."

Lucien nodded and looked at Ranulf. They had to do the closing ceremony. He didn't feel like it and knew Ranulf didn't either—not without Eris.

A frantic voice crackled over the nearby walkie-talkie, "Attention, everybody. Get Lucien or Ranulf or both to the archery range. Now! We've had an accident. Repeat. There's been an accident."

"Emergency medics are in route," a female voice, a little calmer than the previous, said.

Another voice yelled, "Oh shit! It's Ms. Brue."

Lucien and Ranulf moved in perfect synchronization. They ran for the golf cart. Lucien jumped in and hit the gas just as Ranulf sat.

The CB in the cart crackled. Ranulf snatched up the receiver. "We're on the way."

Lucien pushed the cart to its top speed. He took a shortcut through the woods to avoid the crowd he knew would be present for the last day of the ren faire. They arrived at the same time as the ambulance, which had had to push its way through the crowd.

Both men ran to Eris's side. Lucien barked, "What happened?"

Eris lay on the ground unconscious with a broken-off arrow in her left shoulder. It was just as Lucien remembered. Even her left her was still tied to her side. He couldn't believe it was her.

The man closest to them shook his head. "We're not sure. It was weird, almost surreal. It was the last volley of the archery contest. Just as everyone fired their arrows, a freak wind came out of nowhere—I mean this was like hurricane force or something, it ripped the tent stakes out of the ground and blew over the podium—and blew all the arrows toward that bush." He gestured to the crop of bushes nearest Eris. "We heard the scream and knew someone had been hit. When we saw who…" He looked at Lucien.

Ranulf asked, "Whose arrow?"

"You'll have to figure that out later, gentleman. We've got to get the arrow out and get this bleeding stopped." The EMT directed the others, and they loaded Eris into the waiting ambulance. "It was smart thinking binding her arm to her side so she doesn't move it."

Everyone looked around but no one took credit for the act.

The EMT didn't seem to notice the confusion. "Who's riding with?"

"I am," Ranulf and Lucien said in unison.

"We've only got room for one, and you need to decide quickly."

Ranulf said, "You go. I'll get the car."

Lucien hesitated. "What if she wakes?"

"We're leaving," the EMT called.

"Talk to her then," Ranulf said, shoving Lucien toward the ambulance.

Lucien climbed in, and the tech slammed the doors after him.

As the ambulance sped away, Eris whimpered, which made Lucien jump. He'd laugh if he could.

He'd faced centuries of new dangers, countless wars, and seen things that would make the hardest man weep—through it all he'd endured and adapted. Looking at Eris unconscious and bleeding made him feel fear for the first time in centuries. Fear that she would never wake and fear that she would.

The conflicting emotions were new to him. He'd only ever wanted to see Eris again, the version that didn't know of his betrayal.

He sighed.

"Don't worry, sir. We'll be there soon."

Lucien nodded. With a shaking hand, he smoothed some dirt from Eris's face. He wanted her to wake. Of that he was sure. And then he wanted to finish the conversation they'd started so many centuries ago.

Police sirens blared around the ambulance, snapping Lucien out of his pity-induced stupor. "What's happening?"

The driver said, "We seem to have a police escort—one in front and one behind."

Lucien's cell rang. "Ranulf?"

"Yes. I called in a favor with local law enforcement to get us to the hospital faster. The hospital is awaiting her with a doctor who knows the situation."

"Good."

"Don't worry, old friend. She will survive this, and so shall we."

Lucien nodded even though Ranulf couldn't see the motion. He snapped the phone shut and turned his attention back to Eris.

They made the trip to the hospital in record time. The ambulance barely had time to stop before the doors were snatched open and Eris was hustled away.

Lucien watched her go but didn't follow. He couldn't make his feet move. Judgment day approached, and he could do nothing but watch.

Ranulf joined him.

"I can't do this," Lucien whispered. "I can't watch her turn from me after all that we shared."

"That's why we did it. We wanted her to go back with memories that would sustain her. Good memories."

"They weren't enough. Nothing will erase her look of loathing." He bowed his head. "You've won."

"Let her tell you that. I already said I wouldn't let you admit defeat because of guilt. Her return hasn't changed that." Ranulf put his hand on Lucien's shoulder. "She needs us."

Lucien walked forward.

The nurses directed them to the waiting room outside of the surgery ward where Eris had been taken. They were given paperwork to fill out while they waited. It was the longest three hours of Lucien's life.

A woman exited surgery. She spoke with a nurse, who pointed toward Lucien and Ranulf. Both men stood.

"Doctor?" Lucien asked.

The woman looked at Lucien, Ranulf and then behind them. "Is her family not here?"

"I haven't called them yet. How is she?" Ranulf said.

"Well, her wound wasn't as bad as we originally thought. The arrow hit nothing vital, but it nicked a vein and that caused all the bleeding we saw."

"Thank God." Lucien let out a long breath. His whole body deflated until he sank onto the chair behind him. "Thank God," he whispered again.

Ranulf patted Lucien's shoulder. "When can we see her?"

"She's in recovery. We'll be moving her to a room soon, and you can see her then."

"Thank you. We'll call her family and let them know the situation."

The doctor nodded and walked away.

"The crisis is over. Now comes the hard part," Ranulf said without a hint of humor.

* * * *

Eris blinked a few times and then opened her eyes. She didn't quite understand what she was looking at so she closed and opened her eyes again.

"She's awake."

That thankful sentiment was uttered by a very familiar voice. She turned her head and looked at Ranulf. He smoothed the back of his hand against her cheek.

"You gave us a fright."

"Fright isn't the word I'd use," Lucien said from her left.

She turned her head and then pulled back quickly with a scared gasp. She looked at Ranulf again and then her surroundings.

"Calm down," Ranulf said in a soothing manner. "It's okay. Shhhh." He continued stroking her cheek. "You're back."

"Back?" She looked at Lucien, and he stared at her, waiting. She reached for him, and he took her hand. He was real. "Lucien?"

"Yes, Eris."

"You're...it's really you?"

"Yes, Eris."

All she could do was stare at him. It seemed he only wanted to do the same to her.

She was back in her time, her present. The last thing she remembered was dozens of arrows raining from the sky above. She'd dodged to the side in hopes of finding cover of some kind only to take a nosedive into the hole that had taken her back in time.

She'd screamed and knew her head-first descent would more than likely break her neck. Everything went black before she felt the impact or any pain. When she woke up...

Tears leaked from her eyes. No amount of eyelid-squeezing could stop them. Sensing an inevitable battle, she gave herself up to the emotions.

Lucien gripped her hand. "Eris, I—"

"How?"

She opened her eyes and looked at him when he didn't answer.

His gaze left hers, and he shook his head. "That's a long story."

She loosened her hold on his hand and tried to release him. Lucien wouldn't let her. He brought up his free hand and cupped hers.

"Eris, I plan to explain everything."

"*We* plan to explain everything," Ranulf said.

She asked, "When?"

"When you're out of the hospital so we can talk in private." Ranulf looked at his watch and then the doorway. "Right now, we're expecting your parents any second. It didn't occur to me to call them until half an hour ago. Cherish was understandably frantic."

She nodded. "Later then."

Again she tried to get her hand back from Lucien. He still refused to release her.

"Lucien." Ranulf's voice had an edge of warning to it. "Now isn't the time."

It was a few seconds before Lucien finally let her go. He looked as though he would say something.

Eris remembered when that look had made her so curious. She remembered when all she wanted was to help him past his pain. After her little trip, all she could think about was the pain he'd caused her.

She closed her eyes and tried to make sense of all that had happened to her. It almost felt like a dream. She would have discounted it as such if not for her wounded shoulder.

Ranulf and Lucien sighed. She watched them sit, one on either side of her. They watched her as though waiting for her to do something. She had nothing to say. Not yet.

* * * *

"I hate hospitals."

Eris jerked awake. She'd been dozing thanks to the anesthesia still in her system.

A Japanese-accented female voice said, "You only hate them because you end up in them so often. Your daughter takes after you."

"Why do you insist she's my daughter alone when she gets hurt?"

Eris tried to call out to her parents but couldn't summon the energy. On either side of her Lucien and Ranulf stood and faced the door.

"Is it this one?" Cherish looked into the room a second after asking the question. Her face crumpled, and fat tears rolled out of her eyes. "Eris."

She rushed to the bed and hugged Eris tight. The hug lasted all of a few seconds before Cherish jerked back. "Oh, I'm sorry, baby. Did I hurt you? Are you okay?"

"I'm fine, mommy." Eris smiled up at her mother then looked at Mariko and her father. She frowned a little. "Didn't Last Mommy want to make the trip?"

Cherish rolled her eyes, but Kaylie was the one who said, "Mom is taking care of Emil and David at home. She hates hospitals more than My Mommy." She faced Olivia toward Eris and waved the light girl's arm. "Say hello to Auntie."

Olivia burbled at her and laughed.

Eris imagined she looked funny to the baby who probably hadn't seen a hospital since her birth. She looked behind Kaylie, but Declan and Benkei entered the room instead of Minnie.

Kaylie said, "Minnie is with Allen. I called her though. She's all frantic and upset that she couldn't cut her visit short to see you. I think she just wanted to see Ranulf again." She winked at him.

All at once, Ranulf and Lucien were the center of attention. Everyone bombarded them with questions. They seemed at a loss as to which question to answer first.

"Everybody, shut up," Gordon yelled. He glared around the room, ending at Lucien and Ranulf. "You two better be damn good and ready to pay for my daughter's pain and suffering."

"Dad!"

"No, Eris. This is unacceptable. You were hurt on their property. That gives us the right to sue."

"I'm *not* suing them." Eris struggled to sit up. Declan helped her and kept a supportive arm around her shoulders. She leaned against him while pinning her father with a stern look. "This was an accident."

"Who the hell uses actual arrows at a competition? Aren't they supposed to use those rounded arrows and foam targets or something?"

"It was a ren faire. You know, re-enactment. You understood well enough when you overhauled my dress. Of course they would have real arrows. They had live steel swords as well."

"That's my point! That's dangerous. What if you'd been hit by an axe?"

She wanted to smack her forehead so badly. "Dad—"

"Excuse me." A nurse walked into the room. "This is a hospital. Your voices are too loud, and you are upsetting my patient. If you can't hold a civilized conversation, I'll have to ask you *all* to leave."

Gordon made a guttural sound of agreement. "You heard the woman," he said to Lucien and Ranulf. "Leave." He pointed to the door.

They didn't move. They hadn't spoken one word or done anything since Eris's family arrived.

Cherish pulled her husband's hand back to his side. "Gordon, stop being an ass for two seconds. Lucien and Ranulf helped Eris."

"They are in the wrong, of course they helped her. That's their way of placating us. I refuse. They should pay." Gordon looked to Mariko, who nodded agreement though she didn't speak.

Kaylie crossed the room and shoved Olivia at Gordon's face. "Look. A baby."

The man took Olivia and cradled her in his arms. "You can't distract me with Olivia. I won't stop being mad about this. They—"

Olivia's face screwed up into a frown and she let loose a long, loud wail. Giant tears flowed down her cheeks and she waved her arms.

Gordon's angry look disappeared. He grinned at the little girl and bounced her. "That's my good girl. Granddaddy isn't angry with you." He made hushing noises.

While he was distracted, Cherish ushered Lucien and Ranulf out of the room. Eris wanted to stop her mother. She looked at her father and knew calling them back would only start the argument all over again. She resigned herself to the situation at hand. She couldn't get the answers she wanted while in the hospital surrounded by her family.

She would get them though.

* * * *

Ranulf wanted to balk as Cherish walked them down the hall toward the elevators. He'd already decided theatrics wouldn't solve anything. Thankfully, he didn't need to convey that conclusion to Lucien.

They stopped walking at the end of the hall. Ranulf faced Cherish. "You're angry with us."

"Not at you." Cherish looked weary. "This whole situation is a nightmare. When I got your call…God, it was like that accident all over again. I never wanted another call about Eris going to the hospital, not ever."

"I'm sorry."

"No, no. You were right to call. I only wish you had called sooner so we could have been there when she awoke."

Ranulf dropped her gaze. He had genuinely forgotten to call her family until after she'd been admitted and the doctors were operating. Once the thought occurred, he'd waited.

He hadn't known what Eris's reaction would be when she realized her journey was over. He decided her family didn't need to see it and had postponed the call until after the doctors had moved her to her own room, knowing it would take the Brues a while to get to the hospital.

Cherish said, "I understand we were the last thought. Don't worry about that. I'm just glad we were a thought at all."

He nodded.

Behind them the elevator dinged. The doors opened.

"Ranulf. Lucien. Cherish."

Ranulf turned and saw Pete. Who had called him?

Pete said, "I got a call from Chad. He was at the faire when everything went down. It took this long to find out details and which hospital. How is she?"

Lucien said, "Well and awake."

Pete heaved a sigh and nodded. "Thank God."

Cherish said, "Pete, could you excuse us?"

Pete looked at them all and then nodded quickly. He gestured behind them. "I see Gordon." He jogged away with a worried look cast over his shoulder.

Ranulf looked at Gordon glaring at them from the doorway of Eris's room.

Cherish turned her back on her husband. "Gordon is very protective of his children. He and his father have that in common. Once Eris is out of the hospital he'll stop being so pig-headed. Until then—" she sighed, "—it would be best if you both left."

Ranulf nodded and noticed Lucien doing the same. "We've taken care of her hospital bills."

"Thank you. We appreciate that." She gave them a quick hug and then gently pushed them onto the elevator.

The doors closed with a finality Ranulf didn't like.

"Why does this feel like the end?" Lucien whispered.

"I want to know the same." He only hoped Eris would give them the chance to explain.

Chapter Fifty-four

Eris took a deep breath. It didn't help. Nothing would, except doing it. She pushed open the front door without knocking and walked into the house.

Lucien stared at her in surprise where he stood near the office speaking with Ranulf.

She didn't blame them for looking at her like they'd never seen her before. She'd taken a month of sick leave and turned off her phone for the duration while she had sorted through her memories of the past and recuperated.

Once the doctors gave her a clean bill of health, she had waited for the following Sunday—so none of her co-workers would be present—to confront Lucien and Ranulf.

Before they could speak, she asked, "Did you two plan all of this? Did you search me out and then hire my company so you could set me up and drop me back through time just to become immortal?"

"No," Lucien said.

At the same time, Ranulf said, "Yes."

She crossed her arms.

Ranulf gestured to the office.

She regarded him for several breaths, weighing her options. They needed to talk. That much was a given. The location of the conversation had never crossed her mind.

Being alone with them made her feel uneasy and a little scared. That didn't sit well with her. She thought returning to the present would alleviate her fear of them. It had only made it worse. She had so many questions.

"Please," Ranulf whispered.

She nodded. "You two first."

"Eris—"

"Ranulf, just get in the office," Lucien snapped, following his own command.

She waited for Ranulf to precede her and then entered.

"The door—"

"Stays open," she said. "There's no one here but us. You two made sure of that."

They nodded.

"Then it's time to talk. Why me?"

"That's a paradox of epic proportions, Eris," Ranulf said. "Yes, we searched for you, but only because we wished to see you again."

"So, you hired CGC to get at me."

"No," Lucien said. "We hired your company to do just what you've been doing—to catalog our comic collection."

Ranulf went to his desk. He rummaged through a few desk drawers before he found a folder that he held out to her. She didn't step forward to take it, and Ranulf's expression turned pained. "Please, Eris. You know we won't hurt you."

"Do I? I just spent the last seven months walking on eggshells around you two. That's not something I'm going to suddenly forget because of a time shift."

He sighed. When he would have approached her, she backed up a few steps. He returned to his previous spot, placed the folder on his desk and then crossed the room away from her so he stood next to Lucien.

Keeping both men in her sights, she went to the folder. She didn't know what it contained, but what she saw was unexpected. "Why do you have pictures of me, Asia and Cynthia?"

Both men looked at her in surprise. Lucien asked, "You know those women?"

"Of course. They're my cousins. Identical triplets born to three different mothers. It's a family running gag that has nothing to do with this conversation." She held up the folder. "What is this?"

"If you look at the time stamp, you'll notice those pictures were taken two years ago."

Ranulf held up his hand, halting what Lucien would have said next. "Do you remember the day I put a hole through the wall in the survey room?"

"I'd be hard pressed to forget."

"Yes." He leaned against the desk. His whole being looked fatigued. "When you mentioned having brown eyes, not hazel, I remembered that picture. Lucien and I hired an investigator in hopes of finding you before two thousand ten. We even offered a generous finder's fee." He gestured to the folder. "That investigator got the closest."

"Why didn't you bring me in then?"

"That would be the reason for my outburst. The investigator said he'd found three girls that fit the description, but two had the wrong name, and the third had the wrong eye color. I didn't bother looking at the pictures. I simply dismissed his findings as another dead end and buried the folder without looking at the contents."

"Until I mentioned my accident." She gasped. "You two...you didn't...were you the cause—"

"No!" Both men yelled the word.

The force of their combined voices made her step back quickly. She looked between them, uncertainty coloring her vision. "How can I be sure?" she asked in a small voice.

Lucien made to step forward then seemed to rethink the idea, and instead, he held out his hand to her. His eyes pleaded with her to understand. "We didn't know about the accident, Eris. You have to believe that if you believe nothing else. We didn't know about it until you told us."

"We do know that our search for you, the wish to have you by our side once more, was the reason you survived it." Ranulf met her gaze without hesitance or flinching.

"What does that mean? Why were you searching for me? What do you want? What are you?"

Ranulf said, "I told you already. It's a paradox. We wanted to see you again, to be with you again. But, for you, it was a first meeting. You didn't know us and couldn't be with us until you'd met us for the second time."

"So you pushed me to wait until after the faire because you knew that was when I'd take my trip."

"We weren't sure of the actual date but had an idea—yes."

"Is that why you started having the faire?"

"No," both men said in unison.

Ranulf waved for Lucien to proceed.

Lucien shook his head. "No. You told us so little that we had nothing to work with. We traveled aimlessly, learning what we needed to survive and then simply learning because it was something to do. The medieval faire was my way of reliving the past, if only for a few days."

"Why would you want to?"

He looked into her eyes and held her gaze. The pain was there full force. She thought he'd hold her gaze, but he looked away.

With his fists clenched at his sides, he said, "The memories are painful, but they are all I had left."

Silence descended.

Eris waited for either Lucien or Ranulf to continue. Lucien was too busy wallowing in his guilt, and it looked like Ranulf was waiting for Lucien to continue.

She looked at Ranulf. "Quit dodging my question. What are you?"

"Immortal."

She slammed her hand down on the desk. Both men jumped at the sound. "Stop playing with me! What flavor? Vampire?"

"No. Simply immortal."

"And what? You woke up one day and thought, 'Gee, I think I'll be immortal today?' *How* are you immortal?"

Lucien made a calming motion that only enraged her more.

Ranulf regarded her with worried eyes. "Eris, please sit. This is all complicated, and you're still recovering."

"Stop stalling!"

Her little outburst winded her. It was all too much at once, but she needed to know. She needed an explanation for all that had happened to her, all she'd endured.

"I'm not stalling. I only want you to sit."

She wanted to tell him she was fine standing, but she wasn't. Her legs didn't feel steady, and all of the revelations were making her head feel light. She perched on the desk. "Happy now?"

"It'll do." Ranulf took a deep breath and then exhaled loudly. "In order to explain how Lucien and I became immortal, we have to tell you what happened after you disappeared."

"I'm waiting."

Ranulf looked at Lucien, but the man said nothing. He faced her and continued, "We ran to the caves as we'd originally planned."

Lucien said, "We laid false trails but that plan would have only kept us safe for a short time."

"Yes." Ranulf glanced at Lucien and then looked back at Eris. "The cave made a good hiding place and an even better dungeon. We had no way to escape and—"

"Stop going for dramatics and get on with it. You may have all the time in the world but I don't." She crossed her arms.

"Forgive me. I am saddened to say Lucien and I fought."

"Huh? Why?"

"I still didn't believe you had traveled through time. I thought Geoffrey's men had captured you and Lucien had left you to them. I was angry and attacked him."

Lucien pointed to his side. "That is the scar you asked me about at Halloween."

She made a get-on-with-it-motion.

Ranulf said, "The grotto was where we met *him*—the one who gave us our immortality and the chance to see you again. In exchange, we had to pledge loyalty and service to him."

"Him who? Do you mean the benefactor you mentioned? And why the hell would he simply give you immortality to meet me again?"

"That's the paradox. We would have never ended up at those caves and became his servants if you hadn't traveled back through time. And you wouldn't have traveled back unless we lived through time to meet you again."

Her head was starting to hurt. It all made sense, but it didn't make sense. It was a Möbius strip in real life.

"Actually," Lucien said in a voice much deeper than his usual, "Ranulf's statement is somewhat inaccurate."

Eris looked at him to ask what he meant and then screamed. She jumped off the opposite side of the desk so it was between her and whatever Lucien had become.

His eyes were missing.

She peered at him. Lucien only smiled at her. The movement made the lights of the room glint off of his eyeballs. They were still there, but they were completely black.

She looked at Ranulf, but his eyes were the same tawny color they always were.

Lucien said, "Hello, Eris."

She pointed at him, partially to keep him away and partially because she didn't know at what she was looking. "What in the hell?"

Ranulf raised a calming hand in her direction. "It's okay, Eris. Calm down."

"Like hell! I'm getting out of here." She ran for the door, but it slammed before she took two steps. She whimpered and hugged her arms.

"You're scaring her," Ranulf yelled at Lucien.

"I do not mean to. She does not leave. You finish your explanation and then she leaves. That is how normal flow presents this situation."

Eris turned and looked at Lucien as though he was crazy. "Open the door."

"I cannot. I am subject to normal flow and thus must obey its rules. You do not leave at this point."

"If you would—"

"Eris," Ranulf yelled over her words.

She faced him.

"Let me finish and then he'll open the door. Yelling at him will do no good."

Though she nodded, she didn't move away from the door. At the first opportunity, she would leave and never look back. She'd played her part. Whoever-Lucien-had-become had what he wanted.

"Not at this point in normal flow," Lucien said.

Ranulf looked at him. "Excuse me?"

"At this point in normal flow I do not have what I want yet, Eris. As said before this point, Ranulf's statement is false. I do not want him or Lucien. My goal is you."

"What?" she and Ranulf yelled at the same time.

Lucien smiled. "You finish your explanation, Ranulf."

"Like hell, I will. Explain yourself. What do you mean *you* want Eris?"

"I forgive your anger because of your shock. It does not mar our relationship."

"I don't give a shit about that!"

"You should. Without my intervention, you and Lucien would be dust. As such an action would only hurt me, I refrain." Lucien looked at Eris once more. A soft smile curved his lips. "This point in normal flow is one of my favorites."

Eris dropped to her knees.

Ranulf rushed to her side, but she pushed his hands away before he could touch her. "Eris?"

"I don't care anymore. I don't. You hear me? I don't care. Just let me leave."

"Finish, Ranulf," Lucien said.

"I don't care!" Eris covered her ears as a way to block out whatever Ranulf planned to say. It was too much all at once. She'd expected a simple explanation of vampirism or something similar. Something easy.

"Your thoughts are chaotic, but you hear his words." Lucien nodded to Ranulf. "Tell her."

Ranulf covered Eris's hands with his. She shook her head at him, not wanting him to talk.

He pulled on her hands. Light tugs, not forcing her. It was the look in his eyes that made her yield. He seemed as reluctant as her and a little fed up.

She lowered her hands to her lap. Ranulf kept his hands around hers and stayed close. He said in a low, soothing voice, "He is Chronos, Eris."

"Chronos—Greek god of time."

"Yes and no. Chronos, the name we use for him though he has thousands, is far older than Greek mythology."

"Time has no age," she mumbled.

Lucien said, "I have an age. The number is incomprehensible to you, thus meaningless."

Ranulf bit out, "Shut up."

Eris looked at Ranulf, trying hard to ignore Lucien—*Chronos*. "What do you want with me?"

"I…Eris, I only did all of this to be with you again. I love you. I loved you then but wouldn't admit it. I took Chronos's offer of immortality because I knew it was the only way to see you again. Lucien feels the same."

"You were going to share me."

"We didn't know what the future held. We only knew that neither of us would back down. Chronos granted us both immortality, made us both his servants. At the time, we thought that was a good thing." He glanced at Chronos. "Now, I'm not so sure."

"Your mistrust is unfounded. We have the same goal." Chronos's words exited Ranulf's mouth. Eris screamed again and scrambled away. Lucien rushed to her side, placing himself between her and Chronos, acting as a shield.

She looked up at him. He glanced back at her, and she saw his eyes were back to normal, but that was because Ranulf's eyes had gone black.

Chronos had jumped bodies.

Lucien spat, "You tricked us. You never said you wanted Eris."

"Such knowledge is not for you. All you know is that *you* want Eris."

"Why?"

Chronos curved Ranulf's lips into the same smug smile he'd had Lucien wearing. "I love her."

Eris stared at Chronos. She'd never even met him. How could he say something like that?

"Easily, Eris."

She touched her head. "Are you reading my thoughts?"

"Yes."

"Stop it!"

"It is not something I can stop. I cease responding to your thoughts, however."

She wanted to leave. It was too much. Two immortal men and trips through time were one thing, but a god? What had she done to gain the eye of a god?

"I am an eternal, Eris, not a god. One of the four eternal truths."

"You said you'd stop doing that!"

"Of course. I do lapse. Forgive me."

He didn't look sorry in the least. His soft smile remained. Though his eyes were black pools, they shined with love for her. It made no sense.

She asked, "You sent me back, right? Not some spell on Lucien's mother's ring?"

"Yes."

"Then what was all that flashing the ring did? Why did one ring shock me when I tried to touch it?"

"A ward. The feeling of unease, the shining, and the shock when you touch it. All so the ring of that point in normal flow does not leave it. Any other action causes a paradox and normal flow collapses."

"You... that..." She couldn't get the words out. In that moment, Chronos resembled Lucien a great deal. They both took unnecessary risks that could have horrific outcomes if they miscalculated.

Chronos said, "I slow many of your body's functions. That causes your constant chill and facilitates the progression of your physical relationship with Lucien and Ranulf. For every month spent in the past of your normal flow, certain parts of your body only age a single day. It is the only way to protect you from the diseases and other maladies present in that period."

Well, that explained why her hair had never grown and why she'd never menstruated in all that time. But he'd done more than slow down her aging. "You also made it so I understood Middle English."

He nodded.

"Why do all that?"

"It is appropriate. The trip causes you enough stress. I endeavor to lessen it in small ways. The only hardship I truly impose on you is the stipulation of your return."

She didn't say anything. He already knew she was going to ask. He didn't need her participation in the conversation.

Chronos's smile widened, but he said nothing.

They sat in silence, staring at each other. She finally sighed and asked, "What was the stipulation?"

"I only obey your command not to respond to your thoughts, dear one."

She glared at him.

"To answer your question—you, Lucien, and Ranulf have to all be in agreement for you to return."

"It wasn't the time of day or the ring or the hole?"

"No. None of it matters. All that is ever needed is a mutual wish shared between the three of you."

It made sense. All the times they had tried sending her back, one of them hadn't wanted her to leave. They hadn't all agreed until her life was in danger.

"Continue, Lucien," Chronos said.

Lucien said, "No."

"Before this point in normal flow, you never disobey me."

"I do now."

"This is the only time."

"Don't bet on it."

Chronos's soft smile changed to a knowing grin.

Lucien stiffened. He glanced back at Eris and then looked back at Chronos. "What does all this mean? Did you use us to get to her?"

"Yes."

"I thought you used her to get to us."

"No. Finish the explanation."

Eris touched Lucien's leg. He faced her, and she pulled back. "I want to go home. Just do as he says so I can leave."

Lucien looked like he would plead with her. He dropped to his knees, facing her, with his head bowed. "We didn't know about this. I thought Chronos was moved by our fervent desire to be with you again and make right all that we'd done wrong. I didn't know he wanted you for himself."

"As you and Ranulf want her for yourselves. Instead of two, there are three."

Eris glared at Chronos. She wanted him to shut up. Every time he opened his mouth things got more complicated.

He bowed to her.

She looked at Lucien. "Go on. You made a deal with Chronos," she whispered.

"Chronos is the master of time. That is the simplest and easiest explanation. To govern it, he cannot live within it. To inhabit linear time, or normal flow as he calls it, he must take a host. He prefers a voluntary host."

"You or Ranulf."

Lucien nodded. "We volunteered simply because it meant immortality and the chance…the chance to apologize properly and beg forgiveness." He met her gaze.

She looked away from him. Of all the topics she wanted to discuss, forgiveness wasn't one of them. In fact, she was done wanting to talk about anything. She wanted to get the whole ordeal over and leave.

She faced Chronos. "They said I survived my accident because of them, which means it was because of you, right?"

"My brother knows you to be my love. He acts at my behest and keeps you with the living."

"Your brother?"

"Destruction. Though most call him Death. He sends your brother Benkei to you because he knows a familiar face eases your fears fastest. I thank him for that consideration."

"Sent my brother? How does Benkei know Death?"

"Benkei is a—"

Lucien yelled, "Don't!" He moved so he blocked Eris from Chronos's view. "That's enough."

Eris moved to the side and said, "Finish. Benkei is a what?"

"Eris, you don't want to be burdened with this knowledge as well." Lucien reached for her, but she pulled away.

Chronos said, "Benkei is a *shinigami.*"

Eris looked at him in shock. "A death god? How?"

"He dies five of your years prior to this point in normal flow. My brother raises him up from that mortal death and makes Benkei one of his messengers. A collector of souls. Immortal."

Eris didn't know what she felt about her brother being dead, or immortal. Technically he was alive and well with his wife and kids. Did his wife and kids know?

"His wife is the *shinigami* who trains him," Chronos said. "Excuse my lapse, my love. It is hard not to respond, even for me."

Eris shook her head. Worrying about Benkei would have to wait for another time. "Why do you think you love me? We've never met before today, right?"

"Normal flow creatures are hard for me to interact with only because all time is known to me." He walked forward, keeping Lucien between them, and stooped to her level. "If I am to define my love in normal flow, it is because of Ranulf and Lucien that I start caring for you. Their love translates into my love." He reached for her.

She wanted to pull back but didn't. Fear coursed through her body, but it wasn't paralyzing. She sensed no ill intent. Curiosity kept her still so he could touch her.

His fingers brushed her cheek in the barest of touches. That contact felt like standing next to a power transformer. She could feel the electricity, his power. Would taking hold of his hand kill her?

"I never hurt you, my love."

"I don't know you."

"As normal flow passes."

"You say you love me because of Ranulf and Lucien, but they only met me because of you."

He smiled at her.

She was about to demand he give her a better explanation, but Ranulf's tawny eyes faded into view and he sighed.

Eris looked at Lucien, but his eyes remained normal. Both men looked at each other.

Ranulf said, "He's gone."

They looked at her.

She stared back. That was not the explanation she'd wanted. Now that she had it, she didn't know what to do with it.

Her whole being ached. Weariness settled into her bones and her soul. All she wanted to do was sleep. A small part of her wanted to go to bed and never leave it. She hadn't felt like that since her accident.

"I have to go," she whispered. Her voice sounded far away. It didn't even feel like she was the one saying the words, more like someone else was making her mouth move.

"Eris," Lucien and Ranulf spoke at the same time. They looked at each other. Ranulf waved Lucien forward.

Lucien placed a hesitant hand on her shoulder. "You can't leave in this state. You might get into an accident."

She reached up to brush his hand away. Instead, she found herself patting his hand. "Would it matter? Chronos will call Death again. I'll be fine."

That at least made sense. Chronos wanted her alive, thus she wouldn't be killed. Hurt maybe, but not killed.

Would he have stepped in and stopped the Lucien and Ranulf of the past from killing her? But that made no sense. He had to already have known Lucien and Ranulf weren't going to hurt her—too badly—and that was why he hadn't interfered.

She looked at Lucien's hand on her shoulder and then his face. Concern creased his brow and made him look older. She touched the fuzz that lined his jaw. "You look better with short hair. You have the face for it."

"Eris?"

Using his chest as a brace, she pushed to her feet. Everything felt all cottony around the edges and not real. She looked at Ranulf. "I'm glad you kept your hair long."

"Do you know what you're saying?" Lucien asked in a worried voice.

She looked at both of them in turn and then nodded. "I have to go. Is the door open now?"

Ranulf rushed and opened the door without argument.

She passed him and entered the foyer.

"Eris—"

"Goodbye, Ranulf."

Neither man tried to stop her. She left the mansion and returned to her car.

No thoughts bothered her as she drove home. She didn't even remember the trip. When she blinked, she was standing in her kitchen staring at the fridge.

Was she hungry? Was that why she'd walked to the fridge?

She didn't feel hungry. Actually, she wasn't sure what she felt.

Something wet brushed her hands.

She looked up at the ceiling, but there wasn't a wet spot from a leak. A quick glance out of the window showed it wasn't raining. She looked down at her hands. When she would have touched the wet spot another droplet hit it, making it bigger.

And another.

And another.

It took her a moment to realize she was crying.

How long had she been crying?

She shambled to her bedroom and collapsed onto her bed. A great heaving sob left her body. Once uttered, many more followed.

The real world returned in cascades, and it hurt.

She didn't know when she had started crying, but a better question presented itself.

Would she ever stop?

Chapter Fifty-five

The phone was ringing.

Eris lifted her head and looked at her clock.

Who the hell would be calling her at five in the morning? Getting a landline was quickly turning into a bad idea. She'd only done it because of the incident with her cell phone disappearing. But, the annoying new addition to her household might have to be removed once more.

Hadn't she turned the ringer off so it wouldn't wake her at odd times?

It didn't matter. She ignored it and stared at the clock. It took her a moment to notice the dot in the upper right corner. It was five at night, not morning. She couldn't be mad at someone calling at five at night.

The phone stopped ringing, and she sighed.

"Thirsty," she mumbled.

She reached for the water bottle closest to her bed. It was too light to have anything in it. She shook it just to be sure. No sloshing noise of liquid greeted her ears. She tossed the bottle away and it landed near the growing pile at the end of her bed.

There were no other bottles on the dresser. That meant she'd have to get up and go to the kitchen. Why hadn't she brought all of the bottles to the bedroom?

Oh, that's right. Getting out of bed to get more water was the only motivation she had to get out of bed. That and going to the bathroom.

Just as she reached the kitchen, her cell phone rang.

She didn't plan on answering that either. Whoever it was would have to leave a message. She retrieved a bottle and walked back toward her bedroom.

Once the liquid replenished her body, she'd start crying again. That had been the routine for the last week.

"Geez, I feel like a bill collector. Don't you ever answer your phones? Why even have them if you won't use them?"

Eris whipped around and faced the woman who had spoken.

"Hello," the woman said with a bright smile and half a wave.

Eris backed up quickly, looking around for something she could use as a weapon. "Who are you? How did you get in my house? What the hell do you want?"

"Calm down, chicky. I'm not going to hurt you. Besides, I never hurt people named after me. I'll screw around with them, but I don't hurt them." The woman walked into the living room. She eyed the furniture before sitting on the ottoman. "Come take a load off and chat a spell."

The woman was nuts if she thought Eris would sit and talk with a housebreaker.

"I'm not nuts, and I didn't break in."

"What?" Eris touched her head. "You…you read my mind."

"I'm Errita, the entity known usually as Chaos and Chronos's older sister." She held out her hand. "Nice to meet you."

"You're Chaos?"

"Call me Errita. And sit down while you're at it. I'm not here to hurt you. I want to talk."

"About?" Eris sat on the arm of the couch but stayed ready to make a run for it.

The woman before Eris lived up to her name, visually at least. Her features kept changing. Various strands of her hair shimmered from one end of the color spectrum to the next in a random pattern. In fact, her whole body was doing it—her eyes changed shape and color, her nose morphed from one shape to the next, and so on. The changes were slow and subtle. It made Eris think there was something wrong with her eyes, but no amount of blinking made it stop. The effect was making Eris sick to her stomach.

Errita snapped her fingers and suddenly her body stopped shifting. It was like she had hit the button on a slot machine but hadn't gotten a matching set. Her eyes were Asian slanted and blue, while she had a sharp English nose, and the full lips any black woman would envy.

"I can change it," Errita said.

Eris held out her hand with a shake of her head. "It's fine. Just stop changing." She sighed when Errita nodded. "What did you want to talk about?"

"You and your boys."

"What about them?"

"Why are you making them suffer like this? You want them, and they want you."

"I'm being stubborn."

"I'm glad you know that about yourself."

"And, I'm scared. Chronos said he did all this for me. That he wants me. How am I supposed to react to that? Do you have a husband?"

"Me? Married?" Errita laughed, slapping her thigh. "The man who could marry me doesn't exist, though there is one who likes to think we're married. I did play mortal for a bit about fourteen millennia back and got married to a fey that thought he loved me. We had a baby, a little girl. The annihilation of her entire universe is held within her name so she always goes by her title. Her powers and potential were obvious from birth, and the hubby got freaked out when he realized I wasn't a fey like him but something much more powerful."

"Fourteen millennia? I like how you say that like it was only a few days ago."

"And a few millennia back, I had a fling with Jormungand."

"Who?"

"The Midgard serpent. You know? Norse mythology."

"He's real?"

"In another universe, yes. All the gods are real in one universe or another. How their stories travel between universes is still a mystery since the nagas have strict rules about crossing dimensional cultures in their travels. It's probably just a few select individuals who project their astral forms while they're sleeping, or something like that, and then wake up thinking they've seen God or came up with the greatest story known to man."

"Huh?"

Errita waved her hand in a dismissive gesture. "Don't worry about it. Jormungand and I had a son. He's not as powerful as his older sister, though. His capacity for destruction is limited to a single planet, not the entire universe, and it's held within his voice, so he whispers all the time."

"Um…sorry?"

"I think it was all the partying I did while I was pregnant with him. It stunted his growth or something."

"But you're Chaos. Why are you having kids that destroy everything?"

"It's the way of us siblings. We have each other's children. I beget Destruction. Destruction begets Order—that's Chronos, by the way. Order begets Creation. And, Creation begets Chaos. You've met Creation."

"I have?"

"Genevieve."

Eris recognized that name. She gasped as the memory took hold. A well-manicured redhead in a no-nonsense business suit, high heels, and an attitude a mile wide came to mind. The woman Lucien and Ranulf had said was the sister of their benefactor. Now that she knew who their benefactor was, Genevieve made a bit more sense.

"You got it. And you're right about her attitude. Stuck up little snot said she's never having children because she didn't want more of me running around."

"The mind reading again."

"There's no help for that. Even if Chronos says he won't, he's still doing it. Even if your mind wasn't an open book for me and mine, we've existed forever—me the longest—so there isn't much you could do or think that we don't know about. It comes with being eternal."

"That's what I mean. You all are forever. Chronos could stop loving me one day and then what? Where does that leave me, Lucien and Ranulf?"

Errita pulled Eris into her arms and gave her a squeeze. "That's what I love about you humans. Everything is going to happen to you tomorrow, but today is when you worry about it." She let Eris go. "Let me tell you something about my brother he may have overlooked mentioning—he resides outside of time."

"He mentioned that."

"So let me explain in layman's terms so you understand what that means. For Chronos, everything is now—past, present and future are all right this second for him. That's the reason he always speaks in present tense—annoying as that is. When he says he loves you, there is no greater guarantee than that. It won't end."

"Why me?"

"Because Lucien and Ranulf love you."

"Why them?"

"Nah, I'm not getting into this with you. You're trying to make this whole situation linear when it's not. This isn't about the chicken and the egg, chicky, because neither of them exists in this scenario—or they both do simultaneously. It's the chicken and the egg, but it's not."

Clear as mud made of volcanic ash. Eris wanted to understand, wanted to be with Lucien and Ranulf, but it was all too big for her.

She met Errita's gaze. "Say I accept all of this and…him. How long before this stuff makes sense to me?"

"I don't know, but Chronos does. He won't tell you or me, so don't ask. I can tell you this—Lucien and Ranulf still have issues with it."

"Oh, that's just great." Eris rolled her eyes.

"It may annoy you but know that you will understand in time, because that is something he gives you."

"Time?"

Errita grinned. "One of the perks of loving an eternal is immortality."

"So I'll look like this forever. I mean, if I accept this?"

"You can look any age you want once you learn to control your gift. You had to have noticed Lucien and Ranulf look younger than when you met them in medieval times."

"Yes."

"And another thing that will freak you out and help you make up your mind."

Eris raised an eyebrow.

"At some point you start visiting Chronos in his realm for some one-on-one time without the middlemen. That's how we siblings first met you."

"His realm. Outside of time and existence?"

"That's the place."

"When? I mean, not when I go there but when did you meet me?"

Errita grinned. "I shouldn't tell you since Chronos worked real hard not to mention it, but I was talking to you before I decided to drop in here and say hi."

"That doesn't make any sense."

"*Outside* linear time is all time all at once. In other words, I've known you for quite a while. That's why seeing you like this is so fun." Errita pinched Eris's cheek.

"Quite a while."

"Yup."

She was about to ask Errita to define "quite a while" but didn't. Errita wouldn't answer, and Eris wasn't sure she wanted to know. "I'm there now?"

"Stop trying to make it linear and your head will stop hurting."

Eris touched her forehead. She didn't think her head would ever stop hurting if she let a relationship develop with Chronos.

But there was no "let" about it. The relationship was happening even as she sat talking to Errita. She shook her head. "You're right. That does freak me out."

"Simple question."

"Go for it. I need simple right now because my brain is fried mush."

"Sounds tasty." Errita turned Eris's chin so their gazes met. "Do you love Lucien?"

"Why are you even asking if you already know the answer?"

"Humor me. Do you love him?"

It was a simple question, and it had an equally simple answer. Eris may be mad at him, but she was tired of denying her heart. She whispered, "Yes."

"Do you love Ranulf?"

"Yes."

"Do you want to be with them?"

"Forever."

"Chronos is good at forever. But don't worry about him. Let Lucien and Ranulf be your only concern for now and the other will work itself out."

Eris digested Errita's advice. It was so simplistic and right in front of her. She hugged Errita. "Thank you."

"Oh, don't thank me. This is my apology for screwing with you earlier on in your relationship. And the only reason I'm apologizing is because you threatened to tell Chronos on me."

She pulled back. "I did? When did I…"

Errita grinned.

"Never mind. What do you mean screwing with me?"

"The computer eating your work, your car not starting, the cell phone that walked, the tardy tow truck guy…" She trailed off with an etcetera motion.

"That was you?"

"That was child's play. You should see me when I'm really putting some effort into it."

Eris didn't know what to say. None of the things Errita had done were particularly malicious, so she couldn't be angry. She shrugged.

"Oh, I'm never mean to people who are named after me. I may play with them, but I'm never mean to them."

"Why do it at all?"

Errita shrugged. "Everyone needs a hobby."

"My mother loves saying that."

"Oh, I know. Your mother invokes my power so often I couldn't help but notice her."

"You're the reason for her accidents?"

"In a roundabout way. I'm not doing it purposefully. As I said, your mother invokes me, especially when she's near the family computer." Errita slapped her legs. "We're getting way off topic. You need to get back to those men of yours and start with the loving."

Eris agreed but didn't move. She stared at Errita, trying to put some kind of explanation with the woman that her brain could comprehend. "You know, for a being of chaos, you're not very chaotic."

"Chaos isn't my job, it's who I am. The thing exists because I exist." She stood. "Besides, who knows how long you would have sat here moping if I hadn't stopped in and talked sense into you."

"But—"

Eris couldn't ask her question because Errita disappeared. Eris stood and walked to the spot Errita had occupied, but the woman was gone. She turned in a circle.

"Thank you, Errita."

"Any time, chicky," Errita's disembodied voice said.

The matter was solved. The only thing left was for her to go be with Lucien and Ranulf.

Chapter Fifty-six

Like last time, she didn't knock. Eris waltzed into the house then the office and closed the door. Lucien and Ranulf looked at her. Their twin looks of sad resignation only made her want to hug them all the more.

It may have been painful to wait for her to come to terms with everything, but she had no sympathy. They had centuries to cope. She'd only gotten a few days, and whether that was enough remained to be seen.

Errita had summed up the entire situation into two simple questions. If Eris only focused on her answers to those questions, she didn't need any more time.

She smiled.

Time…Chronos.

"Eris?"

She looked at Lucien. Before she realized it, she was walking toward him.

He stood slowly. When he would have rounded the desk to meet her, she held up her hand. He immediately froze.

"It would have been easy to say, especially in those last few hours before I returned to the present."

He frowned at her in confusion but didn't speak.

She nodded. "I could have forgiven you then." She shook her head to stop him from talking. He snapped his mouth shut. "You torched your home and became a fugitive for me. Because of that, I felt my anger at you leaving. I didn't say anything, though. I could have taken the burden you carried all this time and let you live through the centuries in peace. But I didn't." She stopped.

Lucien stayed silent.

"Ask me why?" she whispered.

"Why?" His voice was a rasp filled with accusation.

It made her want to laugh and cry at the same time. Tears threatened to flow down her cheeks even as she smiled at him. "I wanted you to suffer."

"Obviously."

She sucked in a breath to help hold back her tears, though they still colored her voice. "You owed me that. Your guilt, the unease you felt when I first entered this house, and everything else in between was owed to me."

He sighed, his shoulders sagging, and then nodded. "Yes. You're right. I…I spent so many nights, especially after you had gone to the past, trying to think of a way to earn your forgiveness."

"This is your debt repaid." She opened her arms to him.

Lucien looked at her in surprise.

Then, she did laugh. "Come here, Lucien. I won't bite."

He didn't go around the desk but over it. Lucien's strong arms surrounded her, and he crushed her to him. "Tell me this isn't a trick."

"It's not." She gasped when his hold tightened. Given the circumstances, she could deal with a little shortness of breath.

It felt good to be in his arms. She had missed the security of his embrace—both past and present versions.

"Ranulf." Lucien released her quickly and looked at his long time friend.

Eris followed his gaze.

Ranulf remained seated at his desk, watching them. His expression was blank.

Despite that, Eris could see the pain. She pulled away from Lucien fully and walked to Ranulf's desk. "Would you really sit here and do nothing? Would you really let Lucien alone have me?"

"Lucien wouldn't be alone. There is still Chronos."

"Answer the question."

"If…if it's what…" His lip quivered, and he bit it. After straightening his spine and clearing his throat, he tried again. "If that's the way you want it."

She leaned on the desk so her face was close to his. "If that's not the way I want it? If I want to complicate my life with three instead of two? What then?"

"Do you?"

The question hung between them.

She reached out and caressed his cheek. He turned into her hand, kissing her palm. That was all he did. He didn't try to touch her.

When she pulled back, he grabbed her hand in a crushing grip. Real emotion entered his gaze, and that emotion was need. Every sense of the word—physical need and emotional need—was there for her to see when it hadn't been moments before.

She tugged on her hand. Ranulf didn't release her, and she'd known he wouldn't. He followed her, climbing over his desk much as Lucien had. When he stood before her, she brought his hand to her cheek. "You owe me," she whispered.

"Anything."

"Are you sure about that?"

"Anything, so long as I can stay with you."

She nodded. "Remember you said that."

"I've forgotten nothing else about you. I won't forget this." He bent to press his lips against hers.

She turned away. "This is..." Her words petered to a halt as she tried to think of how to phrase her thoughts.

A hand clutched her shoulder. She let her gaze trail up the hand to the arm and up the arm to Lucien's eyes.

"This is weird."

Both men nodded in agreement.

"I'm glad you both think so too." She smiled at them. "Not only is it weird, but in some ways, it's really wrong." She moved from between them. "It's way more than any one person should have to deal with."

"Eris, please, don't—"

"You can't mean after—"

She held up her hand. Both men watched her with fear. She lowered her hand. "That said, I still love you both and want to be with you. If that means I'm suddenly with Chronos as well, then so be it. I'll get used to it, I guess."

Lucien asked, "You're sure?"

She nodded.

"Be sure," Ranulf said. "Once you say yes, we're never letting you leave us again."

"Yes." She stepped back quickly when they would have surrounded her, and the men pulled up short with a question in their eyes. "I'm sure I love you both, then and now."

"We feel the same," Lucien said.

"Do you?"

"How can you doubt that after all that's happened?"

"It's been so long for you."

Ranulf took a breath then stopped and smirked at her. "I'll refrain from saying something corny if you stop looking for reasons not to let us make love to you."

She backed away from them. "Maybe I want you to say something corny."

The men followed her step for step.

"We can recite sonnets," Lucien said.

Ranulf added, "Or write them, if you like. I'm no Lord Byron, but my words were always well received when I cared to pen them."

Eris shook her head. "Tempting, but no."

"What then?"

They'd made it out of the office and across the foyer before she stopped walking. When she stopped, Ranulf and Lucien stopped as well. She held up her hand to keep them in place and then turned from them and climbed the stairs.

Once at the top, she looked down one hallway and then the other. "I've never been one for sonnets." She faced them. "How about a race to the top to see which room we use?"

She thought they would hesitate or at least ask for an explanation. Both men ran. Lucien reached the top first, but Ranulf didn't admit defeat. He grabbed her in his arms and ran with her to his room. Lucien chased him, and Eris laughed.

There was a frenzy as clothes were removed then two sets of hands roamed over Eris's body followed by two separate mouths. She found herself lying on the bed but didn't remember moving there. Ranulf and Lucien had definitely gotten better over the centuries. She felt close to release already and they had barely done anything to her.

"I have a gift," Ranulf whispered. He eased off of the bed and retrieved a small bottle from his bathroom.

Eris said, "I'm not into perfume."

He grinned and drizzled some of the viscous liquid over his fingers. "Oh, this isn't perfume. I spent a few decades perfecting it just for you."

She looked at Lucien, and he grinned as well. At least it wasn't a surprise he didn't know about. But then, she doubted Ranulf and Lucien had many secrets from each other anymore.

Ranulf returned to the bed and her. He slid his fingers between her rear cheeks and circled her puckered opening. Eris shivered as the silky smooth liquid heated and tingled. He slipped a finger inside her, and she gasped.

"Do you like it?"

She nodded, biting her lip so she didn't cry out.

He held the bottle to her nose.

She sniffed then looked at him. "Roses."

"Oh yes. I cherished that memory and worked to have this little concoction ready for when we would be together again."

She clutched at Lucien and moaned when Ranulf added another finger.

"I plan to market it, but I wanted to know what you thought of it first."

"Love it." The heat and tingling only made Ranulf's movements that much more pleasurable.

"Once you name it—" he kissed her back, "—I'll let my company sell it." He kept his fingers moving inside of her as he rained kisses over her back and shoulders.

Lucien's fingers entered her center as he suckled at one breast then the other.

She was about to let herself go into bliss-filled oblivion when she remembered one important thing.

"Wait!"

Ranulf and Lucien stopped their movements and looked at her.

"One thing."

"Condoms. You don't want to get pregnant," Ranulf said. He removed his fingers and left the bed, headed for his bathroom again.

"Oh, you're way too late for that," Eris said, grinning.

Lucien sat back, and Ranulf stumbled to one knee. "What?" they both said.

"I'm pregnant already. Chronos said he slowed my body so it only aged a few days, and in that time, we had a lot of sex, relatively speaking. Once my body resumed normal function, I should have started my period a few days later, but I didn't. I did a pregnancy test, and it came up positive. I had my doctor make sure when I went in for a checkup on my shoulder."

"Whose is it?" Ranulf asked in a shaky voice.

"I'll forgive stupid questions at the moment since you're both in shock. But, really. Do you honestly think I'd know when you both shared me on a regular basis—once you stopped fighting?"

"This is…this is…"

"It doesn't matter," Lucien said. He hugged Eris tight. "It doesn't matter whose child it is. We're both its fathers and you're its mother."

"I could tell you if you like," Ranulf said in a deep, rumbling voice. The shocked, shaking Ranulf had disappeared. In his place, a black-eyed Ranulf stood tall and calm.

Eris wasn't as freaked out seeing Chronos. "I don't want to know."

"As you wish."

"There is something I do want to know though. Why me? What's so special about me?"

Chronos smiled. "You do not ask this question of Lucien and Ranulf, only ever me."

"It's not the same."

"They are human."

"No, they aren't."

Chronos lifted his hand but stopped just as he had started reaching for her and moved his hand back to his side. "Compared to me, they are as human as you. Their love is no mystery to you. Only mine."

"You're a god."

"I'm an eternal. Gods hold less power than we four."

"That makes it even worse."

"Worse?"

"You know what I mean." She tried to keep herself calm.

Behind her, Lucien rubbed her back. That soothed her. She noticed that he didn't interject. He probably wanted to know the answer as badly as she did.

She asked, "Why me?"

"We are together for all eternity. You ask the same question of me millions of times. Each time you ask, I give a different answer and yet no answer I give satisfies you or soothes your anxiety that I will someday stop loving you."

"I still want an answer."

"My first answer." He moved a few steps closer. His face took on a soft look of wonder as his gaze roamed over her face. "You draw my attention. Trillions of women on billions of planets in hundreds of alternate dimensions, and it is only you who catches my eye. I see all of time all at once and yet it is only the times where you exist that interest me the most. All else is merely—" he stopped with a small smirk, "—time passing."

He was right. His answer didn't satisfy her. It didn't calm her fears that his love would wane, which could possibly undo all that she had with Lucien and Ranulf.

Yet, heat bloomed within her heart just hearing his words and knowing, for that moment, Chronos meant them.

She beckoned to him, and he came closer to the bed. When she motioned him closer, he put one knee on the bed and leaned into her. She searched his eyes, still scared at the deep nothingness but a little curious.

"This isn't an invitation," she said.

"Of course not."

"You knew I was going to do this already."

"Yes, but every time you accept me is joy. That never changes for me."

"That's what Errita said."

He frowned a little and then smiled. "I shall thank my sister."

"Shall? What do you mean shall? You always speak in present tense. That's what Errita said."

Chronos caressed her cheek. "Errita is the eldest for a reason. Of all that exists in creation, she alone is immune to the rules of my domain. As such, I cannot know her actions until she does them."

Her confusion must have been evident. Or he simply read the question from her thoughts.

"I introduce order into chaos, not the other way around. Thus, she must act before I can react. When I deal with my elder sister is when I know the feelings of normal flow creatures."

Lucien snorted and grumbled under his breath, "I'd like to *deal* with her, all right."

Chronos smiled and nodded.

Eris didn't ask.

She leaned into Chronos, keeping her gaze locked with his, and pressed her lips to his. He took the kiss she gave him and didn't make it more. She expected him to but was happy he didn't. The lips were Ranulf's, but it didn't feel the same.

Against his lips, she asked, "May I have Ranulf back? It's been so long for him and Lucien. I'd like them both to be present and aware."

"As you wish." Chronos backed away.

Eris caught his arm. He actually looked a little sad. Did she really mean that much to him?

"Oh yes, sweet Eris. Very much."

"Next time, but only for a little bit. I'm still getting used to this."

Chronos caressed between her breasts. "Your heart that is so kind is one reason I love you. That is my second answer." He bent and kissed her cheek. "Do not force yourself and feel no guilt. I am fine, though I pout."

That confession made Chronos seem a little more familiar—more human. She smiled at him. "It'll take…well, you know."

"Until you next see me, my love."

Ranulf eyes bled back to their normal shade. He blinked a few times, sagged, and sighed. After a moment, he smiled. "You are kind-hearted, Eris."

"Is that bad or good?"

He returned to the bed and kissed her lips. "Very good."

"Delicious, in fact," Lucien said, turning her so she kissed him next.

Eris went limp and let the men do as they pleased. This was her family now. Two men she loved, one entity she would love and a baby on the way.

She hadn't thought her definition of marriage and family could get much weirder, and it had. As it turned out, weird worked for her.

THE END

ABOUT THE AUTHOR

Whether as D. Reneé Bagby or Zenobia Renquist, Reneé lives in her imagination. When not traveling through her fantasy worlds, she can be found in MD living with her husband and two cats.

She is an Air Force brat turned Air Force wife, which means she's accustomed to travel and does it whenever possible (so long as she doesn't have to fly). Her favorite pastime is torturing her characters on their way to happily-ever-after for the enjoyment of her readers.

On the few occasions her muse flees the scene of the crime, Reneé likes to read (comics, manga, and romance), go to the movies, play a few levels of whichever puzzle game has hijacked her interest or experiment with a new chain maille weave.

Siren Publishing, Inc.
www.SirenPublishing.com

Breinigsville, PA USA
13 September 2010
245268BV00004BC/4/P